Cathy Williams can remember reading Mills & Boon books as a teenager, and now that she's writing them she remains an avid fan. For her, there is nothing like creating romantic stories and engaging plots, and each and every book is a new adventure. Cathy lives in London. Her three daughters—Charlotte, Olivia and Emma—have always been, and continue to be, the greatest inspirations in her life.

Annie West has devoted her life to an intensive study of charismatic heroes who cause the best kind of trouble for their heroines. As a sideline she researches locations for romance whenever she can, from vibrant cities to desert encampments and fairy-tale castles. Annie lives in eastern Australia with her hero husband, between sandy beaches and gorgeous wine country. She finds writing the perfect excuse to postpone housework. To contact her or join her newsletter list, visit annie-west.com.

Also by Cathy Williams

Her Boss's Proposition
Billionaire's Reunion Bargain
Heir for the Holidays
Maid for the Italian

Also by Annie West

Ring for an Heir
Queen by Royal Command
Stolen Pregnant Bride
Forbidden Princess's Billionaire Bodyguard

Discover more at millsandboon.co.uk.

A PASSIONATE PROMOTION

CATHY WILLIAMS

ANNIE WEST

MILLS & BOON

All rights reserved including the right of reproduction in whole or in part in any form. This edition is published by arrangement with Harlequin Enterprises ULC.

This is a work of fiction. Names, characters, places, locations and incidents are purely fictional and bear no relationship to any real life individuals, living or dead, or to any actual places, business establishments, locations, events or incidents. Any resemblance is entirely coincidental.

Without limiting the exclusive rights of any author, contributor or the publisher of this publication, any unauthorised use of this publication to train generative artificial intelligence (AI) technologies is expressly prohibited. HarperCollins also exercise their rights under Article 4(3) of the Digital Single Market Directive 2019/790 and expressly reserve this publication from the text and data mining exception.

® and TM are trademarks owned and used by the trademark owner and/or its licensee. Trademarks marked with ® are registered with the United Kingdom Patent Office and/or the Office for Harmonisation in the Internal Market and in other countries.

First published in Great Britain 2026
by Mills & Boon, an imprint of HarperCollins*Publishers* Ltd,
1 London Bridge Street, London, SE1 9GF

www.harpercollins.co.uk

HarperCollins*Publishers*, Macken House, 39/40 Mayor Street Upper, Dublin 1, D01 C9W8, Ireland

A Passionate Promotion © 2026 Harlequin Enterprises ULC

Out-of-Office Temptation © 2026 Cathy Williams

Boss's Marriage Agenda © 2026 Annie West

ISBN: 978-0-263-41826-2

04/26

Printed and Bound in the UK using 100% Renewable Electricity
at CPI Group (UK) Ltd, Croydon, CR0 4YY

OUT-OF-OFFICE TEMPTATION

CATHY WILLIAMS

MILLS & BOON

To my wonderful and inspiring daughters,
Charlotte, Olivia and Emma.

CHAPTER ONE

ERIN'S PHONE BUZZED. She didn't bother to look at it because she knew exactly who was texting her. That made it six texts since she had arrived at her boss's mansion in Chelsea, where a celebratory cocktail party was currently in full swing.

Raffaele Rossi had just closed a major deal and the champagne was flowing. The company he had acquired was small but in rude health. They needed his financial clout to take the next step and he wanted them because in under three years, he anticipated their stock skyrocketing with his judicious investment, bringing yet more millions into his already healthy coffers.

More than the money, though, Raffaele Rossi would be celebrating the new challenge of taking something small and turning it into something huge. Every new acquisition had him as excited as a kid in a candy shop.

Thirty people were milling around in his living room while waiters and waitresses circulated with trays of exquisite canapés and, naturally, the finest champagne on tap.

Lawyers, most with other halves, accountants, most with other halves, the CEOs of the firm Raffaele had taken over, *all* with other halves—and Erin. With no other half and text messages that kept coming through.

She caught Raffaele's eye across the crowded sitting room and he winked at her. Erin's mouth tightened in response, and she saw him stifling laughter.

She swiped a passing canapé and turned to one of the young lawyers next to her, a guy she had met several times over several deals. He had been trying to engage her in conversation while she distractedly banked down rising impatience with her boss. This time, she wouldn't be making her excuses early and leaving, which was her usual approach to these dos. No, she would be sticking it out, because she intended to have a word with her boss and for once, to heck with the consequences.

Enough was enough.

'Your phone seems to be buzzing again.'

'I know.' Erin smiled apologetically at Colin. He was a bit older than her, with a neat, tidy appearance that belied a sharp legal brain. She might only have met him a few times but she'd always liked what she'd seen.

'Maybe you should just answer whoever keeps trying to get in touch.'

'No. I won't be doing that, Colin.' Erin smiled at him when he reddened. 'And I don't mean to be rude. What do you think of the company merger? Are you exhausted after working solidly for the past week?'

'Comes with the fat salary, doesn't it?' He grinned. They looked at one another in a moment of wry agreement.

'That and loyalty.' Erin wondered how loyal her boss would think her once she'd given him a piece of her mind.

'Everybody knows that Rossi Holdings is the golden ticket. Pays the most and in fairness, we only have to work mega long hours now and again. People would kill for my job so even if I was collapsing on my feet, I'd know better than to complain. What do you think the next big deal's going to be?'

'You know I can't breathe a word about what's in the pipeline.' Smiling, Erin met his eyes and made a shushing gesture with her finger over her mouth.

'What's it like working for Raffaele every day, Erin? I only deal with him when something like this happens and it's all hands to the pump. Is he as tough as everyone says?'

'Tough but fair.'

'Tough, fair and with a different woman on his arm every other week. Sorry.' Colin looked at his champagne flute ruefully. 'Too much of the fine stuff. I'm gossiping.'

Erin laughed but didn't carry the conversation further.

A different woman every other week? Maybe not quite that…but it definitely wasn't a million miles away from the truth.

She stole a look through her lashes at Raffaele, who was standing across the room. She knew very well that if he caught her eye, he would raise his eyebrows and stifle another amused grin.

He thought Erin was dull.

Dull but incredibly capable, incredibly efficient and probably indispensable. She caught a glimpse of herself in an impressive oval mirror sandwiched between two abstract paintings. Shoulder-length chestnut hair, hazel eyes, short, straight nose and full lips. Not unattractive, she knew, but definitely not in the same ballpark as the string of women who entered and exited Raffaele's life with monotonous regularity.

She suspected, in addition to *dull but incredibly capable, incredibly efficient and probably indispensable*, she could likely add *plain*.

The perfect secretary from Raffaele's point of view.

Certainly, before Erin had arrived four years ago, her boss had managed to burn his way through six PAs, all of whom, he had later confided, had to be dispatched because they'd ended up having a crush on him.

He'd confessed that he was in perpetual mourning for the sixty-something-year-old lady who'd worked for him for years before inconsiderately inconveniencing him by emigrating to New Zealand to be with her daughter and grandchildren.

Erin had stepped in, killed his curiosity about her personal life before it could really take root, and now they couldn't have had a more harmonious working relationship.

Except for the times when she'd had to grit her teeth and remind herself of the size of her pay cheque.

Like now.

Except this evening, she was going to do a little bit more than grit her teeth.

'What are you doing after this?'

'Huh?' Eric blinked and looked at Colin with surprise. 'What do you mean?'

'Fancy coming to a bar with me? Or we could go have a proper meal somewhere? These canapés are amazing, but I could eat ten times what I've already eaten and still be hungry.'

'Colin, that's very nice of you...'

'I can sense a *but* coming after that.' He smiled at her. 'Can I add a *but* of my own?'

'Of course.' Erin could feel herself blushing.

'Okay, *but* if you do change your mind and ever fancy having a date with a lawyer two floors down, promise me you'll get in touch.'

'I will,' Erin said warmly, still pink. She drained her glass, only her second for the evening. She was still all hot and bothered as Colin gave her a little half salute, then headed away to join everyone else who hunting around for bags and jackets.

Raffaele's cocktail parties were always lavish and always brief. He opened his house in a show of generosity but there was always the unspoken understanding that no one outstay their welcome.

Erin watched the gradual exodus of people but remained where she was, standing by the bay window with the empty glass in her hand.

Her boss's house was magnificent, an exquisite, vast Georgian mansion in one of the best postcodes in London, with grand Corinthian columns and ironwork balconies as intricate as lace. The floor-to-ceiling windows that they guarded were impressive from the outside and even more impressive inside because of the light they let in.

They had all been ushered through to the largest sitting room in the house, whose marble floors with handmade inlays oozed opulence. Lots of pale colours everywhere and an abundance of paintings, all vaguely recognisable and all priceless originals.

Erin had only ever been into a couple of rooms on the ground floor but she imagined that the rest of the magnificent house was the same—cold, elegant and luxurious. Not her thing, if she was honest. She thought of where she had grown up and stifled a smile. *Definitely* not her thing.

She blinked her thoughts away and found that Raffaele was seeing out the last of the fast-departing crowd. Then he turned, lounged indolently against the wall and looked at her with raised eyebrows.

The man was stupidly beautiful.

Six foot two inches of pure, sexy alpha male. His Italian heritage was evident in his classically beautiful features, in the dark hair which he wore slightly too long and in his Mediterranean colouring. Only his eyes, a deep navy blue, suggested other roots. Those eyes were fixed on her now in a lingering, amused stare.

He began strolling towards her.

'Why are you still here?' was the first thing he asked when he was towering over her. 'Shouldn't you have been at the front of the queue when everyone started leaving? You're usually the first to go. Plus...is that an empty glass I see you holding?' He looked at it with an unduly shocked expression.

'I'm not teetotal, Raffaele. Why wouldn't I be holding an empty glass?'

'You didn't drink at the last do I had. I noticed.'

'You *noticed*?'

'It's my job to notice what my employees are getting up to. You didn't touch a drop—although, in fairness, you had a cold and spent most of the evening trying not to cough. I notice things like that. It's why I'm so successful and such an amazing boss.'

'That's very modest of you.'

'You still haven't answered my question. Why are you the last to leave? No, before you answer, let's get out of here. Let's have a drink in the blue room. I want to talk to you about something interesting that came up in one of my discussions with Archer.'

Typically, he didn't give Erin time to answer. He spun around on his heels and headed to the door, grabbing a bottle of champagne on his way 'I'm taking it that you're not in your usual rush to leave?'

'I can stay for another drink.'

Raffaele grinned approvingly and Erin was cross with herself for reddening.

He got to her. She hated to admit that, even to herself, but the man got to her. Even though she never, ever showed it. She was utterly professional in her dealings with him, fully aware that anything else would be as good as signing a death warrant on her very, very well paid and very, very satisfying job.

The blue room was one of the smaller sitting rooms that led into an expansive conservatory and out to the back lawns which, by London standards, were ridiculously big.

'So,' Raffaele said, the second they reached the blue room, 'what's going on with you and the lawyer? Was that why you were hitting the bottle?'

He nodded to one of the sofas. Erin obligingly sat down and waited for him to join her—much as she didn't particularly want to have him so close to her right now. She was fine sitting next to him, arm brushing arm, if they were poring over a report or looking at something on his computer, but in this setting...

Instead, though, he topped up their champagne glasses, then strolled over to the gleaming console by the window. He perched against it and looked at her with keen interest.

'I beg your pardon?' Erin said.

'You and the lawyer. Something else I noticed. You can tell all, although I have to warn you that I'm not a fan of intra-office affairs...'

'What are you *talking about*, Raffaele?'

'Colin. Grey suit...neat hair...good brain, I admit, but looks like his social life might revolve around dogs and long country walks in bad weather...'

'There's nothing going on between myself and Colin. And, by the way, that's not a very nice description of him! He happens to be a lovely guy! Also,' she spluttered furiously, 'it would be none of your business anyway if Colin and I were dating!'

'You both work for me.'

'There would be no conflict of interest! And I don't even know why we're talking about this because…because…' Erin gulped down a mouthful of champagne and then waved one hand in a dismissive, annoyed gesture.

'Okay! It was simply an observation. I wouldn't want my invaluable secretary to start hearing wedding bells and thinking babies.'

'I don't believe I'm hearing this. And not that it's at all relevant, but I'm not the sort of woman who goes on one date with a man, hears wedding bells, thinks babies and immediately decides to hand in her resignation!'

'Thought not,' Raffaele said smugly. He sipped the champagne and walked towards her, sitting down and relaxing back on the sofa next to his PA.

She looked, he thought, a little ruffled but he was pretty sure that she was telling the truth. Not that it really was any of his business if there was anything going on between her and Colin. Co-workers were free to date one another. It was hardly as though Erin could clamber onto Colin's shoulders to get a promotion or to be given any special treatment. The clambering on shoulders would have to be for a different reason entirely, he thought, slanting a wicked, sideways glance at her.

Still, he felt quietly satisfied that they *weren't* dating, or about to start dating. Was he possessive when it came to his prim and very proper secretary? Only, he decided, insofar as he didn't want to lose her to any heady romantic nonsense. Who else could fill her shoes?

He looked at her for a few seconds through lowered lashes. He could understand Colin's interest in her. Underneath the neatly groomed exterior, Erin Fisher was a lot sexier than first impressions seemed to suggest. Something about those calm, greeny hazel eyes, the silkiness of her poker-straight shoulder-length chestnut hair, the slightly cool expression, the surprisingly husky voice... and the fact that she did nothing to promote herself.

She could be as sensual as any woman a thousand times more overt.

He shifted and cleared his throat.

'So onto the Archer business. Seems like there might be a prospect of another takeover in the offing although this one would be completely out of my comfort zone. Wouldn't mind hearing your thoughts on it but nothing leaves this room. Understood?'

'Before we get onto work, Raffaele, and I do wonder if we should stick to talking about another acquisition on Monday in the office...'

'Those walls have ears. And, like I said, this is just something I'm toying with...'

'Right. But I stayed behind because there's something I wanted to talk to you about.'

Erin noted the way Raffaele stiffened, the way his eyes narrowed. 'I'm not sure I like the tone of your voice. Tell me you're not handing in your resignation.'

'Why would I be handing in my resignation? What makes you say that?'

'It's not like you to pull me aside to have a word.'

Erin took a deep breath. Was she so predictable that

deviating from business talk was something that might set off warning bells in his head? Yes, she was, because she was the employee with no personal life. She was one-dimensional. Maybe that was why he'd been so disconcerted to see Colin flirting with her.

'I happen to be very happy in my job,' she told him firmly.

'If it's a pay rise you're after...'

'I'm not after a pay rise and maybe you could just let me finish?' She'd brought her small cross-body bag in with her and now she dived in, retrieved her phone, unlocked it and handed it over. The screen displayed the relevant thread of texts, the same messages that had been making her phone beep at her throughout the cocktail party. All from Raffaele's ex-girlfriend.

'Ah.'

'"Ah"?' Erin parroted. 'Is "ah" all you have to say, Raffaele? "Tell Raffa I adore him... Could you arrange a meeting...? I know I could get him back if I get the chance..."' She took the phone and stuck it back in her bag. 'Is "ah" your only response to all those texts that have been pinging every five minutes while I've been here?'

Her lips thinned and she drew back and folded her arms.

'You're doing your head-teacher look.'

'This isn't a joke, Raffaele. I resent the fact that your ex-girlfriend thinks it's okay to text me about your relationship!'

'We don't have a relationship.'

'I know that,' Erin said, torn between unbridled resentful sarcasm and a modicum of restraint because he was, after all, her boss. 'I know that because you get me to do the dirty work for you *all the time.*'

'Sorry? I'm not following you.'

'Raffaele, how is it that I always seem to know when you change girlfriends?' She met his perplexed frown with a look of frustrated impatience. 'I know because at the end of every fling, you get me to send them some kind of overblown parting gift.'

'Ah, yes. Occasionally I admit I've asked you to buy them something…'

'"Occasionally" is an understatement.'

'Well,' he said thoughtfully, 'you're a woman. Wouldn't you instinctively know what another woman might like when a relationship comes to an end?'

'*That,*' Erin snapped as temper overrode restraint, 'is possibly the most sexist thing I've *ever* heard you say.' She saw his lips twitch and realised that he was gently poking fun at her, which only made her angrier. 'Buying parting gifts for all those women who enter and exit your life through a never-ending revolving door was never in my job description!'

'"Never-ending revolving door"? I had no idea you had such strong views on the matter, Erin.'

'Well, I have.' Jumping in and out of relationships wasn't Erin's own style. She had been brought up to respect the sanctity of love. Her parents might have had their unusual ways, might have had a taste for moving around and for adventure that was a little too highly developed given they were parents, but they adored one another and they adored her. In their own, eccentric way.

'But that's not even the point. All this…these texts from Alexa. Raffaele, it's an invasion of my privacy.'

'Why would she have decided to text you? Have any

of my exes texted you in the past? Tried to get in touch? You've never mentioned a word of it to me. If you were unhappy about the situation, then you should have said something, Erin. You don't find me that unapproachable, do you?'

Erin realised that she had drained her glass of champagne and that he was pouring her another, his expression solicitous and concerned.

Was she overreacting? She cast him a jaundiced look and accepted the glass, gathering herself to get to the point she was determined to make. That any involvement in his fast-paced, superficial love life was beyond the bounds of her employment and that the endless string of texts tonight had only brought that home to her.

Was she now supposed to play ad hoc therapist to all those women he picked up and then dispatched the minute he got bored with them?

She had met Alexa a couple of times. A very nice girl with an excellent clothes-horse, legs-up-to-armpits figure and a posh cut-glass accent. She had been to the office a handful of times and Erin had always winced at the unconcealed adoration in her big, blue eyes every time she looked at Raffaele, knowing what must be coming all too soon.

Honestly, Erin had often thought, *he really doesn't deserve it.*

She'd said nothing, of course. But now she was determined to lay down a few laws. Better late than never.

'I don't find you unapproachable,' she said coolly, 'which is why I'm now taking this opportunity to tell you that you need to find someone else to do the present buying for you. I'll continue to arrange the theatre and the opera and wherever else you want to take those poor girls you date, but buying them farewell gifts to ease your guilty conscience isn't something I want to carry on doing.'

She saw the shutters instantly slam down on those hooded deep blue eyes. His expression cooled and Erin flinched, not only because she thought that she might have crossed a line but because...

Because this was an area into which their relationship never strayed and she didn't like it. She was accustomed to his careless teasing, the warmth of his charm. Not this remote expression in his eyes as he looked at her unsmilingly. This was an expression he had always reserved for other people, people who didn't live up to his exacting standards. Never her.

'I apologise for...overstepping the mark, Raffaele. I suppose those texts from Alexa were the final straw and also...'

'Also?'

'Nothing,' Erin said quickly as her thoughts turned to her parents again and this time anxiety nudged past the rose-tinted memories.

'In that case, let's go ahead and establish a few boundaries right now. No more favours.' He held up both hands in a light-hearted gesture but his blue eyes were steely. 'I won't be asking you to buy any flowers or jewellery or whatever else I've asked in the past. I will instruct any woman I date to refrain from making personal calls to my office. If anyone gets through, feel free to cut her off without explanation and you can simply tell me that there's been a call. Likewise, there's no need for you to make small talk if one of them happens to inadvertently stray into my office. That way, none of them will be encouraged to think that they have any kind of personal relationship with you. You can be what you're paid to be in situations like that...namely, my very efficient gatekeeper.'

'Raffaele, that's not what I've been saying. Because I... I mentioned that—'

'Let me finish,' he interrupted coolly, 'on another note and while we're setting down boundary lines, you should refrain from making personal observations about my life choices when it comes to women. They're not "those poor girls"...'

'I didn't mean—'

'Oh, but I think you did, Erin. Don't think I haven't glimpsed a certain expression on your face when you haven't seen me looking, an expression of disdain. Why do you think that the women I date are poor girls?'

'Perhaps I used the wrong phraseology.'

'They're anything but poor girls. In fact, I'm a one-woman man and when I date a woman, she has one hundred percent of my focused attention. She has whatever she wants, money no object. You know that well enough because of the things you've booked, which I now discover you booked with simmering resentment.'

Erin could only look at him miserably, hating the horrible vibe between them, desperately wishing they could return to their familiar footing.

But things had to be said. She told herself this and swept aside her discomfort.

'Okay,' she agreed. 'You won't hear another word from me about what I think about your love life.'

'I don't use any of the women I date, Erin. It's not a revolving door, as you put it, of tormented, discarded exes weeping into their hankies and thinking that their lives are over.'

'I never said that!'

'I'm not interested in commitment and I tell that to every single woman I date from the outset. I make it crystal clear that while I'll enjoy them, *enjoy us*, for a while, it's never going to last. Alexa was upset when we broke up but she knew from the outset that it wasn't going to lead to a walk down the aisle, so guilty conscience? You couldn't be further from the truth. Block her from communicating with you and I'll contact her and repeat what I patiently told her four months ago when we started dating.'

'Two and a half months ago.'

'Come again?'

'Nothing,' Erin said quickly. His eyes were still flint hard. She loathed it. She took a deep breath and went for it.

'I probably wouldn't have mentioned anything about the texting, Raffaele, but…' Erin hesitated because this would be the first time she'd ever said anything really personal to him and it felt as though she might be jumping off the edge of a precipice. Yes, she might tell him vaguely what she did on the weekend, share one or two details about a holiday she might have had, but that was where the sharing ended.

'But…?'

'I've been a little stressed lately.' She lowered her eyes and felt her heart begin to thump. 'It's…it's my dad…'

'What about your dad?' Raffaele looked at Erin's downturned head, the glossy hair dropping in a heavy curtain to her shoulders. This was the first real awkwardness to ever crop up between them, which was amazing considering the length of time they'd been working alongside one another.

He knew that he could be a tough taskmaster but not once had he ever thought that she didn't keep pace with him.

She'd opened a can of worms by telling him what she thought about his private life. Naturally he had had no choice but to pull up the drawbridge. He was as transparent as a pane of glass when it came to the world knowing what woman was on his arm, but judgement on how he conducted his private affairs? Out of bounds.

He certainly wouldn't be lectured on commitment. It wasn't on the table. Never. Not for him. From nowhere, he thought of his parents, a marriage that was a sham, a pretence that made him realise a long time ago that behind what passed for love between two people was often a very different reality underneath. And into that cold union, a child with wants and needs could get lost and forgotten.

He slammed shut the door on those uncomfortable thoughts. Erin could make her own decisions, but for him, safety lay in relationships that promised nothing.

Still, it was inexcusable that she have to contend with the fallout from a relationship gone wrong. He was also shocked at how much it cut to the core to have had this stupid spat with her.

He didn't like to see that wounded look in the eyes of someone who was always so calm and cool and composed and efficient. He didn't like to see the slump of her narrow shoulders.

She was about to confide in him and maybe, he mused with a spike of interest that he instinctively knew had always been there, the sound of a door slightly opening between them was a good thing...

It was bizarre that he didn't have any insight at all into her personal life. He wasn't asking for a ring side view of what she did and thought but a few details might not be a bad thing...

His curiosity ratcheted up a few more notches.

He could sense her hesitation. Didn't she realise, he thought wonderingly, that the more she hid the more he wanted to probe?

Especially now that she had offered him this once-in-a-lifetime opportunity?

'Is he okay? Your dad?'

There was genuine concern in Raffaele's voice and that alone was sufficient to make Erin relax into the conclusion that she had done the right thing. It was ridiculous to act as though she had to fight to the death to protect every square inch of her privacy. She wasn't a secret service spy facing a firing squad if she didn't!

'He's had a fall and broken bones in his ankle. He's going to be off his feet for a bit...'

'Well, that's not too bad, is it? I thought maybe there might be some serious illness involved. You've never mentioned your father to me...or your mother, for that matter. I'm presuming that you have both your parents?'

'I have,' Erin replied briskly. Her eyebrows shot up. 'Come to think of it, *you* haven't mentioned your parents to me either.'

'Valid point.' He flushed. 'You can take a few days off, Erin, if you want to go see them. Where do they live?'

'On the coast.'

'Now if that isn't a broad-spectrum kind of reply,' he drawled. 'Surely you can be a little more forthcoming? I don't intend to drive to wherever they live and pay them a surprise visit if that's what you're scared of.'

Erin shot him a grudging smile. 'Sussex. It's very pretty. I've actually been going there for the past couple of weekends to help out. This is the first weekend I haven't been.'

'I didn't know! You should have said something. You could have made them into long weekends without using up whatever holiday allowance you have.'

'I... Yes, thank you, but there's only so much I can do at the moment and I've put...well, certain things in place that will help him out until he's back on his feet.'

'Is your father at work? What sort of help did you have to put in place? Surely his company is taking care of everything necessary? Giving him time off and making sure he continues to be paid, arranging whatever physio he needs to have. If they're not, tell me immediately and I can put that right.'

'No, no.' Erin felt a film of perspiration break out. She thought of her parents and their nomadic lifestyle. Until she was twelve, they had lived in a commune not a million miles away from where they now were. It had been a settled and happy time for her, surrounded by families who had all supported one another.

After that, a serious dose of wanderlust had finally got the better of her parents and they had headed out to explore the big, bad world. They had done pretty much every corner of the country, including a stint in the icy wastes of Scotland, and had, only a handful of years ago, arrived in their trusty camper van back where they'd started but in a different part of Sussex.

Thanks to her, they now owned a tiny little house and a small freeholding where they grew their own vegetables, selling the surplus to the local shop. Planning for the future had never been one of their priorities and it had become crashingly obvious that life in a camper van wasn't feasible as a retirement option.

She felt a little faint at the thought of describing her parents' hippy lifestyle to her elegant, sophisticated, sexy boss. She fidgeted with the collar of her shirt, tugging at it, suddenly hot and bothered.

'You don't have to talk about this if it's going to give you a panic attack,' Raffaele said, vaulting upright and hunting down the bottle. He poured the remnants into their glasses.

'Of course I'm not having a panic attack! I... I'm just saying that I've been a little stressed out about my dad and... Look, it's no big deal, Raffaele, but he doesn't actually have a job. As such.'

'What does "as such" mean?'

'He... My parents live a simple life...'

'I'm really not following you.'

'They own a small freeholding and they're self-sufficient. They grow all their own food, or try to. My mum makes jewellery and has a side job upcycling furniture. I... With my dad's ankle out of action, he hasn't been able to get to do the crops and there's only so much Mum can do so I've been a little stressed out but I've got someone along to help out until my dad is back on his feet...'

Raffaele digested this in silence for a few seconds, unreasonably shocked by the picture she had painted.

Self-sufficient? Selling jewellery? Upcycling furniture? He couldn't have imagined a different background. Actually, he'd pictured accountant married to schoolteacher. Now that she had opened up about a more colourful childhood, he was downright intrigued.

However, he could see that she was already half regretting letting him have that fleeting glimpse of Erin Fisher the woman, as opposed to Erin Fisher his dependable secretary, always kitted out in neatly tailored clothes, always wearing sensible shoes and always sticking to the straight and narrow.

He thought about her flirting with Colin and realised that he didn't like it. Maybe that was why he'd been so relieved when she'd shot his speculations down in flames.

Or had that been a case of the lady protesting too much? Was there something going on there, a furtive romance kept under wraps because they both worked for him? He was irked at the thought of the other man knowing more about his enigmatic PA than he did.

'Sounds like a great life,' he said non-committally as he stood up, waiting for her to follow suit. He was definitely going to dig deeper now. He lowered his gaze so that she couldn't see just how curious he was in the woman who now seemed so much more fleshed out after only a few remarks, a few revelations that most women would never have considered keeping to themselves.

'Maybe.'

'At any rate, keep me in the loop and I'll be at hand to help if you need anything at all.' He smiled lazily at her as she faffed around sticking her bag over her shoulder and adjusting it, her silky chestnut hair swinging across her delicate face. 'And can I say something now that we've been a little more open with one another?'

'What?'

She looked at him warily and he could tell that she

had already retreated back behind the facade he was accustomed to.

But they were in new terrain now and just as he felt when he made a new deal, he was filled with the excitement of a challenge. The challenge of getting to know his PA better. Why not? It could only make their harmonious working relationship even better because it would be a more rounded relationship.

'You think I play the field and leave a string of broken hearts behind me,' he murmured, stepping towards her and fleetingly wondering what it would feel like to sift his fingers through that silky hair.

'I never said…'

'Well, I think you should live a little. From the sounds of it, your parents have lived quite the adventure…so how is it that you haven't? Or maybe you have and I've just never seen that side of you…' He tilted his head to one side and wasn't surprised when there was no answer forthcoming.

Was even less surprised at the realisation that seeing those other sides to her was something he really rather wanted to do…

CHAPTER TWO

ERIN HAD NO idea what to expect when she pushed open the door to her large, airy office on the Monday morning at eight sharp, half an hour before most of the workforce began making an appearance but usually a couple hours after her workaholic boss had been at his desk.

Her office was linked to Raffaele's via a bank of sleek walnut sliding doors with panes of smoked glass. If he happened to be in a meeting and needing privacy, the doors would be shut but mostly when he was in, they remained open so that she could, with a glance, see whether he was busy or not.

If her office was large, his was five times the size, large enough to incorporate a separate seating area and a scaled-down boardroom. Many an evening had been spent there working to wrap up a deal.

Right now, as she divested herself of her cardigan, she was relieved to see that the doors were shut.

It gave her more time to continue going down rabbit holes berating herself for confiding in him, when she'd spent so long avoiding that particular trap.

Amid all her heated thoughts as she'd tossed and turned in bed the evening before, the one that jumped out at her was the one she was least willing to confront.

Feelings for her boss, which she had only ever entertained now and again before stuffing them away and pretending that they didn't exist, could no longer be ignored because they went a long way to explaining why she was so rigid about maintaining her privacy with him.

Yes, she disapproved of his antics when it came to the opposite sex. She scorned the way he picked women up, enjoyed them for a while and then discarded them before moving on to the next one. And of course she knew that however attractive the man was for her on a personal level, he could never prove a serious temptation because she could never emotionally engage with a commitment-phobe.

She wanted that love her parents shared. She wanted the guy who would lie down on the railway tracks for her. She might be realistic when it came to her parents' life choices, living on the road and kidding themselves that tomorrows were never going to get in the way of their enjoyment of the present, but on the emotional front…? They had set a template for her to follow and it was firmly embedded in her.

She'd had one stumble, a stumble that was in the past, a stumble, she liked to think, that had been a valuable learning curve. A broken heart had stiffened her resolve never to fall for the wrong guy again, to look carefully at the man she would one day trust with her heart.

Raffaele, with his casual disregard for permanence, represented everything she found unappealing.

So that being the case, why should she have such strong opinions on what he did or didn't do? On any of the choices her boss made? Shouldn't she be indifferent to whatever chaos ensued from his unregulated private life? So what if he asked her to buy presents for the women he always ended up walking away from? It was hardly a back-breaking chore. In fact, it often allowed her an afternoon off, scouting through stupidly expensive stores she would never otherwise have entered, and that was sometimes very entertaining. So why the ruffled feathers?

And why should it matter what her boss knew about her background? She was aware that it was an unorthodox one but she wasn't ashamed of her parents. Yet the thought of him teasing out the details of her personal life made her feel vulnerable, made her feel as though she was advertising herself as a woman rather than as an automaton created solely to play the role of Personal Assistant.

Her rebellious eyes were fond of straying in his direction and only she knew her darkest fantasies, so deeply buried that they were only allowed out at night, when her mind was allowed to wander.

They were forbidden and delicious but they were *contained*.

Was there a disturbing jealousy swirling around inside her at the thought of him and the catwalk models he was so fond of?

She eyed the closed door, took a deep breath and then briskly walked towards it, gave a perfunctory knock and slid it open.

Raffaele was sitting behind his desk, which was as big as a single bed. He was sprawled in the leather swivel chair, his long legs extended, his eyes closed and his hands folded behind his head.

The minute Erin walked in, he opened one eye, then both, then sat up, pulling the chair towards the desk and looking at her with his head to the side.

'You haven't brought my coffee,' he said provocatively. 'I'm very thirsty.'

'The doors were shut. I thought you might have been in a meeting.'

'Only with my thoughts.'

'I didn't realise,' Erin said politely, 'that having a meeting with your thoughts necessitated closed doors.'

'Anything to improve the thinking process. How was the rest of your weekend, Erin? How's your father doing?'

Erin was instantly disabused of the hopeful notion that he might have forgotten what she had told him.

'Good. Thank you.'

'Which bit? The weekend or your father?'

'Both. Shall I fetch you some coffee, Raffaele? There are a few things I wanted to ask you about the Saudi investment fund. I had a look at it, as you asked, on Friday and—'

'Coffee first, Erin. My mind isn't on hedge funds at the moment.' He shot her a smile without taking his eyes off her face.

'Now that we've entered this new and exciting phase in our working relationship, I think it's vital we keep the connection going. I've always thought that it's important that co-workers have more than just a superficial relationship. A three-dimensional relationship really expands our ability to work productively together.'

'Really? I don't remember you mentioning anything of the sort in all the time I've worked here.'

'Haven't I?' He frowned with an expression of puzzlement. 'Perhaps,' he continued as his expression cleared, 'that's because you've always encouraged me to keep my distance and naturally I would never have disrespected your boundaries by being curious about you in any way, shape or form...'

'I'm not the sort of person who spends a lot of time trading confidences,' Erin said impatiently.

'Which I'm sure is something we'll get to in due course.'

'I don't think so,' Erin countered as politely as she could.

Raffaele grinned, stood up and took his time stretching. 'Been here since six,' he said. 'Stiff joints from sitting in a chair for too long.'

Erin didn't say anything. She thought that his joints might have been a little less stiff if he'd made *himself* a cup of coffee but actually she welcomed the opportunity to regroup in private. Of all the things she had expected, a direct reminder of what she'd told him hadn't featured.

Why she would expect subtlety from her outspoken boss she had no idea, but as she scuttled out of his office, half sliding the doors shut behind her, her head was in a whirl.

She'd been comfortable watching him from the sidelines. She had been very happy having her harmless fantasies, safe in the knowledge that theirs was exclusively a working relationship. And if, in the deep recesses of her mind, she saw the possibility of something more, then there was no sign of such wild abandon in her dealings with him.

Having moved from pillar to post during her formative years, sometimes attending school for months on end, sometimes home-schooled by her parents or else just burying her head in books and doing the learning herself, Erin had become a private person.

It had been difficult to make friendships when she wasn't around long enough for them to flourish and although she had had a couple of boyfriends, one reasonably serious when she'd been at university, she had always found it difficult to open up, to show the softer, more vulnerable side of herself.

She knew that that was why the guy she'd dated for over a year had broken up with her. He'd wanted more of *her* than she'd known how to give. He'd wanted someone, he had thrown at her, 'less inhibited, less uptight'.

'You're a nice girl,' he'd said from halfway out of the door, shaking his head in frustration, 'but I don't know who you really are, Erin Fisher, and no one ever will unless you learn to open up! You're bloody hopeless! What man is ever going to be interested in a woman who can never let her hair down! Complete waste!'

How his parting shots had stung, had made her feel incomplete and helpless. Those biting words had made her scared to take more risks on love just in case she made another mistake, another misjudgement. She would take her time and not be rushed into having her choices dictated by her biological clock.

She would only risk loving if certainty of that love being returned was as guaranteed as was humanly possible. She would do her utmost to protect her heart and never let it be damaged again. *Never.*

A crush on her boss, because that was what it was, was perfect because it had allowed her to press Pause on doing anything proactive about her love life.

Abruptly finding herself on the receiving end of his curiosity was a lot less perfect, especially as she only had herself to blame.

Erin made the coffee. Suddenly, after years of pleasant hibernation from dipping her toes in the dating game, she wondered how she had ended up where she had.

She was nearly twenty-nine!

She'd vaguely known that at some point in time she would find the guy she wanted to settle down with, but she'd been in no particular hurry to get there.

Maybe, she thought ruefully as she headed back to the lion's den, there was more of her parents in her than she'd thought.

She'd always considered herself so responsible. She'd stuck to the straight and narrow like glue, unlike her forever wandering parents, who had never really paid attention to how their thirst to roam the world had affected their only child.

Yet when it came to finding a soulmate, it seemed as though she was as meandering as them. The one guy she'd hoped might be the soulmate her heart sought had turned out to be a disaster and so she had hidden away behind a silly secret crush.

How did that begin to make sense? There was a life out there waiting to be lived. She thought of Colin asking her out and wondered now whether she should have taken him up on his offer.

'Just what the doctor ordered,' Raffaele said as soon as she returned to his office with the two mugs of coffee.

Erin didn't say anything but she felt a surge of anger that all this tortured self-analysis had been instigated by her boss and the way he was encroaching on her private terrain.

'You're not completely helpless, Raffaele,' she said a little more acidly than she'd intended. 'You know how to make a cup of coffee for yourself. You don't need to wait until I come.'

'Bravo. I like it!' Raffaele came over and took a mug

from her hands, but didn't draw away, a wicked glint in his eyes. As always, he towered over her.

'What? What do you like?' Up close like this, Erin could see the deep blue of his eyes as he stared at her with satisfaction. She could smell the vaguely woody scent of whatever cologne he was wearing. Her heart picked up speed as she stared, doing her best not to flinch away from the directness of his gaze.

'I like hearing you really exercise your voice.'

'I have no idea what you're talking about.'

'You're standing up for yourself!'

'I didn't think I was ever *not* standing up for myself, Raffaele. I've always told you what I thought when I haven't agreed with something you've said…or done.'

'Ah,' he returned, 'but only when it came to work. And naturally, whilst I've appreciated everything you've had to say, it's heart-warming to hear you find your voice when you challenge me on a more personal level.' He nodded to the chair in front of his desk, and Erin obediently sat down.

'You told me that I wasn't allowed to have opinions on your private life, Raffaele. Or have you forgotten that you said that?'

'That's in a different category,' he said smoothly. He still hadn't sat or moved away, so that Erin had to crane her neck to stare up at him. 'What I'm talking about here is you being authentic when you rebut something you don't like. Of course, this doesn't mean that you're excused from making my coffee. On a practical level, you're a much better coffee maker than I am.'

He finally moved to sit back down in his swivel chair and Erin felt her breath return and her pulse normalise.

So he welcomed *her voice*.

Well, she thought, this might actually work for her. If she felt free to answer back to him, then surely it would break the spell he seemed to exert over her? Was he right? Was a more easy-going, well-rounded relationship between them something that was desirable? Had she put Raffaele—or his attractiveness, at least—on some sort of pedestal and fed into that unhealthy addiction by shying away from him? Like some kind of adolescent unrequited crush?

Something easy, something safe she could retreat behind because, after her break-up all those years ago, she was scared of risking her heart with another man? Scared and, unlike so many girls her age, not petrified of entering her thirties without a guy by her side and so in no rush to fix the situation by actually going on dates?

'So,' Raffaele continued, looking at her over the rim of his cup as he sipped the freshly brewed coffee. 'No, no, no…don't get out the laptop just yet. Didn't I just tell you that I'm not having a hedge fund moment? And don't look so alarmed. I haven't suddenly taken leave of my senses.'

The dark, semi-sexy, lazy charm flowed around her and she was more conscious of it than she usually was because they weren't relating to one another in the usual way.

She stared at the space just over his shoulder but it was still far too easy to take in the white shirt, cuffs rolled up to the elbows, the strong, bronzed forearms, the dark hair curling around the strap of his dull matte silver watch strap, the sharp contours of his beautiful aristocratic face.

For a second she thought of her own appearance, regular features, her straight chestnut-brown hair, green eyes, slender and neat and serious. If he was an eagle, she was a sparrow.

'I had no idea there were times when you weren't thinking about hedge funds or investments or company takeovers or exciting mergers.' Erin liked the way this sudden openness between them felt because it gave her a chance to be sarcastic, to gently take him down a notch or two.

'I hope you're not too disappointed.'

'I'm surprised,' she said honestly. 'You're such a workaholic.'

'But I'm not really, am I? You of all people should know that, considering you've only recently staged a rebellion at buying goodbye gifts for the women I go out with.'

Erin flushed.

'I just want to say at this point,' Raffaele murmured soothingly, 'how glad I am that you finally got it together to tell me how you feel about buying those trinkets for my ex-girlfriends. I admit that sermonizing about my relationships is out of bounds, but buying presents? Definitely good of you to remind me that that's not in your remit.'

'Not exactly *trinkets*, Raffaele.'

Raffaele shrugged. 'They are to me,' he said kindly. 'Or maybe a better way of putting it is… I may not commit to permanent relationships, but when they're over, it's my way of thanking the women for the time they've spent with me and the enjoyment they've brought to my life.'

'That's very noble,' Erin said politely, and Raffaele grinned.

'I've never been called *noble* before but I'm more than happy to run with that. But now, moving on to other things…'

'Yes!'

Back to work, Erin thought with relief. Relating to her

boss like this was out of her comfort zone and she was keen to return to where she was more sure-footed. Even if it made sense to build a more three-dimensional relationship with him, this was an early stage and she would need time to get used to the subtle shift in their relationship.

Gradually.

She could feed him small sound bites on a day-to-day basis, always with the proviso that she didn't have to confide any more than she felt was necessary, however much his curiosity might have been piqued.

A Pandora's box hadn't been opened. Far from it.

She felt much better after this bracing internal pep talk. 'Do you want me to prioritise the emails that came in at the end of last week? I know you've scanned them all, but there are quite a few I can handle and dispatch myself. You can sign them off by the time I'm ready to leave this evening.'

Raffaele looked at Erin from under his lashes for a few seconds in thoughtful silence.

She looked exactly the same as she did most days, bar slight variations in colour schemes. Neat skirt, grey, neat short-sleeved shirt, pink with fine white stripes, neat black flats, hair glossy and tucked behind her ears, secured on either side with tortoiseshell clips, and yet the more he looked, the more intensely pretty she seemed. Those delicate features and the huge hazel eyes that were so good at revealing nothing whatsoever. Or had been, until two days ago. That change had been very satisfying indeed.

Outside it was a balmy summer day but where everyone else her age might have turned up the volume on colour, dusted off the cobwebs and brought out the flowered dresses, Erin was as background as she always strove to be except...

She wasn't really background at all, was she?

Raffaele felt the kick of curiosity about her again, this time a little harder. An internal alarm rang distantly, but it was easy to ignore. He was well practised when it came to self-control. This intense curiosity might jar a little because it was out of the ordinary but when it came to women, he was immune to being thrown off course.

He waved aside her enthusiastically professional response. 'Sure. Of course I'll sign off all those emails and by the way, much appreciation for your diligence on the weekend.'

'Is there something more important that you'd like me to do? Before I finish up what I started working on on Friday?' she asked.

'Now that you mention it...'

'Yes?'

'Remember my little drinks party on Saturday?' It was a provocative introduction to what he wanted to say, and Raffaele was amused at the way she unconsciously stiffened.

Yep, she certainly remembered it and he knew why—it was the first time she'd opened up to him about anything. It had made him realise, with surprise just how work oriented their conversations always were and just how cleverly she had always avoided mentioning anything significant about herself.

Her reticence, he now thought with a certain amount of admiration, was a refreshing change from women who were always keen to tell him anything he wanted to know about themselves.

He decided on the spot that a closed book could be a lot more alluring.

Her cheeks were pink and she'd lowered her eyes and was twiddling her fingers on her lap.

'Remember I mentioned a conversation I had with Archer?' He rescued her from her discomfort and saw her breathe a sigh of relief.

'I can't remember who Archer was, I'm afraid.'

'Tall guy…grey hair and a lot of it…some might call it a mane…much younger wife with enough jewellery to open a store.'

Erin smiled and Raffaele realised how much he liked to see her smile. They were a rare sight, and lit up her face in a way that was infectious.

'She did jangle quite a bit. The upside of which was that you always had fair warning of her approach. Sorry, very catty remark.'

Raffaele laughed and looked at her appreciatively. 'Archer's disposing of one of the arms of his leisure business. He wants to specialise in casinos and he needs to sell his chain of hotels so that he can reinvest the money into expanding the gambling side of his business, both the physical premises and creating more of an online presence. I'm thinking of branching out of the money markets and dabbling in something a little less predictable. I'm getting a tired of dealing with tech and hedge funds.'

'Really?'

Raffaele shrugged.

He thought of where he was and what he had inherited. Enough money at the age of twenty-one to take his first-class degree in Maths, convert it into a Masters in Business and not have to worry about the cost. Enough money to decide where he wanted to set his sights and pursue his end goal, without fear of being thrown into poverty if he failed.

Wealthy parents...substantial trust fund... He had increased that original trust fund a hundred times over since he had come into it. He had devoted his career to what he had known and what had come easily to him. A flair with numbers had set him up to turn straw into gold when it came to the money markets, mergers and acquisitions. There had been no need to be a workaholic but he had nevertheless been compelled to throw himself into work, because work was always going to be more reliable than emotions. Work would never disappoint him the way people continually had. He was, he thought bitterly, the archetypal man with the privileged life whose soul was empty, and no amount of money could fill that void.

He was the guy who had never known the real warmth of parental love even if he had been the recipient of everything that money could buy. He couldn't remember either of his parents ever hugging him. And that was before he'd discovered that his parents' marriage was nothing more than a sham, his father's affairs protected from scrutiny in the name of the status quo and power.

Still, that hadn't been enough to kill off his juvenile illusions about love. He had stupidly thought that still... there might be hope for him. Had idiotically ventured into a relationship that had conclusively shattered what little remained of his rose-tinted view of the world.

Disconcerted by this sudden plunge into introspection, Raffaele frowned and dismissed the past with the ease born of habit.

'I can afford to get bored and try my hand at something else,' he said smoothly.

'You're so spoiled,' Erin told him drily. 'I hope you

never say anything like that in the public forum, Raffaele, because that's a sure-fire way to lose friends and *not* influence people.'

'Since when do I care what other people think of me?'

'You care what the women you go out with think or else you wouldn't spend a small fortune buying them trinkets when you break up with them.'

'Don't you mean getting *you* to buy them trinkets when I break up with them?' He grinned. 'Okay, we won't go there. I don't want another sermon from you.' His grin widened when she glared at him. 'Maybe,' he added as an aside, 'I buy them expensive trinkets to acknowledge the Herculean feat of putting up with me.'

Erin raised her eyebrows. For a few seconds as their eyes tangled, she wondered whether she could sense an underlying seriousness beneath his throwaway remark.

He was so cavalier about his relationships, so grounded in the certainty that he didn't want any of them to go anywhere.

Why? He had always lived a gilded life. Shouldn't he have been rushing to get the next bit of the jigsaw puzzle in place? The wife and the kids and the houses here, there and everywhere?

It was a question she would never ask. Even the thought of stampeding through that kind of barrier made her skin prickle.

'You're right. Let's talk about you getting into the hotel business because you're going through a bored patch.' She smiled, easing back into the familiarity between them she was so accustomed to.

'Interesting way of putting it. I'll email you the list of hotels. Not many. Five, to be precise. One in the Caribbean and the rest in Europe. The one in the Caribbean is dragging the other four down because it needs extensive refurbishment. Has promise to more than pay for itself but Archer's not willing to put the money in because of the casino business he wants to expand.'

'But would five hotels be worth the time and effort?' Erin asked dubiously.

'I'd probably get them at a knock-down price. He's keen to sell and wants them to remain as hotels and not be converted into flats or housing. I've promised to maintain their integrity. I gather the hotels were his first foray into big business and he's sentimental about them. Written into the contract would be a clause allowing him and his wife to continue to stay at any one of them free of charge. He doesn't think there are many potential buyers who would concede to that.'

'But you would.'

'I can afford to be lenient.' Raffaele shrugged.

'Okay...'

'Why do you sound so unconvinced?' Raffaele said with a touch of irritation.

Erin paused. Perhaps he had a point. 'I'm not sure,' she confessed truthfully. 'I suppose... I suppose I always associated you with the business of making money and a lot of it, so five hotels, one of which needs a lot of work, doesn't seem to fit the pattern. Also all the stuff you do is wrapped up in the business world. Either money or tech.' She smiled. 'It would be a challenge, and I *know* you said you want a change and *of course* a change is as good as a rest but even so...'

'It's not all about money,' Raffaele said gruffly. 'Is that what you think? That I'm driven by the desire to make more and more money?'

'I haven't given it much thought.' The conversation seemed to have suddenly drifted into uncertain territory and she couldn't understand why. Surely it had been a harmless enough question?

There was a brief silence and in that silence something fizzed, a tiny electric current zapping between them like quicksilver. It made Erin shiver with a mixture of apprehension, wariness and low-level excitement.

'But—' her mouth was suddenly dry and her thoughts felt muddled and sluggish '—it doesn't matter.' She laughed shortly, breath hitching in her throat because he was still looking at her, his navy blue eyes unrevealing. 'It's certainly not my business what motivates you. I think hotels would be a great thing to get into. I mean… the world's getting smaller and smaller, and people are getting more and more adventurous and the cost of travel is getting more and more competitive. Er…have you had any ideas on what you would do to change the dynamic of what already exists?'

'Small steps.' Raffaele waved a hand although his eyes remained firmly glued to her face. 'Early stages.'

'I could set up whatever meetings you want,' Erin suggested.

'Already had a more lengthy chat with Archer yesterday. He's definitely on board. Of course, the money may not be of a make-or-break figure but that doesn't mean that I'm going to go into something like this without any due diligence whatsoever.'

'No…'

'Which brings me to the interesting part of this deal.'

'Yes?'

'I think step one will be seeing what I'm letting myself in for and the best place to start will be with the hotel that needs the most work.'

He switched attention to his computer and after a couple of seconds he swivelled the screen so that it was facing Erin. She leaned towards it and focused on the online brochure in front of her.

She scrolled past a picture of a tired hotel in a spectacular setting, amid lush rainforests. She flicked through to images of faded plantation-style elegance and then speed-read some of the copy, all touristy bumph.

'So here's where I tell you to make sure your passport's up to date.'

Erin looked at him blankly as her brain registered the question.

'Sorry?'

'Because—' he sat back and spread his arms wide in an all-encompassing gesture '—the sooner we go and see what the deal is with hotel number one, the sooner I can start putting things in place. I've never been involved in the leisure industry. It should prove to be an interesting gamble.'

'We?'

'You'll be coming with me,' Raffaele said comfortably.

Erin's eyes widened with sudden alarm and her heart picked up pace. 'That's not going to be possible, I'm afraid.'

She'd gone on a couple of business trips with him in the past. Short, intense breaks in Paris, Lisbon and Milan, where they had worked solidly alongside the usual consortium of lawyers and accountants. She'd never thought twice about accompanying him but that was before...

Before things had changed between them...

Those subtle changes had shifted the dynamics. It felt

ridiculous that telling her boss a tiny bit about herself had altered their relationship so much, but it had. She couldn't quite put her finger on why, because nothing she had said had been very important and yet…

'Why not?' Raffaele asked bluntly. 'Is it because of your father? I know you've been going down to help out for the past few weekends but if your presence is going to be missed so much, then I'm happy to get someone in to do whatever needs to be done outside…harvest whatever needs harvesting. What needs harvesting anyway? You never specified.'

'No!' Erin was even more appalled at the thought of further inroads being made into her private life. 'I mean—'

'So if it's not concern for your father, then why the hesitation? Do you have any inconvenient pets that might need sitting? That can always be arranged. Kennels exist, to the best of my knowledge. You don't have a dog, do you? Or a cat? Why don't I know this about you? Seems a small detail. Birds? Tropical fish?'

'Raffaele, no pets! No dogs, cats, fish or birds!'

'So where's the problem?' He let the silence settle between them for a few seconds. 'We'll be gone for a week and you'll be richly compensated for the inconvenience, just as you always have been on the few trips abroad you've done with me. So, Erin, all you have to do is sort out the flights and book us a couple of rooms at the hotel. Honestly? I have no idea why you're so alarmed.' He tilted his head to one side and stared at her. 'It won't be any different than any other business trip except this time, we're going somewhere hot.'

CHAPTER THREE

EIGHT DAYS LATER, Erin found herself staring, with trepidation, at the suitcase sitting by the front door of her little rented two-up, two-down terraced house on the outskirts of London.

Fortunately, considering the fact that she would shortly be flying to the Caribbean with him, the discomfort she had briefly felt in Raffaele's presence ever since the cocktail party had faded as they once more settled into the usual routine of work, work, work.

No more curious questions about her private life. No more provocative remarks that made her feel hot and bothered and on edge.

Raffaele had returned to the grindstone and indeed, she hadn't seen him at all for the past four days. He'd disappeared to New York on business.

Yesterday, he had emailed her to tell her that he would send his driver to collect her and take her to the airport. Normally, she managed all his travel arrangements but he knew her well. She suspected that he'd worked out that presenting her with a fait accompli would do away with her predictable protests that she would be more than happy to arrange her own transport, which was what she'd done on every other occasion when they'd travelled anywhere together on business. Fine when it was a short hop at a civilised time during the day. Less fine for a transatlantic long-haul trip at an ungodly hour in the morning.

'I'll be waiting for you in the first-class lounge,' he'd instructed her. 'We can take some time to discuss the nitty-gritty of the hotel accounts and expenditures so that we're prepared for the meetings we'll be having with the hotel manager and his lot and Erin—' even as she'd read the closing sentence of his email, she'd had no trouble picturing the amused grin on his face '—don't forget it's going to be boiling hot and humid over there. Feel free to jettison the woolly tights and starchy skirts.'

Right now, at a little after six in the morning, she was dressed in a loose pair of cargo pants and a short-sleeved T-shirt. She'd thrown the grey cardigan she usually wore to the office over the T-shirt in a nod to the fact that this wasn't going to be a holiday. It was going to be about work and meetings.

She would have felt more comfortable in her usual uniform of a skirt, a blouse and her black pumps, but even she had to acknowledge that that look wouldn't do in searing tropical heat. Not unless she wanted to pass out with heat stroke.

Her case contained an assortment of similarly summer clothes, most of which hadn't seen the light of day since last year when she'd had a two-week holiday in Cyprus with two girlfriends.

She was hovering in her small sitting room, glancing anxiously at her watch, when the doorbell rang half an hour before she was expecting it to. Overtaken by a sudden flurry of nerves, she leapt to her feet and headed for the front door.

She glanced at her reflection in the mirror in the tiny,

narrow hallway. She looked young and fresh-faced and not much like Raffaele Rossi's PA heading off for a week of high-level meetings and writing up reports. With one hand on her case and her bag slung over her shoulder, she pulled open the door—and drew in a sharp breath, her eyes widening in shock.

'Raffaele!'

Her boss stood on her doorstep lounging against the door frame, hand raised as though on the verge of ringing the doorbell again. He was casually dressed in black jeans, a black polo shirt and uberexpensive tan handmade loafers. The absence of all logos proclaimed just how pricey his clothes were.

'What are you doing here?' Erin asked.

'I thought it might be fairly obvious. I've come to collect you to take you to the airport.'

'I was expecting George!'

'Sadly George had to pull out at the last minute. His wife's been rushed to hospital with a burst appendix. I thought it might be a little insensitive to tell him to drive us to Gatwick first before going to the hospital to hold her hand. Open up and let me in. I have time for a quick coffee before we head off.'

'That's awful!'

'What's awful? George's sudden health crisis with his wife—' Raffaele grinned '—or my unexpected appearance on your doorstep?'

'George, of course!'

'I'll be sure to pass on your condolences.'

'I could have taken public transport,' Erin huffed as she continued to guard the door with folded arms.

'I wouldn't dream of letting you take public transport to the airport, Erin. How would you get to Gatwick from here, anyway? I don't recall passing any Tubes on the way. Or maybe I passed one a thousand miles back.'

He nudged the front door and Erin reluctantly stepped aside.

Raffaele had never been to her house. There had never been any reason for him to have visited. Now that he was here, she could feel a tide of mortification rising up inside her.

So there *wasn't* a Tube. There was a mainline station which she took to Waterloo and then it was easy enough to connect with whatever Tube she wanted. Granted the mainline station was a hearty walk away but there was no such thing as too much exercise.

The area was respectable enough and the house was acceptable enough, and her landlady was a dream who had allowed her to paint the walls and hang one or two pictures and plant whatever she'd wanted to plant in the back garden.

But as she looked at her boss turning a full circle in the small hallway, she mentally cringed because she knew that this wouldn't have been what he would have expected, not given the amount he paid her.

'I can make you a coffee if you like,' she offered, breaking the telling silence briskly, 'but perhaps it might be a good idea to get to the airport early? We'll be less rushed if we discuss business once we're there.' She remained where she was, arms folded.

Raffaele focused his eyes on her for a few silent seconds.

Frankly, he was shocked.

Why was she living here? In a faceless, nondescript suburb miles from public transport, never mind cafés, restaurants, shops and any sort of buzzy infrastructure suitable for a girl of her age? The nearest he had found to any sort of life had been a strip of uninspiring shops on what passed for the high street. Several had been boarded up.

She was paid a small fortune!

Where was the money going? How many more layers were there to peel away to reveal the real Erin Fisher? How was it that in *four years* he had succeeded in finding out less about her than he'd found out about the guy who delivered his post?

Curiosity tore through him but he nodded slowly and agreed.

'Good idea. You can fill me in roughly on any background information you've got on the hotel group. General stuff. We can hit the details later when I've got my computer in front of me and I'm not behind the wheel of a car. Where's your bag?'

'It's okay, I can carry it.' Erin grabbed her compact suitcase, which she'd left by the front door, glanced around her one last time.

As he passed by her through the front door, Raffaele could see her mind working—making sure she hadn't forgotten anything, mentally double-checking that everything that should be turned off was turned off and everything that should be turned on was turned on. Everything he never had to consider when he left on trips; he had others to worry about those things for him.

Finally, Erin stepped out and locked up.

'Sure you have enough in that small case?'

'It's not a holiday. It's a work week, so I've taken pretty much what I would wear for a work week.'

'But excluding,' Raffaele murmured, sliding an amused sideways glance at her, 'the starchy skirts and blouses...'

Erin huffed her way into the passenger seat of Raffaele's sleek, black Ferrari and didn't respond to the jibe.

'Well?'

He turned to her when he was in the car, flicking on the engine but staring at her for a few seconds as he waited for her to answer.

'No starchy skirts. Raffaele, you made that clear in your email. I've googled the weather over there so obviously I haven't packed my tights and fleecy jumpers and overcoat.'

Raffaele burst out laughing and pulled away from the kerb.

'What about swimsuits?'

'What about them?'

'Any tucked away in your very small case?'

'I had no idea I would be needing those for a working holiday,' Erin said tartly. 'Are we planning on conducting meetings in the ocean?'

Raffaele was still laughing as she fetched her notebook from her handbag and began prepping him on all the non-essential details of the hotel chain that might not seem immediately relevant but which might hold the key to whether he acquired the properties or not.

This was something Erin was especially good at.

She'd worked hard to get to university and she'd known, the minute she started doing her research, that the best courses would be the ones that led to concrete jobs. She'd studied accounting and finance with a view to becoming a chartered accountant but along the way had got spooked at the promise of a job that would require very long hours doing things that seemed too repetitive to be satisfying, at least for her.

Plus, her parents had been entering an unstable time of their lives, ready to settle down but without the money to buy anywhere at all. They were getting older, with their mobile home looking like it might be their forever home, so she wanted a job that paid well but didn't consume her every waking moment. She needed to be there for them when they inevitably needed her.

When they'd been younger, they'd managed just fine but now that they were no longer moving around, Erin could see how much they had aged over the years.

They'd had her very late in life and now were both in their late sixties and bewildered by modern life, which seemed to have passed them by in their colourful, adventurous travels. Their computer was a thousand years old and only used for the most basic of tasks.

She'd had to introduce them to technology bit by bit and had realised that any job that demanded all of her time wasn't going to work, and besides she wouldn't enjoy it.

She'd had some interesting temp jobs while she waited for just the right one to come along and sure enough, the role as Raffaele's assistant had fallen into her lap and had been sheer perfection. She'd been able to use everything she'd learned at university and had enjoyed delving into the details of projects without having to devote her entire life to them. She'd loved having the challenge of new things happening week after week whilst also maintaining a switch-off mode so that none of those new challenges became onerous.

She rattled off her findings as he drove, satnav guiding them on the fastest route. Raffaele listened with his head tilted to one side, interrupting to ask questions, nodding in agreement with some of her conclusions and then congratulating her on a thorough job when she'd finished.

'My perfect little PA,' he eventually murmured with satisfaction, 'what would I do without you?'

'I'm guessing you wouldn't curl up in a corner, sobbing and crying and thinking that the sky had fallen in. You'd just find someone else.' Erin glanced across at him with a wry smile and then kept looking, first at his aristocratic profile, the crooked smile on his mouth and then at the capable, long fingers holding the steering wheel. She had to tear her eyes away.

'Took me a while to find *you*. Do you remember what I told you about the long line of failed applicants?'

'You mean the ones who just couldn't help falling in love with you?'

'Inappropriate crushes, I believe is what I said.'

'Maybe you just made them a little nervous, Raffaele. Or maybe if you'd widened the pool to include a few candidates over the age of thirty, you might have had a little more luck.'

The scenery was whizzing past them. She lived closer to Gatwick than Raffaele did and they were well on their way now, speeding towards the airport and with next to no traffic on the roads because it was still early.

'You weren't over the age of thirty and I don't make *you* nervous,' he pointed out. 'You settled in to my routine like a duck to water from day one. No blushing every time I looked at you…no stammering if I asked a question…no showing up in inappropriate outfits…'

'Sorry, but I thought you were quite critical of my dress code.' Erin settled back against the plush leather seat and half closed her eyes.

It was a stupid car. Who needed something this fast in London? But she had to admit that it was comfortable. Raffaele had once told her that he didn't get to drive as often as he liked, so she could understand why he hadn't delegated the task to someone else even though after New York he surely would have been a tiny bit jet-lagged.

People stared, mouths open, as the black Ferrari rushed past their more pedestrian cars on the motorway.

It was ridiculous to be tickled pink by that but Erin was.

'Your dress code is perfectly acceptable. Although I've questioned it when you've shown up at Christmas parties in pretty much the same outfits as you wear to work.'

'I don't have wardrobes filled with cocktail dresses.'

Raffaele slanted a sideways glance at her.

Erin's delicate, pale face was drawn. He took in the outfit, her interpretation of 'casual'. Workmanlike cargo trousers, a T-shirt and a cardigan which she'd wrapped around herself.

He was only now realising just how little she put herself out to impress him on the physical front and just how surprising that was. Nearly every woman Raffaele had ever met had always done their best to impress him. Given the chance to show up in casual gear, Erin had chosen the least feminine outfit she could have got her hands on, even though the loose, unfussy clothes suited her slender frame, made her look incredibly feminine.

With a small jolt, he realised that being in her presence soothed him somehow. When he considered his life, the relationships he'd had... First, there was his cold, distant upbringing, carrying with it those hard lessons of hurt, sadness, disillusionment and eventually the erection of icy walls behind which his heart would forever be locked. Then that one crazy fling with a woman all those years ago who confirmed his belief that romantic happiness was beyond his grasp. It had been a painful reminder of his own inability to love; he'd tried but he just hadn't had enough to give. After that, he had walked away from anything that required too much emotion of him. And now there were the women to whom he gave trinkets when everything ended. Fun, energetic, temporary.

Between all that, Erin occupied a special place.

She stimulated him intellectually and without a physical connection…yes, she soothed him, made him feel safe.

And now, more than that…she intrigued him.

What had she meant when she'd said that she didn't have wardrobes full of cocktail dresses?

Did she hate cocktail dresses?

Because on her pay grade, she could certainly buy as many as she wanted. That thought brought him back to her house. What was going on there?

He dumped pointless introspection about his past and focused on the here and now. The suddenly very invigorating here and now with his once-predictable secretary. She had her secrets and he'd find out all about them in due course. It was a very pleasant prospect.

They were going to have a week together and not all of it was going to involve sitting in front of a computer or having back-to-back meetings with hotel people.

Next to him, Erin yawned.

'You're tired,' he said.

'I got up really early,' Erin agreed. 'Plus I went to bed really late. I wanted to finish doing as thorough a job as I could on researching the hotels and it took me a bit longer than I thought. I never knew the hotel business could have so many nooks and crannies. It's not straightforward at all. The profit and loss columns are, but then things can change at the turn of the dice. If the restaurant in one of the hotels gets a new chef and the menu isn't popular, business could fall off and that could affect the profit margins in a matter of weeks. If something happens that spooks the clientele, same could happen...'

'Something like what? Murder in the building?' Raffaele grinned but he was still half thinking about her living circumstances and tempted to ask her what was going on there.

'You'd be surprised. I started checking out all the things that could go wrong in hotels, impacting their profits, and there's a lot.'

Erin shifted so that she was half turned to look at him.

'I still don't get it, you know,' she murmured drowsily, on the edge of nodding off in the sleek, powerful car.

'Don't get what?'

'Why you're interested in buying this chain of hotels. It feels like a real departure for you. And feel free to tell me to mind my own business but I'm just looking at it from a practical point of view. I know you said that it's not about the money but I always figured that, with any luck, people end up doing the things they really enjoy and are good at and then they stick to the programme and don't really deviate. And you've always seemed to thrive on the challenges of the financial world.'

'A change is as good as a rest, as you said. Is that what you did? Never deviate? Were you never tempted by any other career choice?'

'I...' Erin blinked. She seemed to think for a second. 'No. Financial security is important to me,' she said firmly. 'I also didn't think that we were talking about me.'

'Now that we're getting to know one another a little better, I think that conversations between us should be fluid, don't you? Airport up ahead. We made excellent time.'

The conversation was lost in a whirlwind of valet parking and checking in and then, within half an hour, they were in the first-class lounge, ushered through the opulent, semi-empty space like royalty to a group of comfy chairs and brought coffee and breakfast by one of the uniformed staff who was clearly in awe of Raffaele.

And then they carried on chatting about work.

Her comfort zone, Raffaele mused. He looked at her from under his lashes as she busied herself on her laptop, swivelling it occasionally to corroborate whatever point she was making. He intended to dig much deeper into his guarded secretary than she might anticipate.

Why the sudden fascination? Had it always been there, lurking under the surface, waiting for the right key to unlock it?

Or maybe he was bored of his standard-issue women. Bored with ridiculously good-looking women who were always too eager to please. Maybe he needed the safe distraction of someone like Erin, someone clever and restrained and, even more important, someone who wasn't in awe of him, who would never want any sort of romantic involvement with him. Why shouldn't he give in to curiosity about his disciplined, guarded secretary with all those enticing layers?

One day he would settle down, although right now the thought alone was enough to bring him out in a cold sweat. Too many associations with his parents and their dysfunctional marriage, two people wandering around their mansions, barely connecting on any meaningful level. Too many memories of his youthful hopes shot down in flames because the girl he'd thought he'd loved just couldn't put up with a guy who had no heart to give. He thought of all the many ways love could fail and his mind went blank.

Why was the past resurfacing right now and with such

vigour? Raffaele didn't know, but it made no difference. He was firmly rooted in the way he was. He would never change.

He was here, Erin was here and she had challenged him by revealing just a little bit more about herself than she ever had before. He'd never been one to resist a challenge so right now, Erin was irresistible.

'Are you listening to what I'm saying, Raffaele?'

Raffaele smiled slowly at her. 'I'm always listening to what you say.'

Erin reddened. For a couple of seconds, she appeared to be lost for words. She stared down at her computer; Raffaele watched, lazy and amused and interested.

'Good,' she told him huskily when she finally dragged her gaze back to him, 'because I've done a lot of work on these hotels...and a lot of background research into the hospitality trade.'

'I'm getting the picture. Definitely beyond the call of duty. No need for you to have stayed up working into the early hours of the morning to collate all this material. I may be a hard taskmaster but even I have limits. You told me you were curious about my sudden interest in branching out from the well-trodden path.'

Someone came around to tell them that they could board and Raffaele stood up and waited for her to follow suit.

'I'll tell you why...' He picked up where he had left off and fell into step alongside her, looking down at the smooth, silky, chestnut-brown hair that swung in a shiny curtain on either side of her face. The little clips restraining it were somehow prissy and sexy at the same time. 'I came into a sizeable trust fund when I was twenty-one, enough for me to play around and take my time discovering what

I was really good at. It was a privilege. I had the luxury of only needing brains and drive to get where I wanted to go. A very gifted guy I met a few months ago, Alessandro Barbieri, had equal amounts of brains and drive but he also had obstacles to deal with that I never had. My trust fund was brilliant but there's no such thing as a free gift, at least not in my corner of the world with my wealthy parents.'

'How so?' Erin looked sideways at him with wide, curious eyes and shivered as his deep blue gaze lingered on her face.

'Part of the condition of my trust fund was to continue working for the family company as a form of long-term repayment of the money being granted to me at such a young age. Had I chosen to take my trust fund later, when I was in my early thirties, it would have come with no strings attached. My parents could have waived that condition but they chose not to.'

'So there was no rush for you. You could have gone to work for your family company, knowing that you would come into a lump sum when it was time for you to settle down and get married.' She smiled. 'You're an only child. Maybe they couldn't bear the thought of an empty nest.'

Raffaele's lips thinned. She couldn't have been further from the truth. His father had always enjoyed power over other people and that had included him. For Franco Rossi, love was control and control could be cruel.

Somehow he had got lost in his explanation but now he found that he was enjoying the rare experience of opening up to someone else. This wasn't weakness. He had casually mentioned something that could be found anywhere on the internet if you could be bothered to sift through all the bumph about him that had been posted over the years.

The details of his background were all there for anyone to see. Erin knew that he was an only child and he couldn't remember ever having mentioned that to her. It was just general knowledge.

If he had elaborated on the bare bones, then it just came under the heading of chit-chat with a woman he actually spent the majority of his life with.

'Empty nest? No. You haven't quite got that right.' His voice was bitter and as their eyes briefly met he noted her startled look. He forced a tight smile. 'I actually paid back every penny of the trust fund as soon as I was financially able to so that I could sever any hold my parents might have felt they had on me. Then I worked furiously to replenish my resources. But now that I have more than I could ever possibly need, I fancy doing something I was never geared to do but was always interested in pursuing.'

Walking at pace and not looking at him, Erin felt a slow flush of heat within her. This sharing of confidences felt incredibly intimate.

She wondered whether Raffaele was aware of the change in his tone of voice, the disillusionment that had seeped through at that passing mention of his parents.

'That's brilliant,' she said warmly but she didn't glance across at him because she realised that she didn't want this moment to be over quite yet. It was like having a taste of forbidden fruit—exciting, irresistible…dangerous.

She'd always had a lot of insight into his work ethic, into his many and varied relationships with the opposite sex… into his utter lack of commitment on that front, but she had never had any inkling of his buried dreams or unfulfilled desires, had never once heard him mention his family.

Was that what she was now glimpsing? *The real Raffaele that no one ever saw?*

Or was she letting her imagination get the better of her?

Was this stuff he routinely told other people but had never told her because she was his employee? She always suspected that Raffaele only revealed what he wanted to reveal, that he was, at heart, an intensely private man. But maybe he was, in actual fact, the sort who spilled his heart out to every one of those women he hopped into bed with.

Maybe there was nothing he loved more than a bit of post-coital breast beating and emotion sharing.

No.

Her gut told her that the things he'd just told her were feelings he'd probably never shared with anyone and the heat spread through her again.

'I admit I love what I do and I've always been invested in the importance of having financial security...' Thoughts of her parents and their casual disregard for anything that smacked of putting down roots or planning for a future sprang to her mind. 'But I've always been interested in painting...'

'Painting?'

'No need to sound so shocked, Raffaele,' Erin laughed. She'd barely noticed that they'd been checked through and were now heading to board the plane.

She'd travelled first-class with him before on business trips and every time she'd been impressed all over again by the sheer luxury. The plush bedding, the flat bed, the gourmet à la carte dining and the all the little extras as well, none of which she had ever taken advantage of.

Now, though, as they were shown to their seats, which were side by side and as comfortable as armchairs, Erin barely noticed the opulence around her or the fawning of the good-looking crew eager to hand them flutes of champagne.

As she settled in and half turned to look at him, she felt the thrill of danger zip through her again.

Tomorrow she would *definitely* put all this wild curiosity to rest but in the meantime...

Her eyes drifted treacherously to Raffaele's forearm resting on the wide leather armrest between them. Bronzed, muscled, strong.

She looked away guiltily.

'I've always absolutely loved drawing but with all the travelling we did...'

'Travelling? What travelling? I always got the impression that the Greek islands and Rhodes was the extent of your travels.'

'I meant...' Too late, Erin realised that she was on the verge of sharing way too much.

What was going on here, she thought with a flare of panic? Had she forgotten that Raffaele was *her boss*? She had worked hard to make sure that boundaries between them were always maintained. She had known from day one that he didn't tolerate inappropriate behaviour from the women who worked for him. That had suited her fine because she was, by nature, guarded and self-contained.

So what was happening here?

Did she really want to jeopardise her job for the sake of satisfying her curiosity?

Worse, was she beginning to think that because she had shared a little more of herself with Raffaele and because he had said a couple of things about *himself*, that they were somehow striking forth on some kind of relationship? That they were now going to be sharing little confidences and eyeing one another across their laptop computers?

Had she *taken leave of her senses*?

She thought about the crush she'd had on him for *years*. Had that managed to scramble her brains?

She strapped herself in and reached into her bag for the book she had brought with her, a pointed reminder to herself that she wasn't here to make incessant small talk and tell him all the ins and outs of her private life.

The thought of having to face him in an office setting after a series of indiscreet confessions filled her with dread.

'I meant that I've always *wanted* to do a lot of travelling, landscape painting. It's an impractical dream but yes, I suppose if I could have, I might have chosen to study fine art but…' She shot him a wary look and began opening her book to her bookmarked page. 'Not many of us have a trust fund to be going on with.' She smiled at him, one of her practised cool, unrevealing smiles. 'Do you want to carry on working on the flight over? I know it's going to be a long one. Or is it okay if I read my book?'

She turned her focus to the page, even knowing that Raffaele was still staring at her. Only when he tilted the book, forcing her to look up, did she meet his amused gaze.

'What are you reading?'

Their eyes tangled and he grinned. 'Looks verbose.'

'How can you tell anything from the cover?' Erin tugged the book and he released it but carried on looking at her.

'I can't. I'm going on the blurb at the back. I can't say that "a moving and epic poetic masterpiece" is the sort of thing I would find captivating.'

'It's riveting. Can I ask what does interest you?'

'Nothing poetic or epic. Feel free to devour your book

on the flight over. I have a lot of work to attend to so you can settle down in comfort without fear of being interrupted. You'll probably fall asleep on the flight over.'

'I don't think so.'

'Even with a bed? You can also change into pyjamas. There's a luxury pair waiting for you so that you can really relax.'

'I'll stick to my book.'

'Of course you will but I'd be shocked if it doesn't put you to sleep.'

He was still grinning as he flipped open his laptop and she settled into the enormous seat and made herself comfortable.

Fall asleep?

Pyjamas?

She'd rather drink twenty cups of black coffee and prop her eyelids open with matchsticks.

She stared at her book while her mind chattered away, diving off in a million different directions.

The next sound she heard was the captain's voice congratulating himself on an excellent and turbulence-free flight.

She was nudged into consciousness and blinked her way to the surface to see Raffaele's face way too close to hers for comfort. There was a cushion under her head and, horror of horrors, she was propped up on his shoulder.

'Ah, Sleeping Beauty's awake!'

'You should never have let me fall asleep!'

'And deprive myself of the chance to hear you snoring? Wouldn't have dreamed of it. But it's wakey-wakey time now. Our adventure's waiting just around the corner!'

CHAPTER FOUR

WITH THE TIME DIFFERENCE, dusk was already gathering pace as she and Raffaele cleared customs at the tiny airport on the island.

A handful of hours on a plane had transported them from the pleasant warmth of an English early-summer day to blistering tropical heat.

Around them, people were coming and going and talking and calling out to one another. Taxi drivers were hunting down customers, but without any real sense of urgency, taking refusals good-naturedly. There were fragrant smells of food in the air and over the road, Erin could make out a bustling strip of shops selling souvenirs and food.

She stared around her.

It was wondrous—he smells, the heat and the indigo, purple and orange sky blazing above them as night fell.

'Now aren't you glad that you listened to what I said and didn't decide to wear your suit?'

'I've never worn a suit in my entire life, Raffaele.'

But she was too absorbed in this alien, spectacular environment to rustle up much of a response to what he'd said.

'A jacket...a blouse...a skirt... That's as good as a suit. The hotel's arranged a driver for us while we're here.'

The words had barely left his mouth when a smiling man approached them with a clipboard and then they were being ushered through the milling crowd away from the airport towards a car park.

In the distance, she could see the sea, black and still. The heat was like being in a sauna, and it made her slow down.

She felt Raffaele's hand on her back as he gently but firmly propelled her along and she cast one last backwards glance over her shoulder, taking in everything, wishing she could have stayed a bit longer just breathing in the swirl of new, different smells.

She'd travelled so much with her parents. She'd seen every corner of England. For six memorable months of lazy home-schooling, they had explored northern France against a backdrop of incredible spring and summer weather. There had been lots of barbecues on their portable camping stove, weaving in and out of small villages in their caravan, enjoying the scenery and a culture which was different from their home and yet very much the same.

She'd never, ever been anywhere like *this* and every adventurous cell in her body which she hadn't even known existed was fired up with excitement.

They slid into a small, black four-wheel-drive jeep and then they were off, windows down so that a warm breeze blew through.

The hotel was tucked away in the lush rainforest in the opposite direction of the main drag of tourist hotels and motels. She'd glanced at the blurb about it on the internet and knew that it was divided into a handful of little cabins and then the main hotel for guests who didn't like the thought of being too cut off.

Erin couldn't get enough of the scenery passing them by even though, as darkness settled fast, the canopy of towering trees and the dense foliage by the side of the road was reduced to shadows and mysterious dark shapes that harboured the vibrant sounds of tree frogs and crickets and the last of the daytime birdsong.

'This is amazing.' She turned to Raffaele, who was leaning against the passenger door and looking at her. In the darkness, she could only make out the angles of his face and the glitter of his eyes.

The road was bumpy, narrowing in places, widening in others and swinging around corners that were barely discernible in the darkness. She had to hang on to the door handle to steady herself from falling against him.

Ahead, their driver was concentrating on the twisty road to the exclusion of everything else.

'Never been to the Caribbean?'

'No. A bit of Europe and... No, I've never been anywhere like this at all in my life before. Have you? No, strike that. Silly question.' The breeze was blowing her hair across her face. She held it back with one hand and looked at him. 'I bet this part of the world is like a second home to you.'

'Not quite,' Raffaele said drily, 'but I'm not unfamiliar with it.'

The car jolted and she half fell against him, then quickly pulled back as he reached out to steady her.

'I don't know how I'm going to be able to focus on work while I'm here,' she confessed breathlessly.

Something about the fragrant air, the salty smell of distant sea and the unfamiliarity of their surroundings was filling her with a heady sense of adventure that she knew she had to bank down. She distantly recalled the feeling from way back, when she and her parents would be on the road to some new, unexplored destination—a time before she'd woken up to the reality that no amount of adventure could ever be worth the insecurity of never knowing what lay around the corner or the loneliness of an adolescence in which friends were always just passing through.

She thought she'd ruthlessly killed any streak in her that might have been tempted to follow in her parents' footsteps, but it was obvious that in her soul a bit of their influence lingered. She could feel it now.

'You won't be on call 24/7,' Raffaele murmured. 'And remember what I said about *living a little*?'

In the semi-darkness, the deep blue eyes resting on her were lazy and speculative and Erin felt her pulse begin to race.

'I can do that in my own time.' She cleared her throat. 'Not on company time.' She winced at just how prissy she sounded. Like a middle-aged woman instead of a girl in her late twenties. 'By which I mean,' she rushed into embarrassed clarification, 'of course I'm going to take time out to enjoy myself while I'm here. I know it's not going to be around-the-clock meetings and there'll be a lot to explore.'

'I'll make sure you have a driver to take you on tours.'

'Really?'

'The public transport infrastructure here is basic, Erin, and I'm pointing that out now, before you tell me that you can manage perfectly on your own just so long as you can locate the nearest Tube.'

'Very funny, Raffaele.' But his throwaway remark suddenly stung. He was just teasing her. She knew that. It wasn't out of the ordinary and normally she would have swatted his teasing away without really noticing it at all. But for some reason, out there with the smell of excitement in the air, it seemed to compound the sudden image she had of herself as stuffy and inhibited and dull. The person her ex-boyfriend had been considerate enough to describe in great detail.

'Who knows? I might even come with you on some of your out-of-hour tours. Might be useful to gauge the infrastructure, if I'm to take over Archer's hotel business.'

'I thought you were familiar with this part of the world.' She thought of them touring the island together without the benefit of a laptop acting as chaperone and her stomach lurched.

'I'd be looking at it from a slightly different standpoint,' Raffaele drawled. 'On the few occasions I've been to this part of the world, it hasn't been in the capacity of a fact-finding mission.'

'I can imagine.'

'Can you?'

Erin shrugged and turned away to look out of the window once more although she could feel his eyes on her. Eventually, with the silence thickening between them, she returned her reluctant gaze to his face.

'What will be the timings for tomorrow? I know we have a schedule but I'm not sure how much we're going to adhere to it. Do you want me to be up and running at the usual time? Eight? Maybe we could discuss the day's projections before we have the first meeting?'

'I've noticed something about you, Erin.'

'Really?'

'The second you begin feeling a little bit uncomfortable with a conversation, you swiftly steer it back to work. Have you noticed that about yourself?'

'I've noticed that the hotel is up ahead.'

Their eyes met. He smiled slowly and half nodded but she wasn't sure whether he was nodding in agreement or nodding because she'd just proved his point.

He looked at the approaching bank of lights and Erin could sense the change in him as his business mind took over. Even from a distance, he was already assessing the venture he might eventually be sinking money into.

The bumpy road wound its way towards the hotel. Through the rustling trees on either side, Erin could see various paths leading out into the forest to the individual cabins she had read about.

Lanterns lit up the veranda of the main building and people were sitting outside, eating and drinking. Only a handful, fewer than she might have expected.

'Hope you remembered to book cabins, like I asked,' Raffaele turned and said. 'I thought that separate cabins might be more relaxed in terms of work, more convenient for private debriefing. Everything we discuss will be informal, just a matter of useful observations, and then if I decide to go ahead, I can get my legal team involved along with the useful suspects. If you'd rather stay in the hotel, then that's fine. The entire resort caters for approximately fifty guests but from the looks of it, it's not running to full capacity.'

'It's such a shame because the setting is amazing. And yes, I did remember about the cabins and no, I'm happy with the cabin. It makes sense in terms of work to be away from the hustle and bustle, as you say. Not that there seems to be much of the hustle or the bustle.'

Raffaele hmmed. 'The place has potential but I doubt it'll ever make millions. Fortunately, I can afford to take the hit if I decide to go ahead with this. It's late but feel free to head to the restaurant for something to eat or have something delivered to your cabin. I'm going to catch up on work and we can reconvene tomorrow morning eight sharp in the hotel foyer. Sound acceptable?'

'Perfect.'

'The first meeting is with the guy in charge of running the place. We'll meet him at nine thirty and aside from showing us around, he'll give us a general feel for how the hotel is doing financially and what improvements would need to happen to take it forward.'

'Wonderful.'

'And no need for the swimsuit just yet. The meeting won't be ocean based.'

He was still grinning at his own wisecrack, she noticed, as they headed into the hotel to be greeted by staff who fussed over them as they checked in.

It was a charming open space with large windows protected by white shutters and overhead fans that made the heat just about bearable—although now it was much cooler than it had been when they'd arrived.

Through the open windows, the light breeze brought in the rich scent of the tropical flowers and the sounds of an orchestra of night creatures lurking in the encroaching forest outside.

The decor was colourful with a huge painting of tropical birds behind the reception desk, and the wooden planters by the entrance were filled with cascading ferns and lush, vivid flowers that were bigger than anything Erin had ever seen before. Like everything else around her, they seemed exotically, fantastically alien, reminding her of just how little she'd seen of the world, despite her parents' wandering feet.

She glanced across at Raffaele, who was signing the usual check-in forms, asking a few questions about their accommodation, and was struck at the enormous gulf between them.

He'd barely looked around him. He'd seen it all before even if, as he'd said, it hadn't been on 'fact-finding missions'.

She imagined his trips to the Caribbean had been more along the lines of playboy-having-fun-in-the-sun excursions.

All of a sudden her childish crush…those little shivers of awareness…the warmth that had flooded her when he'd thrown her some breadcrumbs of personal information about himself… They all seemed pathetic and embarrassing.

'Right. Ready?'

Erin blinked and focused on the drop-dead-gorgeous guy staring down at her.

'We're all checked in?'

'Certainly are.' Raffaele handed her back her passport and began heading out, waiting for her to follow him. One of the staff members led the way, chatting as he walked ahead of them, telling them about the restaurant, about the availability of car rentals or driver services, about the capital, which was by the sea and excellent for local restaurants and interesting souvenir shops.

They left the main hotel behind. Here, lanterns lit various diverging pathways into the forest and under the canopy of overhanging trees, the sounds of the insects and night animals seemed more insistent.

Erin unconsciously sidled a little closer to Raffaele.

It was now after nine yet the air was still hot and sultry and everywhere smelled of lush, rain-washed foliage. That made sense; it was supposed to be the wet season—although, as the hotel porter leading the way to their accommodation observed, there was no real difference between the wet and dry months. Sometimes rain in December and sun in July. Only the Big Man up there knew what was going on, he said.

'I'll walk you to your cabin,' Raffaele said as soon as their porter retreated back into the darkness of the forest.

Erin hovered, looking around her anxiously.

Her cabin was close to his, separated by a bank of thick bushes which were dark, rustling silhouettes under the semi-moonlit, star-studded sky. The hotel they had left behind a mere handful of minutes ago felt like a million miles away.

'Do you think we're safe here?'

'Come again?'

'Safe.' Erin cleared her throat nervously.

'We both live in London. I'm going to be bold and say that it's probably going to be a lot safer out here on a peaceful island in the middle of a rainforest. Rampant knife crime tends to stick to big cities.' He made a show of looking around him for people carrying knives and Erin could see the glint of his teeth as he tried to control a mix of indulgence and amusement. 'Erin, there's no need to worry. Honestly. I don't hear any suspicious noises. Have you decided what you're going to do about eating? I'm not sure if you heard me ask when I was checking in, but there's room service out here although the hot food stops at nine thirty and after that it's snacks and sandwiches. The place is also well stocked with snacks and drinks.'

They were at the door of her cabin. It was small but perfect, with a small wooden patio at the front. To the side, a hammock was strung between two posts. There was also a similar set-up next to Raffaele's cabin and the clearing was washed under the mellow light of the lanterns strung between the trees.

'I'm not hungry. And I'm not talking about knife crime. I'm talking about creatures,' Erin told him flatly.

'Creatures? What about them?'

'I… There are noises… Can you hear noises? Pretty loud, actually.' She cleared her throat. 'Insects, maybe? Harmless little insects?'

'Ah. I'm getting it.'

'I've never been anywhere like this in my life…'

'You're really scared, aren't you?'

'No!'

He wasn't smiling anymore. The genuine concern in his voice stiffened her spine because, weird noises or no weird noises, her boss wasn't there to hold her hand and calm her nerves.

She fumbled with the old-fashioned key and pushed the door open into a cosy space, easily big enough for two people. She stepped into a sweet sitting room, with a low sofa and a television and small kitchenette. Beyond that, she could see the door that led to the bedroom. Through the open shutters, the breeze gently billowed the thin curtains.

She looked around to see that Raffaele had followed her into the cabin to deposit her bag on the ground and when she switched on the overhead light, his face was gentle.

He walked towards the phone on the rattan console in the small sitting area outside the bedroom and pointed to it.

'Call me if you're spooked by anything, Erin. I mean that. There will also be a phone next to the bed. Believe it or not, there's Wi-Fi here. The password is in the bedroom on the dressing table, according to the guy behind the desk. You can call me anytime on my mobile. I understand that if you've never been to the tropics before, it might seem a little overwhelming. Are you going to be all right?'

'Yes.' Erin folded her arms, mortified at the stupid fuss she'd made. 'Storm in a teacup.'

'Shall I get you assigned a room in the hotel? You might feel more comfortable there.'

'I'll be fine.'

He hesitated, looked at her in silence for a few seconds, then walked towards the door.

Hand on the doorknob, he said with utter seriousness, 'Just as long as you're not too proud to knock on my door whatever the time of day or night if you need me. Understood?'

'I appreciate the offer, Raffaele, but *I'll be fine*. I just need a couple of hours to adjust. The long flight...the heat... It's all been a bit overwhelming...'

That said, within seconds of him shutting the door behind him, Erin set about checking the entire cabin just to make sure there weren't any creepy-crawlies bedding down for the night next to her.

It was a lovely space. Rattan furniture and cute local paintings on the walls and a sofa covered in bright floral patterns. Still, even with her nerves ratcheted up, Erin could detect the signs of wear and tear. The circular rug on the ground was clean but threadbare, the phone Raffaele had indicated earlier was a hundred years old and the small kitchenette looked tired. She was sure that were she to dig a little deeper, she would find far more fundamental issues which would point to failings through the entire hotel. She made sure to firmly shut the connecting door between the sitting area and the bedroom, which was beautifully air-conditioned.

She fell asleep quickly. The flight, the darkness and

the array of emotions that had been churning inside her ever since she'd opened her front door to find Raffaele standing on her doorstep had resulted in sheer exhaustion.

She awoke just as quickly and surfaced at speed, momentarily confused and disoriented by unfamiliar sounds. The room was cool but beyond the low hum of the air conditioning Erin was all too aware of the forest pressing against the cabin. The sounds that had been insistent background noise when she'd entered four hours previously had now become a cacophony.

And there was something banging around in the sitting room.

She could *hear* it through the thin wall separating the bedroom from the sitting area.

At first, nerves paralysed her but after a lifetime of frozen fear, she finally managed to leap out of bed, step back into her flip-flops and race into the pitch-black space of the sitting area. When she banged on the light, she caught the swoop of wings racing up towards the high rafters.

She didn't stop to think.

She scooted at lightning speed out of the cabin and only felt safe when she was banging on Raffaele's door.

Raffaele woke fast, muscles reflexively primed before his brain had even come back online.

He didn't run. He walked purposefully to the door and pulled it open. Only then did his brain really engage and, disconcertingly, it engaged in a way he had least expected.

Erin was there. Wearing next to nothing.

Some tiny shorts and a sexy little vest. He could see the rounded shape of her small breasts. Everything that she had managed over the years to conceal under an array of drab clothes was revealed now, from the slenderness of her arms to her smooth, shapely legs and *the tiny span of her waist...*

He felt his breath catch and blood rushed to a place that hadn't been active since he'd broken up with Alexa of the infinite text messages.

Swiftly he moved slightly behind the half-open door because he was only in boxers himself and, *hell*, he had an erection! Rock hard, utterly inexplicable and highly embarrassing. 'Erin...'

'There's something in the cabin!'

'Wait..."something in the cabin"?'

'Raffaele, I'm sorry... I know it's...it's...'

'After three in the morning?'

'I...'

She was close to tears. *His perfect, coolly controlled, unflappable secretary was close to tears!*

Another punch of raw arousal hit him, making him wonder what sort of dinosaur he was if he could be actively turned on by a damsel in distress. Although, in fairness, not just any old damsel in distress.

'Okay. Come in. I'll grab some trousers and don't worry... I'll sort it out.'

He spun around on his heels and disappeared quickly into the adjoining bedroom before his body could betray him even more than it already had.

Erin stepped into his cabin and it was only when he had vanished that two things struck her, temporarily banishing the fear and panic that had gripped her as she'd flown to his cabin.

The first was that Raffaele had answered the door in just his boxers. For the first time her fantasies had crashed slap bang into reality and the body she had idly and guiltily daydreamed about had been there right before her eyes. No amount of daydreaming could come close to the magnificence of the real thing.

Broad, muscled shoulders, sexy dark hair on his chest and a flat belly that tapered to narrow hips.

She'd felt the air leave her body in a whoosh when he'd answered the door and then, before she could really absorb what she was looking at, he'd somehow manoeuvred himself behind the door, probably in an act of kindness to spare her blushes.

She knew he thought she was all those things a brilliant secretary should be—smart, efficient, professional— along with all those things a woman should never be as far as femininity went, *smart, efficient, professional*, equalled *drab, unexciting, uptight*...

The second thing that struck her, hard on the heels of her semi-naked boss and his glorious body, was the fact that she had scrambled over to his cabin without bothering to shove on anything over her pyjamas. The sensible dressing gown she had brought with her was still hanging pointlessly on a hook on the bathroom door.

And here she was...

Appalled, she folded her arms, covering as much of her breasts as she could, and waited for him to emerge from the bedroom.

With a sinking feeling, it was dawning on her that whatever had been flapping around in the cabin would have been easier to deal with than this.

'Ready to face the monster in the room?'

Raffaele appeared decently clad in some grey jogging bottoms and a loose T-shirt and flip-flops.

Their eyes met and he smiled reassuringly.

'I shouldn't have rushed over here at this ungodly hour,' Erin said jerkily.

'Why not? Something obviously petrified you and naturally I'm here to help. I can't have you cowering under the blankets until you get rescued by room service in the morning. I'm being serious here, Erin. Want me to carry you back to your cabin? Because I will.'

'Just get rid of whatever's flying around inside the room.' She cleared her throat, eyes darting between his cabin and hers in expectation of just about anything that might lunge out at them. There was a myriad of noises coming from the trees and the bushes all around them. 'Please.'

'Your wish...my command.'

She led the way to her cabin. It was literally seconds away from his. She could feel the blades of grass on the ground brush against her flip-flops and fronds from the ferns tickle her legs. They both heard the sound of furious flapping the second she pushed open the door.

Raffaele didn't give her time to protest. He swept her off her feet, kicked the door shut behind him and carried her straight through to the bedroom.

'Stay here.'

'What are you going to do? What is it making that racket?'

'I'll find out soon enough.'

'Are you scared? Should we call the manager?'

'At this hour in the morning?' Raffaele laughed. 'No and no. By which I mean no manager, and no, I'm not scared.'

He headed out of the room, shutting the door quietly behind him, and Erin curled herself into a ball in the chair by the window and tried her best to block out the muffled sounds outside.

It had been a mistake coming here. She should have made up some excuse and dug her heels in and stayed put in the safety of her office in London. If she had, she wouldn't be here now, trembling at the thought of whatever was out there, not to mention all the other *whatevers* that might be lurking in the bushes and the trees and the rivers, waiting for some unsuspecting English girl with zero experience of the tropics to wander along.

And if she had dug her heels in her boss wouldn't be playing knight in shining armour at her request, and wasn't that the bigger problem?

How had the dynamic between them changed so suddenly? How had one stray confidence turned into...into *this*?

She was only aware of Raffaele's return to the room when he was standing in front of her, casting a long shadow.

She looked up at him with a sigh of resignation, resentful that she was now the damsel in distress.

'What was it?'

He squatted down on his haunches so that they were on eye level.

'It was a fruit bat. Harmless and more scared of you than you were of it. One of the windows was open behind the curtains and it must have got in either accidentally or because it was attracted to the fruit in the bowl on the table. You were really scared, weren't you?'

'I overreacted. I'm sorry. I should never have run over to your cabin and banged on your door.'

'Why not? You were scared and I could help.'

'Raffaele...this isn't me.'

'It is now,' he returned with a crooked smile. 'I like this new Erin Fisher. I like the fact that you can drop the mask now and again. It's definitely an improvement.'

* * *

Erin met his eyes. She felt the thrill of her illicit attraction fighting against the *need* for her to return to the person she had been, safe and controlled and in charge of her emotions.

She just couldn't allow a childish crush to overwhelm common sense. She would never make another mistake with a man again. Finding love didn't lie down that road. She'd made one mistake. *She was wiser now.*

But Raffaele was so close to her. She could smell him, breathe him in, reach out and touch him.

She balled her hands into fists. 'I was temporarily thrown off balance. Like I said, I have no experience of what it's like in this part of the world. Tomorrow, once I begin to find my feet, believe me, I won't be a shaking wreck at the sound of a silly bat flapping around in the living room.'

Brave words. In reality, she honestly wouldn't care whether the bat was popping over to make friends with a cup of tea and some scones; just thinking about it appearing again made her shiver.

'For the record, despite the fact that the hotel is set in a forest, there are remarkably few venomous creatures.' He stood up, flexed his muscles and dragged the chair by the dressing table over to where she was sitting.

Erin watched him warily. If anything, his presence felt more suffocating now, with him leaning into her, forearms resting on his thighs, knees practically touching hers.

'Is that right?' she asked faintly.

'There are snakes but most are harmless. They'll slither away in fear if they hear you coming.'

'What about the less harmless varieties?'

'Don't worry. You won't come across them. We won't be doing any deep-jungle exploring and actually, even if we chose to, I don't think there have been any tales of deadly snake bites on this island in living memory. Anyway,' he said and grinned, 'I'm here.'

'And you have a lot of experience in dealing with venomous snakes?'

'None, but as you can see, I'm good at dealing with the unexpected. The fruit bat won't be bothering you again.'

'No, it won't.' Erin clung to politeness but her heart was thumping as she looked at him, remembering way too clearly how he had looked in his boxers and nothing else, 'because I'll make sure all the windows are shut when I go to bed.'

'Wise precaution.' He stood up, headed to the bedroom door but then he turned to look back at her over his shoulder. 'Now, before you protest, I'm going to settle down in the chair outside and make sure you're okay before I head back to my cabin.'

'Raffaele!'

'Tut, tut, what did I say?' He reached out and before she could pull back, his finger was on her lips in a silencing motion. She felt the blood rush to her face. 'No protests or you might find that I stay for the rest of the morning. Understood?'

Erin didn't protest. She physically couldn't. Her vocal cords had tightened up because all she could imagine was this big, powerful, sexy guy in the room outside keeping watch over her while she slept.

She nodded silently. Even after he'd let himself out of the bedroom, she could still feel where his finger had briefly been on her lips.

But, weirdly, within ten minutes she was fast asleep.

CHAPTER FIVE

IN THE LIGHT OF DAY, Erin's panic the night before seemed like a massive over reaction. She cringed when she thought of the way she'd raced over to Raffaele's cabin like—fittingly—a bat out of hell and flung herself at him, trusting him to deal with the situation with just the sort of helpless, stereotypically feminine reaction she honestly had never had time for.

She could change the washer in a tap, hang a heavy picture and put up shelves! So why had a bit of wing flapping sent her shrieking with terror straight into the arms of her boss? How did this tally with the woman who had privately scorned the many women who'd fallen under his spell and treated him like an Action Man hero every time they were within smelling distance of him?

She also cringed knowing that he had checked on her before he'd left her cabin. She knew he had, because the socks she'd worn to bed just in case she stepped on something in the dark had been slipped off her feet and neatly placed on the chair, and she'd been covered with the cotton blanket which had been folded at the foot of the bed. He had placed it over the thin sheet she had fallen asleep under, knowing that at some point the cold from the air conditioning unit would probably wake her up.

She decided that she would face the day and the upcoming week without dwelling on any of that. It was the only way she would be able to get through their confinement together and work the way she had always worked—professionally and efficiently.

It was a perfect day and jet lag had not yet put in an appearance. At a little after eight, the sky was already a cloudless blue and as she headed out of the cabin, the scenery that had been shrouded in darkness when they'd arrived was spectacular in all its Technicolor glory.

It was hot but the clearing beneath the towering canopy of trees was cool and shady and there was nothing sinister in the gentle rustle of the breeze through the leaves.

The paths they had followed through the forest to their cabins had seemed bewildering when the only light had been from the lanterns strung between the trees but now, in the bright light of a sun filled day, the winding pathways were all visible between the borders of bright tropical flowers and giant, oversized ferns.

She headed straight to Raffaele's cabin and banked down the nerves as she raised her hand.

He opened the door on the first knock.

'Erin.'

'Good morning.' Erin smiled distantly and he grinned.

'It certainly is. Come in, come in. Don't stand there hovering by the door. First meeting isn't until eleven so we have time to brief and grab breakfast.'

He turned on his heels and Erin reluctantly followed him in. He was dressed casually. Navy blue collared T-shirt and a pair of light cream linen trousers and flip-flops.

In her short-sleeved lemon blouse and neat cotton skirt and with her laptop firmly tucked under her arm, she felt inappropriately stuffy.

'So?' he called over his shoulder. 'Sleep all right for the remainder of the night—or should I say morning? I stayed on for about an hour then went to check on you and you were fast asleep.'

'Thank you for...the babysitting duties,' Erin said politely.

'It was no bother,' Raffaele returned with equal politeness but with a wicked glint in his eyes. 'As babysitting duties go, it was stress free. In fact, all I did was remove the socks and throw a blanket over you.'

Erin gritted her teeth as the very subject she'd hoped to dodge was flung at her with an amused smile and raised eyebrows.

'Won't happen again. I can already see how ridiculous and misplaced my brief panic was. Everything always looks so much less threatening in the daylight. What will we be covering in this morning's meeting? I've brought my laptop so that we can maybe have a look at how the costs of running the place are broken down?'

'Excellent. Let me grab mine and we can go have some breakfast in the restaurant. Unless you'd rather we stay here? Have someone deliver something for us?'

'No! The restaurant will be fine.'

Raffaele smiled and shrugged.

Erin was as formally dressed as it was humanly possible to be given the heat and the humidity. Unassuming flowered skirt, loosely falling to mid-calf, and a neat shirt with tiny buttons. Very impractical, he decided. She would be drenched in sweat within the hour.

He knew just what that was about. She was desperate to put distance between the woman he had seen in the early hours of the morning. The woman half scared to death, wearing the sexiest little vest and shorts imaginable. The woman who had banged on his door looking tousled and pink faced and very, very cute. The woman who had painted toenails—a sweet pale pink that somehow gave the lie to her being the ultimate professional with all girlie traits stamped into oblivion. She was as slender as a ballet dancer and, having seen her in her nightwear, he could now attest that she had the shapeliest legs he'd seen on a woman in a long time.

The woman with the background he'd never have guessed who had roused his curiosity to the point where his curiosity had no intention of being put to bed, at least not just yet.

The restaurant was a charming wooden pavilion attached to the side of the main hotel, open to the birds which flitted in and out, pecking whatever scraps had been left on plates before they were cleared away. Their plumage was bright—blue and yellow and orange—and they filled the air with song.

'This place is amazing,' Erin admitted as they were shown to a table. Around them various other couples were having breakfast and poring over maps and making plans. Shorts and T-shirts with beach bags on the ground. She fidgeted uncomfortably in her more formal gear.

'Yes, it is but there's a lot of work that would have to be done to get it up and running. I was out and about at six thirty and the only real thing it's got going for it is its location, which is stunning. There's a waterfall about twenty minutes' walk away. Beautiful. Very private. These are the sort of things I'll want us to check out because it's the added bonuses that can sell a hotel like this and my feeling is those have been bypassed as Archer's goals have shifted away from his hotel business.'

Erin was busy taking in the birds and the flowers curling on green tendrils over the white wooden railings of the sitting area, where the tables were arranged in no particular order.

She nodded absently and only surfaced when breakfast began appearing.

'Did I order?' She frowned.

'No menu. You get what's freshly baked.'

'That's something else that could be used as a selling point. A lot of people like the idea of the food being locally sourced on a daily basis.'

'So you *were* listening to what I was saying.'

'I always listen to what you say. I'm your secretary. That's what I'm paid to do.'

'Ah...because for a while there you were a million miles away.'

'I was admiring all the birds,' Erin admitted. 'I've never seen anything like it.' She thought of the life she'd led, which she'd always considered eccentric and ridiculously adventurous compared to everyone else she had known along the way, the other pre-teens and the teenagers who had passed in and out of her life like whispers. For a while it *had* been both those things but being here...

It was in places like this, she thought, that the adventure really started. It was here with all the new sights and smells and tastes, where nothing was like anything else that had gone before, that the imagination could take flight.

The predictability of her life at home hit her like a sledgehammer. After her break-up a million years ago, she had retreated into the safety of her carefully curated comfort zone, the very one that had become part and parcel of her life from as far back as she could remember.

She had put *adventure* in a box that wasn't for her and that had included adventures with men.

She'd been moulded by her wandering parents and hurt by her ex-boyfriend, hurt by the things he had casually thrown at her. Protecting herself had become the most important goal in her life.

They were disturbing thoughts and it was easier, surrounded by all this untamed beauty, to shove them aside.

'And this breakfast is delicious. The bread…is there coconut in it?' Their eyes collided and Erin blushed. 'This is what I meant when I said that the food could be a pulling point here.' She cleared her throat and looked away.

'Definitely something I will mention to Gary, the manager, when we meet him later. How did your parents take you being absent from another weekend because you're here with me?'

Erin was thrown by the abrupt change of subject and she blinked like an owl for a couple of seconds.

'Meant to ask at the airport,' Raffaele drawled, sitting back to look at her with his head tilted to the side. 'But we got wrapped up in work chat. How dependent is your father physically on you being there on the weekends? I know you said something about arranging for someone to come and help him…' He paused and looked at her thoughtfully for a couple of seconds. 'Which suddenly makes me wonder something…'

'Shouldn't we stick to working out what we're going to concentrate on when we meet the hotel manager in…' Erin glanced at her phone, which was on the table, and was gutted to see that they still had over an hour before they were due to meet Gary. 'Er…soon?'

'I think our time would be better used having a stroll through the grounds and assessing the property and the outbuildings. Finished here?'

'Yes, sure...'

'Good!' He smiled brightly at her and vaulted upright, waiting for her to follow suit. 'We can start with the cabins,' he said, waiting while she faffed and got her things together.

'My laptop...'

'I'll get someone to stash it in the room we'll be using for our meeting.' He nodded to a member of staff who came along and obligingly whipped it away, leaving Erin feeling vaguely deprived of an essential prop.

'But getting back to what we were talking about a minute ago,' he murmured, slowing his pace so that she could fall in alongside him. 'Can I ask you something?'

'I'd rather you didn't.'

'Really? Why?'

'Because I'd rather we stick to work. Feels like there's a lot to discuss without us getting bogged down in chit-chat about other stuff.'

'Oh, we can spare a few minutes, Erin. Relax and go with the flow for a change.'

'I relax *all the time*, Raffaele.'

'Really? You don't seem very relaxed now. I'm just making conversation. There's honestly no need to get hot under the collar. This isn't an interview and your job isn't going to be on the line depending on what answers you give me. In fact, you don't have to give me any answers at all. I know we agreed that it would a good idea if we moved our relationship along a notch or two, got it into a more normal place, but if you feel a little panicked at the thought of that, then of course I'll back off and we can return to where we were.'

'Where we were?' This was to buy time, because the ground underneath Erin seemed to have suddenly turned to quicksand. *Why?* 'And I'm not *panicked* at the thought of making conversation with you, Raffaele!'

'I can't tell you how pleased I am to hear that. I feel that we're more than just boss and secretary. I feel that we're *friends.*'

'Friends...' Erin thought of the way her body responded when she was around him, the way her mind soared off into fantasy land with him playing the lead role... *Friend* didn't come close to describing his interaction with her in all her forbidden imaginings.

'So why is it that you had to be the one to arrange help for your father?'

Erin sighed. He was like a dog with a bone. It was one of the many reasons why he was so successful. He was primed to tenaciously pursue what he wanted until he got it. She'd known that; it was just that that tenacity had never been directed at her. But now it was and there seemed to be little she could do about it without giving the impression of being scared, which inevitably would lead him to question why that might be.

Besides, the heat and the sounds of birds and insects, the smell of the sea in the air, the exuberance of the trees and bushes and flowers all around them...it was all having a lulling effect on her.

Could she bother to be on her guard?

Why should she?

The lesson she should take from all this wasn't that she had to keep her defences up around him just in case he caught a glimpse of her inappropriate crush.

Nor was it that she might shatter into a thousand pieces if she wasn't scrupulous about who she decided to let into her life.

No, what she should take from this was that she needed to get a move on, needed to *start living*.

What Raffaele did or didn't know about her was irrelevant because she wasn't involved with him.

Outside the work arena, he had no impact on her life. She would never tell him how she *felt* about things, what her thoughts were on *love* or *marriage*, and he would never know anything of her dreams or fears or desires.

But questions about her dad?

Not a problem!

Still, that was easier thought than believed...

She idly noted the bees buzzing lazily around giant deep pink trumpet-shaped flowers that seemed to grow wild all around them.

A clutch of cabins was just ahead of them, each private and separated by trees. All had hammocks identical to the ones she and Raffaele had, although these hammocks were knotted, unused because the cabins were empty.

She swatted away some tiny insects from in front of her, realising that she was baking hot in her skirt and blouse.

Bypassing the cabins, they chatted idly about the state of the overlong grass and the signs of decay in the wood, but Erin knew that the topic of her father would reappear. Sure enough, once they'd explored some of the forested area beyond the main hotel and begun to trudge back to the cool of the hotel, Raffaele shoved his hands into the pockets of his lightweight trousers, turned to her and picked up where they had left off.

'I'm too hot to answer any questions,' Erin said irritably, breathing a huge sigh of relief when they were back in the hotel foyer where the overhead fan was generating at least a smattering of cool air.

Raffaele grinned. 'I did think that your outfit might have been a little much for this heat,' he said. 'Did you bring anything lighter?'

'Sort of,' she sighed, sweeping her hair back and feeling it damp with perspiration.

'Sort of? You mean *sort of cotton shorts*? Or *sort of loose clothing*? We'll wrap this meeting up quickly, head into town and get you clothes that will be a little more comfortable while we're here or else you'll find yourself completely overwhelmed by the humidity. In fact—' he glanced at his watch '—you skip the meeting and I'll meet you outside your cabin at twelve fifteen. You can change into something more comfortable. We're not going to discuss anything important anyway so it's not essential you attend. I'll arrange transport into town…'

'Raffaele…'

'No protesting, Erin. The last thing I want or need is a secretary who can't function because she's overcome by the heat.'

'No, I'm sure you don't,' Erin said testily, 'especially considering you've already rescued me once already. How much more rescuing can you be expected to do before your trusty steed collapses?'

He grinned broadly at that and she glared back, too steaming hot to do much else.

As soon as he headed off into the hotel, she flew to her cabin. She'd packed two pairs of shorts but they weren't decent enough to wear to a meeting. Too old and way too short.

Her skirts, which would have been perfect for an English summer, were ridiculously out of place when it came to coping in a furnace. Buttons on blouses were maddening.

She had a quick shower then changed into another of her stupid skirts and this time one of the old T-shirts and her flip-flops instead of the canvas shoes she had been wearing.

Raffaele knocked promptly on her door at twelve fifteen.

Annoyingly, he looked cool as a cucumber.

'That looks a lot more suitable' was the first thing he said in an approving voice. 'Why didn't you wear that this morning? Don't feel that you have to dress formally while you're here, even if it *is* something of a working holiday. I've got a driver to take us into town. Ready?'

'Guess so.'

'Don't sound so thrilled.' His voice lightened with amusement as he led the way to the jeep that was on standby. 'Don't women love shopping?'

'Not all.'

Once in the back seat of the sturdy little jeep, Erin relaxed back and half closed her eyes.

'All the women I've ever dated have loved shopping. In fact, I'd say that they were all passionate about it, the sort of passion top scientists might feel in pursuit of the cure for cancer.'

'That says more about the women you choose to date than the female species as a whole.' She slanted a sideways glance at him to find him staring at her with a lazy half smile on his face.

So, so unfairly sexy. Her thoughts were sluggish and she didn't look away, not even when he slowly raised his eyebrows in a question.

The car bumped along the very uneven road that had brought them to the compound the day before.

The breeze was lovely and she felt as floppy as a rag doll.

When she finally glanced away from his face, she realised that her hand was on the seat between them as though begging to be held. Honestly, she still felt too lethargic to whip it away. It was as though the intense heat had formed gaping cracks in her usual defence systems.

'Do you financially support your parents, Erin?'

His voice was low and serious and Erin met his eyes without flinching and nodded.

'I was surprised at where you live,' he mused. 'Now it makes sense. You never said.'

'Why do you think I should have said anything?' Erin asked with genuine curiosity.

'Because, like I said, I thought we were friends. Maybe not the confiding-intimate-secrets kind of friends but surely friends who share financial troubles...'

'You would never have any financial troubles to share, Raffaele, and honestly, we're not friends. You're my boss and lines have to be drawn.' She thought of her inappropriate crush which couldn't have been further from the friends category he mistakenly thought they might be in. 'You're used to women who love shopping and who probably can't wait to tell you all about themselves but I'm not any of those women. What's more, I work for you. Don't forget all the girls you had to sack because they started blurring the boundaries.'

'If you'd told me that your father was out of work, then I would have gladly given you whatever money you needed to tide him over until he found something else. Was he made redundant? What did he do for a living?'

Erin looked at Raffaele coolly.

He truly lived in an ivory tower. Born into a life of privilege, handed a healthy trust fund when he was barely out of nappies. Whatever disagreements he might have had with his dad over time, he would never have known inconsistency. He had always been cocooned. From the top of Mount Olympus, it would be impossible not to look down on the ones who lived below without a certain amount of incomprehension and pity.

He would never have had self-doubt and would never have suffered. A squabble over when to repay a trust fund that would set you up for life didn't count.

She thought of how her parents had agonised when they had finally decided to put down roots only to discover how unprepared they were for the reality of what that process entailed.

Her father had cried and apologised to her when she had told them that she would use her own money to ensure their future security. They'd had next to no savings of their own by then. Living in the present had made zero allowances for life in the future.

'You wouldn't understand,' Erin eventually said.

'Try me.'

Erin looked away for a few minutes. It was a slow journey because the roads were narrow, twisty and occasionally perilous, with steep drops into dense forest on either side. She couldn't imagine what would happen if someone happened to be coming in the opposite direction. Strung overhead in a seemingly random fashion, electricity cables bowed under twisting vines. The heat was like a blanket around them, dense and filled with humidity.

'Okay, yes, I have financial obligations,' she finally confessed, because the whole story was going to be better than half a story. If she dropped it all, he would be left thinking that her parents were irresponsible layabouts who exploited her good nature, and just thinking that made her feel angry on their behalf.

'My parents have never been good about money and it's not because they're stupid or lazy. It's just that…' Her voice trailed off. She thought about her colourful childhood. Exciting, unpredictable, joyful…but what a learning curve in the end. And she thought about his: predictable, wealthy, privileged and with zero learning curves beyond how much more money it was possible to make.

'Just that what?'

And suddenly Erin felt her lips twitch and she looked at him with raised eyebrows and grinned.

What would her billionaire boss, who had always been protected from the hardships of life, who'd probably never glimpsed any life too far removed from the one he'd led, what would he think of hers?

Her smile broadened when he frowned and she could tell that he was bemused and disconcerted by her sudden change of attitude.

'Raffaele, this might come as a shock to you but until I was twelve, I grew up in a commune.'

Erin stifled a laugh when his mouth dropped open in shock. She'd shocked him once when she'd mentioned that her parents had a small holding and a tiny cottage industry…and now she'd shocked him again with this revelation.

'A commune…'

'It was wonderful, to be honest. I'm not sure how my parents drifted into that lifestyle but I think they'd both been hippies from the very beginning and commune life appealed to them once I came along, which was quite late in life for them. I think they spent so many years just enjoying one another and enjoying their wonderful nomadic life that they only decided at the very last minute that they'd quite like…well…me. A child. And along I came, at which point they joined a commune. We lived in the middle of nowhere but it was a vibrant community and we were all home-schooled.'

'Home-schooled…'

'You look a little dazed, Raffaele. Is this all too much for you? Should I get the smelling salts out?'

'Is that the sound of you being patronising?'

'I'm afraid it might be.'

'And then what? What happened after the commune life?'

He was leaning against the door, staring at her with his long legs splayed and his hands loose between his thighs, which for some reason made her unexpectedly remember the sight of him in his boxers. Solid, muscled and way too sexy for his own good.

She quickly looked away.

Her brief flirtation with amusement at making him uncomfortable now felt dangerous.

'We travelled,' she said abruptly. Her voice softened with memories. 'I think my parents stuck it out being in one place when they had me but in the end, the wanderlust gene was too much. It was embedded way too deep in both of them. Maybe if one of them had wanted security, then life would have been different, but they were absolutely both on the same page.' She half closed her eyes and enjoyed the warm breeze blowing her hair this way and that. 'Unfortunately,' she said drily, twisting to look at him and noting that the dazed expression still hadn't quite left his face, 'travelling didn't come with the usual stuff like pensions and savings. They worked as they moved around, sometimes for a while in one place if it took their fancy but...'

'But then the time came for them to put down roots and they found that their... What did they do all this travelling in? Whatever it was, it wouldn't do as a permanent roof over their heads.'

Erin tried to take offence and bristle at that remark but found she couldn't, because there was clearly nothing malicious behind it. He sounded genuinely curious and interested.

'Actually, we changed homes several times.' She slanted a glance at him and smiled wryly. 'Almost like normal people moving house. When we left the commune, I remember a brightly painted mobile home and then an old four-wheel drive with a caravan. My dad could turn his hand to most things. He was really clever, and especially gifted with cars. Some of his jobs paid enormously well and we would hang around for a while, reaping the benefits. Sometimes we did actually stay put long enough for me to go to school somewhere, but we were never anywhere longer than a handful of months.'

'And how was that lifestyle for you?'

'Had its ups and had its downs.'

She looked at him seriously, establishing boundaries. No matter how much she was attracted to him, she still knew he was her boss—utterly off-limits—and it felt important to subtly manoeuvre the conversation so that he was aware of that. Just because some of the barriers between them had been eroded, she didn't want his finely attuned antennae picking up any signals that would set alarm bells ringing.

'It made me resilient, I think,' she mused thoughtfully, eyes half lowered but still keenly gauging his reaction to what she was telling him. He looked frankly fascinated and she felt a kick of something pleasing in that. 'It also made me really value the importance of financial security. Thank goodness for that, as things turned out. It also made me value even more the importance of...emotional security. My parents adore one another but for me love would have to be with a guy who was committed to settling down, in one place. A house with a picket fence and a couple of apple trees in the back garden.' She grinned. 'If you get my drift.'

'Sounds dull.' He grinned back at her. 'Sure there's no longing for adventure waiting to break through the picture-perfect future you have all mapped out?'

'None,' Erin said firmly. She thought of him, yet again, in those boxers and sucked in a steadying breath. 'Absolutely none *whatsoever.*' She smiled blandly as they hit tarmac and the jeep picked up a bit more speed. 'Thanks for bringing me into town. I have an idea, why don't you look around the place while I grab a couple of things more suitable for the weather? I can meet you back in half an hour or so.'

Holding her bland, unrevealing gaze, Raffaele nodded and returned the smile with an equal measure of politeness. Underneath, though, he was burning to reject Erin's signature *hands off* change of topic and ask more. The little she had opened up and shown him had kickstarted more questions than it had provided answers, and he was startled at just how urgently his wanted her to keep talking.

She'd told him that the women he dated were shopaholics who needed no urging to tell him all about themselves and she'd been right. He dated open books.

Honestly, that had always suited him. He had no interest in anything long term so if they liked to be indulged and if they enjoyed talking nonstop about themselves, then that had always been fine.

Now, he could feel his brain engage—in the presence, for the first time, of a woman who clearly didn't want to prolong the conversation and who had no interest in him beyond the fact that he was responsible for her pay cheque at the end of every month.

She'd said as much.

Hell, she didn't even *consider him a friend*!

Logic told him that in the face of all that, his best way forward was to drop all interest in trying to get to the bottom of her and return to the fault free, perfect working relationship they had always had.

Or he could pursue it.

Since when had he ever not been up for a challenge?

The week, he decided, was going to be a great deal more interesting than he could ever have imagined.

CHAPTER SIX

'THE TIMING WORKS WELL' was the first thing Raffaele said when they met back at the jeep an hour after their arrival in town. Erin had visited three boutiques, but she could have happily stayed longer: the settlement was compact, a picturesque collection of souvenir shops nudging against places where the locals shopped. Small grocery stores, a chemist, various shops selling fabric all rolled in huge bales and stacked like colourful sausages on counters inside the stores and on rickety tables outside to lure customers in.

'How so?'

Hand on the door, ready to hop in, Erin shaded her eyes and looked up at Raffaele.

He slung the bags of clothes she had bought into the back of the jeep and opened the door for her.

'A family friend who has a yacht moored on one of the islands just north of here is coincidentally around for two days. He's cruising along the chain of islands. My father knew I was here and got in touch with me to suggest a meeting. Something he wants me to discuss about a business the guy is thinking about expanding. The guy's a crashing bore and I could do without the hassle, but needs must. I've arranged to meet him for lunch on his yacht. Of course, you're more than welcome to join me but I'm guessing you'd rather return to the hotel? The pool is very nice.' He looked up at the blue skies, then returned his gaze to her. 'I'd be tempted myself if I had the chance.'

'I wouldn't dream of intruding on your lunch, Raffaele, though I don't for a minute think the man's a bore. If he's sailing along these islands, then he has to be interesting.'

'Your logic escapes me,' Raffaele murmured, his deep blue eyes roving over her flushed face. 'Just because someone has a boat and knows how to handle it, it doesn't make him interesting.'

'No,' Erin mused thoughtfully, 'I guess you're right. To be interesting, he really has to know how to chase a bat out of a room and claim to know how to deal with venomous snakes even though he might never have encountered one outside of a zoo.'

Raffaele threw his head back and burst out laughing.

'I always knew you were sharp, Erin,' he murmured when his full-bodied laughter had subsided, 'but your sense of humour still continues to surprise, especially now that you've released it from captivity.'

Erin's heart skipped a beat. She hurriedly broke eye contact and climbed into the rear of the jeep. The windows were all down and Raffaele leaned half into the car, looking at her.

'Sure you'll be okay?'

'Of course I will, Raffaele. I'll return to the hotel and have a lovely walk around and then, of course, I'll also do whatever work you want done. I'll check incoming emails and make sure nothing urgent needs sorting. I've already played truant going into town and missing our first meeting of the day.'

'Or you could just laze by the pool and forget about work.'

'That's not what I'm being paid to do.'

'I'm your boss, don't forget. If I say you can relax, then you can relax. Relax.'

'I'll certainly think about it. Oh, and before I forget, thank you for the Amex card and for...funding my change of clothes. There really was no need.'

'Erin, do you honestly think I would let you spend your hard-earned cash buying clothes for a week because yours weren't that suitable?'

'Maybe,' she said quietly, 'you might have if you didn't know about my parents, about the fact that I currently... lend a helping hand with their finances. Honestly, it's just until they can sort themselves out completely...' Their eyes met and she refused to look away. 'I don't want the little you know about my background to influence your behaviour towards me.'

'You underestimate me. But still, I can't put what you've told me about yourself to the side and pretend that it doesn't exist. It exists.'

Erin glanced away in receipt of this blunt truth. She had confided. She had told him things that would alter their relationship and now she could only hope it wasn't for the worse.

There was no going back. But she couldn't help but notice that whilst she had been encouraged to open up, he'd seen no such compulsion to return the favour.

Maybe on one occasion she'd sensed something about his background in the intonation of a throwaway remark... But her memory of that whole conversation before their flight was a muddle by now. She could have been mistaken.

She shrugged. 'What are the plans for the evening? Is anything arranged?'

'Funny you should ask. We're going to be meeting a few of the staff and their respective partners. It'll be an informal get-together so that we can try the food and I believe there might be some live music.'

She unconsciously made a face and he slanted her a slow, curling smile.

'Time for that box to be broken as well,' he purred silkily.

'What box?'

'The one you shut yourself in every time something like an informal get-together with good food and live music presents itself.'

'I don't do that!' Erin reddened. 'Can you name one instance when I've done that? I can't remember the last time I was at a party with live music!'

'My point exactly. That's just the sort of thing you should be throwing yourself into, instead of dreaming about picket fences and apple trees in the back garden with some guy you have yet to meet. Unless...' He lowered his voice and the smile was still there, this time a little broader. 'Unless you've already got him stashed away in a cupboard somewhere and you're going to tell me all about him at a later date? Produce him from thin air like a rabbit from a hat? You seem to be full of surprises of late.'

Erin ignored him. 'What time is this event happening, Raffaele, and where exactly? I'll meet you there.'

'Of course.' He grinned, drew back and gave her a half salute, although his deep blue eyes remained firmly fixed on her face. 'Six sharp in the meeting room in the main hotel. Someone from reception will take you through. I'd say I'd walk you over but I'm not entirely sure how long it will take me to get back after lunch with the bore.

You might have to hold the fort for a bit, but you've done that before.'

'No problem.'

'Right then.' He slapped his hand on the side of the jeep, drew back and nodded to the driver. 'Off you go and Erin...don't work today. Have the day off. Gather your strength for the gruelling ordeal of the food and live music nightmare scenario.'

'I'm actually looking forward to it,' Erin purred, steely eyed. 'I really fancy immersing myself in the culture and getting to meet some new faces.'

'That's the spirit!'

The man, Erin thought as the jeep began bumping its way back to the hotel and away from the hot, tiny town, was insufferable.

Brilliant...sharp...edgy...challenging and stupidly good-looking, all of which combined probably explained the highly developed insufferability gene.

He expected her to show up, politely do what she had to do and then leave just as soon as was humanly possible. That was his impression of her in a relaxed environment. So she didn't really like work social dos! Since when was that a crime?

She did her absolute utmost to spend the rest of the day enjoying the hotel grounds, which were more extensive than she'd first thought.

She had some lunch in the same place where earlier she and Raffaele had had breakfast, chatted to some of the guests and then explored the untamed gardens. By midday, there were no thoughts of creepy-crawlies. The sun shone down with searing heat, making her feel lazy and lethargic and not at all in the mood for doing any work. She managed to find the waterfall, which was tucked away in a clearing. It was easy because she just had to follow the voices of a few of the guests enjoying the cool, refreshing water, and as she lingered at the side, watching them have fun, she wished she'd had the foresight to wear her swimsuit.

At the back of her mind, as she strolled through the forested grounds and explored the more cultivated gardens, a huge section of which was devoted to vegetables and beds of fresh herbs, the image of Raffaele lingered. She expected to bump into him at any given moment. The man had a habit of catching her unawares.

She didn't feel as horrifically exposed as she'd always imagined she would after sharing a slice of her private life with him, but she had made a decision. This was her chance to turn over a new leaf. The time had come to put her annoying crush on her boss to bed.

Now that she'd started down that road, it would be so easy to keep spilling little pieces of herself, to parcel out glimpses of her unusual background in the hopes it would win her scraps of surprise and amusement from her sexy boss. But unusual backgrounds didn't always make for anything interesting. Unless she changed her behaviour, she would always still be the sparrow who didn't know how to live life to the full, nursing an impossible crush instead of striking out in search of something real.

The sense of adventure that had swept through her when she'd stepped off the plane straight into the searing tropical heat swept through her again as she had a shower and relaxed and decided what she was going to wear for the meet-and-greet later on.

Why stick to her comfort zone? Here? In this amazing place that begged for her to live, for a moment, in a different skin…?

* * *

Raffaele made it back to the hotel with not much time to spare. He felt borderline traumatised by lunch with the bore who had droned on interminably about every single little setback that had befallen him and his wife on their six-week sailing tour of the Grenadines. Raffaele was sorely tempted to tell him that he should just pack it in because if he couldn't enjoy what everyone else would have given their right arm to do, then he didn't deserve the opportunity to do it.

He'd refrained but had spent several hours trying not to look at his watch too much and swatting away the man's wife.

Bridgette, blonde, leggy and all of thirty-four—thirty years younger than her rich husband—had greeted them at the yacht in a bikini and had spent the rest of her time surreptitiously trying it on with Raffaele.

It had been exhausting.

She'd reminded him a little of the women he was accustomed to dating, the same pouting physical perfection that expected attention from the opposite sex. But in this case, a wedding ring on her finger hadn't stood in the way of her relentlessly flirting.

The thought of seeing Erin, with her interesting background and her intelligent, cool, witty conversation, had had the call of the siren.

Now, as he shut the cabin door behind him to head to the hotel for the drinks party, he debated whether to knock on her door.

But no. He should leave her to it for now. Let her savour her time before the party. She was probably nervous. Strange place...unfamiliar faces...look at how spooked she'd been the night before when a bat had flown into the cabin! She hadn't yet settled into the vibe on this small tropical island. Her normal cool control was temporarily missing in action.

He liked the thought of holding her hand, metaphorically speaking, for the evening. If it came to discussing business, she would be brilliant as she always was, but he doubted there would be much of that.

There would also be a lot more people than originally planned. The modestly sized gathering had swollen to include friends and friends of friends and businessmen who all knew each other because the island was so small. Word of mouth had sent the numbers soaring.

She would be lost.

He idly savoured the pleasurable thought of swooping in as her knight in shining armour once again as he strolled unhurriedly towards the main hotel, which was lit up like a Christmas tree.

The place was much busier than it had been previously. Not only busy with the hotel guests, scant though their numbers were, but busy with people arriving in droves, laughing in groups.

He marvelled at the informality of it all. Back in the UK, no one would have ever contemplated tagging along to any party he threw unless there was an official invite. For starters, they would never have been able to bypass border patrol at his front door.

He spotted Gary, waved and cast one backward glance over his shoulder in the direction of the cabin where Erin was no doubt getting ready and maybe wondering whether she would fit in.

'A few more people than I'd anticipated.' He had to raise his voice as Gary fell into step with him. They entered the main hotel together, Raffaele towering over the smaller guy by at least ten inches and exuding the sort of lazy power that made people spin around to look at him with interest.

He was idly looking around. He reckoned there would be perhaps forty people there in total, excluding hotel guests who would be milling around but not allowed through to the various rooms where the informal get-together was being held.

He could hear the sound of music growing more insistent as they exited towards the back of the main hotel, out to a separate building which was used for functions.

Gary was telling him something about the function rooms. Weddings…anniversaries…private parties…not as popular as it could be…sometimes tourists in particular liked to have a beach on their doorstep…how could a beach compare to a rainforest…beaches were two a penny…every Caribbean island had one…

Raffaele was half listening.

He was busily searching the crowd when he spotted her. For a couple of seconds, his brain simply didn't register what his eyes were telling him.

Erin.

She was dancing! Since when did his well-mannered secretary dance? And she was dancing with a man…

Raffaele stopped dead in his tracks.

The room was cleverly lit. Sultry, shadowy nooks and crannies gave an atmosphere of intimacy, but it wasn't so dark that people couldn't see what they were doing. The crowd was lively, mostly young. On the edges, groups of older men and women were chatting. There was a space in the middle cleared for dancing and on a small rostrum, a trio of steel band players was rocking classic old tunes.

And there Erin was…*dancing*.

And here *he* was, hardly able to breathe as he watched her sway to the beat of the steel band without a scrap of inhibition. In the arms of some young, good-looking guy who was grinning like the cat that got the cream.

She was wearing something and nothing much: a bright yellow vest that clung to her slender body and emphasised her small, rounded breasts, and a flowered wrap-around skirt in shades of yellow and orange and bright green, slit up both sides so that her thighs were visible with every sinuous movement.

And where were her sensible shoes? All-weather and practical?

He remembered the pale pink toenails... Now the shoes she was wearing matched those pale pink toenails. They were tan gladiator-style sandals with beads.

Raffaele had no idea why he was so shocked by the vision of his secretary being twirled on a dance floor by a complete stranger, her head thrown back as she laughed with delight.

She was doing the very thing he had been encouraging her to do and yet...and yet...he wasn't sure he *liked* to see her in action. Of course he had *meant* every word he had said about her needing to relax, to just *let go*, but had she any real idea of how easy it was to give some young guy—and some young guy they didn't know from Adam—the wrong impression?

He realised his jaw was slack and quickly pulled himself together. Briskly, he walked towards her, only stopping when he was towering over her partner.

'Erin!'

Her cheeks were pink and her eyes were sparkling. She looked every inch the carefree girl he'd been imagining she could become when he'd encouraged her to step out of the box she liked to hide in. Although now he wondered whether he had got that completely wrong.

Maybe the box had only ever been for his benefit. Maybe this was the real Erin and she'd simply chosen not to show him.

He sensed that his smile was more of a scowl as he cut in, inserting himself between the couple just as the tempo changed from bouncy to cosy.

He slid his arms around Erin's waist and dipped down so that he was more on her level.

'Having fun?'

Erin felt the sinewy hardness of Raffaele's body against hers and everything in the room disappeared. Suddenly, it felt as though it was only the pair of them on a dance floor that had shrunk to the size of a postage stamp.

'I was,' she managed in a wry voice, edging back but finding that his hold was just slightly too tight to easily disengage.

He looked amazing in a pair of linen grey trousers, loafers and a black polo shirt that fitted him like a glove. He hadn't shaved and his six-o'clock shadow was unforgivably sexy.

'Who's the kid?'

'Kid?'

'The one you were dancing with.'

'He's a year older than me so I'm not sure "kid" would be the right description, Raffaele.'

'Exchanged personal information already? Quick work.' His voice was light and amused.

Erin shrugged.

'I didn't expect to find you here before me,' Raffaele said, sweeping her towards the side of the room so that they were now on their own, away from the hubbub of people.

He stopped abruptly and stepped back to look at her with an expression, Erin noted, that looked a lot like disapproval.

She felt her hackles rise.

Did he imagine that he owned her? That because she'd shared something of herself with him, he could now dictate what she did while they were over here? Maybe he figured that an episode with an errant bat now warranted full protection just in case she had another Victorian-maiden-style meltdown over nothing.

'Why not?' she asked bluntly.

He looked away briefly and raked his fingers through his dark hair.

'I figured that you might have been a little...nervous. I did actually make an effort to get back here so that I could be by your side when you came over to the main hotel but everything just dragged on and on with Clive and his wife getting more and more inebriated over lunch until I finally managed to escape.'

'Oh dear. But wait...why do you think I might have been nervous? Didn't you say that I should head over here to meet and greet and get the lay of the land if you weren't around? Didn't you remind me that that was something I was accustomed to doing? So why would you think that I might have been nervous?'

'Because you're in unfamiliar territory... It can be daunting...'

Erin's hackles rose a little more but she wasn't going to be drawn into self-defence.

'We should be mingling,' she said coolly. 'If you like, I can see what business I can do but it doesn't seem the right place or the right time to try to introduce profit-and-loss discussions into the conversation.'

'Of course I don't want you to work!'

'Thank you. I'll get back to the party in that case?'

'Erin...'

'I'll be up first thing tomorrow morning, Raffaele, and I can meet you for breakfast at eight thirty if that suits.'

'You're overreacting...'

'To what exactly?' She sighed, banking down her annoyance, her impatience, her desire to give him a piece of her mind, because she didn't suddenly need her handsome boss thinking that he had to look out for her. 'Doesn't matter, Raffaele. Let's just drop all of this, could we? I guess we're both adjusting to being in a different country with different customs and—' she looked around her but had to grit her teeth to hide the resentment '—different scenery, not to mention the heat. Gets to a person if they're not used to it.'

She forced a smile. He didn't smile back and with a small shrug at his lack of response, she peeled off back to the party. Her dance partner seemed to be waiting for her, ready to pick up where they'd left off.

Left on his own, Raffaele scowled and stared at the pair of them through narrowed eyes.

Erin shimmered. The bright colours suited her, made her chestnut hair glow with different shades of auburn and brown, emphasised the gracefulness of her slender body and the slimness of her shapely legs.

She moved like a dancer.

Come to think of it, she'd always had that graceful way about her and he had always noticed it. He must have filed the observation away somewhere in his subconscious.

The rest of the evening was fun, lively, busy and he managed to work the room without being obvious.

He may have chatted with Erin a several times during the course of the evening, may have exchanged a couple of comments about the food, the music, the vibe, but whether he was talking to her not, he knew that he hadn't let her really out of his sight and she'd been in his head even when his attention seemed to have been one hundred percent focused on whoever he happened to be talking to.

The place was thinning out by ten and when Erin and the boy—Raffaele had discovered that his name was Thompson—began moving towards the door, Raffaele was hit with a surge of…fierce possessiveness that shook him.

He dumped his conversation with two women who had managed to corner him and made for the door as well, intercepting Erin and Thompson just as they were about to head out.

'I'll take it from here,' he addressed the much slighter guy with a terse smile, while lightly resting his hand on Erin's arm. 'Our cabins are side by side. You're…?'

'Gary's my uncle.' Thompson smiled but his big, dark, liquid eyes were fighting to look away from Erin. 'I have a little sightseeing business. We do the coral reefs in glass-bottomed boats…'

'Great! Sure I'll get around to chatting with you sometime if this hotel sale goes ahead but in the meantime—'

'Raffaele…!'

Raffaele looked at Erin blandly, hand still on her arm.

'In the meantime,' he continued, returning his gaze to Thompson, who was beginning to get the hint and good-naturedly backing away from a potentially awkward situation, 'Erin and I are going to be wrapped up with work 24/7…'

'Sure, man!' He grinned, then looked at Erin and winked. 'You know where to find me,' he said, 'and I'd love to show you around our island, take you to have some real local food at one of the villages you probably would never get around to visiting...'

'I'll call...'

'I'll be waiting!'

Raffaele watched this little exchange with frowning displeasure and as soon as the other guy had been eaten up in the darkness outside, Erin turned to him, hands on her hips.

'What was *that* about?'

'Come again?'

'You know what I'm talking about, Raffaele!'

Heading back to the cabins, they soon left the thick of the departing crowd. The music had wound down and now the night noises were forming their own symphony. The sound of the crickets, the frogs and the screech owls mingled with the music of the brightly coloured birds they'd seen at breakfast, still singing mournful songs in the darkness.

There was a slight breeze but not enough to sweep away the heat and the humidity. The lanterns and fairy lights that had been strung between the trees for additional light sparkled against the inky blackness.

'Let's sit for a bit...'

'Sit?'

'We've barely spoken this evening. I'd like to get your thoughts on anything helpful you might have picked up... from any of the people there. You know how it is...music, alcohol loosens tongues...'

'Raffaele, surely that can wait until tomorrow? Especially,' she added with biting sarcasm, 'as I'm sure you'll have me working flat out 24/7, just in case I might be tempted to see Thompson.'

In the darkness, Raffaele flushed darkly. He felt edgy and restless and unwilling to cut short a conversation that he wanted to have without quite understanding why.

'I may have slightly over-egged the pudding on that front.'

He'd led her to one of the many benches scattered in little clearings in the forest for tourists to sit and appreciate the scenery and watched as she hesitated before sitting down.

'Why? Why would you over-egg the pudding? You made such a song and dance of telling me that this *wasn't* going to be a work, work, work busman's holiday.'

'Because...'

Raffaele raked his fingers through this hair and hesitated as his normally very logical, very precise, analytical mind became fuzzy and soft focused.

'Believe it or not, while you're over here I feel that you're my responsibility,' he said gruffly.

'Your responsibility?'

'Call me a dinosaur.'

'I can think of other words,' Erin muttered under her breath.

'That guy you were flirting with...'

'I was *having a conversation with him*,' Erin corrected impatiently. 'I wasn't *flirting*.'

'He was all over you like a rash.'

'Raffaele, are you *jealous*?'

For a few seconds, the silence stretched like elastic between them and Erin felt her heart in her mouth, felt her pulse race with treacherous desire.

'Of course I'm not *jealous*,' Raffaele gritted. 'I've never been jealous in my entire life. Have I ever said anything to you that would indicate that I'm the sort of guy who gets jealous?' He laughed shortly. 'Just because I'm telling you that you should be careful, it doesn't mean that I'm jealous.'

'"Be careful"?'

He *was* jealous. Erin could sense it in her bones, somewhere deep inside her. She had no idea why. Did he think that she was his possession because over the years he had never known her to be distracted by another man? Have a social life? Because, from his perspective, her life was devoted to him?

Her blood boiled and yet there was a treacherous thrill in thinking of herself as his possession. She was a feminist through and through and had always been proud of her determination and her drive and her independence and yet…right now in the heat of the tropical night, excitement threaded through her veins like quicksilver.

'What do you think I should be careful about?' she queried. 'Did you think that Thompson might have made a pass at me and I wouldn't have known what to do about it? That it might have been another bat-flying-in-the-cabin scenario, demanding an urgent rescue from you?'

'Who knows?'

'Well, believe it or not, *I* know.'

'I wouldn't want you to find yourself in an awkward situation,' Raffaele said heavily, his voice laced with discomfort as she continued to look at him, steely eyed.

'Well, thank you very much for your concern, Raffaele. That said, it was misplaced.'

'I'm not sure you were aware of just how…how…'

'How what?'

'How beautiful you looked tonight, Erin. There wasn't a man in that room who wasn't staring at you.'

In the sultry heat, with the rustle of trees around them and the darkness turning everything into shadows and shifting angles, Erin stared at him and was ensnared by the glitter in his eyes.

Her heart skipped a beat.

She wondered whether she'd misheard what he had said. Was her mind playing tricks on her? Was she feverishly hallucinating that he had said the very thing she'd always imagined him saying in those wild fantasies she'd had about him?

'I... I...' she stammered. 'S-sorry? I'm not...uh...following you...'

'Okay, then I guess there's no harm in making it clearer. You looked amazing tonight, Erin. Stunning... beautiful...sexy. Any more descriptions you might need to get the picture? Every eye in that room was on you, including mine.'

The silence lengthened between them, stretched to breaking point.

'I could see what that guy wanted to do from a mile away. He wanted to touch what he was staring at. Maybe you didn't see that but I did. He wanted to do...exactly what I wanted to do...'

CHAPTER SEVEN

RAFFAELE HAD NEVER found himself in a position where he was making a pass at a woman without being absolutely certain that it would be a reciprocal situation. In actual fact, women were often the ones who did the pass-making, with him in the role of obliging recipient.

But that was what he had just done, wasn't it? Made a pass at Erin? She was staring at him in dumbfounded silence and he couldn't blame her.

If *he* couldn't understand what had just happened there, then what were the chances that she would? Had telepathy ever been one of her many skills?

He stared back at her, gauging her reaction in the steamy darkness and utter silence.

He should have been kicking himself but he wasn't. In fact it was a struggle not to reach out and do what his body wanted: reach out and trail his finger over her lips and then bring his mouth to hers so that he could taste her.

Sex. Lust. Desire. A place he'd never thought he would ever want to explore with Erin Fisher, but right now it was the only thing he wanted. The alluring pull of the woman who made him laugh and made him think had collided with the intense drag of attraction, one that had roared into life with sudden, blinding ferocity when he'd seen her dancing.

'It's late,' he said abruptly. He stood up and remained standing as she stumbled to her feet.

Erin took a step back from him, desperate to put some distance between them because what he had just said was ringing in her ears. *He thought she was sexy? Beautiful? Since when? Had she failed to notice that pigs had started flying?*

'It's late, yes,' she said feebly, 'and I'm guessing that you must have had more to drink than you imagine. That rum punch was really strong.'

But even as she spoke, the glittering intent in his eyes had her spellbound.

'I never drink more than I should. Do you think I must have had too much to drink because of what I've just said to you?'

'Yes, if you really want to know.'

'Why wouldn't I find you sexy? Beautiful?'

'Because…'

'Because…?'

'Because I don't think that this conversation is appropriate.'

'That's not an answer. Give me an answer.'

'Oh, for goodness' sake! Because that's not the sort of thing that's ever happened to me!' Erin burst out in a rush. 'Satisfied?'

'No.'

'What do you mean by that? What do you mean by *no*? You can't say that.'

'You fascinate me, Erin Fisher, which is why I want to find out more about you. And yes I can say it. I just did.'

They stared at one another.

When he reached out to trace the outline of her jaw, she audibly gasped but the thrill of his touch was...electric. It turned every bone in her body to jelly. She wanted to subside right back onto the bench but weirdly, she was incapable of any movement at all. She could only stare at his beautiful face, cast in shadows. That feathery touch had come and gone in seconds but the heat from his finger lingered, and she had to resist the temptation to cover the spot with her hand.

She longed to touch him back. Yearned for it and yet the awareness of the danger of going there roared through her with the force of a volcano.

This was a risk she couldn't take. *Wouldn't take.* She wanted love and this road led to...despair. She knew this man, knew herself...knew the two should never, ever merge.

'Since when do I fascinate you, Raffaele?' she scoffed weakly.

He shrugged and looked up to the dark, cloudless sky, the hundreds of thousands of stars studding it, then gazed at her thoughtfully for a couple of seconds.

'I don't know and you're right. Ridiculous conversation. You don't have to answer anything.' He smiled crookedly. 'Sometimes curiosity gets the better of me and yes, add to that that I happen to find you sexy and it's a combustible mix. You go back to your cabin. I'm going to remain out here for a bit...get my thoughts in order.'

Faced with a choice, Erin dithered, watched as he sat back down, stretching his long legs in front of him.

This was about as exciting as life had got for her in... in as far back as she could remember.

She'd played it safe. She always had. With her love

life, with her work life, with her plans for her future. As she'd learned from her parents, choosing not to walk the straight and narrow might lead to adventure, but there were too many downsides for it to ever appeal to her.

But now, under a velvety black sky studded with a million stars and the man who'd featured in too many of her fantasies over the years... She could barely breathe as excitement reared its head, beckoning her to explore.

Somehow she found herself sitting on the bench next to him. Succumbing to something more powerful than all her internal back-and-forth reasoning.

'I work for you.' She turned to him and heard the pleading in her voice.

'I get that and like I said, you don't have to indulge me.'

'This is just a simple conversation.' *Was it?* 'I suppose I've been working for you for quite some time so it's only natural we end up sharing a little more than just the superficial stuff... No big deal.' The steamy, sultry air made her lazy, challenged her to step out of her comfort zone for once in her life even though she continued to tell herself that a conversation was just...a conversation.

She sighed into the stretching silence. 'My life...on the road so much of the time...it was difficult to form friendships, to form relationships. My mum and dad only ever saw it all as a huge adventure but really, for me, my most secure time was when we were at the commune and things were the same every day. I missed that when we took to the road. I missed the routine, I missed the sameness. I missed the faces that would be there every morning when I woke up and every evening before I went to bed, and those times when we settled for a bit... when I managed to go to school...it was hard. The other kids... You know kids, they can be cruel. They sometimes laughed at us, called us names. That said, there were a lot of amazing times, a lot of friendly faces but even so...' She turned away, mortified at her outburst but when she moved to stand up, he stayed her with his hand.

'Keep talking, Erin.'

His voice was low and serious, the voice *of a friend*. Except he wasn't a friend, was he? Or if he was, then this was no longer an innocent friendship. A Pandora's box had been opened and she was struggling to put the lid back on it. Her head was saying one thing but her body was exerting a power that was too strong.

'What else is there to talk about?' Erin breathed in deeply at the memories of her younger years. 'Is this all information overload? I'm guessing you don't have a lot of stamina for women pouring their hearts out to you.'

Raffaele was caught up in a moment he couldn't have foreseen in a thousand years.

Frankly, she was right about his usual appetite for heart-to-hearts. Zero. But right now, right here, she could have kept talking forever because he wanted to keep listening forever.

'Besides,' she chided good-naturedly, 'I notice I'm the only one doing the talking.' Another laugh. 'Fine by me but I think I'll call it a day now before you start thinking that you have to fish around to find a hankie to mop up my tears.'

'Confiding...doesn't come easily to me...' Raffaele said roughly.

'Doesn't to me either, it has to be said. Just another one of those things learned along the way. You never really get the time needed to build the sort of friendships that encourage girlish confidences.' She shrugged but her voice was sad. 'So you learn to keep things to yourself. You don't have to share anything with me. In fact, it's a good idea if you don't. I've already said too much.'

'You think my life was perfect,' Raffaele said on a wrenched sigh and then was astonished. He hadn't meant to say anything about himself. That was the program he'd always stuck to.

'No one's life is perfect but some of us have a bit more to contend with.' Erin smiled kindly.

'Fair enough.' He smiled back at her crookedly. 'I didn't live on the road, travelling wherever the wind happened to blow. I wasn't isolated from my own peer group because I never stayed in the same place long enough to establish a base but...'

'But?'

Raffaele peered forward into the unknown, into the possibility of handing himself over to someone else. His early-warning systems were ringing in his ears but he wanted to ignore them.

It felt like an act of wild courage.

When he looked at Erin, her head was tilted to one side and her expression was curious but gentle.

Maybe if he'd seen anything else but that gentle curiosity he wouldn't have taken a deep breath and said, 'My parents have a loveless marriage. It was always a union that made sense between two powerful families, but love? No. I barely saw them. I was sent to boarding school almost as soon as I was out of nappies. Maybe if I'd been around them I would have stopped hoping for a show of affection that was never going to come a bit earlier than I did. But I just kept on hoping, until I didn't. Eventually, I wised up to my place in the pecking order.' He shrugged. 'I was a teenager when I discovered my father's affair.'

He laughed shortly. 'Why it came as such a shock I have no idea but it did.'

'How awful for you.'

'These things happen. Their marriage weathered it, though. I later found out that their marriage had, in fact, weathered my father's *numerous* affairs. My mother told me when I asked her. She didn't really see why it mattered. Their marriage was everything a marriage should never be, held together because neither of them wanted to abandon their precious status quo.'

'That's a dreadful learning curve for anyone, far less a vulnerable adolescent. Raffaele, I'm so sorry. That must have been devastating for you. We look to our parents to define the road we'll end up travelling down, at least emotionally.'

'I handled it.' He raised his eyebrows, forcing his expression to resume its usual cool. 'You know why I don't get wrapped up in relationships that lead anywhere? Because I learned that I wasn't capable of it… I can do *sex* better than most but love is something I have no interest in. Like you say…the road I have ended up travelling down was defined for me by my distant parents in their loveless union.' He laughed mirthlessly. 'I have no idea why I've just told you that but…' He shrugged indifferently. 'Learning curves are wonderful things. I know mine have made me as tough as nails. Handy when it comes to doing business.'

But not, Erin thought, her heart constricting, *when it comes to anything else.* He had retreated from that window of vulnerability and she knew better than to try to continue the conversation.

He had let her in briefly and now the door would be

shut. But she'd had a striking glimpse of a guy who would never commit to loving anyone when the example set had been devastating for him.

'I should head in.' She stood up and feigned a yawn. He stood as well, towering over her and giving her hammering heart no respite.

'Have a drink with me. In my cabin. Or yours.'

'A *drink*?'

'It's a thing, I hear. Some call it *a nightcap*.'

She hesitated. Part of her wanted to do just that, to have a drink with him, but then she shook her head briskly. Immediately, he backed off, raising both hands in a gesture of amicable surrender.

'Until the morning, in that case.' He spun around on his heels and began heading towards their cabins. She fell in alongside him, still unsettled.

'And the plans are? I mean for tomorrow?'

Raffaele answered readily enough, and Erin could tell that he was as relieved as her to dive into the details of the meetings they had lined up tomorrow. After whatever rogue impulse that had propelling him into opening up to her, talking about work was a return to known terrain, a safe and comfortable refuge.

But then they were standing outside her cabin, and his eyes drifted to her.

'It'll be a hot day,' he murmured as she inserted the key. 'Dress as light as you can and wear a swimsuit under your clothes. The waterfall will be on the menu and it'll look very strange if you hang back.'

Erin quailed.

After everything that had happened tonight…how he had looked at her tonight, that he had told her she was sexy, the way her senses had been roused… And even more dangerous than that, that shared moment between them when the world had stood still...

After all that, the thought of parading around in a swimsuit was unsettling. But if she were to be successful in moving on from tonight's revelations, then she would have to act as though it didn't matter. And the swimsuit she had brought with her was the last word in prim. If he'd suddenly found her sexy in her new-found peacock clothes, then he'd soon be catapulted back to square one the second he spotted her in her black one-piece. That was some consolation.

If he never mentioned those low, murmured confidences again, she would be happy to pretend that they didn't exist. Things would settle back into place with maybe just the odd jarring reminder here and there.

'I wouldn't dream of hanging back.' She lightened the mood with a cheery laugh. Something wicked stirred inside her. 'For starters, Thompson would never forgive me if he's there! See you in the morning, Raffaele!'

To Raffaele's intense annoyance, he found himself spending the following day of meetings and socialising on high alert for the Thompson kid. He didn't sit on the managerial board of the hotel, so should if Thompson appeared, then obviously Raffaele would be within his rights to send him on his way. Very satisfying to savour the thought of that.

He also found himself surreptitiously watching out for signs of flirting from the team, most of whom were young.

Erin had shown up for work very modestly dressed in some neat, soft navy cotton shorts, a daffodil-yellow T-shirt and some flat tan sandals. But somehow she still managed to look as tempting as she had the night before in her brightly coloured outfit. It felt as though a thought had taken root in Raffaele's head, and now that it had, it was intent on sprouting all sorts of tendrils.

She had also reverted to her usual polite self, controlled, smiling and helpful. He should have welcomed that. He didn't. He wasn't going to return to any of the touchy-feely, kumbaya nonsense he'd strayed into last night. But he also wasn't going to pretend that he wasn't aware of her as a woman either.

Last night he'd done nothing but think of her until finally, unable to sleep, he'd got up and worked. Or at least tried to.

Thoughts of her had driven him mad. The things he'd told her…the things she'd told him…the way their eyes had locked together, two people trying hard to fight the obvious.

All he could see in his mind was her. As a man to whom the adulation of women had always been a given, he simply hadn't known how to handle the one woman who eluded him.

He had always had a policy of never actively pursuing any woman. At the end of the day, there were plenty of fish in the sea. But after a couple of hours of fitful sleep he had awoken to the realisation that that particular policy no longer held true.

There was only one fish in this ocean and that was the only fish he wanted.

God, he wanted her so much, as if a dam of dark, desperate want had been swirling under the surface for a million years and had now, finally, burst.

The intensity of what he felt didn't disconcert him at all.

When it came to women and his lack of faith in long-term relationships, there was always an underlying unease that they might end up wanting more than he would be prepared to give them. He always came clean from the start that he wasn't in it for marriage but even so...

Well, just look at Alexa and how that had turned out. She had ignored his warning completely.

With Erin, however, there would be no such fear. She knew him in a way no other woman did; she knew how he felt about longevity in relationships. The things he'd shared with her would only have reinforced what she would already have known. Love wasn't on his agenda and never would be. He could keep it physical, just like he kept all his relationships with women physical. That was a given.

More than that, when it came to a life partner, he simply wasn't her type.

In an ideal world, a fling on the other side of the world would be something they could both indulge in and then, once it was over, lock away in a box never again to be revisited. Their working relationship would resume the peaceful course it had once taken.

This wasn't an ideal world, of course, but Raffaele still thought they could navigate this situation. He had the perfect solution.

It was something he had been vaguely thinking about for a while. And now that their circumstances had changed, that vague thought had crystallised. It was waiting to be pulled out of the hat, magician style.

'Hope you're wearing your swimsuit,' he had murmured to Erin during their lunch break, as they stood at the buffet bar helping themselves to some of the delicious local food. 'As soon as the next round of meetings comes to an end, off we all go to sample the local beauty spots.'

'Of course I'm wearing my swimsuit!' She had looked at him with astonishment. 'Isn't that what you asked me to do? Or have you forgotten?'

Now, lunch done and the final meeting wrapped up, Raffaele stretched back in his chair and looked around at the eight men and women assembled at the table with him.

They were an efficient bunch. They all knew their numbers and even though they'd all been fully cognizant that the hotel had been gradually being sidelined by its current owner, they'd all maintained their enthusiasm to see it do as best as it could, given the financial restraints they'd been dealing with for the past couple of years.

'Okay.' Raffaele stood up and strolled through the boardroom, all eyes on him. 'Good work and I want to say that if I go ahead with this purchase, you'll all be in line for generous remunerations. You've been loyal to this hotel despite the fact that not a huge amount of money's been poured into it over the past two years.'

He paused behind Erin's chair and rested both hands on the back of it.

Automatically, Erin stiffened, feeling his presence behind her and reacting to it with every fibre in her being.

Playing it cool had taken everything out of her.

She'd barely slept the night before. Her head was stuffed full of images of her boss's dark, handsome face, that curling smile, the lazy intent in his eyes that challenged her to step out of the box and explore the unimaginable, those whispered words about the troubled boy behind the controlled man...

She realised she was holding her breath when she felt him straighten behind her and stroll away until he was standing at the head of the conference table, gazing at them. Only then could she breathe out.

'So I think I've done all my due diligence.' He moved to perch on the edge of the boardroom table. He was so mesmerising, so exquisitely good-looking that it felt as though everyone else there was also holding their breath waiting for him to finish talking. 'I have all my facts and figures so thank you all for your cooperation. No need to extend your hospitality further. Erin and I will now do a little exploring of the area on our own.'

Erin's mouth dropped open.

He caught her eye and his eyebrows shot up, feigning innocent surprise at her expression. 'We've already been to the town but there are a couple of beaches, I've been told, which are only accessible by boat…?'

Voices faded to a blur.

She was doing her best not to look appalled but wasn't sure what sort of job she was making of that.

She knew that at some point she was standing up, shaking hands with lots of the people there, making smiling noises about seeing them all again before she and Raffaele headed back to London.

When the door to the conference room was opened and people started filing out, she felt the blast of hot air rush in, cutting through the cool of the air conditioning.

Then the door shut, and she and Raffaele were alone in the room.

'They've worked hard,' Raffaele said. 'They don't need to keep disrupting their timetables to entertain us.' Erin looked at him, her expression carefully guarded, as he walked slowly towards her. 'I'd…like to have a chat with you, Erin.'

'What about?'

'Can't be summed up in one word. It's something of a spectrum.'

'I have no idea what you mean by that. Should I be concerned?' She laughed nervously and stared up at him.

'I guess it's a wait-and-see scenario.'

Erin kept a polite, curious smile pinned to her face but her heart was beating wildly as a million unpleasant outcomes raced through her head.

Top of the list was the sinking dread that he had somehow sensed her attraction to him and had been spooked by it. He might enjoy a bit of light flirtation here, in a place that was alien to both of them, but was he now backing away at speed from the terrifying possibility that she might be yet another woman greedy for love and commitment? Especially after what he'd shared with her?

All her insecurities rose to the surface with suffocating urgency.

She'd told him so much about herself and now she felt trapped by those unwitting confidences as though he could read her soul by putting together the path of breadcrumbs she had laid down. As though he could just *see* that his idea of light flirtation with the secretary he now knew a little more about had provoked a disproportionate, inappropriate reaction within her.

'How I love wait-and-see scenarios,' she said with an attempt at her usual dry humour and he obligingly smiled.

'Why don't we take a walk? We can head in the direction of the waterfall. It's probably quiet out there at this hour. People taking it easy after a day in the sweltering sun.'

'Sure.'

It was cooler than it had been, with rain in the air. Still steaming hot, though, and here, without any pretty lanterns and fairy lights, the forest around them felt wilder and lusher.

There was no one on the path they took. No locals, no tourists. They walked through a shadowy twilight semi-darkness under the canopy of trees with the squish of fallen leaves underfoot. Occasionally the fading sun would penetrate the canopy, sending shards of pale light through the branches of the trees. After a handful of minutes, during which they had walked in silence, they emerged into a glorious clearing where the waterfall, not very big at all, crashed over dark rocks into a crystal clear pool empty of people.

Erin walked down to the water, mesmerised by the thunderous sound of the falls and the way they cascaded down, rippling outwards until the turmoil gave way to ice-cold water as still as a swimming pool.

She felt Raffaele next to her and her whole body stiffened with tension.

'Spit it out, Raffaele,' she stated as she spun around to face him. 'The suspense is killing me.'

'I want you.'

'Sorry?' She twisted to look at him but he continued staring out at the water, his jaw clenched.

'I want to sleep with you, Erin.'

'What? Wait. What are you saying? No!' Her voice shook. 'That can't happen!'

'Because you don't want to sleep *with me*?'

'I don't want to have this conversation. How on earth would we ever be able to carry on working together if we…if we…?'

This time he did face her and Erin's pulse raced at the absolute seriousness on his face. The very face she had longed to touch for so many years.

Her lips parted and her treacherous body took a step towards him. She saw just the ghost of a smile on his face. It should have been a signal for her to break the electric connection between them, but she couldn't.

He wanted her.

No misreading of signals, no imagination playing tricks on her. *He wanted her and she wanted him right back.*

She knew the dangers. She'd listed each and every one in her head a million times but crushing desire made a nonsense of all those rational concerns. Crushing desire was already making an argument for doing exactly what they both wanted, was telling her that this was just lust, that lust couldn't end up hurting her or derailing her hope of finding love with the right guy.

She trembled, her breath hitching, as Raffaele lowered his head, and the cool feeling of his lips on hers kick-started a cyclone of pent-up arousal inside her. She moaned into his mouth and stepped closer to him, her slender body pressed against his hard, masculine, much bigger one. She reached up and sifted her fingers through his dark hair as he continued to send her senses into spinning meltdown, first with his mouth, his invading tongue lashing against hers, and then with his hand, moving underneath her top and finding the cup of the swimsuit she'd worn under her clothes.

'This is too much,' he growled. 'We have to get a room.'

'Raffaele...'

'Come... I know where we can go... Jesus, I've never felt so turned on in my life before... I can barely get my thoughts together...'

Erin followed him blindly. He was saying something about the ledge he'd found behind the waterfall when he'd been on one of his earlier journeys of discovery.

The noise of the waterfall thundered around them. Sure-footed and agile, he held her hand as he led the way to the smooth, cool ledge behind the falls, big enough to sit and have a picnic with friends. Hidden from view by the wall of water a mere handful of feet away.

This was peace, privacy, a cool, misty respite from the stifling humidity.

There was nothing cool between them, though. Erin was burning up.

Her clothes were sticking to her like glue.

She began stripping off. Part of her could scarcely believe this was happening. Another part revelled in it, revelled in the freedom of being reckless for the first time in her life.

The ledge, smooth and flat, should have been uncomfortable, but it was lovely and slippery and cold underfoot. Erin found herself wondering how many couples had sneaked behind this waterfall over the decades to do exactly what they were doing now.

They didn't speak. The sound of cascading water feet away from them would have drowned out their voices anyway.

Erin liked it that way because she just wanted to feast her eyes on Raffaele and enjoy him in perfect, blissful silence.

When the last of his clothing was off, her mouth fell open. He'd worn swimming trunks underneath, black and navy blue, and as he kicked them to the side, to join the rest of his discarded clothes, she breathed in sharply and trembled.

He was impressive and there was no mistaking the fact that he was turned on.

She had begun undressing already. Now she couldn't

wait to get her clothes off completely. She scrabbled at them while he stood exactly where he was, watching her with his hand resting idly on his erection.

She had never been so turned on.

He walked towards her and then held her. Their bodies glistened with perspiration and spray from the waterfall. She could smell the humid air and the scent of earth.

It felt as though time stood still as he began touching her, exploring her nakedness slowly with his hands while he kissed her. She had to reach up to him, half on tiptoe, her hands wound around his neck so that she could pull him tighter towards her.

Her breasts pressed against his hard chest. She felt the scrape of his hair against her nipples and rubbed herself against him so that the sensation was amplified.

He cupped her rounded bottom and massaged it, ran his hands along her waist and felt her shiver and then curved them around her breasts, inching slightly away from her so that he could rub the stiffened peaks of her nipples with the abrasive pads of his thumbs.

'I don't want to rush this,' he groaned. 'Would you rather we take this to a bed in one of our cabins? Although I'm not sure I can make it that far…'

'I want to stay here.'

'Then let me spread some of clothes out… We can lie down…'

It took Raffaele seconds to haphazardly spread some of their clothing in a reasonably good semblance of a sheet, but it felt like hours. Finally, it was done and they were staring at one another across the tumble of clothes on the ground.

Naked. With the spray from the waterfall on them and the cool of the grotto on them.

They moved towards one another in unison, eyes locked.

'I want to take this slowly,' he breathed into her ear, wrapping his arms around her in a caress that was almost chaste. 'I've been thinking about this...wanting it... wanting *you*... I want to take my time and pleasure you until you want me to carry on forever...'

Forever...? The word lingered in Erin's head, pernicious and heady, until she dismissed it because she wondered whether that was a word Raffaele would ever really understand.

They lay down together, adjusting their bodies until they found their comfort zone and then they began to explore one another.

Tentative...eager...slowly...hungrily...

They clung and kissed, at first urgently, limbs tangling but then the kiss softened as they tasted one another, neither wanting to break apart but both eager to explore more, to touch more.

Raffaele had never felt anything like this, anything so wild and powerful and consuming. Each time Erin whimpered, he had to steel himself against rushing everything because all he wanted to do was to reach his orgasm as fast as he could.

Every tiny movement she made against him sent his senses reeling.

He cupped her small breast in his hand as he trailed kisses along her neck and when she arched back, he obligingly took her pert nipple into his mouth and sucked hard on it.

She was so slim that he could feel the outline of her ribs under his hand, could feel every thrilling response to what he was doing, every small shudder.

He touched her lightly, ran his fingers in a feathery motion over her stomach as she sucked in her breath and then he dipped his fingers into her, into her wetness, feeling a slippery way to touch the spot that made her groan and begin to buck against his hand.

'We can't take this where I want to take it,' he groaned with anguished frustration, even as he continued to tease her, tickling the stiffened bud of her clitoris and feeling it pulse to his touch.

He briefly propped himself up to look down at her flushed face.

'Don't stop.'

'I don't have protection with me.'

'Arghh!' Erin likewise propped herself up on her elbows, her chestnut hair tumbling around her face, her mouth parted with desire. She pushed her hair from her face and stared at him. 'And I'm not on any contraception.'

'Wouldn't matter. I always make sure to be responsible for my own protection. You're beautiful, Erin.' He smiled when she blushed. 'Never mind. I know a million other ways we can satisfy one another and when we get back to my cabin...we can pick up where we left off. Might be fun to have some delayed gratification.'

'Says the guy who's probably never had to experience that in his life before?' she teased huskily.

He smiled back at her, appreciatively, eyes devouring her. 'Change is as good as a rest… I'm certainly finding the idea of delayed gratification a big turn-on.'

He stopped talking and began exploring, this time with his mouth and his tongue. He pushed her thighs apart and smelled her musky scent as he delicately licked her.

When she trembled, he could feel something intensely

and gratifyingly masculine tear through him, a feeling of powerful possessiveness.

The thought that this was his prim and proper secretary was a turn-on like nothing else he'd ever experienced in his life before.

He stroked her thighs as he continued to tease her clitoris and then when he knew that she could no longer fight the surging, pulsing need to come, he thrust his fingers into her so that he could pleasure her with more than just his mouth.

Erin was taken to Heaven and back.

She arched back, detached from everything around her, lost in sensation, barely recognising her own guttural moaning as she came against his mouth.

The wall of cascading water cocooned them. It made the experience feel unreal and yet incredibly erotic.

Outside, the fading sun threw everything in that intensely private space into misty twilight.

It was surreal.

The noise of the waterfall…the humidity…the spectral light…and, as Erin surfaced back to reality, this glorious, beautiful man who had only ever existed for her like this in her deepest, darkest dreams.

She touched him all over, the way he'd touched her. Every bit of his naked body was a revelation and a delight.

She explored him, eyes open so that she could see what she was touching. She lost herself in the feel of him, hard and muscled under her exploring fingers. When she licked her fingers and gently stroked his flat, brown nipples, she thrilled to the way he shuddered and then gripped her hand, guiding it to his erection because he couldn't stand being teased any longer.

She enjoyed him the way he had enjoyed her, and loved pleasuring him the way he had loved pleasuring her.

She had no idea where this freewheeling sense of freedom was coming from. Maybe because for the first time in her life, she was giving herself permission to do exactly what she wanted without counting the cost.

She was expunging the crush she had had on him for such a long time. She had never foreseen any of this happening but he had extended his hand. She had taken it without thinking about repercussions because, at least on the emotional front, she was safe.

He was a commitment-phobe. He could never be the sort of guy she would ever contemplate being a lasting feature in her life.

On a work front… Well, that posed a number of thorny issues, but for the moment, Erin decided that she would delay thinking about that.

There was a cabin to get to. There was hot, steamy, wonderful, wild, taboo sex on the menu…

Thorny issues were for another day.

CHAPTER EIGHT

'MY PARENTS WOULD give their eye teeth to see what I'm seeing right now.' Erin was lying on a lounger, looking out at a sunset that lit up the clouds in tones of sherbet. A soft, impressionistic swirl of orange, pink and lavender was rapidly being swallowed up by a star-studded, velvet blackness.

Raffaele's lounger was right next to hers and she felt his hand move to lightly rest on her stomach.

The yacht they'd rented four days previously was bobbing gently beneath them to the rhythmic lull of the waves lapping against the sides of the hull. They were both lying on their backs, looking at the same sunset, the same expanse of sky and the same calm ocean all around.

'Do they know you're here?' Raffaele asked curiously.

'Of course not.' Erin wriggled onto her side so that she could look at Raffaele. He was naked. Completely naked. So was she. They were miles from any of the islands that made up the Grenadines. If she peered through the gathering darkness, she might just be able to make out the silhouette of Bequia, where they had spent most of the day, but from here?

Just the ocean all around them. She could smell the salt from the sea. The horizon seemed to stretch forever. It was dreamlike. A bit like everything that was happening between her and Raffaele. Dreamlike. She didn't want to wake up.

'You haven't told them that you're having a fling with your boss?'

Erin heard the smile in his voice and shivered.

'Of course I haven't.'

'Think they'd disapprove?'

'I know they would.'

'Why?'

Raffaele shifted so that he was lying on his side, looking at her. He ran his hand gently along her side, feathered over the dip of her waist and then stroked her flank until the usual responses were firing up.

Lust...desire...the spreading wetness between her thighs that longed for his touch, for his mouth...for the hard thrust of him inside her, filling her up.

Her breath hitched and she saw his eyes darken as he recognised what he was doing to her.

It was definitely a two-way street. She could see exactly what she was doing to him as well.

She felt languid. She wanted to be teased. She wanted to tease him. To talk while they touched one another.

'Oh, you know...'

'They disapprove of intra-office relationships?'

'They'd disapprove of me doing this...just having sex without any commitment...' She mirrored his stroking, running her hand along his thigh and liking the abrasive feel of hair-roughened, muscled skin.

He was fully erect and she teased the tip of his erection with her finger and smiled when he shuddered and clasped his hand over hers for a couple of seconds.

'From what you've told me about them, I'll admit I got

the idea that they might have been a little more liberal in their thinking.'

'Because they led an unconventional lifestyle?' Erin thought about her parents, still crazily in love with one another. 'They were soulmates. They literally only had eyes for one another. They had me later in life but honestly…they're great believers in the power of love and all they've ever wanted for me was to find my own soulmate.' Erin hesitated. She'd told him a lot, but she hadn't mentioned David, the guy she'd dated, the mistake she'd made. 'Especially after David.'

'Who was David?'

Erin flopped back onto the lounger and stared off into the distance. Darkness had roared in, extinguishing the russet colours of sunset.

'Oh, he's someone I thought was the real deal. I was inexperienced. I built castles in the sky.' She smiled. 'It was never the real deal. We were never a match and when we broke up, he said some pretty harsh things…' She sighed. 'I got over him and it didn't take long to realise that he was toxic, passive-aggressive a lot of the time…moody when he didn't get his own way. I don't think I was really myself when I was with him and never relaxed into the relationship. I was in love with the thought of being in love so decided that it was okay to ignore red flags. When we broke up, he was pretty callous, pretty scathing about me and that hurt. A lot. So while that break-up was the best thing that could have happened to me in retrospect, I think it made my parents realise, and me as well, that the next relationship should be something healthy, a relationship with a future. My parents might have been hippies and still are, to be honest, but they'd see this as me wasting my time.'

'And do you? Think that you're wasting your time with me?'

The conversation was suddenly very serious. Thoughts that Erin had barely voiced to herself now rose to the surface.

Where was this going? How had that bridge to be crossed at some point in the future suddenly materialised under her feet? Was it because feelings she had dismissed as no more than a trivial crush were turning out to be something a lot more dangerous?

Her heart picked up pace.

Was she falling in love with a guy whose only commitment to her had been to take a few days off work? All so that they could prolong their time in this little bubble where reality could be suspended?

Raffaele hadn't even discussed what would happen when their time on this yacht was at an end!

And she'd just gone along for the ride because he was addictive. She'd squashed all her qualms when they'd tried to nudge through and told herself that she was in control. And why had she done that?

Because she loved him.

And the alternative of stepping back and taking stock was inconceivable, so she'd pretended there was no need to look beyond the moment. She'd dumped every principle she'd had when it came to men, lock, stock and barrel.

And now she was terrified.

Her mouth suddenly felt dry. 'Why would I think that?' she managed to say.

'Well, it sounds as though after the break-up, you programmed yourself to think that the only way forward would be with a guy with an engagement ring in his back pocket.'

His voice was light and amused but Erin thought she could pick up something in his voice, a wariness, the cautious testing of the ground. The hint of unspoken questions. *Was his secretary beginning to get unrealistic ideas about what they had? Which was, essentially, nothing? Should he be worried?*

It wasn't as though he'd said anything about a future... no plans beyond how they would occupy the next hour or so...

'Programmes have a way of changing,' Erin mused thoughtfully, absently, while her heart beat fast and wild against her ribcage. 'Your programme also changed, didn't it? But here we are.' She shrugged and smiled and then provocatively traced a line with her finger along his arm. 'I reckon this is just what I need. Something temporary...a fun stepping stone to the committed relationship I really want. I mean, I fell into the habit of taking time out from guys after my break-up. It was easy and it was lazy and I'm honest enough to admit that.' She smiled ruefully, something in her chest aching.

She loved this man... How could she have let this happen?

'"A fun stepping stone..."'

'That's it. A wonderful game. Wouldn't you agree? I mean, neither of us saw this coming and now we're here, it's almost as though we're not actually in the real world.'

'I can agree with that.' Raffaele smiled, trying to cover over the unsettling realisation that it was pretty much the only thing Erin had said that he was inclined to agree with.

Wrong. He could theoretically agree with all of it. He just didn't *like* every word he'd just heard.

A stepping stone? A bit of fun? Before she found Mr Right?

Was that the sound of a woman who was using him?

And why was it such a big deal? It was discomforting to think that that was precisely how he usually approached his relationships, although he baulked at the thought that he was *using* those women. Fair was fair: he always warned them in advance of his intentions, or rather the lack of them.

The perfect gentleman.

He didn't feel like being the perfect gentleman with Erin, and that confused him. He wanted something more...but what? Not to be written off as an amusing footnote? Was he that much of an egotist?

He wanted to shake his head clear of a murky swirl of thoughts he couldn't quite pin down and couldn't quite rationalise.

'You asked me if I'm wasting my time. Not a bit of it,' she reiterated.

'My feelings precisely.'

He skimmed her thigh with the flat of his hand and decided that there was such a thing as too much conversation.

He was a doing kind of guy. Sex was much easier. He didn't want to tackle uneasy thoughts.

Two loungers weren't ideal when it came to making love but they could have a little fun on them for a while.

He toyed with her breast, teased her nipple until it was stiff. When she began breathing quickly, he moistened his finger with his tongue and continued to play with her nipple. He was propped up on one elbow, looking at her with intense satisfaction.

Why was she so obsessed with the perfect guy? Couldn't she see that that was all just an illusion?

He cupped the mound between her thighs and then levered himself off the lounger, never removing his hand from its resting place.

Night engulfed them but a full moon threw her slender body into silvery relief.

Want slammed into him. He gently tugged her a little, urging her to slither a little lower down the lounger, legs splayed on either side so that she was open like a flower for his mouth.

He wondered, fleetingly, whether he could ever get enough of the taste of her. For a second, he just breathed her in and then darted his tongue along the slippery groove that shielded her clitoris.

He peeled the delicate folds gently apart, opening her up even more to his questing tongue, and he took his time rousing her, taking her so close to the edge and then pulling back until she began begging him to stop teasing her, whimpering that she couldn't stand it any longer, breathily panting that she needed to come.

Every uttered plea filled him with visceral pleasure. He could feel the steady pulse of his erection, demanding satisfaction.

He didn't speak as he stood up and swept her off the lounger in one smooth, hurried movement.

'You're driving me mad,' he muttered in a driven undertone. 'How do you do that to me, woman?'

He looked down at her small, perfect breasts, at the nipples still glistening from his tongue, and wanted to come on the spot.

He made it to their cabin on the yacht in the nick of time.

The bedroom on the yacht, with its luxurious, high-end en suite, was huge. The bed was king-sized and indulgently comfortable. The air conditioning had been left on and it was cool as he nudged open the door with Erin still in his arms.

He had to clear his head to slow himself down, to make time for the little foil packet of condoms he kept by the bed.

Most of all he had to make sure not to look at her, naked and flushed on the bed. One glance at her and the unthinkable might happen.

He donned protection with shaking hands and didn't bother trying to play it cool or to take his time. He simply thrust into her, long and hard and deep on a guttural groan of fulfilment and only just managed to hold off his climax until he felt her body moving in tune with his and her orgasm tearing into her. Immediately, he came with a long shudder that left him weak in the aftermath.

He collapsed onto his back and let his breathing do its best to return to normal then he flipped onto his side and looked at her.

'You look as though you're falling asleep,' he teased. 'Is that what I do for you? Send you to sleep?'

Eyes closed, Erin smiled but then she wriggled onto her side as well and drowsily opened her eyes to look at him.

Her busy thoughts were returning.

Raffaele might enjoy this vacuum but sooner rather than later reality was waiting for them and they would have to confront it.

When he had suggested staying on in the Caribbean, sailing down the Grenadines and taking a little time out, she had played it cool on the outside but inside, she had jumped at the idea.

He'd mentioned something about a week. He needed a break, he'd told her, holding her and kissing her, and since he was the boss he could do as he damn well pleased.

He'd grinned and told her that as his secretary, she was duty-bound to agree with him.

'We let this run its course,' he'd said with infectious confidence, 'and then we put it behind us. But if we don't see it out…it'll stay there, eating away at both of us, making it impossible to work alongside one another.'

She'd agreed.

It had sounded simple enough.

It wasn't simple now and truthfully, it never had been. She'd just kidded herself because the thought of saying goodbye to him was overwhelming.

'I guess,' she murmured without any hint of anxiety in her voice, 'we should talk about where this isn't going and start thinking about getting back to real life in London. I've been checking my emails daily and there are things waiting to be done that can't be done here, even with an internet connection.'

'Where this *isn't* going?'

'Let's not play make-believe, Raffaele,' Erin said drily. 'I know you. Don't forget I've sent many a Dear John token to girlfriends who were ushered out the back door so that you could open the front door to their replacement.'

She stroked his cheek and knew that she was mentally saying goodbye. How could she just carry on as though nothing had happened when they returned to London? He would be able to do that because he hadn't emotionally invested, but she wouldn't and that was a deep, devastating ache in her she would have to deal with over time.

She just suddenly needed to know how much time she had left with him.

'That's a little on the harsh side!'

'But untrue?'

She saw him shift uncomfortably, saw the dark flush stain his cheekbones. He couldn't deny it even if he found it a little too blunt for his liking.

'Define *untrue*.'

'You're an idiot, Raffaele.'

'I don't have a revolving door of women! And besides…you know why I never promise commitment. I've told you about my parents, their dysfunctional marriage…'

'You don't have to be afraid of committing to a relationship because the example that was set for you was a bad one.'

'No? Is that the sound of you trying to psychoanalyse me?'

'It's the sound of me trying to be logical.'

'Erin…'

'What?'

'You know who I am, don't you? You know that I'm not someone who's spent his life thinking he can't commit because he hasn't happened to find the right woman. I mean, Erin, you know that I'm not interested in commitment…'

Erin knew that this was a warning. A gentle one. This was a fling and nothing more than that. *Don't go getting any ideas.*

'You bet. And sure, I understand that you feel you have to be careful…but will you never be tempted to settle down one day? Have a family? I don't care whether you remain a confirmed bachelor for the rest of your days. I don't care if the only companions you have when you're a wizened old man are a bunch of cats. I'm just curious.'

Raffaele couldn't help but burst out laughing. 'That's a very seductive picture you paint of me. Wizened old man? Well, if that turns out to be the case then it'll be no great shock if the only creatures that actually want to hang around me are a bunch of cats.' He paused and then said with a slight shrug. 'I expect the time will come. An heir will have to inherit the throne.' He smiled with self-irony. 'But when that time comes, I won't be doing it for love. I'll be doing it because it makes sense. No illusions that could lead to disappointment.'

'Yes, but isn't that what your parents did? Married to unite two powerful families? No illusions there that could lead to disappointment?'

'Who said either of them are disappointed?' His mouth curled derisively. 'I assume they both accepted certain terms and conditions within their union and one of those just happened to be infidelity. You'll find that there are many uber wealthy families where a lot is tolerated for the sake of the status quo.'

'But you would never tolerate that.'

'I've always been a one-woman man. That won't change if and when I ever decide to tie the knot. That said, within those parameters, I would need a woman who wasn't in search of romance, who was practical about what I could bring to the marriage. Stability, monogamy and a great deal of money. In return, I would want a calm home front, someone undemanding, there to raise whatever children we might have. Someone who would accept that I work long hours and wouldn't nag to do things I probably wouldn't have time to do.'

'Things like what?'

'Time off work for spontaneous picnics in a park somewhere…chocolate and flowers and love notes left under pillows…'

'That sounds very specific.'

Raffaele hesitated. 'I took a chance on love once upon a long time ago,' he said heavily. 'I was in my early twenties and obviously hadn't yet bought completely into the mindset I now have. Unfortunately, it didn't end well.'

'What happened?'

'She was very sweet, very wide-eyed and romantic. She was everything I wasn't and I honestly believed that if anyone could persuade me that love was possible, then it was her. I thought I could give her what she wanted but it turned out that the lessons I'd learned had been too well ingrained to be cast aside. I was building my own empire and time was in scant supply. She wanted more than the guy who worked all hours and I was puzzled by her growing demands for more of…me. When I did make an effort…she complained that I was still too wrapped up in work to give her my full attention. The sweet-natured girl turned into a shrew and I could hardly blame her.'

'How sad.'

'Timely,' Raffaele said flatly. 'We could have been married…had kids, and then the whole situation would have been a million times more complicated. As things turned out, we ended the relationship and after a few months she actually got back in touch with me to say exactly what I felt at the time we ended things.'

'Which was?'

'That it was better the end came sooner rather than later. All's well that ended well. You'll be excited to know that she found her dream guy a year after meeting me and is now happily married with two kids. She invited me to the wedding but I thought it tactful not to go.'

Raffaele heard the cool, detached indifference in his voice when he recounted this story. Inside, though, he could feel, once again, the pain of finally accepting that that life would never be his. A life of love, vulnerability, of sharing hopes and dreams with the anchor of a woman he loved by his side.

This, what he had now, his work and his women, was his life and always would be.

And now Erin was a part of that life. He liked that. Liked the thought of them continuing what they had. And he'd figured out a way to make it possible.

Yes, it was just another relationship based on sex, but it was good, and he wasn't ready for it to be over. He'd shared a lot with her and against all odds, he had more to share. She'd got under his skin in ways he hadn't predicted and he wanted to keep her there.

His head told him *for the time being*.

His heart…? Perhaps the story was a little more nuanced. Did he dare explore those nuances?

Raffaele frowned as blurry, uneasy feelings tried to break through the logic of his thoughts.

He wouldn't allow that to happen.

'What a tender moment we're having.' He grinned, eyebrows shooting up so that she could clock the jokey sarcasm in his voice that would nullify any seriousness.

Erin looked at him in silence for a few seconds. She felt that the last of the jigsaw puzzle pieces had now been slotted into place.

Raffaele wasn't just the product of his dysfunctional family. He was also the product of a broken heart, of a relationship that had crashed and burned at that very point when hope in love had still stood a chance.

He was never going to love and as she accepted the finality of that, she realised that somewhere she had still been hoping that her impossible, ridiculous feelings would be returned.

'Yes, it's certainly very, very exciting for me to find out that the significant ex in your life is now happily married to someone else. Any more joyous anecdotes up your sleeve?' Her jokey sarcasm matched his.

Raffaele laughed under his breath. 'You have no idea how liberating it is being with a woman who has no expectations, who really and truly can live in the moment.'

Erin maintained eye contact and did something she hoped resembled an airy smile.

'We've drifted away from the topic I originally brought up,' she murmured. 'It's about time to start thinking about getting back to London. I really need to go visit my parents, make sure they're doing all right.'

'Oh yes. Not to mention those pesky emails you've checked that need urgent attention.' He grinned and smoothed her side with his hand. 'It's going to be a bit more difficult to pretend all of this never took place when we return. I thought it would be easy…a brief fling, a need sated…'

There spoke the man with the revolving-door approach to women, Erin thought sourly. However pious he might get on the subject. In Raffaele's easy-come, easy-go world, there were never any lingering after-effects once *needs were sated*.

'I've been mulling this over and hear me out because it's something I actually considered a few months ago, and this seems the perfect time to put it into practice especially since...'

'Especially since what?'

'I don't want this to end.'

Erin felt her heart skip a beat but before irrational hope could start putting feelers out, he continued, 'Not yet.' He leaned into her, kissed her, a deep, bone-meltingly thorough kiss, and at the same time he cupped her between her legs, rousing her all over again.

'And I can tell you feel the same way. Don't try to deny it. I can feel it in your wetness and I know just how turned on you'll get if I do this...'

He dipped his fingers inside her and found the beating clitoris with no trouble at all. He teased it with the expertise of a man who knew her body, knew just how to take it where it wanted to go.

Erin moaned and lost herself in sensation.

She didn't want to. There was a conversation waiting to be had but right now her body had different ideas. He moved his fingers harder and faster, and she bucked, arched and came quickly and on a long, shuddering groan of satisfaction.

'There,' he said with satisfaction. 'That's why I just can't stop this yet. Why neither of us can but...'

Erin didn't interrupt. She had no idea what he was about to say but it didn't matter because he was right. Of course they could no longer work together. Of course she would have to hand in her resignation. Even if she was greedy and decided to continue this situation, sneaking past one another during work hours and sharing hot, surreptitious glances over the computer...it would end one day and when that happened, she would be left with even more broken pieces of her heart to piece together.

He, on the other hand, would always escape unscathed because he would never be emotionally invested.

'Want to hear my plan? I think you'll love it, Erin, and honestly, it's something I should have done, like I said, some time ago.'

'Okay. What's your plan? Tell me. I'm all ears.'

'I promote you. You earned a promotion a long time ago and I'm not talking a salary increase. I'm talking about a complete change of job title.'

He paused and in that pause Erin understood. She saw it all in an instant, how he'd worked things out.

The details, the job title, they weren't important: what it boiled down to was that Raffaele planned to pay her to continue their affair. Although she had no doubt that he would never see it that way.

'Really?' she said, trying to keep her devastation out of her voice.

'I want you to take full charge of a number of clients, including this chain of hotels if I go ahead with the purchase, which I probably will. Your clients will all be familiar to you and you'll have full responsibility to see the ongoing projects through to their conclusion. Naturally, with the title will come a substantial pay increase. Erin, you'll be able to afford to move out from that peculiar place you live in, to give your parents whatever financial help they need…to lead a life of comfort doing the thing you love.'

'Oh wow.' She wasn't tempted for a second. Money could never buy what she really wanted.

'I know! You'll be reporting to me, Erin, but you'll be on a different floor completely so there will be no awkwardness.'

'I see.' Conveniently relocated—near enough to be accessible for as long as it took before he got bored but far enough so that he didn't have to face her on a daily basis once the whole thing had ground to a halt.

'I've started the ball rolling with HR,' he told her comfortably. 'I hope you don't mind? So here's what I'm thinking...a couple more days here and then back to the grindstone except...the grindstone isn't going to be quite what either of us left behind. No...it's going to be a lot more exciting now... You can take a week or so off, go visit your parents, and by the time you return to the office, you'll be the proud possessor of a shiny new desk in a shiny new office on the fourth floor.'

'That's all very speedy, Raffaele.'

'I like to think of myself as a man of action.'

'I see.'

'Am I detecting a certain lack of enthusiasm?' Raffaele frowned and drew back to look at her. 'Aren't you excited? Don't you *want* what's on the table?' His voice roughened with sincerity. 'You get the job of a lifetime, Erin, and we get to keep this going, to sleep together, to touch one another...'

There was just the briefest of hesitations. Erin looked down then back to him. She smiled.

'Keep it going,' she murmured. 'Yes...we both still want one another...so why not keep it going?'

For precisely the length of time they remained on this yacht. Why not indeed? A couple of days of being greedy, of having Raffaele all to herself. And then the minute they returned to London...the only thing on the table would be her resignation.

CHAPTER NINE

Erin was tempted to email her resignation letter. So much easier. Something brief and anodyne with a few vague words about the many challenges the job had given her but alas…circumstances dictated that she now seek alternative employment. Something high on waffle and low on detail.

Then she would cite holiday time still owing, which would allow her to resign without having to set foot in the office again.

In the end she decided to hand the letter to Raffaele herself and deal with the consequences head-on.

How bad could it be anyway? As far as she knew there were no dungeons in the building into which she could be flung because his offer had been rejected. She expected he would be startled but then he would shrug and accept the inevitable.

She'd never known Raffaele to beg for anything in all the time she'd been working for him. When it came to women, he was good at walking away. His nose might be put out of joint because the walking-away schedule had not been set by him, but habit would kick in and the only thing he would really miss would be her efficiency in the office.

She was a bundle of nerves on the Monday morning as she strode into the lift and headed up to the top floor.

Cruising down the Grenadines felt like a lifetime ago even though they'd only returned two days previously, from the sticky humidity to the uncomfortable heat of the city.

Her resignation letter was burning a hole in her bag.

How was it that everything around her was so familiar, from the people greeting her to the buzz of employees ditching their jackets and settling down for a day's work, and yet she felt as though she was having an out-of-body experience?

Raffaele was, of course, already in. There was something about the atmosphere on the floor when he was in, a certain alertness, a tacit awareness that the big guy was around, which meant everyone went into hyper-focus mode.

She waved and nodded to people she knew as she walked towards the office she and Raffaele shared. It was at the very end of a corridor that housed the various directors behind smoked-glass walls.

She breathed in to steady her nerves, pushed open the door and then walked straight through the connecting door. Raffaele was on the phone, his seat pushed back from his desk.

He came off his call with alacrity and looked at her with intense satisfaction before vaulting to his feet to perch on his desk, the very picture of an alpha male in possession of just what he happened to want.

'I thought you were taking some time out to go visit your parents. How are they, by the way? Told them about us yet?' He grinned and moved to shut the connecting door, locking them into his office space.

'I decided that my time might be better served coming in to work today.'

'Got it. Fully on board with that one.' He reached to sift his fingers through her hair. 'The sun loves you. You're an incredible golden colour after a couple of weeks in it. Brings out your freckles.' He deposited a kiss lightly on her lips and for a couple of seconds, Erin's world stopped and she was besieged by memories of how her body felt whenever he touched it.

As though he could literally control her ability to think or not think.

Right now, he barrelled straight through her defences and she felt herself go weak at the knees.

She put her hand on his chest, felt the beating of his heart underneath the white shirt and pushed him away although it was a very wobbly, unconvincing push.

'I know,' he breathed, not budging. 'I get it. Very reckless of us to carry on within the confines of the office. Much better for us to meet outside. Office gossip can spread faster than a flu virus, but which of us would be able to resist if we happened to be within ten metres of one another? Hence why working on a different floor might help our blood pressure.' He slanted a wicked smile. 'But I get why you had to come in. Believe me, I'm on the same page. The thought of not being able to touch you for another fortnight was bringing me out in a cold sweat. I realise I might not be a fan of delayed gratification after all. I might have had to spring a surprise visit on your parents.'

Erin was temporarily distracted by that appalling thought.

She wriggled away from him and moved to her usual chair in front of his desk in a pointed attempt to put some distance between them. Not much but any small amount of distance would do.

He, in turn, returned to perch on the desk, which left her with the heart-stopping sight of his muscular thighs and the fabric of his trousers pulled tight across them. She stared, dry mouthed for few seconds, at his hands hanging loosely between his knees and cleared her throat.

'That would have been a terrible idea,' she croaked distractedly.

'Under normal circumstances, yes,' Raffaele agreed. He didn't take his eyes off her for a single second. 'Under normal circumstances, the last thing I've ever been interested in is getting to know the parents. But then your parents are in a league of their own.'

'Am I supposed to take that as a compliment?'

'Insofar as that would be a first for me,' he murmured without skipping a beat. 'But then, in so many ways, you're a first for me.'

'I'm duly flattered,' Erin said politely. She wasn't. Being seen as a novelty was no great compliment and that was what it came down to, wasn't it? Plus, did he really think that seeing her parents as oddballs in 'a league of their own' was going to have her heart racing? That she was going to be bowled over by the fact that he might want to meet them the way a scientist might be interested in meeting someone from another planet?

Erin knew that she was being unfair.

Raffaele was a naturally curious person and he was genuinely curious about her parents. In a lot of ways she couldn't blame him. They couldn't have been further removed from his own stuffy, cold family, the people too rooted in tradition to give their only child the basic love and affection he had once craved.

No amount of money could buy love and affection.

'So how are we going to play this?' Raffaele murmured silkily. 'Heads down until five thirty and then we go our separate ways and meet up at an agreed time at my place?'

'Since when have you ever left this office at five thirty?'

'Since when have I ever had an irresistible and compelling reason to?'

'Wait, is that another compliment, Raffaele?'

'Now that you mention it, I do believe it is. I'm very tempted to lock the outside door and make love to you right now on my desk.'

'Raffaele...' She drew in a deep, steadying breath and edged her chair a couple of inches back. 'I'm not actually here because I couldn't bear the thought of being apart from you for a week and a half.'

'No?' But his smile told her that he wasn't fully convinced.

She rummaged in her bag and pulled out the envelope.

'What's that?' He frowned but didn't actually take it from her.

'An old-fashioned method of communication,' she said, buying time. 'Only just a little more advanced than carrier pigeon.' She cleared her throat and stared at the envelope. 'Raffaele, it's my letter of resignation.'

The silence settled between them like lead. She watched his expression turn from amusement to disbelief to shock.

Erin had known what lay ahead and she had made sure to enjoy every second of the time she had left with him. Their love-making had been intense...hot...incomparable. Once or twice, in the throes of passion, she had come so close to telling him how she felt about him but she had held her tongue.

Her dignity was important to her. She had already revealed so much of herself to him but that last secret would be hers to hold close to her chest forever.

'Are you going to take it?' she asked.

'No.'

'What do you mean *no*?'

'You're not going to resign. I can scarcely believe I'm hearing this at all!'

He leapt to his feet and strode to the huge bank of floor-to-ceiling windows that dominated his massive office. For a few seconds she stared through him, his body taut with tension, then he spun around and looked at her narrowly.

'What's happened?' he demanded. 'What's changed? No, don't tell me. You've told your parents everything and they insisted that you keep your distance. Is that it?'

'I'm not following you, Raffaele.'

'It's easy enough!' He raked his fingers through his hair and smiled grimly. 'Your parents want the best for you. You've told me often enough how attached you are to them, how anxious they were when you broke up with that creep years ago. I expect you told them that you were involved with someone who wasn't into walking up the aisle anytime soon and they promptly told you that the best thing you could do would be to walk away. Did you tell them about the deal we had? The promotion? Did you mention the fun we have together? *Did you bother to make the point that having fun is a pretty damn important part of being alive?*'

'Raffaele…'

'Let me meet them. I'll talk to them. I'll convince them that what we have is good for you!'

* * *

Was that desperation Raffaele heard in his own voice? Was this him? Were these his insides tearing to shreds at the thought that she was leaving him?

The last thing he'd expected was for Erin to walk away. After his generous offer, after the promotion of a lifetime, after establishing that they still wanted one another.

Especially after those last few days they'd spent together.

Magical.

Just when, hell, he'd begun to see those nuances... begun to feel things he'd never thought he was capable of feeling.

No! The thought of his own weakness was enough to have him balling his hands into impotent fists. He *refused* to lose control, *to lose perspective.*

'No! Raffaele, I haven't told my parents about us although I'm pretty sure you're right. I'm pretty sure they'd be horrified. I'm leaving because what we had was great and it was fun but I want to move on with my life and that life doesn't have you in it. If I stay here, having this fling with you, I'm going to soon start thinking that I'm wasting my time.'

'Wasting your time?'

'Don't sound so horrified. Although I'm guessing this is the first time any woman has said something like that to you.'

'How can having fun be *wasting time*?'

'I suppose,' Erin said thoughtfully, 'I was in a deep freeze when it came to men...and then this thing happened between us. And it was terrific and I had a lot of fun but I realised that to come back here, to return to reality, and then to just awkwardly carry on having fun that was going nowhere would be doing myself a disservice.'

The ground under Raffaele's feet, that rock-solid confidence in himself and his impregnability when it came to his emotions, was shifting.

He refused to let go of the philosophy of total independence that had ruled his life for so long. *Absolutely refused.* But inside, his heart was no longer playing ball with his head. 'You're saying you want some kind of a long-term relationship with me? A ring on your finger? Marriage and two-point-two kids?'

'No!'

Yes!

Raffaele didn't know how close he'd got to the truth, that Erin couldn't be with him because he wasn't into commitment. He just thought that her parents were to blame. In reality, Erin secretly suspected that they might be happy for her to be having fun…might actually agree with Raffaele if he showed up on their doorstep bringing tales of adventure and excitement.

What would he do if she were to tell him the truth? That *she* was the one who wanted too much, that she'd had her fun and now it was time to move on because here, back in the real world, those snatched moments of joy would quickly become a growing groundswell of the pain of unrequited love.

They stared at one another in momentary silence.

'In short, you believe you deserve better than me,' Raffaele said heavily.

Erin's heart constricted. She gazed at his downturned mouth, the lowered eyes fringed by those thick sooty lashes, eyes that were so good at concealing what he didn't want the world to know.

That there was a well of emotional insecurity inside him, the legacy of cold, distant parents who might not have been cruel but had been emotionally neglectful. The boy whose heart had sealed up had become the young man whose one attempt at love had failed. Now here he was before her...the adult who had locked his heart away for good because the lessons he'd learned had been just too hard.

He was right.

She did deserve better. She deserved to love a guy who could actually return her feelings. When she tried to picture this mythical creature, her mind went blank.

'I know what I want,' she said, tilting her chin, voice firm, 'and yes, it's someone who really does want the whole deal and that's what I intend to do now. Dave was a creep and for a while I decided to think that all men were creeps. It was easy and lazy to take a step back from dating, in case I just so happened to run into another man like that—I know that now. But those days are gone, thanks to you.'

'Good to hear I've been useful.'

Erin heard the cynical edge to his voice and could already sense the distance he was putting between them. Pride was slamming into place and his desire to find an explanation for the inexplicable was being ruthlessly stamped out.

'I have some holiday saved,' she said, 'quite a bit, as a matter of fact. Of course, if you want me to train my replacement up, then I'm happy to oblige but—'

'I think I can handle that myself.'

He moved back to his leather chair behind the desk,

establishing the boundaries between them, returning to his role of boss and relegating her once again to her role as his secretary. Putting a full stop to anything else that had existed between them.

'I'll spend the day making notes on the accounts for whoever replaces me…contact names and so on…'

'Whoever replaces you will survive fine without notes.'

Raffaele was still reeling. Through his shock and angry bewilderment, he was already being forced to acknowledge just how deeply Erin had burrowed inside him. He didn't know what to do with the tumult of raw emotions brought to the surface by her casual dismissal of him as a guy she'd just *had a little fun with*.

He'd seen her walk through that door unexpectedly and his heart had lifted. He hadn't been able to stop thinking about her, projecting to when she'd be back to take up her new role…and to pick up where they'd left off.

When she had appeared in the doorway to his office, he'd felt a wave of intense satisfaction that she was on the same page as him.

That surge of pleasure felt like a lifetime ago now.

He couldn't believe that he'd patted himself on the back at the arrangement that was now in place, one in which they could carry on seeing one another, sating this weird, powerful need that was driving them both, without the awkwardness of being within the same four walls.

And it wasn't as if he had created a superfluous role to accommodate their affair! He'd simply done what he'd been thinking of doing for a while, promoting her to the level of her potential.

All around could there have been a more satisfying conclusion? No.

He'd been so pleased with himself. He'd enjoyed imagining her happiness at what lay ahead of them. Not just a continuation of this compelling, addictive relationship but a promotion for her that would come with a hefty salary increase, more than enough for her vacate her sad rented accommodation and to think about buying somewhere without sacrificing the financial help she was committed to giving her parents.

But now...

How wrong he'd been about everything. For the first time in his memory, he'd had the rug pulled from under his feet and he didn't know what to do about it.

The one thing he wasn't going to do was beg. He would deal with whatever was going on inside him later, in solitude. He had access to huge resources of inner strength. He would call upon them in due course to combat the tsunami of frenzied, inexplicable, tumultuous emotion rushing through him.

'When?' he asked in a roughened undertone, as she remained hovering indecisively in front of him.

She'd effectively dumped him. No fuss, no warning. So why was he bothering to prolong the conversation?

Because he cared. Jesus, how and when had that happened? How and when had he *allowed* that to happen?

'When what?'

'When did you decide that the deal on the table wasn't going to do?' He scowled at his own weakness.

Erin sighed and reddened.

Was this going as expected? Sure, she'd known that his pride would be hurt but she'd figured that he'd recover fast and shrug it all off.

She *had* expected him to try to talk her into staying.

That was why she'd had the *holiday time left outstanding* on the tip of her tongue, as a way to wriggle out of spending more time in his company, which would have meant more time absorbing him, breathing him in, falling harder and deeper in love.

It stung to realise just how disposable he thought she was.

Her defence mechanisms swung into place and she looked at him coolly and distantly.

'When you made that offer... I knew that I wasn't going to take you up on it.'

'Right.'

'I guess it put things into sharp focus.' *One hundred percent true.*

'Understood.'

'There was also a part of me that felt...as though you were paying me, somehow, to continue with what we had because you weren't quite ready to end it.'

'Paying you?'

'You can hardly blame me for thinking that.' But her colour mounted at the outrage in his voice and it made her feel small that she had even harboured that treacherous thought, even though *it made perfect sense*.

Although, she now thought, didn't it make just as much sense that she might have *wanted* to see the worst in him? Because doing that gave her the courage to walk away?

'I told you that was something that was already on the cards. It was a well-deserved promotion. When have I ever lied to you?'

'You haven't but—'

'But you decided that it would be a good idea to turn me into the bad guy? I thought you knew me better than that, Erin.'

'Raffaele...'

He waved his hand in a dismissive gesture but for a few seconds, she remained where she was, dithering, filled with a sickening sense of deep loss.

It was devastating for her to think that she would leave this man forever and with the impression that, for all that he'd told her about himself—and it was probably more than he realised—she'd never really known him at all.

He shrugged, his face cool and remote and striking at the very core of her.

'One last thing,' he said, 'and this from the guy you thought had fabricated a job opportunity as some kind of coercive piece of bribery...'

'Raffaele, please...don't. I...'

'You won't see me again. We're done and dusted. But the job is still yours for the taking.'

'What do you mean?'

'I mean the job I offered you...still stands and it has nothing to do with whether we were lovers once or not. It stands because you would be good at it and you deserve it.' He stood up, bringing the conversation to a close. 'You can think about it and let Human Resources know if you're still interested. If not, you can rest assured that the reference you get from me will be of the highest order.'

'Thank you,' Erin whispered, tears stinging the back of her eyes. She spun around before they could start streaming down. When she looked over her shoulder, one last, quick glance, it was to see him binning the envelope with her resignation letter inside. He hadn't even bothered to read it.

Raffaele heard the sound of her shuffling in her office, clearing her stuff out. He could picture her so clearly, could see the soft curve of her neck, the slenderness of her arms, the delicate bone structure of her face with those freckles that had appeared from nowhere in the heat of the sun.

He slammed his fist on his desk, strode restlessly to the window and looked down at the streets below. From here, he had a bird's-eye view of the people entering and leaving the building. He felt nailed to the spot.

Erin had left her office. He'd heard the quiet click of the outer door closing. He wondered whether she would say anything to any of her colleagues, or whether she would just disappear into a future that no longer included him or anyone else she had spent the past four years working with.

His heart *hurt*. He only had himself to blame. That was what came from being foolish enough to lower your guard.

He remained where he was, looking down, waiting to see her hurrying out and away from his orbit.

He wanted to tear himself away, return to the pile of emails waiting for him, but he realised that ever since this three-dimensional, fascinating, sexy, addictive woman had entered his life, work had taken a back seat.

But what would staring through a window do for him? Except ratchet up his levels of frustration? Frustration and basic incomprehension. He had made her an irresistible offer. They still wanted one another. To him, her reasoning for walking away, for *dumping him because he'd served his purpose*, made no sense.

But then again...

Raffaele frowned and thought about them both, thought about his own life experiences and about hers.

His formative years, spent cocooned in wealth but

lacking the joy of loving, demonstrative parents, had toughened him and his doomed love affair had snuffed out any last remaining dregs of hope that love was for him.

He realised with a jolt how little real interest he had ever taken in the backstories of the women he had dated in the past. He had entered all those relationships with his emotions sealed off and, unable to share anything of himself, had never sought to discover anything about his partners.

He wined and dined them and pleasured them and then when it was over, he walked away intact.

But he had found out about Erin. He had begun to feel…things stirring inside him, like small shoots wanting to grow.

But as she had made perfectly clear, he'd never been her type.

She was someone whose entire background had geared her towards the eventual goal of a long-term relationship. Where he was content to have fun until the fun ended, she wasn't. Their intense physical connection had made her realise that she wanted more. Who could blame her? He was cut from completely different cloth.

She did deserve better than him.

All told, it was a good thing that she had broken things off. However disoriented he felt at the moment, he would and could never be the straightforward kind of guy who wanted the neat house and the picket fence and the apple tree in the back garden.

Raffaele stared sightlessly down for a few seconds.

His heart picked up pace.

Yet what might it feel like to have had her love? To have seen that soft smile turn to him with tenderness as well as passion? To see love in her eyes as well as desire? To know that she had his back?

He gritted his teeth in frustration. He'd tried all that in the past and it hadn't worked. He didn't have it in him to return that depth of feeling. He was too conditioned by his past, however weirdly she'd made him feel.

About to swing away from the window, something caught his eye. The navy blue outfit, so severe considering it was summer. The glossy chestnut hair tied back in her attempt to look professional. How could she not know that when he saw that, he also saw it loose and tumbling as she moved beneath him, flushed with lust?

Erin...and next to her...

Raffaele squinted, his entire body stilling at the figure by her side and then freezing as she fell against the man standing in front of her and was enveloped in an embrace that brought a surge of primitive jealousy exploding in his veins.

He spun away and walked to his desk and sat down, everything inside him in turmoil as he replayed in his head what he had just seen.

Best forgotten, he told himself fiercely.

She'd made her choice and he would never beg for anyone.

'I'm so sorry,' Erin pulled back from Colin, shocked at how easily she had blurted everything out to him.

She'd been hurrying out of the offices with her few possessions in a carrier bag and there he was, coming in as she was going out, and the second he had seen her white face he had pulled her to one side and asked her if she was okay.

And the floodgates had opened. A few concerned

words from a guy she barely knew and she had burst into tears.

'This isn't me,' she sniffed, rummaging in her bag for the packet of tissues she always kept there. 'I don't blab and I don't... I don't blub either. And I really, *really* don't share the sort of stuff I've just shared with you. I... Please, you must promise me that you won't say a word.'

'Of course I won't. You forget I'm a lawyer. Lawyers are very good at keeping their own counsel. I kind of knew something was up between the two of you,' he said thoughtfully. 'Not sure how but it was a feeling I got when I glanced over at one point at that party at his house and saw the body language between you. Erin, want to go somewhere and talk?'

'I... No... I should go back home. I need some time on my own.'

'Sure?'

'You're very kind, Colin.' She struggled with a smile and he laughed ruefully.

'I'm not convinced that that's such a great thing to be. What do they say about nice guys finishing last?'

'There's everything right with being a nice guy. You're just the sort of man I should be looking for.' Erin was oddly comfortable saying that.

'But sometimes life doesn't work out that way.'

'No.'

'Will you do me the enormous favour of keeping in touch?'

'Of course I will. I've made loads of good friends here and as soon as I've got my act together, I'll be in touch with all of them.' She sighed. 'In the meanwhile, I shall take a little time out of London.'

'Erin...this probably won't do you much good but... he's a guy who breaks hearts.'

'I know. Don't worry. This heart will mend.'

But would it? And if it ever did, how long would it take?

She was mentally and physically exhausted by the end of the evening. It had been a long day. Life had changed irrevocably in a matter of hours and even though she'd thought she'd braced herself for it, even though she'd spent those last few days on that yacht *knowing* that she would be handing in her resignation as soon as they returned to London, she *still* found that she was unprepared for the enormity of the decision.

Should she have accepted Raffaele's offer? Would another month or so made such a difference? Would her heart have hurt any the less?

He had offered her riches beyond her wildest dreams. A promotion that would have taken her physically out of his orbit, so that she wouldn't have had to see him on a day-to-day basis. She could have carried on there once their *situation* had come to an end, continued with a high-flying career that would have sorted all her financial problems and given her the sort of job satisfaction she could never have found anywhere else.

Had she been *stupid* not to have bitten his hand off for that job promotion?

But no.

A clean break was what was necessary. Anything else would have been the equivalent of the alcoholic thinking that just one drink a day would be okay.

The shock to her system would fade but if she'd chosen to stay, bumping into him now and again...seeing some woman click-clack her way up to his office in passing...

Well, she would have lived in a state of semi-permanent misery.

A little break would do her good and when she returned to London, it would be time to start hunting down another job and getting back to the dating scene!

It sounded good, she tried to tell herself. She couldn't wait.

It was after ten in the evening, when being alone with her thoughts was driving her crazy, that she phoned her parents.

'Hi, Mum?'

'What's wrong, Erin?'

Erin's voice wobbled. 'I'm coming home.' She looked around her, looked at her rented place with its dreary four walls, as unlived in as if she'd only moved there an hour ago. 'And I might just be staying for good…'

CHAPTER TEN

ONE WEEK.

One week of torture. Raffaele hadn't been able to sleep. Worse, he hadn't been able to work. He'd cancelled meetings. Had delegated the search for Erin's replacement to one of the PAs who worked for his finance director and was indifferent to whatever qualifications they came with.

'Just as long as they're competent, can tell the difference between a computer and a microwave and over forty-five.' Man or woman, he didn't care.

He stared, scowling at his office door, which was shut. The adjoining office where Erin used to sit was empty. He could still remember the soft sound of her packing her stuff and the gentle click of the outer door as she'd let herself out of the office and out of his life for good.

He pushed himself away from his desk and swivelled the chair so that he was staring out of the window then clasped his hands behind his head and succumbed to yet another pointless bout of thinking.

How much thinking could one guy do? Shouldn't thoughts run out sooner or later?

For the millionth time he thought of Colin, the guy who'd been flirting with Erin at the party he'd thrown a few weeks back. Mr Dependable Lawyer, who was probably just the sort of solid, reliable man Erin should go for.

Not him. Not Raffaele Rossi, the guy with the broken background who had only ever reliably lived up the dubious role of heartbreaker.

He was the last man she should go for, which was why he'd been good for a bit of fun but nothing more.

Had he wanted more than that? From her?

The question, which had been plaguing him for the past week, inserted itself into his consciousness once again, and Raffaele leaned back against the chair and sighed.

He knew that answer to that. Why bother fighting it? He'd tried. He really had. She'd walked out on him and he'd immediately told himself that it was for the best. He'd seen her with Colin and also immediately told himself that that also was for the best.

Women came and went and if she'd left a hole in his life then it was because she had been the one to leave prematurely, because she'd worked for him, because their arrangement hadn't been the usual one he was accustomed to.

Blah, blah, blah.

Underneath all of that, the feelings unleashed in him had refused to go away and hadn't paid a scrap of attention to the voice of reason.

He'd opened up his heart to Erin and he couldn't seem to escape the consequences of that.

Each line of thought he'd taken to try to avoid that fact had crashed into a brick wall, a dead end. Now Raffaele, in the quiet of his office at one forty-five on a Tuesday afternoon, finally accepted what he'd been dodging for the past week.

Longer.

He'd fallen in love with her. And what he'd wanted in return hadn't been *fun*. What he'd wanted in return had been her love.

And now another man was on the scene.

Some guy she deserved. Who deserved her.

Raffaele banged his fist on his desk and shot up to his feet. He didn't give a damn who deserved who, and he was done with this game of pretending that everything was just fine and that all he wanted was the best for her. Yes, he damn well wanted the best for her! Just so long as it included *him*...

Step one...he'd find Colin, do his best to keep calm and find out what she was up to, whether there was something there, some budding relationship. If there was? Well, that would change nothing. He needed to see Erin, needed to tell her how he felt, and no one was going to stand in his way.

Erin was watching telly when the doorbell went.

Her parents were out and she was guiltily pleased about that.

'You deserve to have a bit of time out,' she had urged them both the evening before. 'Dad, I know you think you have to be careful with money all of the time but you don't. Having dinner out now and again is a good thing. It's not extravagant. Not unless you go to that place by the town hall where you have to remortgage your house to afford a starter.' She'd laughed. They'd laughed. But it had still taken a lot of persuasion to get them to make a booking somewhere and to propel them through the front door an hour ago.

They were both so grateful to her for her financial input even though she told them that there was no need. They were also so concerned about her, about her break-up, about her career now that she had fled London with no plans to return unless it proved impossible to get work locally... The weight of their anxiety was wearying. Now, with them both out of the house, for the first time in a week Erin felt that she could actually stop pretending to be okay. She could stop smiling till her jaw ached.

She could relax as much as it was possible to react when the only thing on her mind was Raffaele. He occupied so much of her thoughts that she had occasional moments of despair, when she wondered whether she would ever be able to clear her head of him.

The memory of clearing out her office, gathering up the few personal bits and pieces and stuffing them into a carrier bag, was as vivid as if it had happened minutes ago.

She'd stood outside, talking to Colin, unwilling in some weird way to break the connection with the place she had worked for such a long time, with the man to whom she had lost her heart. She had felt scared and overwhelmed and adrift. But then Colin had finally and reluctantly left, and she'd taken one last look up to the bank of glass through which she had peered through countless times, hoping for a final glimpse of Raffaele. But of course he wasn't there, staring out like some lovelorn teenager.

He'd was already behind his computer, already putting her to the back of his mind the way he'd done with all those other women he'd dated in the past once their time with him had come to an end.

The sound of the doorbell ringing again, this time more insistently, finally cut through her memories and she reluctantly stood up.

It was a little after seven thirty in the evening, the sun was shining outside and it was still warm enough to be sitting out in the back garden. She felt lazy and slothful cooped up inside wearing some faded cotton trousers with ridiculous cartoon characters all over them and an old T-shirt she had found in one of the drawers in the bedroom she used whenever she came down to see her parents.

She didn't want to answer the door. She didn't want to speak to anyone. She wanted to wallow in dismal thoughts and then lose herself in whatever terrible television show she could locate on the few channels her parents had on their telly.

She was ready with her excuses when she pulled open the door to find…the very man she'd been thinking about standing on the doorstep.

Or was it?

Was she hallucinating? Had her fevered thoughts conjured up the one person in the world who was occupying all the space in her head?

'Erin.'

'Raffaele? What are you doing here?'

'Will you let me in?'

'How did you find out where I was? How did you get hold of my parents' address?'

'I asked the lawyer. Told him I had some confidential papers to give you and I wanted to deliver them personally in case you had any questions.'

'Who are you talking about? What lawyer?'

'The one who was chatting you up at my party.'

'The lawyer has a name and you still haven't told me what you're doing here. You can't just *show up on my parents' doorstep* without warning.'

'I thought that if I warned you I was coming, you might have not wanted to see me.'

'Why?'

Belatedly, Erin remembered that he knew nothing of her broken heart, nothing of her feelings for him. To Raffaele, everything was as it should be and if he was standing on her doorstep now then it was because there was some work-related issue he wanted to discuss.

Or maybe he wanted to plead with her to fall back into bed with him. He could be a dog with a bone if he wanted something that wasn't going his way.

For a few treacherous seconds, Erin played with that tantalising thought before reluctantly boxing it up and shoving it to the side.

'Why wouldn't I want to see you, Raffaele?'

Raffaele's mouth had been dry ever since he'd seen her standing there in the doorway. She was wearing some pyjama bottoms with gaudy cartoon figures splashed over them and a T-shirt that had Bargain Basement stamped all over it and he had never seen anything sexier in his life before.

'Because of the way things ended between us. Felt like we parted on a regrettably sour note. Look, let me in. Are your parents here? I won't be long. You have my word.'

Erin shifted and Raffaele stepped into the small, attractive house and had a quick look around him.

It was quiet here. The cottage was at the end of a peaceful lane and was surrounded by hedgerows and low stone walls. Inside there were beams and whitewashed walls and clutter.

Lots of clutter. A pile of books stacked by the side of the front door, pictures on the walls and lots of them, all framed family photos. Through the open door he could see the sitting room with squashy sofas and a rug and yet more framed family photos and in the background he could hear the sound of the television.

He liked open space, clean lines and absolutely no clutter whatsoever. He should have hated this, but he immediately felt at home.

'Things ended fine between us,' Erin quickly contradicted. 'I told you I wasn't prepared to carry on sleeping with you until the whole thing fizzled out and then I packed my stuff and left.'

'Afterwards I wondered whether you might have been offended because I offered you that promotion.'

'Why would I have been offended? It was a very generous offer.'

'Could we sit? Maybe I could have something to drink. I've spent quite some time on the road.'

Erin sighed.

She didn't want him here and yet she felt as though she'd never wanted anything more in her life. She didn't want to look at him but her rebellious eyes couldn't help but stray, and oh, how beautiful he was. He was an assault on the senses and she could feel herself spinning back to square one. The pain of not having him in her life was hitting her all over again, full force.

Maybe he'd come to check in on her.

He was naturally intuitive and yes, he might have sensed that after their amazing time together, there had been something cool and remote when she had said goodbye. Maybe her unhappiness had somehow got through to him and, as the friend he had always been, he'd felt compelled to come and find out what was going on.

But with the parameters altered between them, he'd felt awkward about announcing his intention.

She didn't care, and she hated herself for second-guessing.

'Colin should never have told you where I was staying. It was out of order for him to give you my address.'

She walked towards the kitchen, keenly aware of Raffaele just behind her. Every nerve in her body was alert to his towering presence behind her.

'I can make you a coffee and you can tell me why you're here and then you can head back to London, Raffaele. Or else there's a hotel in the village if you'd rather check in there and save yourself the trip back. My parents are out at the moment and I'd rather you weren't around when they get back.'

'Why?'

'Why what?' Stretching up to reach a mug from the cupboard, Erin spun around and looked at him with undisguised hostility. She didn't care what he read into her expression.

In a rush, she felt a tidal wave of resentment that he had shown up here, in the very place in which she had come to take refuge. She needed to get him out of her system but right now, with him crowding her in the small, cosy kitchen, every inch of her system was lit up by him.

'Look, Raffaele, if you've come to discuss some stupid work thing, then there was no need to trek all the way down here to sort it out. I did offer to stay and do a handover if that was what you wanted, but you refused.'

'I know. I'm not here about some stupid work thing, Erin. Come. Sit. Forget the coffee. I'll survive without it. Please.'

Erin hesitated. He looked exhausted. Haggard. She hadn't really noticed before because she'd been too wrapped up with dealing with her own emotions.

'I've been a fool' was the first thing he said when she was seated on the chair at the pine kitchen table, facing him.

His hands were resting loosely on the table and he had

spoken so softly that she'd had to strain to hear what he was saying.

'What are you talking about?'

'I let you go.'

Raffaele looked at her and as their eyes tangled, he realised that he'd never felt more vulnerable.

He also realised that this wasn't the first time he'd felt this way. She'd unlocked a piece of him a long time ago. He just hadn't realised it until they'd become lovers. Then all those things he'd shared with her had, piece by piece, unlocked more and more of his frozen heart.

But still he'd refused point blank to admit it.

'You didn't *let me go*, Raffaele,' Erin said, sounding confused. 'I decided that I couldn't carry on working for you because I would have found it too awkward even if we weren't physically sharing the same space, and because I felt it was a good time to branch out. So...'

'I've never shared myself with anyone the way I shared myself with you.'

'You've had a million lovers.'

'A million might be just a tiny bit of an exaggeration.' But he half smiled and held her gaze without flinching. 'Erin, I never shared any of myself with any of them. I took them out, wined and dined them, had fun with them but they remained strangers, even if they didn't take a similar view. With you...? I think I've been sharing bits of myself for years without paying the slightest bit of attention to it. And then when we became lovers... I foolishly assumed that I was going to remain immune to any woman having influence over my emotions.'

'You're saying...' Erin whispered. 'I don't get what you're saying.'

'I'm saying that I fell in love with you, Erin. I never saw it coming but then, when I think about it, it came in small steps and all those small steps were invisible at the time.'

'Fell in love...?'

'I had so many opportunities to tell you. When you said that you were leaving, when you handed me that resignation letter, the bottom of my world dropped out. But even then I was in denial, too afraid to admit that I'd given my heart and soul to someone, that I had relinquished power over my own feelings and emotions, which was something I swore I'd never do.'

'I just can't believe that you're saying all this, Raffaele.'

'I know. I also know that I took a chance coming here. When I saw you standing outside the office with the lawyer—'

'You *saw* me...? With Colin? But when? I haven't been back to London since coming down here.'

'On the day you left,' Raffaele said, flushing. He'd never felt more exposed but now he'd started, there were no signposts showing him how to veer off down another road, not that he wanted to. No, he wanted to share all of himself with the woman sitting opposite him, revealing nothing but on the other hand not turfing him out.

It gave him a glimmer of hope.

And then hope took wing and really began to soar when she reached forward and covered his hand with hers, then linked their fingers together.

He held those fingers tight, never wanting to let go.

'I was jealous as hell of the man,' he admitted gruffly. 'And I was jealous of him at the party as well, even though I swept that aside, barely acknowledged it. It took everything inside me to be civil when I went to ask him about your whereabouts. It even occurred to me that I could have him transferred to another office—New York appealed—so that he was no longer competition on my doorstep.'

Erin smiled.

She squeezed his hand. If she could have bottled this moment forever, she would have.

'You have no idea how tough the past week's been for me,' she confessed, her voice low, her heart beating fast as she strove to match his honesty with her own.

She'd spent so many years holding on to what she'd thought was a harmless crush, only for it to blossom into something far more dangerous to her peace of mind. Now she felt as though her emotions were waiting impatiently to burst their banks.

'Tell me,' Raffaele urged.

'You've been honest with me so I'm going to be completely honest with you,' Erin confided huskily. 'I've had a crush on you for years.' She reddened at the confession. She half turned away from his reaction but after just a second of surprise, his face registered satisfaction that thrilled her to the core and gave her the confidence to continue.

'Tell me more. I'm all ears.'

'That's more like it.' Erin grinned and then leaned forward to kiss him delicately on the side of his mouth only to succumb to something deeper and hungrier and more demanding when he cradled the back of her neck and properly returned her kiss.

'What do you mean?' he murmured, drawing back but keeping his hand on her neck, holding her close.

'The brimming-over-with-self-confidence guy I ended up finding irresistible.'

'Nope. Don't recognise myself in that description.' He

kissed her again, a lingering kiss that left her trembling for more. 'Although I'm very much liking the finding-irresistible part of what you just said. I think we should explore that line in a little more depth.'

'You're so full of yourself.'

'And yet you fell in love with me...'

'Yes, I did. I just thought that it was a harmless crush, a reaction to a broken heart, a safe refuge until I got my act together and started dating again. But the weeks became months and I guess I should have stopped and asked myself why I was stuck in a routine of fantasising about you instead of getting on with finding a guy...'

'It's so easy to work things out in retrospect. I could say the same about myself, about the way I found myself confiding in you without wondering how it was that something I loathed doing with other women came so easy to me when I was doing it to you. Signposts ignored.'

'Yes.' Erin nodded. 'And then we became lovers...and I actually thought that once you were out of my system I would be able to move on. Of course, out there, I finally accepted the truth. I'd fallen for a guy who couldn't love... The more I learned about you, the more I realised that.'

'I never thought I *could love* until I did...'

'It's why I handed in my resignation. I knew that was what I was going to do when I returned to London because I just couldn't envisage being in the same building as you, even if it was a couple of floors down, without my heart breaking over and over every day. Just knowing that you were only a heartbeat away, knowing that at some point I would bump into my replacement...it was too much...'

'I was a fool, my darling, but I came to my senses and I'm just glad that I did, that I finally stopped letting my past to dictate my future. Although, if I'm honest, no woman had ever captivated me the way you had…so…'

'Is there more?'

'Much more. Or maybe not *much*. But the rest is very important, the rest of what I want and need to say. Erin… I can't live without you.' He leaned into her and clasped her hands. 'I want to go to sleep with you by my side and wake up with you by my side. I want to hear your laughter every day and I'm addicted to the way you don't mind telling me what you think. You make me a better person. Erin…' He flushed and briefly looked away but then, when his eyes returned to her face, they were utterly serious. 'I never thought I would hear myself say these words with love in my heart, vulnerable and not caring that I am, but will you marry me? Be my wife? Never leave me?'

'Yes!' She smiled tenderly at him. 'After that wonderful prelude, my darling, I thought you'd never ask…'

* * * * *

Were you captivated by
Out-of-Office Temptation*?*
Then you're sure to enjoy these other sparkling stories by Cathy Williams!

Snowbound Then Pregnant
Her Boss's Proposition
Billionaire's Reunion Bargain
Heir for the Holidays
Maid for the Italian

Available now!

BOSS'S MARRIAGE AGENDA

ANNIE WEST

MILLS & BOON

This story is for the many readers
who have told me how much they enjoy the
drama and suspense of my amnesia stories.

Thank you!

I hope this one provides all the emotion and drama
you crave.

With special thanks to Paula Beavan.

CHAPTER ONE

'You're still on for tonight?' Matt asked down the phone line.

Greer hesitated. The phone was jammed between her shoulder and ear as she jotted a quick note before calling up the document Conall needed for his meeting.

Was she ready for tonight?

Once she wouldn't have hesitated. A Friday night out was a chance to unwind after a busy week. But she wasn't that woman anymore, not fully. The accident had knocked her confidence. She felt different in ways she couldn't explain.

Losing your memory will do that to you.

Five months blanked from your memory would rattle the most confident person and if she let it, that gap would terrify her. All she knew of that period was what Conall had told her. They'd set up the new Sydney office as planned, in between running his hugely successful investment company while most of his staff were still in West Australia.

The last thing she recalled was their move from Perth to Sydney. The car from the airport and Conall dropping her at her new flat before heading to his just-bought penthouse.

Today was the end of her second week back at work after the accident. Before that she'd spent weeks recuperating, first in hospital, then at home. At Conall's insistence she'd only started back in the office part-time but was now well enough to do full days. Her boss hadn't exactly hovered, but she'd seen his assessing stare, his concern about her doing too much. The staff they'd recruited had started downstairs and she'd carefully learned names and roles but still felt she was catching up on her own life.

She was tired of feeling like an invalid. She was fine, the doctors said so.

Fine except for missing a chunk of your life that you might or might not eventually remember.

She repressed a shiver.

No good worrying about what you can't change. You just have to get on with things.

'Sorry, Matt. I'm distracted. I'm in the middle of something. But I'll be there. I'm looking forward to it.'

Fortunately she could still multitask, though she really had to concentrate. She juggled Conall's diary, the challenging projects he'd given her, and everything else that kept his widespread business interests manageable.

But whereas once she'd done so confidently, now she had a niggling sense of something out of kilter. As if she'd missed a vital problem and would discover it too late. It infuriated her, making her triple-check everything.

After they said their farewells, Greer put down the phone and focused on the report filling the screen.

'Going somewhere?'

She didn't have to turn to recognise Conall's voice, deep and easy like the smoothest of single malt whiskies. She felt a tickle of response inside and was torn between gratitude that the feeling was so familiar, and despair that even amnesia hadn't cured her of that weakness.

'Not at the moment.'

She highlighted the section she needed to update before she could send it to him. Only then did she swivel her chair to see him standing in the doorway between their adjoining offices.

Even braced, she felt the impact as her gaze met eyes so dark they looked black. Searching eyes under a frowning brow.

Not that the frown detracted from his charisma. Conall Abercrombie had everything it took to attract. Confidence. An aura of power. Intelligence in that speculative gaze and humour in the laughter lines bracketing his mouth. Strongly carved features that were arresting rather than handsome. Add to that a long, leanly muscled body that looked fantastic in jeans, business wear or more formal clothes.

He'd discarded his jacket, yanked his tie loose and rolled up his sleeves. His dark hair was just long enough to look rumpled from where he'd ploughed his fingers through it.

It was twenty months since he'd taken her on as his assistant yet she still felt a thrill, seeing him. A thrill she worked hard to conceal. If he knew how he made her feel…

Something was wrong. She knew instantly. 'What's up? The new contract or—?'

'Nothing's wrong. Who's Matt?'

Greer stared. She and Conall worked closely together, with an easy camaraderie and mutual respect that allowed them to navigate long hours and intense pressure.

He'd been there for her at the hospital when she was bandaged and feeling sorry for herself. The staff had demanded to know her next of kin and she'd felt shockingly vulnerable, admitting she had none. She'd finally given Conall's number. Her relief when he'd arrived, bringing a sense of normality, had been overwhelming.

She'd never told him much about her background, just as she never commented on the beautiful women he escorted to high-profile events. He didn't talk about his family either, though she'd had the dubious honour of meeting his father, Fraser Abercrombie. The man was lauded as a titan of Australian industry but she hadn't warmed to him.

'Greer?'

'Matt's a friend.'

'A friend? From back in Perth?'

She was going to tell him it wasn't his business but kept the words in. He'd done so much for her after the accident. He'd organised groceries and ferried her to checkups, despite her insistence that he needn't bother. He'd even, she'd been stunned to discover the next morning, spent her first night out of hospital sleeping on her sofa so she wasn't alone.

It had been a relief to return to work and their usual routine. To feel the pieces of her life sliding back into place.

She released a pent-up breath. 'No, he's from Sydney.'

'And he told you you're close?' His voice sharpened. 'It's only been weeks—'

'Since that crane knocked a hoarding onto me. I know.' The accident, where a building site edged a busy city street, was well documented.

'You only have his word for it that you're friends.'

Greer shook her head. 'Don't worry. He's not trying to con me, if that's what you're worried about.'

Much as she appreciated his concern, she didn't need a minder. She was doing fine, if she discounted the feelings of melancholy and loss. 'He's a neighbour. He just moved in a fortnight ago.'

Conall's frown didn't ease. 'That's not long.'

She sat straighter in her chair. 'Was there anything else? Anything *work*-related?'

She watched his eyebrows rise. But it was time to remind him she wasn't an invalid.

'Only I know you want this report before your next meeting, and I need to make amendments. Some of the figures have changed.'

Those gleaming dark eyes narrowed and she felt the

whump of her pulse thud through her body, quickening. But she wouldn't back down.

'Listen, Conall. I appreciate everything you've done for me since the accident. You've been marvellous. I can't tell you how much that means.'

Her throat closed as she remembered that horrible feeling of isolation when she'd woken in hospital, brain-fogged and reeling from the enormity of what had happened.

'But I'm well now. I've lost a few months' memory but that's all.' What courage it took to say that when that gap felt like a yawning abyss. When the idea of not knowing what she'd done in that time haunted her, making her feel vulnerable and, if she let it, fearful. 'If I can run your schedule,' and they both knew it was far more than just his schedule, 'I can manage my own life.'

His gaze bored into hers for the longest time. Then his mouth tipped up at the corner and he raised his hands as if to ward her off.

It was the same rueful half smile he gave when she called him on setting an impossible deadline. Or growing impatient if a new staff member hadn't read his mind and delivered everything he expected, including the things he hadn't specifically mentioned.

'Okay, okay.' His expression turned serious. 'Sorry. It must have been the shock of seeing my invincible Greer knocked off her feet. But I get the message. You can stand up for yourself now.'

For another second their gazes held. Then he turned on his heel, saying over his shoulder, 'Get me that revised report as soon as you can. Meanwhile...' He pulled out his ringing phone. 'Ah, at last. News on the Singapore options.'

Greer watched him take the call and cross his office. Phone to his ear, he stood looking out over the harbour, all thought of their conversation banished as he became completely focused on the call.

She'd never met anyone with such phenomenal drive or the ability to absorb himself totally in business, to the exclusion of all else.

She knew from his decisive nod that she didn't have to worry about him overstepping the mark again. It was a familiar gesture, one that signalled acceptance of a situation and his readiness to move on. When he did that, Conall didn't look back. He always looked to the future.

Exhaling slowly, she spun around to her desktop computer. But instead of pulling up the new figures, she paused, unsettled.

Not unsettled. Disappointed.

She frowned. What was wrong with her? She'd told Conall to back off and he had. She'd got what she wanted.

They'd built a friendly work relationship but they weren't *friends*. He was her boss, even if he'd recently gone above and beyond. That just proved he was a decent guy. And that he valued the work she did for him.

Her mouth flattened. He'd wanted her better and back in the office.

That's unfair. He was worried.
But he's not worried now.

Greer should be glad things were back to usual. Instead she felt flat, as if his easy acceptance when she barred him from her private life disappointed her.

She couldn't *miss* his concern, could she?

There was no pleasing her these days. She might be functioning almost as well she used to, but her emotions seesawed.

Maybe being reminded of how alone she was had affected her more than she realised. Child of a single mother, who was in turn an only child, meant no relatives now her mother was dead. Greer knew nothing about her father except that the thought of him had scared her mother. They'd moved often and Greer had got into the habit of self-sufficiency, reliant only on herself and her mum.

Greer had friends but they weren't so close now. They were back in West Australia and her job left little free time for socialising. As for men, there'd been no one special, given her career focus and innate caution.

Greer surveyed the open document, but her thoughts were elsewhere. No matter what she'd told Conall, she didn't feel in charge of her life. How could she when she had no recollection of what she'd done over five whole months?

She was doing everything she could to look after herself and get better. Yoga stretches and a brisk walk each morning. Time out for lunch, forcing herself from the office and down into the botanic gardens for fresh air every day, whereas in Perth she'd often eaten at her desk.

It's time for you to get out and meet people. Build a network of friends in this new city.

In the weeks since the accident no one had texted or called, wondering where she was, which made her think she'd devoted all her time in the city to business.

That stopped tonight. Drinks at Circular Quay with Matt and his friends was just what she needed.

She sat straighter and reached for the keypad, determined to take a leaf from Conall's book. She intended to get on with her life, building it the way she wanted it to be, rather than worrying about a past she couldn't recall.

Greer ended up working later than intended.

Though she and Conall had worked together for almost two years, since returning to work she'd found it difficult to corral her thoughts when he was in the office. Even on the rare occasions that he shut the connecting door, she was *aware* of his presence, an ever-present distraction.

She hadn't discussed it with the doctors but maybe the brain injury meant she required more solitude to concentrate.

With Conall elsewhere, not expected to return that day, she'd had the executive suite to herself, a rare luxury. Now she was pleased with the progress she'd made. Which tempted her to work on. Conall had been insisting she leave by five and it felt good to catch up with some of the backlog.

Matt had said to turn up any time. He and his colleagues would be at the outdoor bar for hours.

Refreshing her lipstick in the executive suite's private bathroom, she met her eyes, seeing the truth there. Okay, so she was a little reluctant about joining a group of strangers for a drink, even though Matt's cheery enthusiasm was probably the antidote she needed to pull her out of this trough.

Still, the idea of a boisterous group didn't appeal.

What does appeal, Greer? You don't know what you want, that's the problem.

But she needed *something*. Each day she grew more restless.

Eyeing herself in the mirror, she frowned.

Had she overdone it? They were gathering to celebrate Matt's promotion so she'd thought in terms of a party but really, it was casual drinks and maybe bar snacks. Greer had looked in her wardrobe, finding tailored business suits in sombre tones and a selection of exercise wear and comfortable jeans, wishing that for once she had something bright and cheerful. Then she caught a glimmer of colour at the back of the cupboard.

As soon as she saw the midnight-blue dress she wanted to wear it. It had a scooped neckline, narrow shoulder straps and ended high above her knees. She had no recollection of buying it and it was vastly different to anything she *could* remember buying, but just looking at it lifted her spirits.

Now she smoothed her hands down the stretchy fabric that

shaped to her contours. She looked carefree and sexy, something she hadn't felt in a while.

Greer tilted her head. Did the sparkles in the fabric make it too over the top for casual drinks by the harbour?

She didn't care. It was this or the grey jacket and straight skirt she'd worn to work.

She grinned at her reflection. Sparkles it was. But first... She unpinned her long, straight hair and combed it out. Really, she should get it cut. It was overdue. But for tonight she'd enjoy it loose around her shoulders.

Slipping her feet into comfortable slingbacks, she stuffed the comb into her bag, picked up her discarded clothes and walked out.

Straight into a tall body.

She froze, thoughts scrabbling at the feel of a hard, hot male body against her torso. Strong hands closed around her elbows, anchoring her, and she realised belatedly that she wobbled on her heels.

Greer gasped as, in slow motion, her clothes spilled from her grip. That gasp brought a familiar scent. A warm male scent, woody with an undertone of leather. Her pulse skyrocketed, making her heart thud against her rib cage.

Because she knew instantly who this was.

Something intense and shocking shivered through her insides.

Slowly, reluctantly, she lifted her chin, taking in the crisp shirt beneath the beautifully tailored jacket. Up past his open collar that revealed a V of golden flesh and the dark bronze silk of his loosened tie.

He always mangled his ties.

Greer swallowed, searching for something to say. Something light and offhand about being clumsy or him surprising her.

Nothing came. She felt his chest rise on a breath, pushing

against her breasts, but he didn't speak. The friction made her breasts tighten and a hollow feeling open up low in her body.

She needed to move back, break the contact. And again her willpower failed her.

Because this felt so good. Too good.

Despite the heat flaring between them, cold fingers danced up her spine, lifting the hairs at her nape in warning.

Wrong, wrong, wrong.

Of course it was wrong to stand here, soaking up the sensation of Conall's hard frame against hers. But maybe the knock to her head had damaged her willpower too. Since the moment they'd met she'd been supremely aware of this fruitless attraction and done everything to resist it, or at least hide it. Yet no matter how she told her legs to move, nothing happened.

Carefully she lifted her head, seeing the clean, enticing line of his jaw and then that sculpted mouth.

'Are you okay, Greer?' His voice sounded husky, probably distorted by the throb of her racing pulse. 'You seem unsteady.'

Moistening her lips, searching for a semblance of normality, she looked up into concerned dark eyes. *Was* that concern, or something like the exhilaration she felt?

Conall's gaze dipped to her mouth, lingering in a way that sent heat hurtling through her bloodstream. It spread over her breasts and throat, at the same time pooling low in her pelvis.

There was a new sensation too, fine fabric against her palms and beneath the fabric, the solid wall of his chest. She hadn't known she'd lifted her hands until she felt her fingers moulding possessively over tensed muscles and realised she'd nudged his jacket open.

She wanted… How she wanted…

As if in answer to the longing she'd so ruthlessly suppressed, his head lowered to hers. So slowly she didn't actually see the movement, just registered his features getting closer.

Excitement spiked. With it came elation and a hunger so profound it should have scared her.

Yet it felt perfectly, absolutely right. As if the answer to her earlier question about what she needed was simply *Conall*.

Conall holding her close, his body a bulwark against the world, his touch the route to all she craved.

Everything slowed, as it did during life-and-death events. Seconds felt like minutes or hours, while she registered details so thoroughly they stayed imprinted permanently on the memory.

The spiky fringe of his black lashes. The tiny furrow of concentration at the centre of his forehead. The arc of that tiny new scar on his jawline.

She wanted to trace his features. To know intimacies he didn't share with anyone else. Even, foolishly, how he'd got that scar. But most of all she wanted, needed his kiss. She'd never needed anything so much.

'Greer?'

His voice was sharper, his fingers tightening on her arms and abruptly she realised *she* was the one moving closer to *him*. She was on tiptoe, leaning up to reach him, her body pushing against his. One of her hands had crept to his shoulder, a moment away from grasping the back of his head and pulling it down to hers.

Shock blasted her, breath hissing in as reality pierced the haze of desire.

She stumbled back, embarrassment surging as she realised Conall's dark eyes held only concern and a wariness that made her stomach curdle.

Almost as bad was the fact he felt the need to keep hold of her lest she fall.

Wrenching her arms free, she retreated further, coming up against a wall. Her chest rose and fell with each quick, agonising breath and she wrapped her bare arms around her middle, trying to hold in the toxic mix of shock, disappointment and embarrassment.

'I'm sorry. I didn't mean…'

She *had* meant it. That was the problem. For twenty months she'd kept her attraction to Conall under lock and key, never giving in to it. Never even allowing her gaze to linger.

'There's nothing to apologise for. It's okay.'

She stifled a bitter laugh. It was anything but okay. She'd just come on to her boss. Her face, even her ears burned with embarrassment. In the pit of her stomach fear escalated. Had she just thrown away everything she'd worked so hard for?

'Greer, did you hear me? It's all right. It's not your fault you were unsteady on your feet when I surprised you. I probably scared you, appearing suddenly when you thought the office empty.'

Her brows twitched. What about her grabbing him, leaning on him as she tried to get close enough for a kiss?

But she could read nothing in his expression apart from that tiny twist of concern.

He's being kind. He's giving you a free pass. Maybe he feels sorry for you. Believes you're not yourself since the knock to the head.

He was right there. Never in her wildest dreams would she have believed she'd do anything as self-destructive as trying to kiss her boss.

Yet everything she'd felt was real. Those moments in his arms she'd felt more herself, more potently alive than at any time she could remember.

'Now, can I give you a lift home? It's been a long week and you're probably tired.'

She'd rather walk on hot coals than be cooped up in a car with him while he pretended she hadn't just made a complete fool of herself.

'Thanks, but no.' She bent and scooped up her work

clothes, holding them against her chest like a protective barrier. 'I'm meeting someone. See you on Monday.'

Conall watched the lift doors close behind Greer. She hadn't looked at him again, just shoved her work clothes away and strode for the exit.

His gaze had tracked every step of those bare legs. Followed the way the light shimmered on that figure-hugging dress and her dark hair that swayed halfway to her waist with each step. Straight silky hair that mesmerised and made his fingers twitch.

Seeing Greer in that dress... His breath died as a fist slammed into his chest. Or was it a blade? He swore he felt it rip through him, slicing past skin and bone to something raw and savage.

Had he really thought the offer of a lift home would weigh against the lure of her assignation tonight?

He jammed his fists tight into his trouser pockets. She'd felt that spark of attraction, he *knew* it. Standing there, watching her walk away had been tough. As tough as watching her confusion and not intervening when she'd pulled away.

His gut churned at the uncertainty he'd seen in her indigo eyes. No matter what Greer claimed, her memory loss haunted her.

The lift began its descent and he spun away, chest tight as he strode into his office to his vantage point at the corner window. He'd already pulled his phone out, speed dialling his head of security.

As they spoke he thought he caught a glimpse of her on the street, behind a group heading down towards Circular Quay. He couldn't follow her. She'd demanded distance. If she saw him among the end of week revellers by the harbour she'd know it was no coincidence.

She'd even disposed of the note she'd scribbled while on

the phone, with the name of a popular bar there. He told himself it was her habit to leave her desk tidy. Not because she didn't want him to know about her date.

His chest tightened and he yanked his attention back to the phone.

A few minutes later it was sorted. He rarely needed bodyguards while in Australia, despite his wealth and well-known family name. But his security adviser assured him there'd be someone at the Quay straightaway. That was one of the advantages of being wealthy—nothing was too much trouble.

The man assured Conall she'd be seen safely home. No one would take advantage of her tonight. Including her friendly neighbour.

Conall had to be satisfied with that, but he didn't *feel* satisfied. He wanted to see for himself. Greer might think of herself as capable, and in the usual run of things she was. But not now. He knew that even if she didn't.

There was so much she didn't yet know.

She was vulnerable and he needed to protect her.

The recent discovery of just how alone she was had shocked him. Even he, with his dysfunctional family, had people he could technically call on in need, though he'd face almost anything rather than do so since his family was poison. But she had no one, except him.

The doctors had decreed it better not to prompt her memory, that it was best to let things take their natural course without interference.

He shook his head as he crossed to the never-used bar concealed in the credenza. After a moment's consideration he uncapped a bottle of Scotland's finest eighteen-year-old whisky and poured a measure. It was a spirit to be venerated and enjoyed slowly.

Conall knocked it back in one gulp and slammed down the empty glass. That drink was long overdue, but he'd promised himself on the darkest night of his life that he wouldn't use alcohol as a crutch.

Until now he'd held good to that, but the last weeks had taken their toll.

He felt the blast of fire sear his oesophagus. Yet he didn't feel warm, he was cold to the bone. So much had gone wrong, unbelievably wrong. He'd never felt at such a loss.

He planted a palm on the reinforced glass window, peering between the buildings of the business district to the lights fringing the harbour. He refused to go on like this. What he needed was a plan.

His eyes narrowed in thought then he straightened away from the window. He'd promised to let her memory return naturally and he'd do that, but he chafed at the softly, softly approach. It was time for more direct action.

CHAPTER TWO

GREER STARED BLEARILY at the summer sunlight edging her bedroom curtains and cursed her inability to sleep late.

She'd been awake most of the night, only falling asleep as dawn approached. She wanted to roll over, close her eyes and shut out the world, but there was no hope of that. Fully awake, her brain was busily replaying last night's events, as if she hadn't been over and over them for hours.

She tried to convince herself the disturbed night was because her mind was active after socialising with strangers for the first time in... How long? Months? It felt like years.

Despite her reservations, she'd met some interesting people last night and Matt was a nice guy, not pushy, not assuming too much.

One of the women had mentioned a lunchtime Pilates class mere blocks from where Greer worked, inviting her to attend. It had been worth going last night just for that, an opportunity to pursue the acquaintance, perhaps form a friendship.

In other circumstances she'd have enjoyed the lively group more, especially as she'd felt so cut off lately.

But it had been impossible to relax completely. Because all the time she'd smiled and chatted, a great part of her mind had been replaying that scene in the office. When she'd burst out of the bathroom straight into Conall's arms and proceeded to make a fool of herself.

Greer grimaced and hugged a spare pillow to her chest.

Her face burned as she replayed each embarrassing moment in excruciating detail.

The worst of it was that she couldn't, quite, regret her actions. Conall's touch, the strong, steady rhythm of his heart beneath her hand, even the tickle of his intriguing, masculine scent in her nostrils, had felt *affirming* in ways she couldn't explain.

Affirming and reassuring. As if he could conquer the nebulous fear that these days prevented any sense of true wellbeing. She rolled onto her back with a huff of self-disgust and stared up at the ceiling.

It wasn't the white-painted surface she saw. It was his eyes, a gleaming brown so dark it was like looking at the night sky. Eyes that surveyed her without giving anything away.

Did he despise her? Or was he embarrassed by her actions?

He probably felt sorry for her. He had his pick of clever, gorgeous women. Women probably threw themselves at him all the time. He'd been forgiving last night but in the harsh light of day, how would he feel?

Unlikely to want to be assaulted by his assistant. Would he send her back to Perth, perhaps to her old job in accounts? Or would he, come Monday, ask for her resignation?

Conall wasn't like his father, who had a seriously roving eye and a reputation for bending the rules. He wasn't the sort to use his position to importune a woman or indulge in an office affair. Greer had never once taken a call from one of the women he dated. He kept business and his private life strictly separate.

Which meant, despite the good work they'd done together, her time as his personal assistant could be over. The office was for work, nothing else, and she'd crossed that line.

He couldn't really have mistaken her physical response to him for surprise making her unsteady on her feet.

The phone rang and she grimaced, but habit made her reach for it. Her eyes rounded when she saw it was Conall.

Her heart hammered and there was a queasy feeling in the pit of her stomach. She pushed the hair out of her eyes and wriggled higher in the bed, shoving the extra pillow behind her.

'Morning, Conall.' Thankfully she sounded normal, only a slight huskiness betraying her sleepless night.

'Greer. I'm sorry to ring you early on a Saturday, but I knew you'd be up, being an early riser.'

She cast a wry gaze over her rumpled bed. 'How can I help?'

'Something's come up and I want your input. Do you mind?'

I do if you're going to sack me.

She set her jaw. This was the man who, for the past couple of weeks, had scrupulously *not* allowed her to work beyond minimum hours. Who'd rung her at home, but only to make sure she was okay.

Besides, she had nothing planned for the weekend. Nothing at all, and she was used to being busy.

How had she filled her free time in Sydney before? She wished she remembered.

'No, that's okay. Where would you like to meet?'

'Excellent. I'm almost there. I'll see you soon.'

Almost here? Surely not. But the connection went dead in her hand. His penthouse was a ten minute drive but it sounded like he'd already left.

She glanced down at the brief cotton nightie she wore on hot nights. The material ended halfway down her thighs and was so fine as to be translucent.

Fifteen seconds later, clothes in hand, she leaned in and turned the shower on, pushing the bathroom door shut with her foot and tossing her clothes onto the vanity unit. Reefing off the nightie, she stepped into the cubicle, shoving her hair into a shower cap. The water was cold enough to make her gasp, but at least it cleared her head.

It was the shortest shower on record. Soon she was in her underwear, cleaning her teeth as she hung up her towel. She put on light, summer-weight trousers and a fitted T-shirt before trying to tidy her hair. She'd put it into a plait last night but had been so restless it had come loose and tangled.

The doorbell rang and her heart punched hard against her breastbone.

If he'd come to fire her, pride dictated she didn't look like a rumpled mess. On the other hand, she didn't want to keep him waiting, in case he was here for some other reason.

Another couple of quick strokes with the hairbrush and she turned, only to come up short as she viewed herself properly in the mirror, including the dark shadow of her lacy bra under her white T-shirt.

She couldn't remember buying the pretty, frivolous item in midnight-blue but yesterday it had seemed perfect to wear with the blue dress and she'd quickly grabbed it this morning. How she wished she'd stuck to plain beige.

No time to change. Besides, what did that matter if she were about to lose her job?

'Coming!' Closing the bedroom door behind her, she walked to the entrance, slowing her breathing in an attempt to ease her nerves. A tall figure with broad shoulders was visible through the opaque glass at the top of the door.

Conall. Instead of easing, her tension rocketed but she could at least conceal it. Standing tall, she unlocked the door and pulled it open.

Her first thought was that this wasn't Conall, her employer. She'd only seen him like this in the hospital and once, stretched out on the sofa in this very room, features softened by sleep, an undisciplined lock of dark hair tumbling across his brow, making him look...

'Conall!' Her voice was too high. 'I didn't expect you so soon.'

After that one sweeping look, she kept her gaze on his face. It was better not to notice how those faded jeans clung to his long, muscled thighs. Or how the black polo shirt complimented his dark golden skin and showed off his wide chest and flat stomach.

Enigmatic eyes held hers. She'd give a lot to know what he was thinking, but for once she couldn't read his mood. Strange when at work she often sensed what he was thinking and anticipated his requirements.

That only heightened her nerves. As if he'd deliberately cut her off so she couldn't interpret his thoughts.

Greer repressed a shiver, telling herself not to jump to conclusions. He *might* not be here to complain about her unprofessional behaviour.

Fervently she hoped that was the case.

'Can I come in? I've brought gifts.'

She looked down and saw his hands full with a large bakery box and a tray with two large travel mugs.

Automatically she stepped back and waved him in.

Surely he wouldn't bring breakfast if he intended to dismiss her.

By the time she closed the door and followed him, he was at the kitchen end of the open-plan room, helping himself unerringly to plates from the cupboard.

Of course he knew where things were. He'd stayed overnight and shared breakfast with her. His unfussy pragmatism had helped ease her fears that first night out of hospital when she'd been spooked by her amnesia.

She paused between the island bench and the small dining table. Even on a knife edge, wondering about the fallout from yesterday, there was something reassuring about Conall's presence.

His eyes snared hers and her skin warmed. 'Bench or table?'

It took her a second to realise he was asking where they'd eat. She glanced at the small round table, imagined facing him, so close their knees would touch. 'Bench.'

His gaze cut away and it felt as if a thread, pulled taut between them, had snapped. She moved forward, pushing the fruit bowl to one end of the bench, grabbing the travel mugs he'd brought and taking off their lids. Immediately the aroma of rich coffee filled the air. She leaned closer, inhaling the blissful smell.

When she opened her eyes he was watching her. Before she could let herself hesitate, she blurted out, 'About last night—'

'You had a good evening?'

She frowned. 'I did, thank you. But about earlier—'

'I'm sorry I startled you. I should have called out to let you know I was there. Next time I will.' He looked down at the food he'd brought. 'I hope you're hungry.'

Greer stared, perplexed. He was brushing off what she'd done. As if her trying to climb his body for a kiss hadn't happened. Perhaps he thought her head injury made her behave oddly. But if that were the case he wouldn't have her back in the office yet.

She wanted to clear the air with an apology. But she'd done that last night and he'd waved it aside.

Maybe he's so used to women throwing themselves at him, he takes it in his stride.

It took a moment to swallow the sour taste on her tongue.

Instead of speaking, she pulled out a stool and sat down. 'Thank you, Conall.'

He didn't say anything, just nodded. But it was clear he knew she wasn't thanking him for the food.

Something shivered out of her as she exhaled. Relief replaced that terrible wound-too-tight feeling. He was drawing a line under what had happened and moving on.

He took the other stool, sitting close but not too close, and she made herself look away, for the first time taking in the spread before her.

'You didn't get *that* from a corner takeaway shop.'

There was a tub of thick Greek yoghurt, studded with fresh berries and pistachios. There were slices of sweet pineapple, looking like summer, halved passionfruit, mango slices and, her favourite, gleaming red cherries. Plus a large plate of fresh pastries.

The scent rising from the warm pastries and the tangy pineapple rivalled that of the coffee. Greer had a sudden, inexplicable sense of happiness. Of warmth and well-being.

She imagined she felt the sun's heat on her shoulders, the echo of water lapping nearby, and a feeling of utter contentment. She clung to the illusion, surprised to hear the raucous call of gulls overhead.

The illusion of being by the water faded, but that sense of contentment lingered. What was that? A memory? Or just a hope for better times ahead?

She stirred and turned to Conall. But he wasn't watching her face. She followed his gaze and noticed she was rubbing one finger over another, a fidgeting habit she had when distracted.

He'd brought some of her favourite breakfast foods. As he had the morning after she'd come out of hospital. She couldn't remember telling him what she preferred to eat, but her memories of hospital weren't completely clear. However he'd divined the information, it was kind of him to go to such effort.

'Thank you, Conall.' Self-conscious, she reached for a mug, taking an appreciative sip. 'This definitely is first-class coffee.'

'Only the best. Now, what are you going to have first?'

'Fruit then yoghurt.' Yet it was the cherry Danish she grabbed, plonking it onto a plate and putting it beside her. 'Just making sure it's still there when I want it.'

Conall was an energetic man who burned calories quickly. They'd shared enough between-meeting lunches for her to know it was best to claim what she wanted quickly.

She heard his huff of amusement as he added a sultana-studded scroll to his plate. 'In that case, the snail is mine.' Then he reached out again. 'And the cheese twist.'

Greer's mouth curled into a smile. It felt like a wall tumbling between them. The wariness she'd felt easing into something more comfortable.

Was that the worry that had dogged her since she'd woken in hospital finally lifting? That would be a blessing.

She tried not to wonder if that meant her memory might be restored soon. Thinking about that stressed her and she'd resolved not to go there.

Conversation was relaxed. Conall spoke about a possible trip to Singapore and made a few observations about the share market. Easy stuff that didn't require much effort from her.

She was surprised at how suddenly hungry she was when lately nothing much had appealed. Apart from the comfort of late-night chocolate bars.

Finally, the meal was over and she rose to tidy up. Scraping flakes of pastry off the plates, she said, 'You said you want my input. On what?'

He had his back to her as he shrugged so she indulged herself, letting her gaze linger on the lift of his wide shoulders. She shouldn't. It only fed that longing she'd resolved to conquer.

Okay, that's absolutely the last time. Right?

'There's an investment I want your opinion on.'

Greer stilled, pleasure rising. Increasingly Conall sought her input on projects, using her as a sounding board. He said her accountancy training gave her a good eye for detail. His request now meant he really had put last night's contretemps behind him.

His investment business didn't hinge solely on major stock market companies. He also had interests in a range of start-up companies, most innovative and some surprisingly tiny. She'd been fascinated to see him back people, and occasionally communities, that needed an investor to help achieve smaller-scale goals. Unlike his father, it seemed he was interested in benefit to the community as well as reaping financial rewards.

'What is it? I'm all ears.'

Dark eyes met hers and she reminded herself she was inured to their impact. 'Soon. I want to take you to see it. Do you have a hat?'

She blinked at the change of subject. 'Yes.'

'Then get it and we'll be on our way.'

Greer frowned. In the past there'd been reports, interviews of company directors and financial analyses when considering possible investments. There'd been some site visits but that was usually later in the process.

'On our way?'

'Yes. This cost-benefit analysis is best done in person.' A ghost of a smile curved his mouth and something inside her loosened. 'You get ready and I'll finish here.'

He was up to something. She could tell by the glint in his eyes. Mentally she shrugged. She was intrigued and would play along. So instead of protesting that there was no need for him to clean up, she headed for the bedroom. If he wanted to tidy her kitchen, she was happy to let him.

She was crossing to her wardrobe when he said from close behind her, 'Bring sunscreen too, if you have some.'

She swung around to find him in the doorway, sweeping the bedroom with his gaze as if looking for something. She paused. She was only metres from the kitchen. There'd been no need to follow to ensure she heard him.

Greer stiffened, acutely aware of the unmade bed between

them. Crazy how those rumpled sheets made his presence feel...personal.

She was overreacting. She hadn't had enough sleep and her reactions were askew.

Yet her eyebrows lifted at his comprehensive inventory of the room. 'Was there anything else?'

'Can I use your bathroom? I've got sticky hands.' He was already turning away when she nodded.

Greer frowned as she opened her wardrobe. That interchange had felt strange, but she couldn't put her finger on why.

It was only as she slipped on sandals and left the bedroom armed with sun cream and a hat that she realised Conall could have washed his hands at the kitchen sink.

Maybe rich people don't like to dry their hands on kitchen towels.

The idea made her smile. Conall might be rich, but despite his privileged background, she'd always found him down-to-earth.

'Ready?'

There he was, near enough that she felt the sharp drag of air into tight lungs, her heart leaping before settling into a steadier beat.

'Of course.'

She ignored the voice warning that spending time outside the office with Conall Abercrombie was asking for trouble. At least until she worked out a way to inoculate herself against her unwanted feelings for him.

'Okay, I'll play. What are we doing here, Conall?'

Here being the exclusive marina tucked deep into the curve of Rushcutters Bay on the south side of Sydney Harbour. She might be from the other side of the country but Greer recognised the yacht club from countless news reports. It hosted the launch of the world-famous Sydney-to-Hobart yacht race each year.

The landward end of the bay was green parkland, the sides all expensive houses and apartments. The other end of the bay was open to the broad expanse of harbour.

'I told you. We're here to view a possible investment.' He gestured for her to walk with him. 'This way.'

Greer's eyebrows rose as *this way* became a pier between vessels. What was he up to? She couldn't imagine any business investment here.

Still, the warm sunshine and salty air were invigorating. The gentle *ding, ding* sound from the rigging of moored yachts seemed almost welcoming, even to someone who knew nothing about sailing.

Finally he stopped beside a white yacht that looked streamlined and sleek. He looked from it to her. 'What do you think?'

'I think it's not an investment that will give you a solid return on your money.'

He chuckled, the sound trickling through the hidden barriers she'd erected to keep herself safe from his charm. 'Ever the pragmatist, eh, Greer? That's one of the reasons I value you so highly. But we both know not all investments are about financial returns.'

Slowly she nodded. A small but increasing amount of his funding went to what he called his conscience projects, supporting communities.

But a boat couldn't be one of those, could it?

She frowned. 'What are you planning? A sailing school?'

There'd been a couple of schemes to help unemployed people, particularly young ones, develop job skills. Was there a need for yacht crews? Greer had no idea.

'You know, I hadn't thought of that.'

He led the way aboard, then stopped to reach out his hand for hers as she stepped onto the boat.

Something skittered along Greer's senses as his hard, warm hand closed around hers. She was unaccustomed to his touch. That must be why it felt so momentous.

Drawing air into cramped lungs, she fixed on a smile, nodding her thanks but not meeting his eyes as she stepped onto the deck. She turned as if to survey the vessel but in reality the movement was an excuse to slide her hand free.

Because she'd had the bizarre urge to return his firm grip and keep holding.

'Would I go down too far in your estimation if I admitted I'm interested in buying it for myself?'

'A personal investment then?'

Her brow knitted. As far as she knew, all his investments were about delivering results, usually financial, though sometimes charitable. She couldn't remember Conall ever making a major purchase as an indulgence. For a rich man he lived a fairly simple life. He worked long hours and from what she gathered, much of his social life related to business.

'You don't approve?'

Greer surveyed the gleaming yacht. Even to a landlubber it looked beautiful. Her gaze went to Conall, feet planted wide on the deck, his dark eyes crinkling at the corners in the hint of a smile that made her breath hitch.

They looked like they belonged together, this powerful vessel and the man so at ease here. His stance, with his hands planted on his hips, seemed to emphasise the width of his straight shoulders and the power in that tall form.

She shook her head. 'It's not for me to approve. If you want to buy a yacht, you can. What's the point of having money if all you do with it is make more money?'

His response was a bark of laughter. 'Obviously, you don't know my father. Making money and thereby accruing more and more influence and power can be an end in itself.'

'But not for you.'

Conall had the skills and determination to succeed and he used them to great effect. His reputation for nosing out solid investments was well-deserved, and then there were the riskier opportunities, less certain but with great rewards when they succeeded. He had an instinct for those and a reputation for success.

It struck her that from everything she'd seen, influence and power weren't what drove him.

What did? She wished she knew. But his motivation was none of her business. No matter how much he intrigued her. She brushed aside that dangerous thought. She worked for him, that was all. She needed to remember that.

But it was hard to do when he stood there looking like some sexy, modern-day pirate, his eyes glowing with a hint of laughter and his powerful body exuding competence and charisma.

Deliberately Greer surveyed the boat. 'What would you do with it if you buy it?'

'Sail her, of course. I always liked yachting but haven't done much lately.' His gaze touched hers and held it. 'I've been thinking about how unpredictable life is and decided it was time to get out and do some of the things I enjoy. There's no point waiting.'

Despite her best efforts, Greer's eyebrows rose. This was the man who worked seven days a week. Who rarely took a holiday.

But looking into his eyes, she knew he meant it.

He'd realised life was unpredictable. Because of her accident?

It seemed likely. One moment she'd been walking on the footpath and the next she'd been on her way to hospital, unconscious. When she'd woken the last several months had been a black hole.

The idea that her situation had impacted him felt troublingly personal. She'd been grateful for his kindness since the accident but it hadn't occurred to her that her disaster might change him too.

'Would you like a tour before we go?'

'Go?'

He nodded. 'I'm thinking of buying her, so we're going out on the harbour to try her out.'

Greer stiffened. 'But I don't know anything about sailing. I've never been on a boat, just a canoe.'

There'd been no sailing boats in her childhood. That was for rich people. She'd been a netball girl, member of the local team in whichever town she and her mum found themselves.

Conall moved nearer and her pulse ramped up.

'You'll be safe. I know what I'm doing and you'll have a life jacket.' He paused, watching her closely. 'I thought it would make a nice change from being cooped up indoors. To do something fun. I can only guess how difficult the last weeks have been for you, Greer. But if you'd rather not...'

Stunned, she shook her head. He was doing this for *her*? Not buying the boat, of course, but planning today's outing. To give her something to take her mind off the amnesia?

Alarms rang. She'd always been careful to keep some distance from Conall, hiding how he dazzled her. Since her amnesia she'd had to work at that even harder. Her defences were low and she felt vulnerable, as if every emotion sat too close to the surface. She couldn't bear the thought of him seeing that.

But how could she pretend to aloofness now? The idea her well-being was so much on his mind stifled any objection.

Reluctantly she felt her lips curve into a smile. 'It sounds tempting, lolling on a billionaire's yacht.'

A long dimple scored one tanned cheek and it was as if he'd dragged tight a cord that stretched from her throat to her womb. She felt that smile in every needy part of her body.

Silently Greer cursed her weakness for this man. The attraction nothing seemed to budge. Despite all her caution and her determination, it was getting worse, not better.

'It's not mine yet, Greer.' He paused and she fought not to react to the sound of her name on his lips. 'But I *would* like your impressions. There's a gourmet lunch in the galley and I know a secluded cove perfect for a picnic. What do you think?'

It was the worst idea she'd heard in forever.

An outing, just the two of them alone. On an impossibly perfect day. With a man whose smile made her hanker after things she couldn't let herself want. He was her boss. She'd be mad to agree.

The knock to the head must have messed with her sense of self-preservation because she heard herself say, 'Thanks, Conall. I'd love to.'

CHAPTER THREE

THE YACHT MOVED GENTLY, just enough to remind him they were on the water. That was enough to lift his spirits.

The realisation of how extraordinarily good it felt, being out here, only proved what he already knew. Things had been tough lately.

His gaze settled on Greer, half asleep with her wide-brimmed hat low over her face. She'd been full of questions about the vessel and sailing. She'd even offered to help, with an enthusiasm that made up for her inexperience.

He felt a smile hover at the corners of his mouth.

After they'd anchored, she'd shared the picnic lunch as if ravenous. When she ate in the office, she'd often peck at food, getting distracted by work. It seemed to him that since her release from hospital, she was too fragile. The line of her jaw seemed sharper and a slight hollow in her cheeks made him wonder if she were taking care of herself.

Imagine how she'd react if she knew you were trying to feed her up.

The smile became a wry twist of the lips. Which solidified as she sighed and turned in her seat, confirming his suspicion she was dozing.

Her movement drew attention to the rounded thrust of her breasts against that fitted T-shirt.

He knew Greer well enough to realise she hadn't deliberately dressed to provoke him with that sexy dark bra clearly visible beneath the white cotton.

He swallowed. Of course she hadn't.

That didn't stop his thoughts veering in the direction he'd vowed to avoid. He dragged his gaze from her full breasts only to trace instead the line of her body to that slim waist, then the flare of her hips.

His fingers curled into his palms and his pulse thudded too hard as want rose in him.

He jerked his head around to look out across the water. But instead of seeing the glint of sunlight on the rippling surface, his mind's eye pictured narrow, sandalled feet and long legs. She wore a colour he knew from an ex-girlfriend was called French blue. His ex had liked it because it suited her blond hair.

It suited Greer better.

Greer was brunette. Her long, straight brown hair was as dark as mink.

Conall knew that because when he was five, just after his mother died and he'd gone to live with the father he'd never met, he'd discovered a huge walk-in wardrobe, bigger than his old living room. He'd accidentally knocked a jacket off its hanger. It had been so rich and soft it had made him yearn suddenly for his mother and those wonderful soft hugs she used to give him.

When the housekeeper found him he was standing on a chair, tears streaming down his face as he struggled to lift the heavy fur onto its hanger. She quickly tidied up and swept him down into the kitchen before his father could see him crying. His father, a daunting, distant man, didn't like emotion. She'd explained the fur was mink and he must never touch it again. It had belonged to Mrs Abercrombie, his father's wife who'd died. Conall's mother had died too. She hadn't been married to his father or lived in a big house and he'd wondered if that was why she hadn't had anything so soft as a fur coat.

Conall pushed aside the ancient memory. Why he'd thought of that after all these years, he couldn't fathom.

But he could. That had been his first, shocking experience of loss. Events here in Sydney had dragged it to the surface.

They'd hammered home to him how precarious life was.

He remembered the taut, unhappy line of Greer's mouth weeks ago. The bleakness in her blind stare, as if the world didn't make sense anymore. He remembered standing beside her, startlingly bereft in the face of her pain. He'd never felt so desperate to make things better for anyone.

It had been humbling and made him look long and hard at his priorities. What he'd seen hadn't been pretty. What was the point of living for work when life was so fragile? For years he'd forgotten that.

He was thankful she was safe and healing. He couldn't imagine losing Greer.

Conall turned to find stunning, ink-blue eyes staring at him with an expression he couldn't decipher.

'You're awake,' he blurted.

'Was I snoring? It must be the sunshine. One minute we were talking and the next...' She shook her head.

'You only napped for a few minutes. Definitely not long enough to snore.'

Conall saw the warm colour in her cheeks and those glittering eyes and thought how much better she looked. But he knew not to say that. She was touchy about reminders of her injuries.

'So, what do you think?'

She lifted her elbows above her head and stretched as unselfconsciously as a cat.

He was delighted she was so at ease when for the past couple of weeks it had felt like she was on edge around him.

'Think about what? I lost the thread of the earlier conversation.'

'What do you think of the yacht?'

She didn't answer immediately and he noted the tiny vertical fold in the centre of her forehead that signified she was considering carefully.

'It's glorious. Powerful and fast and incredibly exhilarating when the wind caught us and drove us right across the harbour.'

She was exhilarating. The animation in her voice and her face was like summer after the longest, bleakest winter. It was damnably hard, keeping his reaction to her hidden. But now wasn't the time.

'Do you sail much? You never mention it.'

'Not for years. Once I sailed regularly, crewing for friends in races.' But the need to prove himself, make his mark, had meant devoting all his time and energy to business. He couldn't remember the last time he'd been on the water. 'Today's made me remember how much I enjoy it.'

Greer tilted her head as if fascinated and Conall wanted more than anything to keep the conversation going. 'How about you? What sport do you enjoy?'

'I haven't played sport in years. Though,' she added slowly, 'I always wanted to learn tennis.'

'You didn't play at school?'

'The schools I attended didn't offer it.' As if reading his mind she went on, 'And we didn't have money for lessons. But I liked netball. I played it for years.'

His sixth sense told him Greer's change of subject meant they'd veered close to something she'd rather not discuss. Her family's lack of disposable income?

'We didn't have money for extras when I was little either.' He watched her eyes widen and felt surprised himself. He *never* discussed his childhood. But he wanted to further the connection between them. 'My mum raised me alone until I was five.'

She'd kept him a secret from Fraser Abercrombie, afraid the man would take him away. Conall's father went through women like water but had a controlling interest in his children.

'So, the sailing came later. Do you remember your first time on a yacht?'

That was Greer, tactfully not asking about his family dynamics. She instinctively knew *his* no-go subjects. But he trusted her implicitly, more than she realised.

'I do. My half-brother, Jackson, took me out when I was seven. We were in the middle of the river then he turned the tiller hard just at the right moment to tip me in.'

'You fell in? That must have been terrifying.'

Conall remembered his disbelief and terror. 'My life vest kept me afloat while I dog-paddled. And I was almost sure he'd come back and collect me.'

'You mean he did it deliberately?'

'He thought it a great joke. Even bragged about it when we got ashore.' Conall remembered shivering, water streaming off him, listening to his father say he needed to toughen up and hang on better next time. But seeing Greer's horror he smiled. 'I was okay, and it taught me valuable lessons.'

Never trust his half-siblings, Jackson in particular. Friendly overtures were usually a prelude to a trick, especially as Conall was so many years younger than the rest. Never expect sympathy from his father. Rely only on himself.

Reading Greer's questioning look he said, 'It made me practise my swimming and I was so determined to learn to sail, I became proficient young.' Now he wanted to go back to it. It was a spur-of-the-moment decision but it felt right. 'So, thoughts on buying the yacht?'

'As an investment? If you're after long-term profit, I don't think pleasure craft accrue value when compared with other investments, but I'd have to research that.'

'If I didn't care about profit?'

She tilted her head as if to read *his* expression better. 'I don't see how it would fit as a community enterprise.'

'No, though your idea of a sailing school might be worth investigating longer term.'

'So it really would be purely for recreation?'

They'd already discussed this but it seemed she hadn't fully believed it. Did she regard him as a total workaholic?

He couldn't blame her. A year ago he'd never have considered doing anything like this just for fun. Over the years his leisure time had become a casualty of the continual need to pursue business goals.

He'd been raised to take business seriously. His father had deliberately manipulated his children into lifelong competition with each other. The old man's dictum that it was 'dog-eat-dog' out there played out in the family too, at an unhealthy level.

'You're going to take up sailing regularly?' When he nodded she went on. 'In that case, why not? You can obviously handle it alone and it suits you.'

'Suits me?'

Her gaze shifted, settling over his shoulder. 'You looked different. You were obviously enjoying yourself enormously.'

He studied her closely. 'And you, Greer? Did you enjoy it?'

Blue eyes met his. 'I did. Very much.'

'Then I'll have to take you out sailing again.'

'If you buy the boat.'

Oh, he'd buy it. He'd already decided. It amazed him now that he'd stayed away from sailing so long. Another thing in his life he intended to change.

'The question now is whether you're in a hurry to get back.' He watched her closely. 'Did you have anything planned for the rest of the day?'

Like an assignation with her too-friendly neighbour. Conall worked to conceal stirring outrage at the thought.

'Nothing that won't keep.'

Satisfaction warmed him. 'So you'd like another sailing lesson?'

'Only if you have time.' Her expression was diffident. She wasn't to know he'd cleared the whole day for this.

'I've got time.'

His security adviser had reported last night that she'd got home safely. Alone. Conall had told himself then that he could relax. Yet there'd been no let up from the fierce emotions buffeting him.

The news that Greer had accepted a date had floored him. A date! Greer! How could she…?

Easily, goaded that inner voice. He might have told himself to go slowly and not press her. The doctors had made it clear she was still recuperating. But she seemed not to have got the memo. She was getting on with her life while he was hamstrung by the need to let her heal in her own time.

Conall was never hamstrung. He strategised and acted, as he'd done today. He couldn't interfere but he could be with her more, much more.

He'd spent last night imagining her dating other men. Doing more than dating. That, he refused to accept.

His jaw had still been tender from grinding his molars when he'd breezed into her apartment, carrying breakfast.

Even then, when she'd gradually relaxed with him like she used to, he hadn't been able to do the same. Not until he'd checked the other rooms to be sure there was no one discreetly keeping out of sight.

He'd felt like a character in a French farce, sneaking behind her back, making a fool of himself. Yet he hadn't been able to stop himself.

That had been bad enough. But then had come the moment when he'd stood in her bedroom doorway and their eyes had locked across the unmade bed.

Greer's eyes had rounded, her lips parting, and he'd *felt* the quickened thud of her heartbeat pulse between them, a perfect match for his own. He'd carried the memory of that moment like a talisman all day. Surely she'd recognised his need—a need he was doing his utmost to suppress until she was better. Recognised it and responded with an answering hunger, for him.

It had taken everything he had not to stride across the room and pull her into his arms.

At the time he'd been proud of himself for giving her the space and time she needed to work through her feelings in what must be a frightening situation. He couldn't imagine the horror of missing such a large chunk of memory.

Yet the ruthless part of him wished he'd closed the distance between them and hauled her to him. His voice wasn't as light as he intended when he said, 'I've got all afternoon free. Let's make the most of it, shall we? It's perfect weather for sailing.'

And for wearing down that unseen barrier she'd erected. He wouldn't rest until it was obliterated. He planned to monopolise her, staying close enough to convince her she had no desire to look at any other man.

As if to confirm his intentions, she slanted him a smile that made his toes curl and his abdominal muscles tighten. Warmth stroked through him.

'Yes, let's. I'd enjoy that, thank you.'

He felt like punching the air in triumph. Until he remembered how much ground he had to make up. That her handsome neighbour—the bodyguard had sent him a photo last night—was still around, and a day sailing wasn't all Conall needed from Greer.

But it was a start. He'd work with that.

It was evening when she got home, tired but exhilarated. The sailing lesson had been fascinating and fun but had taken concentration. Now she felt weary, as if she'd used both her mind and her muscles and would sleep well.

After they'd moored the yacht, Conall suggested they stop by a place that did terrific takeaway. She could get something for dinner before he dropped her home. Or, he'd paused, if she felt like company they could have an early meal together.

The sensible thing would have been to say she wanted to go home straightaway.

Because the day had been marvellous in so many ways and she didn't wanted it to end. *That* was dangerous.

Because it wasn't just the sailing she'd enjoyed. It was being with Conall. Not as his PA, nor an acquaintance who needed looking after, which she knew was part of how he viewed her. But as his chosen companion.

There'd been an illicit intimacy about the day. As if they were simply Greer and Conall. Two people comfortable with each other, working together to control the beautiful yacht as it sped across the glittering dark water, occasionally laughing in exhilaration. They'd shared an afternoon that seemed brighter and more wonderful than usual.

But Greer had left sensible behind that morning. So she'd agreed to share dinner, wanting to extend the day.

That she'd enjoyed the meal hadn't surprised her. But Conall's choice of venue had. He'd mentioned the place did takeaway, yet she'd thought he'd take her somewhere upmarket.

Instead they'd gone to a little hole-in-the-wall Thai place off a narrow lane. Even at that early hour there'd been a buzz of activity. They'd eaten heavenly food, listening to the clatter of pans in the kitchen and the rhythm of unfamiliar music.

Conversation had been desultory as they concentrated on wonderful flavours with occasional comments about the day. But there'd been no need for chatter. The silences were companionable.

After weeks feeling the unnerving buzz of awareness that something was wrong in her world, Greer finally found herself totally relaxed. Content. Delighted.

Maybe it was the evening shadows, but she'd been almost sure she saw the same contentment in Conall's eyes.

Unfortunately, contentment wasn't all she felt around Conall. Now, leaning her back against her closed front door as he walked back to his car, her heart did a stupid little jig of pleasure that he'd insisted on seeing her safe home.

As if he cared.

Of course he cares. You're his right-hand woman. He relies on you to run his office and his schedule. He has a vested interest in you recuperating and being fit for work.

But that imp of hope danced between the prosaic words, daring to paint another possibility.

Once or twice today there'd been something in his expression, a hooded look, a burning stare, that fed her improbable fantasy. A fantasy in which they were more than CEO and PA. More than friends. Her breath hitched as familiar heat sizzled through her body and—

Her phone rang.

She grabbed it, accepting the call without looking. Maybe Conall...

'Hello?'

'Greer, is that you?'

Something inside deflated. 'Matt?'

'Hi. I hope it's not a bad time to call?'

Greer had straightened at the prospect of talking with Conall but now leaned back against the door, disappointment a solid weight in her chest. 'No, it's fine. What can I do for you?'

'I wondered if you wanted to go to the movies tomorrow.'

'I'm sorry, Matt. I need to catch up on some things tomorrow. Monday's going to be a busy day.'

'Maybe later in the week?'

She opened her mouth then closed it. She liked Matt, but if he wanted more than friendship he was looking in the wrong place.

Despite almost two years of trying, she hadn't been able to get Conall out of her mind. She hadn't been out on a date since she'd begun working for him. Not merely because her job kept her extremely busy, but because his presence cast other men into the shade.

Look at how she'd reacted just now, heart thumping in anticipation, believing he'd called her. That was why she'd accepted Matt's first invitation, because it was time to get over her crush and move on.

But while she liked Matt there was no spark there, nothing to hint they might one day mean more to each other. She didn't want to lead her neighbour on.

Greer bit her lip. 'I'm sorry, Matt. I enjoyed being with you and your friends last night. But I'm not looking for...'

'A relationship?'

She heard his disappointment but couldn't admit she did want a romantic relationship, just not with him.

Maybe it was time to try a dating app. She needed to free herself of her feelings for Conall once and for all.

'I'm sorry. I shouldn't have gone out with you and your friends last night.'

But he'd made it sound like a casual catch-up rather than a romantic assignation. And she'd spent the weeks since hospital hemmed in by a vague sense of unease. She'd decided she needed to get out among people instead of staying in her head, worrying about her faulty memory.

'Don't say that. We were glad to have you there.' He paused. 'If you're not after romance, I'd still like to be your friend. Our paths will cross in the building and if ever you change your mind, you know where to find me.'

Her lips curved in a wry smile. Why couldn't she fall for a man like Matt? She and Conall were from different worlds that only intersected in the office. He came from a phenomenally wealthy background, had a high-flying business, powerful friends and attended high-profile events with glamorous, beautiful women.

Conall valued her work and was concerned for her wellbeing after her accident. But that was *all*.

'You're a nice man, Matt. I'm sorry I—'

'Ah, the death knell of all my romantic hopes. Nice!' Then he chuckled. 'Don't fret, Greer. It was worth asking. Have a good night.'

Half an hour later the phone rang again. This time she checked the caller, her pulse tripping. 'Conall.'

'Greer.' He paused as if debating how to proceed. Or perhaps she imagined it. Conall was confident. She'd never known him to hesitate when he'd decided to do something. 'Would you like to go out tomorrow?'

Greer sank onto a chair, her knees suddenly turning to water.

Was he asking her out? Excitement danced across her skin.

Today had been special. She'd convinced herself Conall had enjoyed himself just as much as she had.

The idea he might now simply want to be with her was wonderful and disturbing.

'Is this you being concerned about my recovery, Conall? Making sure I don't have time to worry about my amnesia?'

'Would it be so bad if I want to…support you?'

Greer exhaled, that jittery thrill dissolving. Protectiveness then. Nothing else.

'I'm fine, Conall.' Despite her best efforts her voice was flat and she looked down to see she was rubbing her finger in that nervous habit she'd acquired. 'You don't have to worry.'

A pause. 'I enjoyed today, very much.' His voice slowed and deepened so she felt his words like a warm eddying pool, low in her body. 'I want to spend more time with you, Greer, and I don't mean working.'

Did he hear her swift, indrawn breath?

Carefully she parsed his words, and still they sounded *personal*.

She'd dreamt of personal since the day she'd met him in the busy Perth office. His PA had left for family reasons and, Greer found out later, the temp filling in until the position was filled had struggled. Her manager had suggested Greer as a replacement, despite the fact her qualifications were in accounting.

She'd knocked on Conall's door and he'd looked up from his desk, smiling. It had felt like a lightning bolt blasting through her body and soldering her feet to the polished floor.

Working together had turned that initial blast of attraction into something deeper. Conall might be a workaholic, but he was considerate, fair, appreciated her efforts and had a lurking sense of humour she found irresistible.

Greer drew a slow breath and found her voice. 'I'd like that too. But I can't tomorrow.'

The words shocked her. She wanted to snatch them back. Yet she knew they were right.

It would be nice to think she'd refused out of innate decency after rejecting Matt's invitation. Or because she'd decided to look for a partner elsewhere.

Instead, she wondered if she were making some obscure point. She'd always been available to work whatever hours Conall needed. When he'd called early today, on her day off, she hadn't hesitated to see him. Her working life revolved around his needs. She needed to make a demarcation from work. Make it clear he couldn't take her for granted.

That didn't stop an inner voice howling that she was an idiot for saying no.

'You have something on? Another commitment?'

She heard tension in those four words but realised that was imagination, a reflection of her own stress. She yearned to say yes, so badly she tasted the salt tang of blood and discovered she'd bitten her lip.

You don't have to explain anything.

Yet she heard herself saying, 'Flats don't clean themselves and I have errands to run.'

'Fair enough.' Did she hear relief in his voice? Now she really *was* imagining things. 'How about later in the week? I can get tickets to the opera.'

'The opera?' She frowned. She knew little about opera, wasn't even sure if she'd like it.

'Yes. You mentioned wanting to attend months ago. You said someone had recommended attending a performance as a chance to see inside the Opera House.'

Greer frowned as something fluttered at the back of her mind. Something tantalising that she couldn't quite grasp. A jovial, deep voice. Something about Mozart and staging and…views from the bar? She could almost hear herself saying she'd never seen an opera and a voice responding—

'Greer, are you still there?'

She rubbed her forehead. As if that would stimulate her damaged brain into remembering! But it was gone, that half memory. Or maybe it wasn't memory at all, just a wish that she *did* remember, conjured by Conall's words.

'I'm here.'

She drew a deep breath then let it out. Hadn't she told herself she had to get on with life? Even though she felt weirdly as if she were in limbo with those months missing from her memory.

Spending more time with Conall could be a disastrous mistake. But everything she'd done to conquer her crush on the man had failed.

Maybe it was time to be brave.

Pressing her palm against her thundering heart, she said for the second time today, 'Thanks, Conall. I'd love to.' It felt like taking a step into a thrilling unknown.

CHAPTER FOUR

'I HADN'T EXPECTED it to be *funny*. You didn't mention that.'

Greer's eyes glowed, bright as gemstones. Her face, which in recent weeks had been worryingly wan, was flushed with pleasure. Around them the intermission crowd buzzed and behind her was a spectacular view of the Sydney Harbour Bridge and the lights of the North Shore. More lights crossed the dark water, marking the movement of ferries and other vessels.

But Conall only had eyes for her as she sipped her sparkling wine. She dazzled.

This was the woman he knew, back again, full of verve. Her energy was tangible. Her smile sent a sizzle of heat straight to his groin. He was torn between relief that she *was* getting better and a hunger that became almost impossible to rein in.

'Don't tell me, you expected them all to die in agony?'

She arched one eyebrow. 'From what I hear, dying is a common theme in opera. But I did my research. I know no one dies in *The Marriage of Figaro*.'

Of course she'd researched. That was his Greer, thorough as always.

'But I thought it would be more serious. After all, the count wants to betray his wife and force himself on her maid. Susanna and Figaro rely on him for their jobs and home. It's about sexual predation. Coercion.'

Something grabbed hard at Conall's gut as Greer's gem-bright gaze turned away. Could that be how she viewed *him*? This evening out? As coercion by her boss?

The number of times he'd held himself back from her, creating barriers. Dating women who should have fascinated him yet left him unmoved. He'd spent such a long time keeping Greer at a distance, because seducing his PA went against every principle. Especially given his father's predilection for pursuing beautiful women, no matter what their circumstances.

'Greer, I don't want you to think—'

She turned back, smiling, then her eyes widened as someone bumped into Conall. There was a splash as his drink sloshed out onto his shirt, followed by a flurry of apologies.

He nodded absently, still focused on Greer. But she shoved her wine into his hand and opened her small evening purse.

'There.' She brandished a handful of tissues triumphantly and moved in, dabbing his lapel and wet shirt. Pushing his lapel aside, she pressed the tissues against him so the heat of her hand spread across his pectoral muscle like a soft brand.

His words died as the light scent of spring flowers filled his nostrils. Spring flowers and the subtle, intriguing scent of Greer. The combination hit so hard he rocked on his heels.

Conall looked down at her sleek, dark hair, falling like a curtain around her shoulders. At the tiny furrow of concentration on her brow that he found intriguing and bizarrely arousing.

He'd never found another woman's frowning concentration alluring. A quick mind and an ability to solve problems should be admirable, not sexy.

He'd known she was trouble the day she'd walked into his office in her sombre trouser suit and pulled back hair, barely concealing her doubts about taking on the job. Greer Munro tempted him too much.

But he'd been greedy. He'd seen how good she was at the work and told himself he could handle a little temptation.

That was the last time he'd underestimated her impact.

Finally she must have noticed how rock still he stood. She lifted her head eyes locking on his, and he heard a wisp of sound as she sucked in air.

Was his hunger so visible?

Yet instead of stumbling away, she stayed right where she was, close enough for her breath to waft across his chin.

'Conall?'

'You know I'd never try to coerce—'

Her eyes turned huge. 'Don't! I'd *never* think that.'

She shook her head, more distressed than he'd ever seen her. Even when she'd lain, bandaged and bruised in a hospital bed, wearing a faded hospital gown and all sorts of medical monitors, she hadn't appeared so upset. *He'd* been the one who felt undone. The shock of his raw emotions around Greer had been a revelation to a man versed in keeping an emotional distance from others.

As if belatedly realising that her palm was planted firmly on his chest, she jerked her hand free of his jacket, balling up the damp tissues.

Conall wanted to grab her wrist because he already missed her touch. But this wasn't the place. Despite his determination to get close, they still had to go at her pace. Nothing else was acceptable.

She retrieved her glass from his hand, inadvertently brushing his fingers. He felt it like a desert plant, soaking up the first drops of a rare rainstorm. The muscles in his arms pulled tight with the effort of not reaching for her.

'I'd never think you'd coerce a woman, Conall. I know you, remember?' A slow smile curved her mouth, easing the tension around his lungs. 'It's one of the things I *do* know, thankfully.'

Yet he said nothing. For even as he returned her smile, an inner voice whispered, *She thinks she knows you, but she's wrong, isn't she? She only knows what you let her see.*

What will she think when her memory comes back?

A bell dinged, loud and continuous. The call to return to their seats.

'Are you ready for the rest of it?' His tone was light, testament to those years in his father's house, learning to conceal thoughts and, above all, feelings. And later, starting up his own enterprise, conscious that half the battle in business was appearing and sounding confident, no matter how he felt.

'I wouldn't miss it. Thank you for tonight. This is just... marvellous.'

He lifted his glass, clinking it against hers before taking a long swallow. 'I can't take all the credit. Mozart deserves some.'

She smiled then sipped her wine and he had to avert his gaze as she swallowed.

There shouldn't be anything sexy about the movement but with Greer, none of the usual rules applied. Especially when she was wearing that dress. The short glittery blue one with the neckline scooped low to the shadowy cleft between her breasts. That left her arms and most her shoulders bare.

He could only be grateful she had no idea how the sight of her wearing it affected him.

'That's the other thing,' she confided, her tone ebullient. 'The tunes are glorious. I hadn't expected that. I thought they'd all be serious, but I'll be humming them tomorrow.'

Her frank approval pleased him. He'd lost count of the gala music events he'd attended and never had he encountered such honest enthusiasm.

From the time Conall's father had brought him to live with him he, like his older half-siblings, had been given the best of everything. The best schools, though he'd hated boarding school with a passion. Access to the finest art, music and sporting events. Even tutoring by professional sportsmen, paid a ridiculous amount to cultivate his skills in polo, tennis and yachting.

Had he become blasé? Of course. But never around Greer.

She grounded him. Yet something about her had always urged him to go that extra mile, imagining possibilities that once he'd never have considered.

But as far as she was concerned, he was simply her boss and he was wary of pushing hard for more. Her accident, her sudden vulnerability, haunted every interaction.

For so long he'd thought of her as indomitable. Yet despite her protestations, she wasn't fully recovered. The doctors didn't know if or when her memory would return. At the same time other men were trying to win her interest! Never had he walked such a fine line. He wanted to keep her close, surrounded by *keep off* signs. But he couldn't spook her by appearing too obviously possessive.

'I'm sure Mozart would have approved.' He put his glass down and resisted the temptation to hold his arm out for Greer to take. 'Shall we go?'

Through the rest of the performance, Conall was only partly aware of what happened onstage. His attention was on the woman beside him. Her occasional sighs of appreciation. Her perfume, her warm, womanly beauty.

And, as ever, the imperative to hide his own response.

Conall had been quiet since leaving the Opera House. Distracted. Greer knew the signs. He had something on his mind. The Singapore deal? The delay in getting exactly the right people for the rest of the Sydney positions? Or something she didn't know about?

Face it, despite the hours you spend with him, you know

virtually nothing about his personal life. You don't even know if he has a girlfriend at the moment.

A sudden, dragging sensation in the pit of her stomach made her gasp.

'Sorry, Greer. Did you say something?'

She shook her head, turning away from the city lights visible through the car's window to look at his profile. Her gaze traced the strong angle of his jaw, the proud lines of his cheekbone and nose. Even in the gloom she could pinpoint the precise place where a long dimple would carve his cheek if something amused him.

Greer shivered as an overwhelming sense of intimacy enveloped her. 'No, nothing at all.'

She could get used to this, she realised with a throb of desperate understanding. Sharing his space in the darkness, away from work responsibilities. Here she could pretend they were simply a man and woman enjoying an evening together.

Not her boss taking her out because he was concerned for her mental well-being.

The people at work, the ones on the next floor whom she'd only got to know again in the past couple of weeks, had been shocked and curious to hear of her memory loss. But they were either busy with their work or totally lacking in imagination. None of them seemed to have guessed how unnerving it was, trying to pick up a life only partly remembered.

Only Conall realised, going out of his way to watch out for her.

She should have told her couple of good friends in Perth, but she'd avoided it so far. She'd have to tell them sometime, but the thought of going through it all via long-distance calls deterred her. She kept hoping she'd wake one morning to discover the amnesia gone. Besides, they were busy with their own challenging careers.

'Here we are.' Conall turned into the private parking for her building. 'I'll see you up.'

The sensible thing would be to thank him but reject his offer.

Greer didn't feel sensible. Music danced in her head, as light and frothy as the bubbles in tonight's sparkling wine. The warm evening air caressed her bare arms and she was tinglingly attuned to the strong, charismatic man beside her.

What harm could it do, letting him walk her to the door? It would give her another few minutes to pretend they were something other than work colleagues.

Then after he left, she really *would* find a way to conquer her inappropriate feelings.

'Thank you.'

She unbuckled the seat belt and opened her door. By the time she grabbed her purse and got out he was there, hands shoved deep in his trouser pockets. He looked big and broad and delicious and she had to focus on the hint of a stain on his shirt to stop herself doing something daft like reach for him.

Greer opened her mouth to say he should soak the shirt as soon as he got home. But he was an adult. He could look after his own laundry. Besides, he probably had a housekeeper.

You're not his keeper.

Abruptly, the evanescence in her blood faded, her pulse became a dull rhythm. 'This way.'

Avoiding his eyes, she led the way. They walked in silence. Every step made her aware of his physical presence. The heat of his body. The intriguing cedar and leather scent of his aftershave. The swing of his arm so close to hers. And with every step her yearning intensified.

Finally they reached her flat. But instead of being relieved, Greer felt wound too tight. As if one unwary move would shatter her composure.

'Thanks for seeing me to my door.'

She was going to add that it was a long time since anyone had done that, when her throat closed with the realisation that she didn't even know if that were true.

There was *so much* she didn't know.

It hit her anew with such force that she wobbled on her high heels and ducked her head, pretending to search her tiny purse for her key.

'Greer, what is it?'

Conall moved closer and she froze. Another centimetre and they'd be touching. She feared that might unleash the longing she worked so desperately to conceal.

'Nothing. I just need to find my key.'

She drew a steadying breath, willing the moment of acute devastation away. But when she lifted her head to fit the key in the lock she was aware of him scrutinising her features. What did he read there?

With a twist of the wrist she unlocked the door and pushed it open, for good measure taking a step into the darkness beyond. Spinning on the ball of her foot she turned and lifted her head, looking at him though avoiding his eyes. 'Thanks, again, Conall. It was a brilliant night.'

Instead of responding with words he took one long step over the threshold that brought him tantalisingly close.

'Something's wrong.' His voice was hard. 'You're trembling. What can I do?'

Hold me.

Greer bit her bottom lip rather than let the words escape. She was stronger than this. She'd had to be.

Yet tonight of all nights, with Conall here to witness it, her nebulous fear that something was badly wrong in her world combined with her fear that her memory loss would be permanent. Then there was the aching need for *him*.

'It's nothing. Really.'

She shook her head and took a backward step into the dark apartment, reaching for the door, needing to close it before emotion really got the better of her.

Conall stopped her with one easy movement. The barely there touch of his knuckle brushing her cheek. 'Talk to me, Greer. I want to help.'

Whether it was the tenderness of his gesture or the soft intensity in his voice, she felt something crack inside and messy emotions spill out. Fear, doubt and the incredible exhilaration that was her body's response to his caress.

'I don't need your pity!' Her voice was sharp and overloud.

'It's not pity, Greer. It's something much stronger.'

'What are you saying, Conall?'

He shook his head, yet he didn't immediately drop his hand. Instead he traced the line of her cheekbone then stroked down to her jaw, as if learning the shape of her face. It was all she could do not to let her eyes flutter shut in bliss.

His husky voice abraded her senses. 'All that matters right now is what *you* want.'

In the darkness she couldn't read his expression. All she had to guide her were his stillness and his touch.

She wanted to tell him, again, that she didn't need his sympathy. Yet the words clogged in her constricted throat. Her eyelids grew heavy, beginning to close as she breathed in his rich scent and his aura of solidity. Certainty. Strength.

How she wished for that strength, and so much more.

She listed forward, like metal to a magnet. She only barely managed to stop far enough to keep a tiny distance between them.

'Greer?'

She'd never heard that one word, a single syllable, carry so much emotion. To her hyper-alert senses it seemed imbued with regret and doubt, with something like longing.

How exhausted she was from second-guessing everything!

Every event, every word and feeling. She just wanted to let go instead of repressing and guarding every emotion.

Which was why she tilted her cheek, nestling it against his big, calloused palm. She was barely even aware of lifting her hand to plant it on his chest, pushing aside the lapel of his jacket to feel the rhythmic thump-thump of his heart. It was reassuring in its steadiness, but exciting too.

She barely even registered the whisper of common sense reminding her she worked for his man. That this was a line she shouldn't cross.

All the tiny hairs on her body rose as her skin tightened. Now she heard the change in his breathing, felt the quickened rise of his chest.

His voice was a low murmur as he shifted closer. 'Is this what you want, Greer?'

His arm slid around her waist, his palm settling at the base of her spine, drawing her forward, so she stepped up against all that lovely heat and hardness.

'Yes. That's exactly what I want.'

No tremor in her voice, no uncertainty now. Maybe tomorrow she'd regret her honesty, but she could no longer hide the truth.

Conall moved in, his encircling arm tightening, wrapping further around her, bringing her up against his body. Greer leaned closer, as if she could drag his essence into her by osmosis.

His thighs were as solid as a wall and between them, pressed to her abdomen, was a rigid weight that sent her yearning into overdrive. She slid both hands up his chest and cupped the back of his neck, sculpting herself against him.

Just as she was thinking she'd have to ask for more, his hand left her cheek to curve around her head and bring her to him. His head dipped. Paused.

Her breath hitched audibly, every cell throbbing in anticipation while outwardly she froze, all the better to absorb each sensation.

The waft of his breath over her mouth, a delicate caress that made her lips tingle. The charged atmosphere as if the very air grew heavy with the expectation between them. The absolute rightness of his touch, as if he'd held her this way before. As if their bodies were made for each other.

And finally, finally, the taste of him. The dark, rich, spicy tang of maleness. His lips brushed hers and every muscle in her taut frame relaxed in relief.

One touch was all it took to smash through old protective barricades and newer doubts. One brush of his mouth and her lips were moving, seeking, eagerly moulding to his.

His kiss was slow, restrained, and while it was the best thing she could remember, it wasn't enough. Not nearly enough.

Greer rose, seeking more, inviting him deeper, pushing up against his hard frame because she needed…

Everything. That was what she wanted from Conall. Tenderness but passion too. Warmth and respect but also fire and intensity.

'Please.' Her voice was muffled against his mouth but he must have heard. Or he felt the same way, because now his embrace was tight, drawing her up his body so she could feel his taut muscles, hard bone and thrumming heart.

His tongue swept into her mouth and she clutched the back of his head, angling for more, meeting his caress with her own. Fire exploded behind shut eyes as sensations she'd once known but forgotten blasted her to the core.

In his encompassing arms, his mouth claiming hers, she felt a swelling heat, brighter and more intense than anything she remembered. Heat and need. Carnal need so intense she shook with it.

She'd wanted comfort and connection. Had wanted to be

seen and appreciated. Held close, so that for once she didn't feel alone.

But now Greer discovered that was just the tip of the iceberg. In Conall's embrace she came alive. These last few weeks she'd been going through the motions, working, completing chores, holding conversations, yet through it all there'd been an air of unreality. As if she were separated from other people by a glass panel. She felt of the world but not *in* it. Physically near people but not connected.

Not anymore. Now everything was so vivid it overwhelmed her. Her fingers dug into warm flesh and crisp hair. She tasted his growl of pleasure, swallowing it as she kissed him back desperately, inhaling his rich, male scent.

Stretching taut against his tall frame was at once paradise and pain because though her body cleaved to his, it wasn't close enough.

Even the way he held her, dominant yet supportive, tapped into a longing she'd tried and failed to stifle.

She shifted her weight, trying to align her achingly empty pelvis with his, and felt her shoes drop as he hoisted her higher.

Something snaked through her then, an uncoiling thread of rapture that made her breasts swell and her muscles clench.

The kiss changed, Conall lifted his mouth a little but before she could protest she felt the nip of teeth against her bottom lip and something exploded in her brain and deep, deep inside her body.

'Greer.'

His voice was almost unrecognisable but the wanting she understood.

His palm moved from the back of her head, down her back, over her hip and lower. One large hand fastened around her thigh, lifting, drawing her leg up over his hip, leaving her open to all that lovely hard heat.

Conall bumped his hips forward, pushing them together and Greer melted inside.

'Conall, I...' They felt so perfect together. She stopped and had to clear her throat because her larynx had seized up.

Greer looked up into the darkness that was his face, outlined against the exterior light outside. Neither of them had thought to close the door. She wished she could see him properly. Did she imagine a change? Did his head pull back?

Yet his hands were firm on her body, one at her waist and one now on her buttock, holding her against his erection so only their clothes prevented the ultimate intimacy.

'Greer.'

Just one word, but again invested with so much feeling. Regret? Or could it be embarrassment? Shock dowsed her.

There was no question about his meaning though as he lowered her to the floor, large hands anchoring her as he stepped away.

Bemused, it took a second to realise her hands still clung. She forced them to drop, her sawing breath so sharp and deep, pain pierced her chest. Even then hope was slow to die because his hands remained, warm on her body.

As if reading her mind he took them away. Pride alone kept Greer standing tall, chin high.

'We shouldn't be doing this. *I* shouldn't be doing this.' His voice was one she recognised from negotiations. His final word on the matter. Conall had made up his mind and nothing would change it.

'Why not? We're consenting adults.'

You know why. You're his assistant. He pays your wage. What working relationship could you have if this went further?

Yet Conall surprised her by not mentioning that. 'You've been unwell. You need looking after, not...'

His hand lifted but instead of reaching for her, he ploughed his fingers through his hair in a gesture so familiar it made her stupid heart clench.

Was that what this was? Her clinging to him out of familiarity? Wanting more of Conall because he was the one sure, steady thing she knew in her life? Because she was scared of the blank space where her memories should be?

Even as she thought it, she knew tonight had been about far more than that.

'What don't I need, Conall? You weren't seducing me. I wanted that kiss.' She wanted a whole lot more than a kiss. 'What happened? Were you trying to make me feel better and went further than *you* wanted?'

Though it had felt as if he wanted her every bit as much as she wanted him. She shook her head, confused and upset.

'I only want what's best for you, Greer.'

Her hands found her hips. 'And you know what's best for me?'

'I'm just saying you've been through a lot. Physically and emotionally. You need time to recuperate.'

'You think I don't know my own mind? That I don't know what I want?'

She didn't know which was worse, being kissed out of pity, or being treated with kid gloves.

'You know what, Conall? I'm suddenly very tired.'

'Greer, I—'

'Thank you for the evening. It was an interesting experience.' She reached to the side, groping for the door, relief coursing through her as she gripped the handle so hard her fingers went numb. 'And thank you for your concern. I know you mean well.' She almost choked on the words.

In the gloom she saw him draw himself higher, his broad shoulders settling somehow wider, as if he prepared himself to take up a challenge.

'It's late and I'm tired. I'll see you on Monday.' Greer

swung the door slowly forward and relief filled her as he stepped back, over the threshold.

He said something, murmured it in a low voice that tugged at something deep inside her. Fortunately, she couldn't make out the words over the pounding of her pulse.

She shut the door, double-locked it and stumbled into the apartment. She didn't turn on the light to search for her discarded shoes, because she didn't want to risk catching sight of herself in the mirror.

Greer found the sofa and sank onto it, drawing her knees up and wrapping her arms around her legs.

What had she just done?

And how could they come back from this disaster?

CHAPTER FIVE

'THE FIGURES JUST don't stack up. Nothing you sent me changes that.'

Conall stared through the open French doors, only half seeing the dark blue of the harbour at the end of the lush private garden. Emerson, now head of the Perth office, was usually on the ball. His investment recommendations were generally sound, if not downright insightful.

'Did you look at the projections in the attachments?'

'Of course.' Conall was always meticulous in his attention to detail. 'I read the whole report.'

'So you weren't impressed with the new income stream starting next year? Or the expansion scheduled for December?'

Conall frowned. He didn't recall that. 'Where are those details?'

'The final attachment. I thought I'd save the best news to last.' His deputy gave a huff of laughter but didn't sound amused.

Damn it! Conall wasn't amused either. He scrolled through the document on the screen and realised he'd missed the last attachment. He swore.

This time Emerson's laugh was genuine. 'Found it now?'

Conall was already speed reading, torn between admiration that Emerson had identified this opportunity before any other investor snapped it up and annoyance at himself.

'Sorry, mate. I couldn't understand why you were so taken with the idea of investing in that company. I should have known better.'

He thrust his fingers through his hair, scraping his scalp as if that might get his laggardly brain cells working properly. What else had he missed today?

'Hard week?'

'Nothing I can't handle. Distracting rather than hard.'

Liar.

'If there's anything we can do over here…'

Conall smiled. 'What, you don't have enough to do?'

'More than enough. Those performance targets we agreed are a real stretch, but they've been good for the team. I'm seeing a bit more lateral thinking in the group. Some of those young hires are really stepping up.'

'Excellent. I look forward to hearing about the lateral thinking next time we catch up. For now I'd better go and reread what you sent me.'

He ended the call, but instead of looking at the proposal, Conall scrubbed his hand over his face. It had been a hellish few days and it was affecting his work, something he'd believed impossible, until now.

He and Greer had tiptoed around each other with exaggerated caution.

Conall had tried to talk to her about that night, that kiss, but each time she froze him out. Normally that wouldn't stop him, but the raw hurt in her eyes, so at odds with her mask of control, got to him every time and he'd refused to pressure her.

He'd feel better for sorting things out, but he wasn't brutal enough to force her to talk before she was ready. Not after everything she'd been through.

Which left him frustrated and antsy.

Over the previous days he'd taken more meetings out of

the office than usual, needing to escape her presence and his conscience. Today he'd decided to work from home, but now it looked like he'd have to double check everything he'd done.

Distracted didn't begin to describe his mental state.

The fiasco was his fault. Greer had needed reassurance and comfort that night. But one touch and *he'd* needed more. He'd been unable to hold back until it was almost too late.

But the doctors had warned she needed time to recover fully.

Greer had wanted more from him and he'd been triumphant and eager to take what he craved, until he recalled she wasn't herself. She struggled to adapt after her accident, and with the many things she couldn't remember.

Despite the extremity of his need, Conall wouldn't allow himself to be like his father, who took advantage of vulnerable women.

Oh, Conall intended to seduce Greer. But it would be a seduction of mind and body. He wanted, needed her to *choose* him, not feel pressured or unsure. There'd be no shortcuts, no tricks. No coercion.

Pain shot through his jaw as his molars ground. He almost welcomed the jab of discomfort. It was better than his regrets sitting low in his gut.

All he'd done in the end was hurt her. Instead of giving her comfort he'd distressed her.

The night he'd taken her home after the opera, the outside light had spilled over his shoulders from behind. He'd read her expression when he finally relinquished her.

Her brittle attempt at composure, and the anguish he read between the cracks, had wrenched his gut and fed his guilt. She was still hurting now, despite the air of efficient calm she wore like a defensive cloak in the office, acting like a polite stranger.

They couldn't keep on like this.

Nor could they turn back the clock. That taste of her had unleashed something dark and hungry and he didn't know what to do with it. Abstinence was no longer working and he couldn't shut himself away from the office indefinitely.

A knock on the open study door made him turn. It was his housekeeper, Alice Robinson. 'Sorry to interrupt, but you have a visitor.' She paused. 'Greer Munro.'

Conall stared, his mind racing.

Greer, here? After days having as little to do with him as possible, she'd come to his home. Why, when she could easily call or text?

His first, instantaneous thought was that she'd come to say she was resigning. What else could bring her here?

Bile rose in his throat. He'd never thought it would come to this. Already part of his brain was calculating his next step. Because losing her was impossible.

'Show her in please.'

'Would you like refreshments before I leave?'

Conall shook his head. 'No, thanks. It's time you left.' Alice was spending a few days off with her sister in the Southern Highlands. 'You go and enjoy your break.'

'Thanks, I will.' She paused, frowning. 'Don't forget I've left tonight's meal ready in the kitchen. And I've been baking today so there's plenty of food for while I'm away.'

Clearly Alice had taken his lack of appetite lately as a personal affront. But then he registered that it was concern not annoyance making her mouth purse and her brow furrow. She looked like a worried grandmother. Not that he'd ever had a grandmother, or anyone much to worry over him.

Except another housekeeper, long ago, who'd taken pity on a shell-shocked orphan, suddenly transplanted into his father's grand, cold mansion. He hadn't known her long. She'd lost her job when his father discovered she'd been coddling him with bedtime stories and warm milk.

Despite the tension gripping his internal organs in a vice, he smiled. 'Don't worry, Alice. I won't forget to eat.'

With a nod she turned away and Conall shot to his feet.

Greer's steps slowed as she walked down the corridor the housekeeper had indicated. Her decision to confront Conall made her nervous enough. But the afternoon had already been unsettling. Even setting aside the curious look his housekeeper had given her.

She halted and looked over her shoulder, watching the older woman walk away. It was hard to shake the feeling Mrs Robinson knew something she wasn't sharing.

Maybe Conall's annoyed enough to start looking for another PA. Perhaps he confided in his housekeeper.

Trepidation shivered down her spine like a trail of ice shards.

Then there was the fact Greer had braced herself to face him, going to the building where he'd had his penthouse, only to discover he no longer lived there.

That had rocked her confidence, after weeks telling herself she was doing fine, picking up the threads of projects at work and learning new faces, only to discover this was something else she didn't know. She'd been involved in the penthouse purchase, not only handling paperwork but actually finding suitable options that met Conall's requirements.

It seemed that in the last five months his requirements had changed. Instead of a new penthouse near the heart of the city, he now lived in a grand waterfront mansion, surrounded by gardens and high walls. Its generous spaces and styling made her think of art deco mixed with Californian Spanish.

And he hadn't told her. Or perhaps he had and it was one of the many things she'd forgotten. Either option made her feel…less. Less capable. Less trusted.

That was ridiculous. The man was allowed to move house and not tell her.

Except they'd had such long discussions about his preferences before the move to Sydney. He'd said afterwards how much he'd valued her input in buying the Sydney penthouse.

But clearly he didn't like it after all, since he moved again so quickly.

Greer told herself it didn't make sense to feel thrown off-centre by this news. But it was one more proof that the confidence she'd once had about her life was now only an illusion. Would she ever claw back what she'd lost?

She set her shoulders and straightened her spine. One thing she did know. Feeling sorry for herself wouldn't help. She'd spent days wallowing in self-pity and it had to stop. She was sick of herself. It shouldn't surprise her that her boss was sick of her too, enough to find working in the office untenable.

She pressed her hand against her churning stomach. Things couldn't go on this way. She had to fix this.

Head high, she walked to the room at the end of the corridor. She raised her hand to rap on the door jamb but didn't complete the movement.

Conall was there, at the vast window, looking dark and enigmatic against the backdrop of green garden and navy blue water. His back was turned to her.

Her heart seemed to still, then just as she began to feel light-headed, jump back into action, pounding fast and hard.

Just the sight of him does that.

She should be used to him after all this time. Yet her gaze devoured him, from his rumpled hair to the dark khaki polo shirt outlining his shoulders and solid chest. To that lean waist and narrow hips, faded denim covering long, powerful legs and the tight curve of his backside.

Her mouth dried and her fingers flexed, imagining—

'Greer.'

She blinked and found herself meeting that black, glittering stare.

She recalled the first time she'd met his gaze, the tickle of excitement that turned into a thrum of awareness. She should have walked away then. But how could she have turned down the chance to work with such a phenomenally successful CEO?

Yet it wasn't just his business acumen she'd stayed for, or the bonuses or the knowledge she could walk into any job she wanted after being Conall Abercrombie's assistant.

'Conall.' She cleared her throat. 'Can we talk?'

'Of course.' Yet that unreadable expression had her on edge. She'd seen it enough times in negotiations, when he refused to give away his thoughts. Usually just before he sealed the deal on *his* terms. 'Come in and shut the door.'

Greer knew a moment's craven impulse to flee but squashed it, closing the door behind her.

He gestured to the pair of leather lounges facing each other between his desk and the window. 'Please, take a seat.' His tone was affable but she hadn't missed his swift glance at her empty hands. She hadn't bought her laptop or even a folder, just her shoulder bag.

Stiffly she crossed the room, but instead of taking a seat, stopped at the end of the lounge. 'Actually, I'd rather stand.'

Conall raised his eyebrows, a frown gathering above those fathomless eyes.

Even that makes your breath quicken. For all the wrong reasons.

Now she was here this didn't seem like such a good idea.

'You moved house.'

It wasn't what she'd intended to say but it was a whole lot easier than the apology she'd been practising.

For a second he didn't say anything, just scrutinised her as if trying to define what went on in her head.

Good luck with that. It's such a mess in there.

Half the time she wasn't sure whether her couple of vague memories from the last months were real or just figments of her imagination. As for her emotions...

He shrugged. 'I find this suits me better.'

Greer stifled surprise. He was a wealthy, single bachelor. He was in demand socially and though she had no idea how many invites he accepted, she'd seen enough photos of him attending galas, nightclubs and swanky restaurants, each time with a gorgeous companion, to know he enjoyed an active social life. A penthouse apartment in the heart of the city seemed more in keeping with a busy bachelor than this stunning, sprawling home.

None. Of. Your. Business.

'How did you find me?'

She blinked. He hadn't told her since the accident about his new address. Heat flushed her cheeks. Maybe he hadn't wanted her to follow him here. Maybe she'd done something that she'd forgotten about that made him want to keep her away from his personal space.

But that didn't gel with him spending so much private time with her recently. The day yachting. The opera. And afterwards, the kiss.

She slicked her lips and looked past him to the private jetty where a familiar white yacht was moored. The sight made her yearn for that carefree day when things had been easy between them.

'I asked one of the staff on the floor below our office. They know my memory only goes back so far. It turns out they'd hand delivered some documents to you here for signature.'

Conall nodded, but the information didn't seem to please him.

'I'm sorry to intrude.' The words spilled in a breathy rush. 'I won't take much of your time.'

He folded his arms, muscles bunching. 'If you're here to offer your resignation—'

'My resignation!' Her blood froze. She'd hoped he'd see past the last few weeks as an aberration and remember instead how well they'd worked together before. 'Is that what you want?' She held on tight to the strap of her shoulder bag as if that might stop her hand shaking.

'No, I damned well don't,' he growled. 'I know you're upset about the other night but it's not worth throwing away a partnership like ours.'

Greer gulped, trying to reconcile his words with the steely ring of anger in his tone. She couldn't ever remember seeing such banked fury in his eyes.

'You don't want me to leave?'

His frown became a scowl as he unfolded his arms and moved towards her. 'Of course not. You didn't do anything wrong.'

She was already shaking her head, pulling the long strap of her bag in front of her with restless hands. 'Don't! Don't be *kind*, Conall.' She already felt guilty enough. Guilty and mired in a situation that felt like it had no way out. But she had to try.

Instantly his laser-sharp stare eased. 'Why are you here, Greer?'

'To apologise.' She dragged in a quick breath and plunged on. 'You've been so supportive and I turned on you as if you'd done something wrong. I'm sorry.' Her mouth rucked up in a bitter smile. 'I came on to you and then *turned* on you, making accusations. You shouldn't have to deal with that, or walk on eggshells in the office because of me. I came to say sorry and see if we could go back to how we were before. If we could pretend that night hadn't happened.'

He was silent so long that her hopes turned threadbare, a weight filling her chest.

'Is that what you really want? To go back to how things were in Perth? Working together as colleagues and nothing more?'

Those obsidian eyes glittered as if he could see past her apology to the secret she'd hidden so long. Her need for him.

Slowly she nodded. 'I like working with you, Conall. My job is challenging and fulfilling.'

And she couldn't imagine not seeing him every day, not being with him.

Maybe she *should* resign. This fixation on him wasn't healthy. She'd told herself that for ages yet the thought of moving on to another position filled her with dread. When had attraction turned into something more?

'Good. I wouldn't accept your resignation.'

'You wouldn't?'

His mouth thinned. 'Absolutely not. And in case you don't remember, your employment contract stipulates a minimum of six months' notice.'

He made it sound like a threat, as if he actually feared she might leave.

'Well that's…good.' She paused, relief stealing her words for a moment. 'And you accept my apology? I know you were only offering comfort that night. I should never have pushed myself at you, demanding a kiss.' She made herself hold his gaze. 'And then to turn on you… It was unreasonable. I know you don't really want me.'

She'd had the week to think it through. She remembered his arms around her and the feel of his erection. But then she'd all but begged for his attention. Just because a man felt physical arousal when a woman threw herself at him, all but scaling his body, didn't mean he wanted *her* specifically. Conall had proved that with his withdrawal.

'You're doing it again, Greer, telling me what I do and don't want.' He paced closer, around the end of the lounge so she had to tilt her head up to hold his gaze. 'Things are complicated enough without you putting words in my mouth.'

The only thing she wanted to put in his mouth was her tongue. Standing so close to him she had total recall of how perfect that kiss had been. But remembering that would only destroy any chance of regaining their old working relationship.

So she stood silently while he took another step, stopping a handspan away. Close enough for his radiating heat to make her flesh tingle.

She remained silent, even when her busy fingers inadvertently tugged her bag off her shoulder to fall on the floor. For there was something in his eyes that she didn't recognise. Didn't dare believe.

'Aren't you going to ask me what I do want, Greer?'

That night at her flat she hadn't been able to see his face. She could now and what she saw made her swallow hard then moisten her lips. Those dark eyes traced the movement and she felt the hard punch of need low in her body.

'What do you want, Conall?'

Heat flickered in that intense stare.

'You, Greer. I want you.'

CHAPTER SIX

CONALL WATCHED HER reactions as if in slow motion.

Shock. Disbelief. Elation. Confusion.

Had he really done such a good job of hiding his desire? It had taken superhuman effort to be patient all this time and not push her too hard.

In the recesses of his mind he heard his tattered conscience scream that he'd promised to hold back.

But when Greer turned up at his door pleading for forgiveness he felt a complete heel. She wasn't the one who should beg for forgiveness.

That knot in his belly tightened, giving a sickening wrench. He wanted to tell her everything and end the constraint between them, but for her sake he had to take this one step at a time.

Unselfish of you, Abercrombie! Sure you're not just protecting yourself?

He ignored the taunting voice. They couldn't go on the way they were. Something had to change and he refused to let her feel guilty for no reason.

As for his own sins… That dreadful burden wasn't going to shift and there'd be a reckoning eventually, he knew. But for now Greer needed more and so did he.

'Conall? Are you talking about needing me in the office, or…?'

He watched her swallow, the movement jerky. Her hands

twisted. The sight of her so tentative killed something inside. He'd always admired her confidence, her willingness to take on any challenge.

Even him.

'I'm talking about *you*, Greer.' He stepped closer, unable to keep away. 'I want you as a man wants a woman.' Her sharp indrawn breath sliced the air. 'I've wanted you from that first day you came to my office, trying to hide your nerves about taking a job you felt you weren't right for.'

Her eyes bulged and, despite the tension racking him, Conall felt his mouth twist in stark amusement.

Yes, for him it had been that quick.

She'd worn similar clothes that day. A straight skirt and tailored jacket over a pale blouse. No doubt she thought it made her look professional, as if he wouldn't notice the firm thrust of her breasts and the way her skirt outlined her hips, buttocks and thighs.

Heat shot through him, a stroking flame, and he had to shove his hands into his trouser pockets, clenching them against the fierce urge to grab her and not let go.

He was breaking a promise to himself by admitting his need. But the one promise he wouldn't break was to let her decide what happened next.

He watched as she considered his words, looking for hidden meanings.

Nothing was as sexy as Greer turning things over in her mind, that tiny half frown on her forehead and the hint of a pout on her lips. From the first her incisive mind had challenged and provoked and beckoned until he was all but slavering for her.

How many times had they sat in a meeting with him hard as a rock, trying not to respond to her allure because she worked for him?

'You want me...sexually?'

'I do.' Still she looked unconvinced so he gave the unvarnished truth. 'I can taste you. Even now I can feel your body against mine. The need for you has been humming in my veins so long, I can't remember what it's like *not* to want you.'

Her mouth gaped but instead of respecting her shock, the devil in him urged him closer. That open mouth was an invitation to glorious intimacy.

Except, he owed her a choice in this.

Who was he kidding? If he had any scruples he'd have found a way to manage the situation without confessing how much he needed her.

He stepped back.

'What are you doing?'

'Trying not to crowd you.'

Her head tilted to one side. 'And that would be a bad thing because?'

'Because...' His voice seeped out between gritted teeth. 'You haven't said how you feel about that.'

She'd wanted him that night in her apartment but maybe she regretted that now. Perhaps she'd just turned to him because she was feeling overwhelmed about other things. He couldn't blame her for that.

He grimaced, remembering everything she'd gone through. It tore at something deep within, a terrible rending sensation. It was something he'd only experienced since Greer. Her pain was his.

'Conall, what is it?'

He shook his head. 'You know I want you, but how do you feel about me, Greer?' He was desperate to know.

She slicked her bottom lip as if preparing to speak, then paused. He forced his gaze away from her mouth and saw her hands work, her thumb rubbing a finger in a nervous habit that always undid him.

'If you weren't my boss, I'd say I want you, so badly it keeps me awake at night.'

A huge breath he hadn't known he'd held escaped in a rush. Aching muscles in his neck and shoulders eased. After so long in purgatory maybe things would be all right after all.

He looked down into dazed, ink-blue eyes and realised he'd closed the space between them with one stride. He swallowed, the movement painful as if gravel lined his throat. He was so close he drew the scent of her into starved lungs. 'And if I said our work situation has no bearing on this? I won't let that matter, no matter what happens between us.'

'Then I'd be…tempted.'

Conall couldn't hold back any longer. The need to touch was too strong. He set his hands on her elbows, skimming up her arms, not slowing until he reached the soft skin of her neck, the underside of her jaw where her pulse throbbed as fast as his own. Her skin was like silk and his hands lingered then slid up to cup her cheeks.

His voice dropped to a bass note that scraped up from his belly. 'Would you like me to tempt you a little more?'

Say yes.

The thought of dropping his hands was unbearable.

Warm fingers covered his and an electric shock jolted him.

Holding his gaze, she pulled one of his hands away and pressed her lips to his palm. A sigh shuddered out of him as the blood left his head and raced south.

'Greer.' The single syllable revealed all his yearning and he didn't care. Nothing mattered beyond the fact she wasn't pulling away. His pulse roared in exultation.

She lifted his other hand and nuzzled the centre of his palm as if drawing in his essence. Fire seared his veins. Her lips moved against his palm, and it was exquisite pleasure and torture combined.

'No need to tempt me, Conall. I want you too.' Her eyes locked on his and his flesh grew tight. 'I think I…need you.'

He wrapped his arms around her, her words shifting the

unbearable weight he'd carried so long. Joy burst free as she moved into his tightening embrace with an easy familiarity that hit him with the force of a sledgehammer.

How he'd held back from her all this time he didn't know.

But then her brow creased. 'Have we done this before? It feels like it.'

'You were in my arms last weekend, remember? I held you and we kissed.'

Slowly she shook her head, hands flattening on his collarbone. 'I don't mean that. Before, were we lovers?'

Her words shook him to the core. All this time, could she have been as tortured as he?

Conall had been leaning forward to kiss her but his head reared back, his heart pounding. What could he say? He'd been told not to force her memories or try to lead her towards them, but to let her recover the memories naturally.

Unless, of course, she never did.

Pain slashed his midsection, lacerating and twisting.

'If you're telling yourself you want me, just because you think we had a relationship in the past, you're doing us both a disservice.' Reluctantly he dropped his hands. 'This shouldn't be about what you think happened before but what you feel now.'

He deserved a bloody medal. Pulling back from her went against every instinct.

'But if you tell me we were lovers...'

'Should that make a difference? The point is what you feel *now*. I want you in my bed but you have to be sure what you feel.'

For him it wasn't *want*, it was bone-hollowing need.

He moved again so they were no longer touching.

For an aching, soul-destroying moment he was alone.

Then she muttered, 'Damn you and your conscience, Conall Abercrombie,' and followed him, wrapping her arms tight around his back and pressing in close.

He considered telling her it wasn't solely his conscience motivating him. Self-interest played a huge part. When she knew the whole truth, things would change irrevocably.

But then she stretched up and put her mouth on his.

She kissed him and he changed in an instant. All reserve vanished. Conall swept her to him in a crushing embrace that felt like heaven. His mouth covered hers with such slow, devastating deliberation that her knees turned to water and her thoughts tangled and frayed.

He was everything. So big, so powerful, so deliciously male. The taste of him was like a drug in her bloodstream, making her crave more with each caress.

Reaching up, she plunged her hands into his thick hair, holding him fast and drawing him close. The instinct to have him, not let him go, wasn't decent or civilised. It was everything.

A wave of feeling rose up and engulfed her, them. For she was sure he felt it too. A shudder passed through them both, rocking them as if the earth quaked beneath their feet. Yet she'd never felt more sure of anything.

So right and so very, very good.

Yet it was nowhere near enough.

Greer shifted her weight, restlessly trying to ease the fever-pitch ache between her thighs. She lifted one leg, only to be stymied by her narrow skirt.

'I need to be closer.'

Conall lifted his head enough to scorch her with those glittering dark eyes. She would have protested him breaking the kiss, except then he was sweeping her up into his arms as easily as she carried her laptop.

Tthere it was again, a mix of acceptance and elation, as if she'd been waiting for him to take her in his embrace. As if it were the most natural thing in the world. Anticipation spiked and she leaned against his shoulder as he turned around.

But instead of carrying her to one of those vast lounges, he bypassed them.

'Conall? Aren't we going to...'

Make love? Have sex? None of those words seemed to fit. Because her need for him felt like the difference between life and death.

He met her eyes with a slanting look that made her toes curl and her body soften.

'Oh, yes, Greer. We're going to do all that and more. But in comfort.' He spoke with a lethal deliberation that felt like he drew his calloused fingers up her inner thigh to circle her clitoris, making her ache and her muscles ease in anticipation. 'But you deserve more than a quickie on a sofa. We're going to take our time.'

He bent and she realised he was opening the door, still holding her against his chest.

She swallowed, her mind rioting at the idea of him taking his time. If Conall were as thorough and focused in bed as he was in the office... She shivered and squeezed her thighs tight.

At least he'd put aside the scruples that had held him back! She knew exactly what she wanted and it was him.

He headed for a broad, curling staircase in the glass-ceilinged atrium. Shards of colour washed the space from the magnificent art deco stained glass above.

'I can walk, you know,' she murmured.

'And I'll enjoy following you up the stairs sometime, watching every tiny sway of your beautiful body in that tight skirt.' His chest rose mightily against her while her own breath stopped in her lungs. When Conall released the brakes he really let go. It was devastating and wholly wonderful. 'But not today. Maybe tomorrow, when we come up for air.'

'Tomorrow?' Her voice trembled with shocked delight. It wasn't even dusk.

'You don't have anywhere else you need to be, do you?'

This time she saw a glint of humour in his midnight gaze and that was almost as enticing as the raw carnality of the picture he'd painted. The man turned her inside out and they were still fully clothed.

He took her to a vast bedroom overlooking the harbour. In the distance she caught sight of a group of yachts, spinnakers billowing. But it was a fleeting glimpse because nothing was nearly as fascinating as Conall.

Even the wide bed with its pale cover was a blurred impression as she held onto his shoulders and he lowered her, impossibly slowly, down his body. As a show of core body strength it was impressive, but then wasn't everything about this man?

For a fleeting moment earlier she'd wondered if she were doing the right thing, admitting her desire. But it was inevitable. Where Conall was concerned there was no choice, there was only him. From the moment they'd met it had been true and her feelings only grew more powerful with time. Now what she felt was a compulsion.

She spared a thought for the future, for how they'd work together after this, but she trusted him when he said it would be okay. They'd find a way. And while her career was incredibly important to her, she'd come to suspect that Conall, and the connection between them, meant more.

That should be scary. It probably would be later. But for now it just felt right in a way nothing else had since she'd woken in hospital, broken.

'Greer.' His low voice reverberated through her. 'Are you changing your mind?'

'No!'

His grin made him look suddenly boyish, delighted and... Was that relief?

'Unless,' she sent him a teasing look under lowered lashes, 'you've changed your mind about what you can deliver. If you don't think you can live up to your promises...'

Hands loose on her hips, he leaned forward, gaze drilling into hers. His voice was soft and his breath a warm caress that made her lips tingle and her nipples bud. 'It's going to be an absolute pleasure delivering on those promises. For both of us.'

It took all she had to stand and not melt into a puddle of pure longing at his feet.

'I'll give you this, Mr Abercrombie, you can talk the talk.'

'But can I deliver?' His lips brushed her forehead, her cheeks, her closed eyes as he slipped the jacket from her shoulders.

Already she was burning up, lit from within by the fire this man ignited so effortlessly. Amnesia or not, she was sure no other man had ever held such power over her. As the daughter of a single mother who'd crossed the country to avoid her dangerous partner, Greer had always been cautious, not wanting to be vulnerable to any man.

She didn't feel vulnerable with Conall, she decided as he plucked her buttons undone with deft fingers. More like powerful. And powerfully aroused.

She dragged her hands down his torso and grabbed his polo shirt, yanking it up and free of his jeans. Seconds later her palms spanned the silky hot skin of his waist in proper skin-to-skin contact. Finally she managed to drag a full breath into sorely worked lungs. Her fingers moulded and skimmed, circling then returning, exploring.

Those firm ridges of muscle, the taut planes and intriguing dips were the best kind of braille.

Except, despite his assurance, Conall grew impatient. Big,

gentle hands brushed her shirt from her shoulders, moving her hands from his body.

She made a sound of disappointment, as if he'd stolen her favourite toy. Her bottom lip pouted at the interruption.

'Soon, I promise.' The words feathered against her throat as he tugged the material down her arms and away.

Suddenly she didn't mind so much because he looked spellbound as he ravished her with his gaze. Her bare skin tightened, her breasts seeming to swell under that avaricious stare.

'I need more.' His arms went around her, hands reaching for her skirt's zip.

'So do I,' she purred, pushing up his shirt.

It bunched under her hands as she revealed more and more of that sculpted torso. His skin was darker than hers and across his chest was a fuzz of hair that, when she brushed it with her fingers, yanked white-hot threads tight between her aching breasts and her womb.

Greer swayed closer, inhaling his clean male scent as she kissed a line up his torso then licked his nipple and felt him shudder. Abruptly his hands moved from her zip, shoving her skirt down her hips before reaching to reef off his shirt.

'That's better,' she sighed, kissing her way across his broad chest and up to his collarbone. He tasted like every of erotic fantasy she'd ever known.

'It is,' he growled in a voice that seemed to vibrate from deep inside him. His chest rose and spread under her palms where they rested above his ribs, soaking up the delicious vibrations. 'But not as good as this.'

With one quick movement he undid her bra, tugging it down her arms, lifting her hands from his body long enough to strip the lacy fabric off her. Then he pulled her to him, bare torso to bare torso, and something erupted inside her.

'Conall!'

'I know, I know.'

She felt the throb of his heart, the tickle of his chest hair teasing her breasts as she leaned up, reaching for his mouth. There. That was better. She felt…anchored with their mouths fused in hungry abandon.

This was so impossibly good, yet she needed more. And he gave it, slipping his hands between them to mould her breasts, his thumbs stroking her tightly beaded nipples.

Greer was all lush heat and splintering senses, and still this wasn't enough. She reached between them, grappling with his belt, moving back just enough to get it undone and tackle the fastening of his jeans.

'Yes,' he groaned against her lips. The yearning in his hoarse voice, the vibration of it from his body to hers, was the most arousing thing she'd ever known.

Quickly she undid the fastening, tugging his jeans down to his thighs then stripping his underpants low enough to curl her fingers around him.

Shock was an unfurling ribbon inside her. He was tall and well-built. Her breath snagged, imagining all that potent length inside her. She found herself spreading her feet wider, internal muscles clenching in anticipation.

Her eyes flicked open as he lifted his head. That lazy confidence was gone, replaced by a look of pared back hunger that should frighten her but instead thrilled.

'I promised to take my time.' His voice ground so low it will rumbled. 'So you'd better let me take it from here.'

He moved her hands away, making short work of the last of his clothes. Then he turned to the bedside table and even that sight was perfection. His broad thighs were so powerful, contrasting with his narrow waist and the twist of his upper body as he reached for a condom, turning him into a living work of art.

Greer hurried to divest herself of her clothes and shoes.

Seconds later she was naked and more than ever aware of

his greater height and strength. She adored it. She wanted to lean in and snuggle against him. Except—her gaze fixed on his proud erection—there were things she wanted more.

She lay on the bed, spreadeagled and bare, her heart in her mouth as she ate up the sight of him. He devoured *her* with a scorching gaze that made her revel in her feminine power and all the differences between them.

Conall took his time moving onto the bed beside her, propping himself up on one elbow as he stroked her face then leaned in to claim her mouth as his hand traced slow, sinuous trails of pleasure around her throat, breasts and lower.

It wasn't enough. She reached for him, only to have her wrist captured and lifted away, then her other one. She opened eyes that had fluttered closed to see him shake his head on a grimace. 'Not yet. I'm too close.'

He shackled her hands above her head, leaving her open to his touch. Greer thought of protesting but she *liked* being vulnerable to him in this way. His hungry gaze and the inexorable slide of his hand down her abdomen only notched her arousal higher.

Then Conall kissed her, slow and deliberate. This time he used his teeth as well as his tongue, grazing sensitive skin then kissing it better as his fingers explored moist folds.

One expert caress and she almost lifted off the bed. He threw his thigh over hers and even that was arousing.

The stretch of her body, the weight of his hand and leg, seemed to intensify every sensation as he kissed and caressed her.

Abruptly, *too* abruptly, her crisis hit. She felt the shock wave engulf her, her body undulating as it crested each peak of pleasure.

Warm arms gathered her close as he moved above her and Greer held on tight.

This was where she needed to be. In a world full of uncertainties it was the one thing she knew absolutely.

'Conall, that was—'

'Just the beginning,' he said with a tight smile. Then he was kissing her again, lulling her rioting senses as she came down from that impossible high.

She was still floating when he shifted his weight back. Instinctively she opened her legs wider. But instead of stopping were she expected, he moved further, halting only when his shoulders wedged between her spread thighs.

Greer shook her head, despite her surge of delighted anticipation. 'I need you, Conall.' The hollow ache inside was still there, despite her orgasm.

'And you'll have me, soon.'

He'd already dipped his head, his lips moving against that most sensitive spot on her body, making it impossible to answer. Her voice disappeared as exquisite sensation overwhelmed her. Not just because of his mouth, but his hand, circling and probing.

Her one cogent thought was that Conall knew exactly how to drive her out of her mind.

Silk teased her palms and she realised she was grabbing his head, fingers buried in his hair. Again her body took on a life of its own, twisting and rising as he coaxed more delight, more impossible pleasure.

Then his gaze met hers and something passed between them. Heat, excitement and... Connection? A second later she found her voice, keening his name with her head thrown back into the pillow and her body arching into his hold.

There was fire and throbbing fulfilment. Soothing hands and murmured words she couldn't catch. She was lost in a world of delight so intense it felt like an out-of-body experience. Except for the way she clung to him as he moved higher, finally settling between her legs.

How long they lay together, unmoving apart from his hand gently stroking her hair, she didn't know. At some point she opened her eyes to find him looking down at her. She smiled, heart full.

And despite the astronomical highs she'd reached, Greer discovered they were nothing compared with the impact of Conall's answering smile. Slow and a little crooked, so tender and understanding she felt it deep within. He'd cracked open another of the barriers she'd erected to protect herself.

She should be worried about that but couldn't be. She lifted her hands, moulding his face like a blind woman learning his features. So familiar, so dear, they made her heart contract. *Surely* this wasn't new.

Thrusting her fingers into his hair, she drew his head closer. 'My body feels like a limp rag but still I need you, Conall. Please take me. Now.'

He'd given her physical ecstasy but instinct told her there was something far better to come.

'You have no idea how much I need you, Greer.'

Propping himself on one elbow, he reached between them and she felt his heavy erection prod her. Then with one slow, smooth glide he joined them.

Her breath escaped in a deep sigh. It was overwhelming, a physical impossibility that she should feel him so deep, as if he nudged her very heart. Yet despite the stretched muscles and the shock of it, nothing in her life had ever been so perfect.

'Greer?'

She opened eyes she hadn't realised she'd closed and found him peering down at her, forehead wrinkled in concern and mouth tight. She ran her hands down his back, feeling the ripple of taut muscles in response. A shudder racked his big frame as she clenched him close.

'Yes.' She bent her knees, planting her feet on the bed beside his thighs and rocking her hips up. 'More.'

The movement, or perhaps her words, cut through his restraint. The next moment he retreated then surged deep again. And again. Each time she met him, thrust for thrust, needing the affirmation of them claiming each other.

His biceps bulged as he held himself above her, but there was enough friction to tease her nipples into tight buds. And the friction lower down was having an amazing effect despite her earlier climaxes.

Greer's senses began to spin. With a final effort she managed to raise trembling legs over his waist, linking her ankles, holding him close as if she feared he might retreat.

All the while Conall's gaze was fixed on hers. As pleasure rose it was shared. She saw the febrile heat in eyes so dark, iris and pupil were indistinguishable. She lost herself in those depths as his movements grew short and hard and she heard his grunt of shock and fulfilment.

Then he was pulsing inside her, the sensation so intimate, so wonderful, her once weary body spasmed and followed him right into the conflagration.

The world disappeared. There was only her and Conall, his eyes on hers.

Greer had never known such a high. Or such connection.

If it weren't so perfect it would have frightened her.

CHAPTER SEVEN

THE SKY WAS DARKENING. From the bed, Conall could see the harbour turn violet in the fading light. But it was the view immediately before him that enthralled.

Shadows accentuated Greer's features, the angle of her cheekbones, the sweep of her eyebrows, the soft curve of her lips. The dark arcs of her long lashes against her cheeks as she slept. He already knew them all by heart yet he could lie here for hours, watching her. Revelling in the fact that, finally, they were together.

That must be why adrenaline still pulsed in his veins, despite that shattering climax. He'd told himself it would happen, the barriers would fall and they'd be together. But he'd learnt not to take anything for granted. Especially Greer.

She lay on her side, facing him, one hand against his chest, her knee on his thigh, a tendril of long dark hair sweeping over her shoulder and around her breast. He wanted to follow it with his hand but didn't want to wake her.

She'd looked so tired this week and he blamed himself. His attempt to comfort her the night of the opera had got out of hand and distressed her. He dragged in a deep breath charged with regret for the mistakes he'd made. But it was impossible to feel guilty when his perseverance and patience had paid off. She was here, where she belonged.

'Conall.' Black lashes rose to reveal eyes of deepest, most beautiful blue, the colour of lapis lazuli or sapphire.

'Greer.' Her dreamy smile made his voice hitch.

How long had he dreamt of her looking at him like that?

A twist of tension behind his ribs disintegrated as she snuggled closer. He wrapped his arm more firmly around her waist, pulling them together. He'd wondered if she might wake to regrets.

'How are you feeling?'

She stretched voluptuously, totally at ease. 'Stupendous. How about you?'

Conall laughed. 'Counting my lucky stars.'

She raised her eyebrows, watching his smile become a grin. 'Flatterer.'

'It's nothing but the truth.'

He stroked her cheek then followed that dark tress down, around her lush breast. Her breath stalled for a second, then she began her own exploration, her hand smoothing up his chest, shaping and exploring.

The steady beat of his pulse became a heavy thud, centring in his groin. But as fantastic as the sex had been, he had more on his mind.

'You're not worn out? No after-effects?'

Her brow furrowed. 'Actually, I feel energised. Are you too tired?'

'Too tired for you? Never.' He paused. 'I mean, do you feel well.'

Greer's confusion cleared. 'You mean my head? The amnesia?'

It was like watching a cloud cross the sun and he silently cursed himself for reminding her, but he had to know. She'd mentioned a couple of times these past weeks small instances of her memory returning. Mainly scents or sounds reminding her of minor incidents. Nothing earth-shattering. So far.

'I wondered...'

'No.' Her mouth flattened. 'Sex didn't miraculously restore my memory. But at least it hasn't given me a headache, if that's what you're worried about.'

Of course she'd have told him if there'd been any new recollections.

'Good,' he said as he slid down her body a little. 'I wouldn't like to seduce you if your head hurts.'

Yet he'd wondered. Their physical intimacy had been phenomenal by any standards. He'd hoped, feared it might be enough to open a door to at least some glimpse of the past. He hadn't known what to expect when she opened her eyes, but had wondered if he'd see a change in her.

But it had only been around a month. The doctors said it might take much longer, if ever. Meanwhile, Greer was here, in his bed, naked and eager.

Conall cupped her breast and closed his mouth over that perfect raspberry nipple, slowly drawing on it, feeling her arch against him, her slender fingers anchoring his head against her.

'You want to seduce me? You're really not too tired?'

For answer he palmed her buttocks and drew her lower body close enough to feel the iron-hard erection he'd been trying to ignore for the last half-hour.

'Conall.' Her sigh was half appreciation and half entreaty. He knew the feeling. She'd only just woken and she had him teetering on the edge.

He tightened his grip, gently scraping his teeth across sensitive skin and feeling her shudder in response. 'Yes, sweetheart?'

How he loved the telltale hitch in her breath and the way she shimmied even closer, the intimate heat between her legs teasing him.

'I need you,' she whispered.

He looked up into half-lidded eyes that glowed like gems. His chest expanded, not on an indrawn breath, but on a swelling feeling of relief and anticipation. He'd hoped, but their recent history had taught him not to take anything for granted.

Conall rose, tumbling her onto her back and kneeling above her on all fours. Her hair splayed across the pillow and a flush of arousal warmed her throat and cheeks.

'I need you too. Desperately.'

He'd never wanted a woman so much. He wanted to tell her exactly how he felt, but refused to move too fast for her. Better to keep this simple for now.

He planted his mouth on hers, rejoicing in her eagerness as she cupped his face and angled her mouth to give him entry, her tongue curling and inviting. She tasted sweet and rich and he could have enjoyed it all night except his primed body had other ideas.

Ignoring her soft mew of protest, he lifted his head to kiss her cheeks, her ear, and that sensitive place on her neck that made her writhe beneath him, hands clutching.

'Sh. Soon,' he promised.

It was tempting to rush but they both deserved more, despite the urgent craving. They'd waited so long and he wasn't going to waste a moment. Greer's pleasure was his and he intended to show her with every kiss and caress how much this meant, since he couldn't use words. Yet.

So he took his time kissing her throat, her collarbone, her shoulders, as he let his hand explore lower and lower. She was writhing now, hips lifting and twisting off the bed, trying to reach him.

His pulse quickened as he reached her breasts. Their contours, their weight, their softness, even the stronger scent of her flesh there, drove him crazy. He couldn't get enough, and the taste of her...

'You have to stop,' she gasped. 'I don't want torture, I want you to make me whole.'

Her words destroyed any hope of teasing her into fulfilment before taking her. He was so close it was a miracle he'd lasted this long.

Conall moved back, kissing his way to her waist, briefly exploring the whorl of her navel before peppering kisses down to the damp, silky hair between her thighs. One too-brief caress there and he rose from the bed, moving stiff-legged to the bedside table for a condom.

He had to pause a moment, and then another, the weight of her gaze on his groin threatening to tip him over the edge.

'What are you waiting for?'

He shot her a look that was part exasperation with himself and her for driving him to his limits. When he finally found his voice it was to speak through gritted teeth. 'Making sure I don't self-combust, trying to put on a condom.'

Her snicker of delight tugged his lips into a smile despite the extremity of his situation. He'd always loved her laugh.

'You won't be laughing if I spill here rather than in you.'

And damn him if she didn't conjure a pout that slammed his body right back to the edge.

Conall closed his eyes, blotting out the image of those full lips. In his head he began going over some of the points he wanted clarified on the Singapore deal. His ordinarily sharp brain was fuzzy and his thoughts strayed but eventually he hauled himself back enough to put on protection. It felt like a miracle of determination over instinct.

After one swift survey of her lying there, he yanked his attention to her face. Her laughter had died, replaced by the same tense eagerness he felt.

He climbed onto the bed, but instead of covering her body with his, he lay on his side, sliding one arm under her head. 'Roll towards me.'

'Onto my side?' She looked confused but complied, and he palmed her hip, stroking down to lift her thigh over his. 'Ah.'

He nodded. 'I've been lying here wanting you but I didn't want to wake you.'

Greer hitched herself higher up the bed, her breasts brushing his chest, and he shuddered.

'You like that?' Her expression told him she'd done it deliberately.

'You know I do.' Conall delved his free hand between them, knuckles caressing her clitoris, and she gasped. 'Do that again.'

She pushed closer and now there was no time for teasing or patient seduction. She was so wet between the legs and he had about twenty seconds before he came apart.

It was like coming home as she opened for him, so slick and tight already he felt the warning prickle begin at his nape and race down his spine. By the time he was seated as far as he could go, the sensation was coiling in his groin.

Conall drowned in the mesmerising depths of her eyes. But he couldn't go alone. He needed her with him.

As he pulled back he found that sensitive nub where her nerves centred, and pressed down as he nipped her ear and began telling her some of the ways he wanted to please her.

By his second surge forward, her breath was a harsh rasp of arousal, her fingers digging into his buttocks to draw him to her as if she didn't trust him to find his way.

Another retreat and surge, and then, just as he feared his body would betray him, Conall felt the change in her. Sharp breaths and the delicious twitch of muscles around him.

'Come for me, Greer. I've got you.'

His arm tightened around her back as his thumb circled and he grazed his teeth along her neck.

Her quivers became a hard rhythmic pulsing that shattered him completely.

Conall flung his head back, shouting his release. He tumbled her onto her back and drove home hard and quick and so desperately there was no finesse, only an urgency that broke out from some primal part of him he'd never known.

Dimly he was aware of her legs wrapped around him, her fingernails digging into him. Then she lifted her hips and he shuddered, bucking out of control.

He felt a sting near his collarbone that shot fire through his veins but he didn't have the energy to open his eyes. He could only finish mating.

For that was what this was, he realised as their movements eventually slowed. He nestled his head in the scented crook of her shoulder, only just remembering to take most of his weight on one hip and elbow.

That hadn't been making love. It had been too desperate, too profound. Too visceral.

His lungs laboured as shock gripped him. He'd taken her as if nothing else mattered, driven by forces older and more primitive than thought or even pleasure. Though there'd been pleasure, so profound it felt like he'd burnt off superficial layers and been reduced to the very essence of himself.

Nothing about Greer was what he'd expected in the beginning. Everything was more. *She* was more.

Groaning at the effort, he rolled onto his side, taking her with him, holding her close, rejoicing in the way she cuddled against him, their bodies fitting together as if made for each other.

Eventually he found his breath. 'Was I too rough?'

Her palm pressed his chest as she tilted her head back, her eyes reflecting the same shattered wonder he felt.

'Absolutely not. I loved it. Besides, I should be asking you that.' She smoothed her fingers along his collarbone then pressed her lips to the spot. 'I'm sorry. I seem to have drawn blood.' She shook her head. 'I've never…'

'Nor have I.' He lifted her chin to gaze into her eyes. 'But I don't mind that you marked me.' He revelled in it. Just as the knowledge she'd bear more than one reddened patch from his stubble made him feel satisfaction. 'That was…' Mind-boggling. He settled on 'Stunning.'

Her slow-curling smile was like a caress he felt all the way to the soles of his feet.

How could a single smile rival for impact the most amazing sex he'd ever had? Conall told himself the unravelling feeling in his belly was the comedown after shattering bliss.

'I'll get rid of this condom.'

Nothing was guaranteed to break the mood more. Except then Greer said, 'Kiss me first. Please.' And how could he resist?

Before Greer, post-coital kisses hadn't been a favourite of his. But she'd changed that. The sharp tang of arousal might have eased but there was a different pleasure to be had in this languorous meeting of mouths, her hands cupping his face and the accommodating curves of her body melding against him.

When he finally broke away she rolled onto her back, glossy hair tousled around her shoulders and reddened lips parted, her breasts rising on a sigh.

'Could you run a bath, please?'

'You're sore?' He stiffened. He shouldn't be surprised. Their lovemaking had been vigorous.

'No.' Something unexpected glinted in her half-closed eyes. 'I've imagined showering with you so often, but I don't think my legs will hold me up. But we could share a bath, don't you think?'

She'd been imagining showering with him?

Despite his satiation and what should be bone-deep exhaustion, Conall felt a tickle stir in his loins. One look, one word from Greer and his hormones were shouting that two orgasms were nowhere near enough.

'I absolutely know we can. Unless you want to wait until your legs have recovered.'

'No. I've been waiting so long.'

He knew the feeling. He felt himself grin like a teenager with his first crush. 'Give me a couple of minutes to run that bath.'

Greer stretched and smiled at the warm, pleasurable ache in well-used muscles. Conall had made love to her tenderly, then passionately, then again in so many ways and with such patience and thoroughness that she'd never dreamt such rapture existed.

It wasn't even the climaxes he gave her, though they'd been spectacular. It had been his hunger for her and his determination to please, put her first and lavish such attention on her she felt like a queen.

If going to bed with her boss was a mistake, she couldn't regret it. Conall was all she'd hoped for and more.

All night and much of the morning they'd been in bed, except when they took that luxurious bath together. She found herself grinning at the memory. When he'd suggested she rest while he got breakfast for them, she hadn't even thought of protesting.

She couldn't remember the last time anyone had waited on her like this.

Except Conall, coming to her apartment on a recent Saturday, bringing food, and if he but knew, the comfort of his presence. That was what she most treasured. She'd been feeling low since the accident, but when she was with him all that changed.

Now it must be late morning, judging by the sunlight and watercraft busy on the harbour.

What a place he had. He didn't even have to lift his head off the pillow for a water view. Yet still it surprised her that he'd moved only months after taking the penthouse apartment.

Conall was a highflying businessman who travelled a lot,

worked hard and seemed purpose-built for apartment living in the city. She'd never imagined him in a sprawling house. But she approved his choice. The little she'd seen of this home, with its generous proportions, gracious style and enormous garden, made her wonder how long before she could afford a house, not an apartment but somewhere with a garden. She'd never manage anywhere like this, but she had her dreams.

'I hope you're hungry.'

Conall appeared in the doorway with a tray. His jaw was etched with dark shadows that made her skin tingle. His hair was rumpled and ridiculously appealing. And he was naked but for the pair of grey tracksuit pants that rode so low on his hips her attention settled on his impressive musculature and stayed there.

One good tug and the fabric would be around his ankles. How could she be exhausted and voracious at the same time?

'Clear the bedside table, would you?'

Greer shuffled up in the bed and saw the surface littered with condom wrappers. With one slide of the arm, she pushed them onto the floor.

Conall's huff of laughter lodged somewhere behind her ribs. 'I've always found your efficiency sexy.'

'You have?' She turned to find his attention not on the gleaming wood surface but on her naked breasts.

She hitched in a sharp breath as her body responded and saw his grip on the tray turn white-knuckled. Finally he looked up to meet her eyes, his expression rueful. 'Always,' he said as he set the tray down.

Greer moved back across the bed, scrabbling for the sheet to cover herself.

'Don't. It's a spectacular view.'

'I could say the same.'

Her gaze flickered to his chest. They'd managed a little sleep last night. She'd spent that time sprawled against him, her head cushioned on his chest, the reassuring rhythm of his heartbeat lulling her to sleep. Abruptly she looked up and something seemed to click into place as their eyes met. The nebulous feeling became a certainty.

'We've done this before, haven't we?'

For a second she thought she saw shock drag at his features. But the impression was gone so quickly she must have imagined it.

'You remember?' His palm covered hers as he leaned close.

'Not remember. But when we…'

How did she put into words the feeling she'd had again and again as they made love? Not familiarity. More a feeling of utter rightness. No, it was more than that. She'd soaked him up with all her senses, shared herself so thoroughly it seemed like even now they were connected, not just by the touch of his hand on hers, but by something deeper she already knew at the most fundamental part of her being.

Surely first-time lovers couldn't reach such transcendent pinnacles?

'When we have sex…' She felt his fingers thread through hers. 'It feels like it's new, but not new. Does that make sense?'

The teasing smile he'd worn as he carried breakfast was gone, replaced by a gravity that caught her breath.

'It does.' Conall paused, frowning, as if looking for the right words. He shrugged those wide shoulders and lifted her hand to his lips, whispering a kiss across her knuckles. 'Your instincts are spot-on, as ever. We've been lovers for a while.'

Greer folded her hand around his. She blinked, hit by an emotion that was part relief that she'd been right and part regret that she couldn't recall something so precious.

'Greer, are you okay?' He wrapped his other arm around her back, pulling her to him.

She was grateful for his embrace, sinking her head against

his shoulder, inhaling that wonderful scent of cedar, heat and male flesh.

'Yes, fine. Really, I am. It's nice to know my instincts were right. It's just…' She shook her head, feeling foolish. 'I wish I could remember.'

The amnesia had stolen so much, including, she suspected, some of her most precious memories.

He tilted her chin up and she lost herself in his warm midnight gaze. 'Don't fret over it. You'll remember in time.'

Greer stifled a protest that there was no guarantee she would. What was the point? It was something she had no control over.

'But however long it takes and whatever happens, I'm here, Greer. You're not alone. You can rely on me. Remember that.'

Her pulse quickened at the intensity of his stare and his words. Wherever this relationship went, she knew Conall well enough to understand he'd stand by her if she needed him.

Strange how good that felt. Better than good. All her life it had been her and her mum together, regularly moving, with her mother concerned Greer's father might locate them. After her mother died, Greer had been totally self-sufficient. She had friends but those friendships had never been really tested.

Instinctively she knew she could rely on Conall's promise.

'Thank you.' She pressed her lips to his, lingering at the delicious familiarity of them together. 'That helps, it really does. But why didn't you say anything?'

'When you came around in hospital you didn't remember anything about us together and you didn't seem to want more from me. I was cautioned against forcing your memories. The doctors stressed patience and one step at a time, so I held back.' He lifted his shoulders on a deep breath. 'Until my control snapped.'

Conall looked almost guilty and she hated that. All he'd done was try to protect her. She pressed her lips to his again, revelling in the freedom to do so. 'I'm glad it did. It's a relief, knowing.'

Given how hard he'd worked to protect her, fighting his own instincts all the time, it must have been tough for him too. 'Are you ready for breakfast?'

'I'm starving. But for details as well as food.'

'Fair enough.' He passed her a glass of orange juice. 'Freshly squeezed.'

'Juice making and coffee brewing? Such talent.'

Conall waggled his eyebrows. 'I thought after last night you might be impressed by something more than my kitchen skills.'

Greer stifled a laugh, the lingering shreds of regret about not remembering them together fading. 'I am impressed, don't you worry. I was wondering if later you might demonstrate some of that considerable talent again.'

His expression turned wolfish and though she knew he was playing, taking her mind off her loss, she was delighted in the idea of him eating her all up.

'That can be arranged. If you finish your breakfast. I don't want you fading away from lack of nourishment.'

Greer drained her glass of tangy juice and passed it to him. 'What have you got for me?' His gaze snared hers. 'I mean food. On the tray.'

She could get used to his teasing, hungry stares. Could definitely get used to sharing his bed.

As they ate she insisted he tell her how and when they'd got together. She'd always been scrupulous about not revealing her feelings for him.

'It was a week after we moved here from Perth. A Friday night.'

He took a mouthful of the cheese-and-herb omelette he'd made. Greer was in the process of demolishing hers. He really did have hidden talents. 'Go on.'

'I was working late and you appeared in my office doorway wearing that blue sparkly dress, the one that only comes halfway down your thighs.' He paused. 'You had your hair loose and said you were going to the Opera House for a drink before a performance. Jarvis Jellicoe had suggested it to you.'

Greer's forehead twitched. Jarvis was a sometime business associate of Conall's. She remembered telling him she was moving to Sydney, and him responding with a list of things she should do, including visit the Opera House.

'And?'

Conall put his empty plate aside and took her hand. 'I was jealous. For well over a year I'd fought my attraction to you, because we worked together and I didn't want to take advantage. But when you'd dressed up to spend the evening with Jarvis—'

'I was going out with Jarvis?'

She couldn't believe it. The man was a decade older and while she liked him, she'd never consider dating him.

'No. I got my wires crossed, but I only discovered that later.' Conall looked rueful. 'I forbade you to go. I blocked the doorway and lectured you about not mixing business with pleasure. And about company loyalty.'

Greer's eyes bulged. She couldn't imagine biting her tongue after that. 'What did I do?'

Conall opened her hand, tracing circles of delight on her palm, his smile wistful.

'You were magnificent. You marched up and poked me in the chest. You said your private life wasn't my concern. Then you reminded me of all the hours and effort you put into my success. You mentioned you'd already had a job offer from a competitor in Sydney, but if I had doubts about your loyalty you could always find me a new PA.'

She blinked, not surprised she'd stood up for herself, but that she'd been ready to leave the job she loved, and leave

Conall. But after so long yearning for what she thought she couldn't have, maybe she'd decided it was time to put distance between them.

'And then?'

He shrugged. 'I said you weren't allowed to resign. Then I blurted out that you were irreplaceable. I also said something about being damned if I'd sit back and watch you go out with Jarvis instead of me. That I'd wanted you from the day you first walked into my office.'

Greer's breathing quickened. How she wished she remembered this. 'And?'

'You accused me of making that up. You said you'd have known if that were true because you'd been attracted to me all that time. We were both so fired up it might have taken ages to sort out, so I took a short cut and kissed you.'

Greer's eyes rounded. She *definitely* wished she could remember that.

He grinned, his expression smug. 'You know that long sofa in my office?'

'We didn't! Did we?'

Conall took her plate and, without looking, put it on the bedside table. There was a clatter and a crash, but neither looked that way. Greer saw in his expression both amusement and something much more powerful. Something that made her yearning heart squeeze.

'Of course we did. We'd both been holding back too long. We've been lovers ever since.'

Greer had so many questions she didn't know where to start, but none were as important as the certainty Conall gave her with the grasp of his strong hands and the open emotion in his face.

'I know it's hard, not remembering. But I'm here for you and I'm not going anywhere. Remember that, Greer. You'll get through this. *We'll* get through this, I promise.'

CHAPTER EIGHT

GREER SECURED THE large towel around herself and left the bathroom. It was mid-afternoon and Conall had reluctantly excused himself to take a call.

The proposed Singapore deal was proving more complicated than they'd thought and he'd booked a long-distance discussion with a key contact there. Greer had offered to sit in but had been glad when Conall had suggested she rest instead.

It had been a momentous twenty-four hours, and though she felt a buzz of well-being, neither of them had slept much.

She was still adjusting to the situation. She and Conall were lovers. Had been for months.

His sincerity when he'd assured her he'd be there for her, through whatever it took to get her memory back, filled her with warmth and hope.

She wished she could remember what her feelings had been for him before the accident. She tried to tell herself she was on a high of sexual satisfaction. That these intense feelings wouldn't be permanent.

Yet it felt like her crush on the man had segued seamlessly into something far deeper than the physical. Even before they slept together, she'd been more than half in love with him. Way more. She'd never felt so much for any other man. Never dared open her heart like this.

She shook her head, her damp hair sliding around bare

shoulders. No one, neither Conall nor herself, could expect her to do more than take one day at a time.

But she'd give so much to remember. Regret filled her at not recalling that first kiss. That moment when attraction had morphed into anger and challenge, and their defences had fallen. Five months she'd missed.

How had their relationship developed in that time?

Or hadn't it? Was it truly purely sexual? Had they decided it would burn itself out given time?

She halted mid-step across the bedroom, her palm pressed to her suddenly churning stomach.

Maybe their relationship had been petering out before the accident. Certainly no one in the Sydney office had given any indication they knew she and Conall were together. Because they were both naturally discreet? Or because they knew what they had was time-limited?

But Conall's lovemaking told her that couldn't be the case. He was invested in this. Whatever *this* was.

It was like walking into a play in the middle of the second act and wondering what her lines were.

No! She refused to be negative. For weeks she'd let those missing months eat away at her when there was nothing she could do about them. Yet here she was, cherished by Conall in ways she'd never dreamt possible. Whether they had a future together or not, life was good. She had the job she loved and she had Conall.

Grinning, she pushed open the door to the wardrobe and found herself in a spacious dressing room. Conall's business clothes hung on one side in a beautifully crafted wooden robe. She made for the first set of drawers. Surely he'd have a T-shirt or something she could wear. She didn't want to put on her work clothes yet.

But as she moved further into the room a pop of colour

caught her eye and she saw that some of the hanging space on the other side was occupied.

Curious, she padded over on bare feet and found herself staring at a collection of women's clothes. The bright colour was a poppy-red dress. A colour she'd always loved but didn't wear.

When she was young her mother had dressed them both in neutral colours, as if trying not to draw attention to either of them. Greer had automatically continued that habit into adulthood, especially when she began working in the corporate sector. She thought she'd be taken more seriously if she looked serious.

Yet her hand lifted towards the bright colour. Whose was this? Riffling through the garments, she felt a jolt, as if from an electric shock. She paused, fingers clenching on the sleeve of a blue-grey jacket.

Greer gulped, fighting a roiling sensation in her stomach as she tugged it closer. Tingles ran up her arm and circled her neck, lifting her shoulders and making her gasp for air.

Holding the jacket to her, she collapsed onto the sofa in the middle of the room. She closed her eyes, bending forward, head almost at her knees as she fought sudden all-consuming wooziness.

Slow breaths out. She propped her head in one hand, the other hand still clutching the jacket. That was when she realised she recognised the feel of the fabric.

Eyes closed again, Greer lifted the jacket onto her lap, running her fingers over it. That sense of familiarity intensified. Without letting herself think, she undid the buttons and put it on, feeling it settle around her shoulders.

Another tingle lifted the hairs on her nape. Snapping her eyes open, she stood and spun around to face the full-length mirror. The jacket wasn't meant to be worn over a towel, but it *was* meant to be worn by her. She'd had the waist taken in because she liked the tailored look.

Greer gasped as she remembered taking it to a little shop for the alteration. Collecting it in her lunch break. Wearing it to work and Conall stripping it off her that evening. He'd kissed her throat and told her he'd been waiting all day to touch her. His voice was thick with longing and she'd been scrabbling at his shirt, tearing the buttons undone as they fell back onto a bed.

Not the bed here. The one in his penthouse.

Greer stumbled back to the sofa and sank onto it again.

Her mind whirled, disjointed images chasing one another, even snippets of conversation.

Her apology for ripping off his buttons. Conall's mock-severe tone as he said he'd have to make her pay for that, his smile slow and lascivious. Her surprise at seeing him, rumpled and sexy, sipping morning coffee on the penthouse terrace while he sewed the button back on.

His father, he'd said, had insisted all his children learn self-reliance. That included everything from changing a wheel to mending, feeding themselves and managing a spreadsheet. But Conall's expression had held a grimness that made her glad she'd grown up with her mother and not his father.

Heart racing, Greer let the memories come, slowly at first. A flow of small, everyday things. She tried not to direct them, but was stunned by how many featured Conall.

He'd been the centre of her world for so long, hadn't he? Now she was getting her answer to how she'd felt about him during those five months.

Her crush had become so much more. She'd tried to be sensible, but once she'd stepped beyond the constraints she'd set herself, it was like opening the floodgates. She couldn't remember everything, but enough to know she'd secretly opened her heart to him.

In each new recollection he was as he'd always been. Focused, hardworking, but with a lurking humour that made her smile. Now there were more intimate memories too. Of his tender touches and powerful passion. Of his husky-voiced midnight loving. His off-key singing in the shower. And his smile that turned her knees to jelly.

Greer breathed deeply, telling herself to be satisfied with the disjointed snippets for now. It was a start. A wonderful start. Proof that her brain was healing and soon she'd be back to normal.

Relief burgeoned. She was light-headed with it. She wanted to race to Conall and tell him. But that was a conversation to be had in private, not while he was on a business call.

Yet she couldn't just sit here. The excitement was too much. She'd go outside, explore the gardens and get some fresh air until he was free.

Greer carried the jacket back and placed it on its hanger. Her fingers brushed the poppy-red dress and she pulled it out, admiring the cut. The sound of laughter echoed in her ears and she remembered a buzz of happiness as she'd worn it. She and Conall had been out to see a play and had eaten later at a tiny Basque pintxos bar and restaurant in a narrow city lane. It had been romantic and fun.

That recollection decided her. She swapped the bath towel for the red dress, smiling as she twirled in front of the mirror. She looked forward to seeing Conall's expression when he saw her in this.

As she turned, something pale caught her eye.

Another dress, another memory? It couldn't be so easy. Yet she found herself cautiously approaching the item that hung by itself.

A step from the hanger she paused, doubt descending.

No, she wouldn't push her luck. She'd be content for now with the memories that had already surfaced.

Yet Greer stood, frowning. She had no desire whatever to touch the dress. In fact, cold fingers gripped her shoulders, pinching them higher as she looked at it.

Which made no sense.

Something more powerful than common sense kept her where she was, a flutter of nerves filling her insides and her palms growing damp as she pressed them to her middle.

It was just a dress, ending around knee height. Fairly plain, but its subtle sheen made her think of raw silk. That seemed fitting, since it was the colour of pearls.

She was turning for the bedroom when a voice spoke in her head. Conall's voice. *For you, to mark our special day.*

Greer's neck stiffened as her blurring gaze caught on a flat, crimson velvet box on a shelf beside the pale dress. A familiar box. Instead of reaching for it, her hands locked in a trembling knot before her and her heart dived.

She shook all over as she remembered opening that box and seeing a necklace made of four strings of pearls. Not plain white but every imaginable colour. Champagne, oyster grey, ivory, lichen green, dark green, silver grey and rich purple. Incredibly beautiful. Stunningly expensive. A statement piece.

She'd lifted her head to look at Conall. His smile was real, but there was something in his expression she hadn't been able to read. Something that looked more like pragmatism than pleasure.

The image disintegrated as understanding trickled in. What *special day* that dress and gift represented. Why Conall had felt it necessary and why she'd agreed.

And why none of that mattered anymore.

Greer's vision darkened at the edges and she braced her feet wider against sudden dizziness, pain exploding in her head and stomach.

Be careful what you wish for.

Now she knew how true that was. If only she'd known how lucky she'd been, forgetting everything.

She staggered into the bedroom then down the stairs, clinging to the balustrade, unsure of each step but needing to escape the room with the beautiful ivory dress and the terrible truth it had reawakened.

Finally she found a door into the garden and pushed it open.

Summer sunshine enveloped Greer yet she was chilled to the marrow. Straight ahead light glinted like mercury on the water. Eyes fixed on that, she stumbled forward, inhaling the scents of salt water and growing things. Vaguely she was aware of seagulls screaming, of large trees and banks of colour around her.

But with each step her senses dulled. By the time she reached the end of the private jetty everything was grey. All the colour had disappeared.

CHAPTER NINE

'THERE YOU ARE.'

The smile in Conall's voice hid his relief. The conference call had only lasted forty minutes yet he'd missed her the whole time. When he hadn't found her in the bedroom or any of the downstairs spaces he'd felt a horrible churning in his belly. As if he'd lost her all over again.

He lengthened his stride down the private jetty.

After everything that had happened he'd felt an almost superstitious fear of letting her out of his sight.

'Greer?'

She must have earbuds in. She didn't hear him approach.

She sat with her back to him, legs over the end of the pier, hair a gleaming dark swathe down her back. Even from behind she was beautiful. And she wore that red dress. He remembered the first night she'd worn it, when they'd laughed together at that little restaurant behind the quay. She'd positively glowed with happiness.

His heart lifted at the memory.

She'd be happy again, he promised himself. He'd make sure of it.

He stopped beside her yet she didn't look up.

He stilled, a prickle of warning tightening the space between his shoulder blades. He reached out a hand to touch her, then paused.

Greer's stillness was unnatural. He wasn't a man prone to

flights of imagination but he'd swear there was a force field around her, an invisible barrier holding the world at bay.

He hunkered down beside her but her head was tilted forward, her hair curtaining her face. Quickly he sat down beside her, all the while a bad feeling brewing in his gut.

'Greer.'

This time she heard him. He saw her minute flinch. Instantly his heart tripped and began to race. This wasn't good. What had happened? It couldn't be…

She turned her head and fear consumed him. Brutal fear and sorrow for the pain he saw. Her face was red and blotchy as if she'd been crying forever. Her eyes were glassy and twin streams of tears cascaded down her cheeks to drip off her chin, darkening her dress.

Conall felt his chest cave in, cracking under the weight of her distress. He wanted to gather her in and take some of her pain. Lessen her trauma. He *needed* to hold her. But when he leaned closer she flinched.

He froze, telling himself she was in shock. Yet a huge chasm opened inside him. A vast, familiar emptiness he'd dared to hope they might conquer.

In an instant that profound feeling of helplessness was back.

'When were you going to tell me?'

Her voice was a cracked whisper but he heard every tortured syllable. They felt like razor blades, scoring his chest and his throat when he tried to swallow.

She knows. Everything.

It was what he'd feared when he'd seen her so still, so… separate. But he'd told himself it wasn't possible.

'That we're married?'

In his peripheral vision, Conall saw the restless shift of her hands. One glance confirmed it was the nervous habit she'd acquired in recent weeks, rubbing her thumb over her ring finger. The finger that had for such a short time worn his ring. Each slide of her hand on that empty finger eroded something inside him.

'No. The reason we married. The baby.'

His stomach went into freefall, plunging deep and brutally fast.

He'd thought he'd hit rock bottom before, all his certainties about his inner strength splintering under the weight of trauma. Now he found he still had the capacity for more pain. He sucked in a sharp breath that couldn't fill his lungs.

His need to comfort her, and comfort *himself* by holding her close, was so great he had to wrap his hands around the wood of the dock, rather than touch her when she clearly didn't want it.

'I'm sorry, Greer. So sorry.' Even knowing it wouldn't solve anything, he felt better, finally being able to say it to her in person. Those unspoken words had been a terrible burden. Never before had he felt so deeply the isolation of his previous life. Or wanted to change it more. 'I've wanted to tell you but couldn't.'

She shook her head, bruised eyes holding his, and he wished there was some way he could take on her pain as well as his own.

'Couldn't or wouldn't?'

Conall stiffened. The fact that she hadn't been able to remember the past meant he'd been able to spend time with her, look after her.

Have sex with her. That's what she's thinking about, that you took advantage of her.

You made her spell out that she wanted sex with you, telling her all that mattered was what she felt in the moment. As if what happened before wasn't important.

He wished he could regret his need for her but couldn't imagine ever not wanting her. He couldn't wish it hadn't happened.

'I consulted the medical staff—'

'About *me*! I deserved to know.'

He inclined his head. 'Yes. But given the trauma you'd suffered, they thought it better you regain your memory naturally.'

Or perhaps he'd won the day, declaring he didn't want more trauma imposed on his wife before she was strong enough to cope with the news.

'It's been torture *not* telling you,' he admitted. 'Waiting for the moment you remembered. Fearing the day when I'd see you like this, hurting so much.'

He dragged in air, pain slicing his lungs as he watched her bright gaze cloud.

Greer had never seen such pain on Conall's features. Not that she could recall. For while she remembered key events, some things were hazy.

But there was stark emotion in his voice too, as if he were stretched to breaking point.

She knew the feeling. She couldn't get her breath. It was as if part of her were missing.

It is. Your tiny, unborn baby. Gone forever.

She hunched forward, arms wrapping around her middle as if that might hold in the keenest pain she'd ever known, fresh as the day of her miscarriage.

The joy of getting your memory back—being able to relive the worst moment of your life as if it had just happened!

Greer tried to sort her still-tangled memories.

All the time she was conscious of Conall beside her, close but not touching, giving her space and time to absorb everything.

She wanted to scream at him to leave her alone yet, at the same time, she needed him there. She'd done this alone once and couldn't face it that way again.

She remembered them becoming lovers. A pang of remembered joy slammed into her, thinking of that heady time when each day drew them closer together.

Then she'd realised her regular-as-clockwork period was late and taken a pregnancy test, telling herself she was jumping to conclusions. Two test kits and a visit to the GP put paid to that idea. It seemed accidents happened despite precautions.

Greer had been numb with shock, not sure how she felt. Starting a family hadn't been on her radar, not yet. She'd spent so long building her career and loved her work. But as the hours turned into a day, then two, she'd begun to feel thrilled as well as nervous.

Her feelings for Conall had been growing deeper and stronger. Now she found an infinite reservoir of love for the unborn child they'd created. She'd begun to imagine a future for them all.

She'd told Conall her news, and that was when harsh reality hit.

Of course he was shocked. They hadn't planned this. But as she waited for surprise to turn into happiness, she'd been disappointed. He'd asked if she were sure. He'd been solicitous about her health, arranging an appointment with a well-regarded specialist.

Later he'd asked if she wanted to see the pregnancy through.

When she'd said yes, he'd nodded and pulled her to him, saying she had nothing to worry about and he'd look after her and the child.

The child, not *our baby.*

Once he knew she was determined to keep the baby, he'd been outwardly supportive. But she'd seen no delight, felt no tremor of anticipation in him.

He hadn't wanted their baby.

He never came out and said it, but she knew him. There'd been a change in their previously easy relationship, a distance about him. He'd been tense, stressed, unhappy but trying to hide it.

When he'd asked her to marry him she'd instantly wanted to say yes. Greer knew her heart well enough to know it belonged to him, though she'd never said the words. But she'd demurred, saying she needed time to think about it, and that marriage wasn't necessary. Because he clearly felt none of the excitement she did at the idea of marriage. He'd proposed because he thought it the right thing to do.

But once Conall set his mind on something, he got it. Obviously he'd thought marriage the best option. He'd talked to her about all the reasons it would be good for their baby to be part of a family. The legal protections of marriage, so if anything happened to him, she and their child would be secure, not tussling with his family over his assets.

Greer wasn't interested in his assets, but he'd been adamant he wanted her protected. He made his family sound rapacious.

Was that why he wasn't enthusiastic about their baby? Had his experiences soured him on relationships?

Finally he'd convinced her. Or maybe she'd convinced herself, telling herself that when he had time to get used to the idea, things would change. He'd realise how much he felt for her, and he'd come to love their child.

They'd been married quietly on a private island off Australia's Whitsunday Coast. There'd been no press, no family and their honeymoon had been idyllic. Apart from the niggling fear that she'd made a catastrophic mistake, gambling that her love would be enough for all of them.

Back in Sydney life had settled into a routine. Conall was as attentive as ever, a colleague at work and a caring lover in private. Except there was an added dimension to him, a reserve that hadn't been there before. A distance when he didn't realise she was watching. As if he were caught up in unpleasant or difficult thoughts.

Then came his trip to the USA. Usually she'd have gone too but he'd insisted she stay and rest. She'd been feeling exhausted and hadn't argued, determined to be sensible about her health and her baby's. Yet on the morning he was due to leave Greer had felt out of sorts. She'd woken to discomfort in her lower back and wondered if she'd overdone her online yoga session.

Worse though had been the inexplicable sense of dread when she thought of Conall's imminent departure. As if she couldn't cope without him! It was so unlike her, but she'd actually asked him to defer the flight. She hadn't mentioned her physical discomfort, thinking it was nothing, only asked him to stay in Sydney.

Conall had held her hands and reminded her that the sooner he finished his business, the sooner he'd be back. He'd promised to streamline the meetings and return early. Greer had wanted to beg him to stay but knew how hard they'd both worked for that deal and how important it was to him.

His flight was only a little way across the Pacific when her back ache morphed into stomach cramps. Despite seeking help as soon as possible, when she left hospital later that day she was no longer pregnant. There'd been nothing anyone could do to save her baby.

Her breath hissed as she recalled the smells of blood, disinfectant and fear.

'Greer? Say something. Talk to me. Please.'

A familiar weight settled at the top of her back, Conall's palm. She wanted to tell him not to touch her, though the feel of his hand, gently circling, felt...welcome. It even seemed to take her headache down a notch or two.

She sat straighter, fixing her stare on the dark blue blur that was the shoreline on the far side of the harbour. 'I'm remembering that day. The day I lost my baby.'

His hand stilled. Did she feel it quiver? Before she could pursue the thought his hand resumed that hypnotic rhythm.

'I'm so sorry, Greer. Our child was a gift and—'

'Please. Don't.' She couldn't bear for him to pretend to feel more than he had. She *knew* he hadn't regarded her pregnancy as a gift. 'Not now. I don't want to talk about the baby.'

She wouldn't blame him for not loving their child but...

Don't you? Isn't that why you ran away from him? Why you moved out of his penthouse while he was still out of the country?

Conall was silent for so long she felt almost guilty at how she'd cut him off. Until she remembered how it had been between them. That he'd felt forced into fatherhood by her determination to keep the baby. When she'd needed him most he'd gone, so she was alone when she lost the baby.

It was one thing for him to regret her miscarriage. He wasn't unfeeling and he clearly realised how devastated she'd been. But the idea of sharing her grief with him when he hadn't really cared about the baby felt wrong. As if it would be a betrayal of that precious life she'd once carried.

That was why she'd left the city after the miscarriage. She'd sent him a message straightaway, telling him what had happened and that she was okay. She'd assured him he needn't cut short his trip because she needed time alone and was going away for a while.

Then she'd switched her phone off, returning to the penthouse long enough to pack a bag and leave, placing the rings he'd given her and her key to his apartment on the hall table. Because surely it was over. He'd married her because he'd felt he had to, for her baby's sake, and now there was no baby. Presumably there'd be no marriage.

Pain tore at her throat and she strove to suppress more tears.

Conall's hand moved again, slower than before, smoothing up and down her spine. The movement loosened knotted muscles and she felt a ripple of something like gratitude.

'Where did you go, Greer? I searched and searched but—'

'To the Blue Mountains. A little cottage.' She'd taken several weeks' leave, effective immediately, trying to sort herself out.

'I worried about you.'

Something in his voice penetrated her misery. She turned to see him staring straight back at her, his eyes dull as if reflecting the searing pain she felt.

Her breath hitched. In the days following her miscarriage she'd half-blamed him. As if he'd have been able to prevent the miscarriage! And for not loving their child, or her, the way she wanted.

It was crazy thinking but at the time, overwhelmed by hurt, she'd felt so guilty and desperate enough to blame someone else. No wonder she'd craved solitude. It had been easier to retreat into herself, telling herself she couldn't rely on him.

Her mother had taught her self-sufficiency and since her mum's death, Greer had learned not to rely on anyone but herself. That was a large part of the reason she'd hunkered down alone after the miscarriage. She didn't lean on others.

'I'm sorry.' Her voice cracked. 'I should have contacted you. I wasn't thinking clearly.' Even now, that time in the quaint cottage was a blur.

'I can barely imagine. I was just relieved when you reappeared.' His voice was as strong and sure as ever but with an unfamiliar quality that made her heart clutch and her shoulders brace.

Because now she saw he'd suffered too.

In the weeks following the miscarriage she'd told herself he was okay. He hadn't wanted their child, and hadn't been emotionally invested, so he wouldn't grieve. He didn't love *her*. They were *close*, intimate, connected, friends with wonderful benefits. But he'd never so much as hinted at deeper feelings for her.

He'd viewed what they had as an affair and had no idea she loved him. Their marriage had only been to secure their child's future from potentially grasping relatives. The diffidence he tried and failed to hide made that clear.

So, logic had decreed, Conall would be okay without her. He'd understand she needed time to herself. He'd probably be grateful he wouldn't have to pretend to a grief he didn't feel.

But reading his features now, she knew that wasn't the case. He didn't look like a man who was okay.

Greer stiffened. Had she been selfish, hiding alone and stopping all contact? She'd needed solitude but she could have contacted him again so he didn't worry about her.

She hadn't even told him when she returned to the city, choosing to stay in her own flat, because she couldn't bear to be in his penthouse where she'd been so incredibly happy, then suffered such devastating loss.

Greer hadn't been able to face questions and explanations, or the sympathy he'd feel obliged to show.

Instead, like a coward, she'd turned up for work on a day she knew he had back-to-back meetings and there'd be little time for private conversation. She'd told herself if she could get through the first day, they could go on from there.

'I'm so sorry I blocked you out, Conall. It was thoughtless of me.' She frowned, realising just how thoughtless and how unlike her it had been. 'I just couldn't...can't face talking about it.'

Slowly he nodded, his face a picture of concern. And something else, fiercely held in check.

That expression took her back to the day she'd returned to the office from the mountains. When she'd said the same thing, that she wasn't ready to discuss the baby.

His features had stilled, his face turning blank. All but his eyes, which hadglowed with a fierce intensity, revealing that she wasn't the only one battling emotion.

'I understand, Greer. It was a terrible time.'

His understanding didn't ease her guilt. Instead it compounded it. He was a wonderful man in so many ways. Even if he hadn't been jubilant about the child, he'd deserved better than to be shunned.

Greer struggled to swallow over the tangle of emotions clogging her throat.

'I won't push you to discuss anything you don't want to yet. It's enough that you're here and safe. And terrible as the memories are, it's an enormous relief that you're beginning to recover from the amnesia.'

He was so...kind.

Fresh tears prickled the backs of her eyes but she held them back.

'It must have been a nightmare for you,' she said slowly. 'When I went to lunch that day and didn't come back.'

The accident had happened on her first day back in the office. The day they'd had such stilted conversations, snatched between meetings.

Greer had sensed his frustration and had been glad to concentrate on work, or try to. At lunchtime she'd gone to buy a sandwich, only to walk into an industrial accident that would land her in hospital. Now she wondered if her mental state had made her too inwardly focused and less aware of danger.

'You have no idea.' His voice ground low. 'I thought at first you'd run away, because you didn't feel able to spend any more time with me.'

His eyes looked haunted and his strong features seemed stretched too tight, as if under immense pressure, making him look almost gaunt.

Greer's stomach twisted in distress for him. 'I'm sorry,' she said again. 'I didn't mean to—'

'Of course you didn't. Don't apologise. It wasn't your fault.'

He raked his left hand through his hair, leaving it dishevelled and ridiculously appealing.

She had an instant flashback to that morning, of her returning to the office, both dreading and longing to see him. She'd been torn between believing their relationship was over and fearing it. Her heart had stopped when she'd seen him through his open office door. He'd been prowling the room, phone to his ear, his hair a tumbled, sexy mess.

In that moment she'd realised that despite everything, she loved him as much as ever.

Some sixth sense had alerted him to her presence and he'd swung around, ending the call and tossing the phone onto his desk. The way he'd looked at her had made her sore heart contract.

'I went to your flat and the penthouse when you didn't answer your phone that day.'

Fortunately his mobile number was one thing she hadn't forgotten in the accident, since she'd known it for years. 'My phone was crushed in the accident.'

He winced at the reminder and instinctively Greer put her hand on his thigh, regret consuming her. Of course the accident wasn't her fault but it seemed wrong that she hadn't realised until now how much he'd gone through, not knowing where she was or what had happened.

She twisted towards him. If the circumstances had been reversed she'd have been desperate. 'Conall, I'm sorry you had to go through that.'

His hand on her spine resumed it soothing caress and his other hand covered hers, pressing it against his denim-clad leg. His touch, she realised, was incredibly reassuring. She'd been so caught up in his passion before, the way he used his body to make hers sing with delight, that she'd almost forgotten this. The simple comfort of his touch, his nearness.

Sitting here, reliving those terrible events, was more bearable with Conall at her side. Even her headache had eased a fraction.

His gaze held hers, unwavering. 'Not your fault, Greer. Besides, things are better now. We're together again, and you're recovering.'

She stiffened. 'Together?'

His eyebrows rose then he looked pointedly down at where she held his thigh and he anchored her palm with his. Anyone seeing them would immediately understand they were intimate.

'Together.' His voice wasn't loud but it held a note of unshakable certainty.

In which case he knew more than she did. Greer didn't have a clue where this left their relationship.

'I didn't know any of this when we slept together,' she protested, trying to slip her hand away, but something, either his firm grip or her own wavering willpower, stopped her.

Conall angled his head as if to view her better. 'When we made love,' he said deliberately, his words stealing her breath. Because for her it *had* been making love. Yet she couldn't afford to read too much into his choice of words.

'But you knew what had happened and I didn't.'

'You think that gave me some advantage?' For the first time she could recall—and she was recalling more by the second—she saw anger flare in his expression. 'You think it was *easy* remembering everything that happened but keeping it to myself, watching you struggle to recuperate, worrying your memory wouldn't return and being unable to help?'

Conall shook his head, his expression sombre. 'You have *no* idea how hard it was to stand back and not intervene. Not to try to force your memory or tell you myself. And that night in the office when you got changed into that sexy, blue dress…'

His stare became a scowl. 'Do you think it was *easy* to watch my *wife* go out for drinks with someone else?'

Abruptly his hand lifted from hers and he snapped his head away to stare across the water. Greer missed the warmth of his touch. It took a second to realise she was free to move her hand and reluctantly shifted it into her lap.

Conall's chest rose on a deep breath. 'I was trying to put you first. As for what happened here…' He jerked his head towards the house. 'I didn't lead you on. I told you what happened had to be what *you* wanted.

'Maybe I should have kept my distance. Would you be happier if I had? If the need to hold you, to have you, hadn't been too much to resist any longer? I'm not cold-blooded.' He raked both hands through his hair then turned, pushing into her space. 'I'm human, Greer. I did my best but I'm not ashamed of wanting you. You're my wife.'

There it was again. *Wife*.

She didn't feel like a wife. She felt untethered. No, that wasn't true. Every instinct screamed that she wanted to be with this man. She loved him.

But for him theirs had been a marriage of convenience. What was it now? Exhilaration whirled through her when he spoke starkly of his need. It gave her hope. Too much hope? All she really knew was that he *wanted* her physically and that he was a decent man who'd worried about her when she was unwell.

That didn't equate to love.

A low-grade headache had harried her since her memory started returning. Now it intensified, wrapping around her head and jumbling her thoughts. Stress or something else? Greer closed her eyes against the water's glare. 'I want to go home. My head's aching and I need pain relief.'

She felt him move and gathered her strength to do the

same, wondering if she could. Suddenly she felt far too unsteady, her limbs weak.

Sternly she told herself not to panic. It was probably just the shock of her returning memory, nothing more sinister. Yet for long moments she couldn't bring herself to attempt rising.

'I'll help you inside.'

Conall's voice came from just beside her and she snapped her eyes open to meet his concerned gaze, too close for comfort. She cleared her throat, about to say she'd manage alone, but the words didn't come. Much as she knew she needed space, she simply didn't have the strength now.

His gaze bored into her as if reading her body's devastating weakness. 'Don't bother to tell me you can walk,' he said, his voice tight. 'You can rest while I call the doctor, then we'll see if you need to be in hospital.'

With impressive ease, he scooped her up into his arms, holding her across his chest. She winced against the light as he swung around towards the house, and rested her head against him, relieved that he was here to help.

From this angle there was no mistaking the pugnacious jut of Conall's jaw. Silently she cursed her body for letting her down so dramatically. But, she vowed, she'd recover quickly. She had to.

'No hospital. Please.'

She still had nightmares about being stuck there, with the kind but firm staff telling her to be patient while she lay, terrified she'd never feel whole again.

Obsidian dark eyes claimed hers and she felt a rush of something hot and sweet. Did his expression soften? But if anything, the muscles in his arms and torso seemed to stiffen, pulling her closer.

'I'll do my best. Trust me, Greer.'

CHAPTER TEN

Conall woke to the feeling of being watched.

Not the nape-prickling alert that signalled danger. This was a wash of sensation, like the lap of a warm wave against bare flesh on a tropical beach.

He recognised it instantly. Greer. Looking at him.

Something surged high and hard in his chest. Delight. Her trawling gaze had always felt like a caress, even in the days when they'd both tried to stifle the unstoppable attraction between them.

His buoyant joy punctured. Those days had been easy in comparison with what they faced now.

Then they'd both struggled, trying not to break the taboo of an office romance, where the imbalance of power between them was so immense. Or so it would seem to the outside world. In reality Greer had just as much power over him as he had over her. Most of the time they worked as partners, and when it came to essentials they were equals, sharing everything.

Until she walked out on you.

Turned her back without a second thought and left you frantic with fear.

The only other time he'd felt anything like that terror was as a small child, told by strangers that his mother was dead. He'd been taken into care then sent to a father he didn't know, all the time struggling to comprehend that his mother had left him.

For Greer to abandon him like that proved she hadn't been herself. The woman he knew was capable yet caring, tender and generous. Yet she'd left him in limbo for weeks, wondering if she were okay... If she were even alive. He'd been frantic about her, and hurt that she'd walked out.

Adrenaline rushed through his blood at the memory, making his heart pound faster while the remembered taste of terror, like rust and blood, filled his mouth.

He'd been frantic, wondering if she'd been so distraught after losing the baby she might harm herself.

He'd told himself Greer wouldn't do that. But he'd never thought her capable of disappearing as if he meant nothing to her. That had cut deep.

He'd been desperate to get back to her in Australia, then desperate to find her and keep her safe. He felt that same urgency now. To fix things. To heal them.

Conall took his time stretching out the kinks acquired from a night in a chair not built for someone his height. When he opened his eyes it was to see that lapis lazuli gaze whip away towards the morning light filtering around the curtains.

'How do you feel? How's your head?'

She looked at him then and at least he couldn't see that haze of pain that had clouded her eyes yesterday. 'Good, thanks.' Then, as he continued to stare, she lifted one shoulder, her mouth forming the tiniest moue, as if regretting being caught out. 'A lot better at any rate. Thick in the head but it's not throbbing anymore.'

He nodded, relieved that at least she'd stopped pretending. 'That's great news.' She didn't want to return to hospital, but any sign of problems and he'd have no compunction taking her. 'Hungry?'

'I am, but I'll wait until I'm home.'

It was a slap in the face. Did she realise how that sounded, or wasn't she thinking?

Only years exposed to the cutthroat business world, first in his father's home, then working for himself, allowed Conall to mask his emotions.

'You really want to do this now?' He'd hoped things would be easier today. He should have known better.

'Do what?'

She pushed herself up in the bed, flinging back the bedclothes as if about to rise, only to stop. Wide-eyed, she surveyed the midnight-blue silk-and-lace nightgown she wore. It was provocative and skimpy, drawing attention to every feminine curve.

Conall remembered the first time she'd worn it, sashaying out of their bedroom, a gurgle of laughter spilling from her throat as the plate he held slipped from his grasp.

The memory faded as Greer wrenched the sheet high enough to tuck under her arms, scooting back to sit against the head of the bed.

'I sold the penthouse. This is home now.'

Greer licked her lips. 'I meant my apartment.'

'We're married, sweetheart. Remember?'

He watched her eyes round as if the endearment surprised her. Every hair on his body stood on end at the realisation of how far she'd receded from him. After everything they'd shared it was the cruellest blow of all.

Conall recalled her words yesterday. Her first thought hadn't been about their relationship but the baby. His jaw clenched as a beat of pain rose in his body. He understood, of course. But what scared the hell out of him was her dismissive tone when she'd referred to their marriage, spelling out that her pregnancy had been the only reason they'd wed.

She'd spoken of losing *her* baby, not *their* baby. He told himself that was natural, yet it didn't bode well. Heaviness settled in his belly, cold and hard.

It was only with the news of the miscarriage, while he was

so far away he was unable to reach her, that it had truly hit him how much the pregnancy meant to him.

He'd never forgive himself for leaving her that day.

They'd lost their child. A child he'd have cherished as his father had never cherished him. 'But I don't feel married. I—'

He didn't want to hear it. Not now. 'This isn't just about you, Greer. There's an *us,* remember?' Her eyes rounded as if stunned but this had to be said. 'The only reason we didn't live together for the last few weeks was so you could gradually take up the threads of your life. Without facing the trauma of what happened straightaway.'

Now Conall wondered if that had been a mistake.

She blinked, her lip wobbling for a second before she got it under control. Conall ached for her. He wanted to fold her in his arms and not let her go but this was non-negotiable.

'I need space. Time alone.'

She voiced his greatest fear.

Even rumpled and with a crease down one lean cheek where he'd slept with his head against the back of the chair, Conall looked so good she had to work to still the quiver of need deep inside.

Greer wanted so badly to be in his embrace. Part of her craved a return to the morning before when she'd found magic in his embrace and his body melding with hers. But the devastating reality she'd woken to this morning, the memory of her miscarriage, meant that what she wanted most was the simple comfort of his company.

That was what scared her most. Because what future was there for them?

With the loss of their child, what was at the heart of their marriage? For her part, love. But she'd seen Conall's reaction to her pregnancy and understood that being a father wasn't a goal for him. It was an obligation he'd accepted because he believed he had to, despite the fact she didn't fit the mould of a billionaire's wife. They came from different worlds that rarely intersected.

Just as she knew his concern for her was based on doing the decent thing. Love hadn't been mentioned when he'd proposed. He'd looked stern, not excited at the prospect of marriage and a child. At least he hadn't insulted her by pretending to feel more than he did. If he'd loved her might he have stayed that fateful day when asked?

But having been pregnant, having begun to imagine a future with her own family, hers and Conall's, Greer realised that was what she wanted for herself. Not just the career she'd focused on for so long, but children. Family. A real home. Somewhere to settle and put down roots. Build relationships. To surround herself with love.

'There's space for you here.' His rough voice interrupted her thoughts. 'I won't crowd you, Greer, but I don't want you to be alone.'

'I'm perfectly capable—'

'That's not in question. You're the most capable person I know. But sometimes being alone with only your own thoughts and no circuit breaker isn't the best option. You were by yourself in the mountains, but I don't think the solitude helped. Did it?'

She frowned. Much of her time in the cottage had been a blur of pain. She'd gone over and over what she might have done to precipitate the miscarriage or prevent it. Even told herself it wouldn't have happened if Conall had stayed with her.

She *hadn't* felt better when she returned to Sydney and work. She'd just known that she had to make a change, move forward and try to concentrate on things other than her grief.

'Only a little,' she admitted.

Her breath caught as memory lodged, of her first night in the cottage. How she'd craved Conall's arms around her, the simple, human connection. How much it would have meant to have his deep voice whispering reassurance, his strength supporting her. Instead he'd been half a world away and she'd felt cut off from everyone and everything.

'I thought as much.' His deep voice rumbled through her. 'Those weeks alone were the bleakest of my life.'

Her gaze caught his, widening in shock as she read the truth in his eyes. It was hard to believe his connection to the baby was so strong. No, he'd been worried about *her*.

'I don't want you to be alone anymore, Greer. *I* don't want to be alone.' His crooked smile that tugged something in her chest. 'It's a big house. You can have this suite to yourself if you really want.'

His gaze bored into hers as if compelling her to admit she'd rather share with him. When she said nothing his smile disintegrated. 'I'll move into another suite. I'll be nearby when you need me and when you're ready, we'll talk.'

She swallowed, her throat dry. The last thing she wanted was to talk about the miscarriage. What she *wanted* was to throw herself into his arms and pretend nothing bad had happened. To luxuriate in the comfort of his embrace while she grappled with grief and her jumbled emotions.

'I…' Greer bit her lip, fighting opposing impulses.

But she knew from the set of Conall's jaw that he wouldn't give up.

She remembered him fussing over her when she came out of hospital with amnesia. And before that, after she found she was pregnant, not letting her carry anything or get too tired.

The man was a born protector.

She grimaced, her eyes squeezing tight shut. He'd have made a wonderful father.

'Greer?'

Shock jolted through her as she felt the softest caress on her cheek. So light she almost wondered if it were real.

But there was no mistaking the feel of his knuckles brushing her face. For the tiniest second she wilted against his stroking fingers, posture relaxing and head leaning towards him.

Even that barely there touch held such power.

She snapped her eyes open and met his black stare. It shimmered with something she couldn't read but felt all the way to her curling toes. It wasn't sexual but it proved the connection between them wasn't dead.

Unable to hold that searing regard, she looked down to her twisting hands and sucked in a breath, realising what she was doing. The way she slid her thumb over one finger again and again. She'd only worn her wedding ring for a short time but she was massaging the place where it had been.

Because she missed it?

The thought shattered her. She wasn't ready to deal with her feelings for her husband.

But running away hadn't helped, had it?

Finally she forced out the words. 'Thank you.' She cast a look his way, careful not to meet his eyes. 'I'll stay.'

She just hoped she wasn't making an enormous mistake.

Days later Greer sat on the terrace, finishing the mango-and-coconut cake Alice had served with her afternoon tea.

Initially Greer had felt uncomfortable around the housekeeper. She'd never had staff, and wondered what the woman must think about a wife turning up out of nowhere.

But Alice was warm-hearted and practical, a soothing presence whose calm efficiency went a long way towards making Greer feel at home in Conall's stunning home. She couldn't think of it as hers. Yet each time she woke to that wonderful view, padded through the gracious, comfortable rooms or strolled in the gardens, she felt some of the tightness around her chest ease. Glimmers of lightness pierced the gloom of loss and hurt.

Conall had been right, insisting she stay.

It wasn't just the peace here, but the company. He'd given her space but had worked mainly from home and she was constantly aware of him nearby. They ate together and Greer discovered that, far from dreading his presence, she looked forward to it.

Her emotions were so muddled!

Today, dissatisfied with reading or lazing in the pool, she'd started working again.

She'd spent the morning in the room adjoining Conall's home office, and after the first hour they'd settled into a familiar rhythm. Each had their own tasks but with the door open between them they often consulted and even spent half an hour strategising on a new investment opportunity.

It had been just what she needed. To feel competent and, she realised, less alone. She enjoyed her work and it was good to have something positive to focus on.

A noise made her turn her head and there he was, ridiculously breathtaking in the suit he'd worn to a meeting in the city.

Her heart seized for a second before fluttering back into something like a regular beat.

Surely she shouldn't still react to Conall with such breathless enthusiasm. But her awareness of him was as strong as ever, if not growing. Their passionate sojourn last weekend had amplified all her restless yearning. Or maybe it was those memories of the months they'd spent together, barely out of each other's sight.

He'd been easier to resist when she had no recollection of the bliss she found in his arms.

Conall shrugged out of his jacket and tugged his tie loose, giving her a blistering smile that made her bones melt. He took a seat beside her and the blood fizzed under her skin. She tugged her gaze away as he undid his cuffs and rolled them up to his elbows. Something about those powerful forearms always made her feel like her insides were melting.

'Alice made coconut-and-mango cake?'

Greer looked at her half-eaten slice rather than stare hungrily at the man she was trying to hold at a distance. It was hard, now, to remember why that distance had seemed so important.

'Would you like some?' She pushed her plate across the glass-topped table.

'At the risk of turning into my father, I might just do that. Thank you.'

He took a bite. His expression changed and suddenly she remembered him tasting *her*, savouring her body as if she were the sweetest treat.

Heat settled low in her body and she shifted, trying to ease that ache between her thighs. She watched the muscles move in his throat and her nipples hardened.

Greer folded her arms, trying to hide her reaction. 'What did you mean about the risk of turning into your father?'

Conall licked frosting from the corner of his mouth and she had to look away. 'He's a big man, not just in size but in other ways too.'

'He's certainly got a forceful personality.'

She remembered the man in Perth. He'd dominated the conversation with his booming voice and an attitude that proclaimed him the most important person at the function.

Conall's eyes narrowed. Was he too remembering that event? The way Fraser Abercrombie had all but ignored her, after that one sweeping survey that made her jaw lock so she didn't demand he keep his eyes above her neckline.

'He has.' The affirmation didn't sound positive. 'He's loud and brash. His capacity for work and success are the stuff of legend. And he matches that with an enormous appetite for pleasure.'

Conall's mouth turned down and she read something in his eyes that made her want to change the subject, for *his* sake. Whatever track his thoughts followed, wasn't pleasant.

'It's as well he has a big frame to match his big appetite, if he has a weakness for cake. Though I did notice last year that he's beginning to grow portly. But I don't think you have anything to worry about. You rarely indulge and you exercise every day.'

She heard a crack of laughter as Conall's expression morphed from disapproving to amused.

'With that ringing endorsement I'll risk another piece of cake.' He took another bite, watching her as he chewed. It felt deliciously intimate, seeing his dark eyes dance with pleasure. 'You're right. He has a sweet tooth. Desserts are one of his weaknesses.'

'But not the only one,' she murmured.

For so long she'd wanted to know more about Conall's family but he'd avoided talking about them, apart from that recent, disturbing revelation about his sailing mishap with his appalling brother. When she'd asked if his family would attend their wedding he'd said their marriage was no business of his family. His tone had made it clear he hadn't wanted to discuss the subject. A moment later he'd distracted her with a mind-numbing kiss.

But a kiss couldn't blot out the suspicion he thought his family would consider her not good enough. Which had fed her concern that they weren't marrying for the right reasons.

'You never speak of him.'

Conall's voice was gruff as he met her stare. 'It's not a topic I like discussing.'

In the past she hadn't pressed for more information because of exactly that reaction. Was it any wonder their relationship had proved fragile when they hadn't been able to discuss such basic subjects?

She looked away, that sense of connection they'd just shared withering.

After a moment Conall spoke again, his tone careful, and that intrigued her almost as much as his words. 'He's famous for his self-indulgence. Fine food and wine, expensive racehorses, expensive cigars, only the best whiskys and…'

Conall paused and she turned to see his mouth tighten.

'You don't have to—'

'I want to. You're my *wife*.'

He said the word with such deliberation it felt like a challenge.

She'd adored Conall for so long but had never felt like his wife. Because he didn't love her, and the way he shut down any discussion about his family or his past reinforced that. Why open up now?

'My father has five children by four different women. He's on his fifth wife now.'

Greer knew about the man, of course. He was a larger-than-life billionaire, dominating both the Australian and international mining industries. She knew about the multiple wives but Conall's expression made her wonder again what it had been like growing up with such a man.

'Your mother—'

'Wasn't one of his wives.'

Greer frowned. What she knew of Fraser Abercrombie came from business articles. She'd never read the biography that came out a few years ago. Perhaps she should have. 'But you have the same surname.'

'When I was five my mother died and the authorities contacted my father. He had my name legally changed to his and I was raised in his house.' Conall's mouth twisted and Greer felt an answering corkscrew of tension in her stomach. 'He's big on ownership.'

There was no mistaking that sour tone. And the way he'd

said he was raised in his father's house, rather than that his father raised him, was odd.

'In that case I'm surprised he waited until your mother died to claim you.'

'He didn't know about me. She kept her pregnancy secret. She gave her notice and moved interstate.'

'Her notice?'

Conall's expression turned sombre. 'She worked for him, one of his junior assistants.'

Greer gasped, her hand pressing against her sternum. The similarities…

He nodded. 'It was one of the reasons I resisted you so long. Because of the need *not* to be like my father. I hated that you might feel pressured because I pay your salary.'

'I'd *never* think that! Not about you.'

It was the second time he'd voiced concern about their respective work situations. It really must have bothered him.

She leaned across and grabbed his arm, wrapping her fingers around the bare flesh of his forearm. She might have doubts about their marriage now the pregnancy that cemented it was finished, but she knew Conall would never use his position of power to seduce or force a woman.

His warm hand covered hers and for a heartbeat she felt again that link, that understanding between them.

'Was that what happened to your mother? Was she pressured?'

Conall stiffened and Greer would have pulled her hand away but he stopped her, long fingers curling around hers, his thumb stroking the back of her hand.

'I don't know for sure. I remember her talking in the kitchen while I played in the next room. She spoke about my father. I remember because Abercrombie seemed such a strange name then. She kept repeating that she'd had no choice.' He frowned. 'I'd never heard her so upset. It scared me. I ran in and hugged her so she wouldn't cry and that's all I recall. But the memory stayed with me because I'd never known her distressed like that. It wasn't until years later that I began to put two and two together.'

Greer's chest squeezed in sympathy for them both. It wasn't proof, but she'd take Conall's suspicions over someone else's certainties any day. She wanted to wrap her arms around him as if he were still that little boy, and hold him close.

'It must have been tough going to live with your father.'
Way to go with the understatements, Greer.

His mouth kicked up in a crooked smile. 'It was…interesting.'

She offered a wry smile. In some ways they were two of a kind with their habit of locking emotions away.

The shadows in his eyes prompted her to change the subject. Much as she loved him sharing with her, she hated those shadows. 'I never knew my father,' she offered.

'He died before you were born?'

She shook her head. 'He was still alive when my mother was. But I don't know his name. She never told me and it's not on my birth certificate.'

'That's harsh. Did she—?'

'She was afraid of him. That's why his name wasn't on the certificate. She thought it safer that way. Whoever he was, she spent her life hiding from him.'

Conall swore, his hold tightening. 'I'm sorry.'

'I was lucky. I had a wonderful mother.'

Returning his concerned gaze, her throat constricted. He mightn't love her, he mightn't have wanted their child, yet he'd tried to protect them both. Every instinct screamed that Conall would have made a wonderful father.

Which made her yearn all the more for what couldn't be.

CHAPTER ELEVEN

A WEEK LATER Greer was in Singapore, accompanying Conall on a business trip.

Negotiations on the investments he'd planned there were nearing completion. Over the last months Greer had put in almost as much work on the deal as he had.

She was working full-time again, though in the last week it had been mainly from his harbourside home. Despite the all-clear from her doctor, her husband was cautious about her not overdoing things.

Her husband. When it came to concern for her well-being, that was how Conall acted. Which made the way he respected her demand for space both admirable and frustrating.

She was glad he abided by her wishes, yet frustrated because her wishes were in direct conflict with each other. Intimacy with him again would be dangerous, because she craved a love he couldn't give. Yet her craving for *him* undermined everything else.

Did he feel the strain of keeping his distance as she did? A week ago she'd have said he needed her as much as she did him, physically at least. But now he made it look easy, maintaining his distance.

Was his attraction to her fading? She shouldn't be surprised, after she'd walked out on him then held him off. And yet...

Greer looked at her bare ring finger, remembering the golden wedding band she'd left in his penthouse. And the solitaire engagement ring with the most stunning sapphire she'd ever seen.

Conall had returned them to her in Sydney but they were still in their boxes. Putting them on again would be a statement of intent she wasn't ready to make.

Much as she longed to resume their relationship fully, she wasn't sure she could cope with the idea of being Mrs Abercrombie. Not when she knew she could have his body and his protection but not his heart.

She remembered too that he hadn't been in a hurry to announce their wedding, saying that she needed time before the press attention began. He'd done everything possible to hide their marriage from the world.

But she'd been convinced, given his tension and his refusal to inform his family, that it was because she didn't fit his rarefied world. That she wasn't the sort of bride he'd choose.

Fed up with her maundering thoughts, she lifted her head and admired the vista from her spot on a garden bench. Conall was playing golf with Mr Lee, the man with whom he was negotiating, so she had this afternoon to herself. She'd elected to visit Singapore's orchid gardens, hoping the fresh air would clear her circling thoughts.

The place was glorious, with meandering paths and exotic plants. Orchids rioted everywhere in a profusion of colour, and as if that weren't enough, jewel-coloured butterflies drifted and hovered. Greer felt her spirits lift in the warm sunshine. Being somewhere new and vibrant helped.

She nodded as a woman pushing a pram took the other end of the long seat. Two children with the woman danced about, chasing a turquoise-and-black butterfly that flitted around a nearby bush. Their laughter filled the air and Greer smiled. Was there anything as joyful as a child's laugh?

Greer was turning her head away when her gaze snagged on the pram.

A pair of serious dark eyes regarded her from a tiny face. The baby wore a lace headband with a yellow bow. Her lips were a perfect rosebud that widened into a gummy smile.

Greer's heart cleaved in two. She snatched a breath, trying to quell the pleasure-pain that swamped her.

One little arm lifted, a tiny fist opening, starfish-like, to bat against the pram's mattress. Chubby legs lifted, kicking, and the baby gurgled, seeing the movement and clearly delighted. Then she looked at Greer, laughing.

It felt like every intense emotion Greer had experienced during her pregnancy, the awe, love, and finally the grief, rose in an engulfing tsunami. Her throat closed. The back of her eyes and her nostrils prickled. Tears welled.

A soft voice said, 'Excuse me, but are you all right?'

No, not right at all.

Greer gripped the seat so hard her fingers shook as she tried to pull herself together. Breaking down in front of strangers was not her style. She managed a crumpled smile. 'I'm f...'

But the word *fine* just wouldn't come. Instead she felt a hot tear spill and run down her cheek, then another and another. Where was her self-control?

It had disappeared with her child and her dreams for the future.

She dragged in a shuddering breath that felt like knives slicing her lungs and forced herself to speak. 'I lost a baby.' She blinked, hearing the unexpected words.

Greer tore her gaze from the chuckling baby to stare bleary-eyed at the two children running around the clearing.

'I'm so sorry.'

'Thank you. It was a miscarriage.' But the grief was still sharp enough to make her spill her woes to a stranger. 'I don't know why I'm blurting this out.'

'I understand,' said that gentle voice. 'I lost two babies that way.'

Startled, Greer swung her head around to meet the other woman's kind eyes. 'I'm sorry. That must have been…' She shook her head.

'It was. I don't think anyone understands how devastating it is to lose a child you're nurturing in your own body unless it happens to them. But my husband was wonderful. It drew us closer. Talking to him kept me sane.' She paused, reaching for the baby whose babbles grew louder. 'I hope you have someone to talk with.'

Another sharp breath. 'My…husband. But we haven't really talked. I was too upset.'

'Really?' She saw and heard the other woman's shock.

Slowly Greer nodded. Conall and she had barely talked about losing their child. He'd been stymied by her amnesia. Before that, and after, she hadn't wanted to watch him pretend to feel regret about the baby when the chances were he was relieved. His concern for *her* was real, but for the baby? She'd convinced herself he'd be a terrific dad once it was born but she'd never know now. For him the baby had only been an obligation to plan for.

Do you know that for sure?

He didn't want the baby initially but maybe his feelings changed. You never gave him a chance to say.

The idea slammed into Greer like a fist.

She *knew* he hadn't wanted the baby. Yet hadn't he deserved better from her?

You didn't give him a chance.

How many times did you cut him off from talking about it? You pushed him away, actually ran away.

You convinced yourself you knew what he was thinking without even asking. How much did you assume?

Her lungs seized as a monstrous idea hit her.

She'd grown up knowing her father was dangerous, a man incapable of loving either his wife or child. Had that translated into an instinctive mistrust of men? A readiness to believe no man would ever love her or want to create a family with her? Had her mother's experience stunted her own relationships?

From her peripheral vision she saw the woman reach out as if to touch Greer's arm then stop and pull her arm back. It jerked her from her whirling thoughts. She swallowed a tight tangle of emotion.

'Thank you for your kindness. It was…good to talk about it a little.'

Which stunned her. There was pain of course, but also relief, a feeling of pressure releasing.

She closed her eyes for a moment and drew a grounding breath. When she opened them it was to see the other woman holding out her baby to her.

Startled, Greer turned to find those kind eyes smiling at her. 'Please. Sometimes a cuddle helps.'

The woman trusted her with her baby? Did Greer even want to hold it? Inexplicable fear rose.

Then the baby's babble drew her attention and innocent eyes met hers. Gingerly, Greer took her, drawn by a force greater than any she'd known. She cradled the bub so carefully she hardly dared move, feeling the warm weight against her breast.

The little girl said something incomprehensible and waved her arm.

Greer carefully lifted one hand to stroke the soft skin of the child's hand. Instantly those splayed fingers curled around one of hers in a surprisingly strong grip. The baby gurgled then smiled, and Greer felt something shift inside, like a knot tugging loose.

Greer decided against putting her hair up for tonight's party. She gave it a final brush, then surveyed herself in her bedroom's full-length mirror.

She'd found the dress unworn and still in its plastic sheath amongst the other clothes in the dressing room of Conall's Sydney mansion. She didn't remember buying it—there were still some gaps in her memory—but one look had told her it would be perfect for a billionaire's party.

A vivid scarlet, it shaped to her body before flaring a little around her knees, flirting around her legs as she walked. The bodice was cut straight across the top of her breasts with a wide, square neckline and narrow shoulder straps. Tiny scarlet beads sewn all across the fabric scintillated under the lights when she moved.

She almost hadn't packed it. It was the sort of dress that drew attention, and back in Sydney that was the last thing she'd wanted. Yet impulsively she'd added it to her suitcase at the last minute.

Greer half turned and watched how the dress caressed her body. She looked confident and sexy.

The way she'd felt when she and Conall were simply lovers. Before her miscarriage. Before the accident that sapped her self-assurance. Before the doubts and second-guessing.

She pressed a hand to her stomach where butterflies the size of dragons swooped and dived. She might look ready to take on the world but she didn't feel it. Not yet.

But she would, she assured herself.

Something had altered today. Pain still shadowed her and she had serious doubts about her relationship with Conall. But she was tired of hiding, for that was what she'd done. Tired too, of expecting the worst. It felt like she stepped out of the miasma engulfing her.

She'd had a long, hard think about her situation and what she wanted. She loved her career but what she *needed* was Conall. The man who'd tried to support her even while she'd pushed him away.

So he didn't love her. But he cared and had refused to let her walk away from their marriage. Unlike her father, Conall was a protector. Surely it was possible caring might turn into more, if she were brave enough to put doubt and hurt aside. If she were brave enough to be more open with him. Greer wanted children and he hadn't but perhaps with time, that would change.

With time. Her mouth twisted.

All her life she'd worked hard, not taking risks but striving steadily to achieve her goals. Maybe it was time to take a gamble on the man she loved. Instead of pushing Conall away, she could fight for the future. He'd stood by her since the miscarriage despite her doubts. Surely there was something worth fighting for there? The idea terrified her because it meant risking her emotions all over again.

Not giving herself time to think further, she grabbed her purse and opened the door into the suite's opulent sitting room.

Conall stood, hands in his trouser pockets, looking at the glittering view of Singapore laid out before him.

He looked predictably mouthwatering in a tailor-made tuxedo and bow tie. His arrogant jaw was freshly shaved and she imagined how it would feel under her hands if she reached up and kissed him.

How it would feel tomorrow morning with a prickle of overnight growth that would abrade her sensitive skin if they—

Conall swung around and her fingers tightened on her silk purse, her breath sighing from her lungs.

'You look stunning.' His husky-edged voice made her think of whisky by an open fire. The timbre peppered her skin with goosebumps and warmed her to the core.

'Thank you. I believe red's seen as an auspicious colour so it seemed appropriate.'

She met his arrested stare and adrenaline spiked, making her pulse thrum. He didn't try to conceal the avid glaze of hunger in his eyes. Conall looked anything but immune and a great tide of relief filled her.

The way he watched her made her nipples tighten against the lace of her low-cut bra and the place between her legs soften. Because she was anything but immune to him.

'You're sure you're up to this?' He sauntered across the sitting room of their luxury suite, his brow furrowed. 'I want you at the meetings but this is going to be a big event. If you feel it's too much I'll understand.'

He stopped before her and she longed to reach for him. Not just because of the physical attraction humming between them. But because she loved him. That had scared her into hiding away with her grief which, she knew now, had done no good at all.

'I'm actually looking forward to tonight. I'm stronger than I look.'

It was only partly a lie. She was daunted by the prospect of attending one of Mr Lee's parties, famed the world over for their extravagance and the net worth of his rich, sometimes titled guests. But Greer didn't care about them, only Conall.

Slowly he shook his head, reaching for her hand.

Was that a flare of shock in his eyes when she didn't pull back? Guilt swirled at how far she'd withdrawn from him. But not anymore. She moved her fingers, feeling the steady pulse at his wrist.

'I've absolutely no doubt about that.' That deep voice curled around her, the most enticing caress. 'Greer—'

'Conall, I— '

A lopsided smile curled his mouth, and a long, enticing dimple grooved his cheek. 'You first.'

She bit her bottom lip and his eyes narrowed on her mouth, making her breath stutter, but she pressed on. 'There's no time now, but later, maybe tomorrow, I'd like to talk. About the baby.'

His tightening hand and the light in his eyes signalled pleasure. 'Whenever you're ready.'

The way he looked at her made her feel strong. Special. Maybe she could be that woman again, strong and confident. She felt that way tonight.

'What were you going to say?'

'Just that I had something you might like to wear to the party.'

He looked down, his expression turning sombre. She followed his gaze to their linked hands, his thumb rubbing her empty ring finger.

A sharp ache started up behind her ribs. Regret? This afternoon she'd thought again about those beautiful rings he'd given her, imagined slipping them on, a sign that she believed their marriage had a future.

She'd had an epiphany today, yet that didn't mean she'd been wrong about their convenient marriage.

But you need to give it and the pair of you a chance.

'Something to wear? That's intriguing.'

The smile dancing in his eyes chased the shadows from his face. 'Says the woman who complains my gifts are too lavish.'

He released her hand and pulled a small leather box from his jacket pocket.

Greer swallowed. Conall's gifts *were* lavish, especially to a woman from a humble background. That engagement ring had stolen her voice. As had the surprise trip by private plane last winter to one of New Zealand's most exclusive private ski resorts.

She loved his gifts. But they reminded her how different their lives were. They didn't just come from different sides of the track but from beyond a social and financial chasm that felt almost uncrossable.

Tonight, for instance, he'd be completely at home in a gathering of some of the world's richest people. All she knew about that milieu was what she'd gleaned from her work, liaising with their staff.

Her thoughts atrophied as he opened the box. He'd bought her hair clips, she decided after a stunned moment gawping. They were identical, each with a row of stars that winked and shimmered with the blue-white fire of diamonds. The design was delicate and utterly beautiful.

'Antique?' she murmured when she found her voice.

'Yes. They were made for a princess.'

'You bought them in Singapore?' When had he found the time? Until this afternoon their schedule had been full of meetings.

'No, I bid on them at an auction. They were delivered when I returned from my last trip.'

His last trip. The day she'd miscarried. Her head jerked up. Conall met her stare and this time she saw the emotion in his features. Emotion he didn't try to hide. Regret. Concern.

Maybe he thinks you're going to reject his gift, the way you've rejected him.

Greer swallowed hard, emotions brimming. She hadn't treated him well. She vowed to make it up to him.

'Thank you, Conall. They're beautiful. Utterly extravagant but stunningly beautiful.'

Heat blazed in those dark eyes. The way he looked at her made her heart sing. 'No more beautiful than you.'

Her mouth trembled. She felt momentarily overcome by the hope rising in her. Maybe, just maybe, he felt more than physical attraction and obligation. Or would one day. Swiftly she looked down, her hand hovering over the box. 'May I?'

He pressed it into her hand. 'They're yours.'

Conall put his hand to the small of Greer's back as they walked towards the towering bronze front doors of Lee's palatial home. Surrounded by manicured tropical gardens and beautifully lit, it was a lavish oasis in the teeming city.

Greer looked stunning, and she was his. He'd do whatever it took to ensure it.

That red dress clung to her body and he felt almost jealous. He wanted to feel her nakedness against his own. To sweep his hands over her and hold her tight.

But it was more than the dress. It was Greer. The way she moved, the way she held herself. The woman she was.

Her expression as she'd accepted his gift made hope soar that finally he was making progress, pushing past her barriers. *And she wanted them to talk tomorrow!*

Elation punched his ribs.

Under the lights of the enormous port cochere, the diamond clip holding back her hair on one side glittered. It drew attention to her profile, the perfect arch of her eyebrow, the angle of her cheekbone and the soft promise of her lips.

She lifted her hand to smooth her hair then let it drop. Her bare left hand.

That punctured his elation. She still wasn't wearing his rings. It felt like one step forward and three steps back with Greer lately.

Maybe it would have been easier if they'd announced their wedding to the world straightaway, instead of keeping it to themselves. Why she should act now as if their marriage wasn't real after all they'd gone through, he didn't know. But he'd had enough of that pretence.

'Welcome to our home!'

Lee and his wife stood in the door, personally receiving their guests, a warm gesture that he saw made Greer less nervous. From behind them came the buzz of voices and music. Conall smiled, returning greetings as he drew Greer forward.

'I'd like you to meet Greer, my—'

'But of course, I know the estimable Ms Munro.' Their

host shook her hand, smiling. 'My own assistant regards you highly, and we spoke recently.'

Before Greer could respond, Conall continued. 'My assistant, yes, but also my wife.'

With his hand at her back he felt Greer stiffen. He watched her exhale slowly, maintaining her smile.

Maybe he should have warned her. But then why? They were married. They both knew it could only be a temporary secret. They just hadn't been out together with people who mattered to them.

Initially he'd been overly cautious, not wanting to make Greer a target for the paparazzi, knowing how unrelenting press interest would be. And as for his family… He'd feared she'd be overwhelmed, maybe even regret agreeing to marry. After all, she'd hesitated long enough to make him fear she'd reject his proposal.

It was natural that he'd inform the Lees.

Plus it ensured the men here tonight understood she was unavailable. She brought out a possessiveness in him he'd never before experienced.

Perhaps it was time to remind Greer too that they were together for the long-term. Lately he felt she doubted it.

The Lees were effusive with their congratulations, especially on discovering they hadn't been long married.

'But you wear no ring,' Mrs Lee exclaimed, puzzled. She was an attractive older woman, elegant and with an obvious fondness for jewellery.

There was a beat of silence before Greer spoke. 'The fact is I'm not used to wearing them, especially the enormous engagement ring Conall gave me. I packed in a hurry. It turned out I'd left them in Sydney.'

At the other woman's gasp, she hurried on. 'They're safe where they are but I *am* wearing another gift of Conall's. He gave it to me tonight.' She turned her head, gesturing to the glittering stars in her dark hair.

The other woman exclaimed in delight, drawing Greer into the vestibule, talking animatedly.

Conall made to follow but his hostess shook her head. 'No, no. You men want to discuss options and deadlines. Let me introduce your wife to some of my friends.' She beamed at Greer. 'A bride, and so beautiful and clever too, if she's able to manage your office.'

At Conall's surprised look the woman laughed. 'I don't mean you're disorganised, only that you have a formidable reputation. Your wife must be very talented to keep everything under control for you.'

'She is.' For some reason his voice acquired a rough edge. 'I couldn't do what I do without her. She's *very* special.'

Greer turned, eyes locking on his, and he felt like he'd dived into an indigo sea. Warmth bathed him and he felt buoyant. How did she do that? His blood effervesced and his pulse quickened. He *needed* her.

Why had he brought her here instead of giving his excuses? They could have spent the evening at the hotel.

'Ah, newlyweds,' their hostess purred. 'It does me good to see the way you look at each other. Don't worry, I'll bring your bride back soon.' Then she ushered Greer past the vestibule's enormous fountain and fishpond and into the vast gold-accented room beyond.

Lee chuckled. 'You must forgive my wife's enthusiasm, but she really will look after your lovely bride. Now.' He held his arm out. 'There are people I want you to meet before our sessions tomorrow.'

Conall bit back a refusal. What had got into him? They were in Singapore to finalise this deal. Yet his mind was on Greer. He watched her move through the throng in the next room. Heads turned to watch her and he had to remind himself she was the most capable woman he knew, in the company of their hostess. She'd be fine.

'Of course. It will be a pleasure.'

Through the next hour or so, Conall kept an eye on Greer from a distance. Any sign that she was distressed or lonely and he'd be there. But she seemed to be enjoying herself, smiling and talking with every appearance of enjoyment. Their hostess led her from group to group, all women, and his tension eased at her happiness.

Conall felt a weight lift. She was beginning to feel better. He'd been worried for her.

Instinctively he turned to look for Greer but there was no sign of her. Excusing himself from a group discussing the Singapore market, he made his way through the crowd filling room after room. There were several red dresses but no Greer. Frowning, he made for the terrace. He couldn't see her and his pulse quickened.

From this vantage point he saw winding paths, lit by ornate golden lanterns shaped like dragons. He heard laughter in the darkness nearby. He was following the sound when a flash of red caught his eye mere metres away. Greer and... Conall halted in mid-stride, eyes rounding at the sight of a familiar figure.

Shock hit like a blow to the solar plexus. Then his eyes narrowed and he stalked towards the pair.

CHAPTER TWELVE

GREER HAD KNOWN almost from the moment he'd introduced himself that she didn't like this man.

But good manners overrode her instinct to walk away. So she'd agreed to follow him to the edge of the terrace, to a seat where they could talk without interruption and where, he said, they'd have a perfect view of the fireworks. He assured her Conall would find them easily before then.

Greer's first billionaire's party was lavish and spectacular. From the displays of precious jade, gold and precious antiques to the handmade crystal glass from which she'd sipped the finest champagne. From the who's who of guests to the extraordinary jewels and designer wear. Even the tiny canapes were exquisite works of art, carried on burnished trays by smiling, perfectly presented staff. As for the intriguingly lit gardens, she'd love to explore, but not with this companion.

Now, as Jason Abercrombie reached for her hand, Greer heeded instinct and pulled away, grateful she'd already risen from the seat and could step back.

'Now, now, Greer,' he said in a voice probably designed to reassure but which to her ears sounded smug. 'Is that any way to treat your brother-in-law? You don't need to worry about Conall. He's used to me taking things from him. Besides, he won't know unless you tell him.'

His smile bordered on a leer and she suppressed the urge to slap him.

Don't make a scene. You can handle him without that. No matter how much he deserves punching.

At first she'd seen the similarities between the half-brothers. The height, thick dark hair and air of confidence as if they owned the world. It was probably something they'd inherited from their father. But over the last ten minutes she'd been cataloguing differences.

Jason was thickset, his neck and head broad and bullish. Grey dusted his temples and he must be at least a decade older than Conall. But those were superficial differences.

Conall had always treated her with respect. But even in the gloom Greer could see the avaricious glint in Jason's eyes, as if she were some prize for the taking. He'd finally given up trying to pump her about Conall's business and his meetings in Singapore.

He spoke down to her, patronisingly assuming she'd got her job because Conall fancied her. He'd even asked if Conall had proposed because it was the only way to get her into bed.

Jason seemed to think that uproariously funny, saying it would be just like his prig of a brother to be undone that way. Then he stepped to block her retreat to the path.

As if that would stop her! She'd scramble through the bushes if she needed to escape his touch. But she wanted tonight to go smoothly for Conall. She refused to be a liability, drawing unwanted speculation and gossip.

Her fears that she'd let Conall and herself down in this unfamiliar milieu had faded. She'd found herself almost enjoying the night. Until Jason Abercrombie. But she hadn't wanted to snub Conall's brother and she *had* been curious.

Curiosity was overrated.

'You're very loyal, Greer. I applaud that. It's rare.' She repressed a shudder of nausea at his cynical appraisal as he loomed closer. 'But I'm not just interested in business, I'm interested in you. I see you don't wear his ring. There's no reason why we can't have a little fun together. If not here then—'

She snapped her mouth open to cut him down to size when a familiar voice drawled, 'Still pushing your luck, Jason?'

Jason turned and Conall walked past, jostling him out of the way without breaking his stride.

Jason Abercrombie might be a big bull of a man but Conall topped him by a couple of inches and the honed power of her husband's body contrasted sharply with the running-to-seed bulk of his half-brother.

Conall wrapped his arm around her waist and peered down at her. She knew that look. Concern.

'I'm okay,' she whispered, planting her palm on his chest, soaking up that delicious sensation of solidity and familiarity. Everything was better with him close. 'But I've had enough.'

'You're sure? If he's touched you or—'

'No!' Greer felt the restless energy vibrating through Conall and read the dangerous set of his jaw. She murmured, 'I don't want a scene. He'd like that. Don't give him the satisfaction.'

Eventually Conall nodded, his eyes never leaving hers. Yet instead of turning to speak to his brother, he drew her closer and dipped his head.

Without a second thought, Greer leaned up, pressing against him as their mouths met, and suddenly everything was all right. The kiss began gently but inevitably the long-banked fire burst into flame as he cradled her head and she opened for him, losing herself in the vortex of passion they created between them.

The taste of him, that rich woody scent and the feel of his arms around her were so dear and exactly what she needed. No wonder her hands clutched his shoulders as if never wanting to let go.

How, why had she kept her distance so long? Had she really needed time to clear her head or was she punishing herself?

Or him? Whatever the reason, distance wasn't the answer. Being with Conall felt as natural as breathing.

When they finally drew apart Jason was muttering something under his breath but Greer didn't listen.

Reluctantly she turned to face her brother-in-law. Discontent made his fleshy face ugly. It was hard to believe the two men were related. They were so different.

Conall drew her towards the path, walking between her and his half-brother. Scowling, Jason opened his mouth but before he could unleash any poison, Conall leaned across and said something in his ear Greer couldn't make out. She saw the older man flinch back, eyes wide with dismay.

Then she and her husband strolled across the terrace, his arm holding her close to his side.

'Let's find our hosts and thank them so we can leave.'

Greer looked up. Even under the bright lights, Conall looked at ease, as if nothing untoward had happened, but he held her so close she felt his rigidity. For a minute there she'd really thought he was going to flatten his half-brother.

'You're sure you want to go?' She glanced around the glittering crowd. Billionaires and powerbrokers were everywhere, even a couple of Serene Highnesses. 'Should we at least stay for the firework display?'

Obsidian eyes met hers with a look that made her fully aware of her feminine needs. It felt as if her skin didn't fit anymore. It was too tight to contain the need clawing at her.

'If you'd like to stay we can. I've done what I needed to do. As for fireworks...' His slow smile was an exercise in seduction. Her core turned molten and she leaned closer. 'We can manage those elsewhere.'

They were silent on the limo drive to their hotel. But, despite his fury over Jason's behaviour, and his impatience at being denied the satisfaction of felling him with one solid punch to his self-satisfied face, Conall's primary emotion was happiness.

For Greer had kissed him the way she used to. Without reservation. With no shadows of doubt.

Sheer elation kicked as adrenaline raced through his blood.

His wife was always the one who ensured everything went smoothly. He could be impatient and tunnel-visioned when focused on achieving his goals. After all, he'd learned at his father's knee. Patience and the ability to listen and consult had taken years of practice. Greer was the one who smoothed his rough edges, should they ever show.

But she hadn't given a damn about social niceties when she'd melted against him tonight. When he'd kissed her he'd have sworn she had nothing on her mind but *him*. All the guests could have been standing watching them and it would have made no difference. Greer *wanted* him.

And they'd held hands all the way back to the limo.

She must have been relieved when he'd interrupted Jason, but relief alone didn't explain her reaction.

He opened the door to the presidential suite and ushered her inside, watching the undulating sway of her walk in high heels with something akin to pain in his lower body.

His need for her was so great but he knew sex alone couldn't restore their relationship. That was what he had to remember, even when she paused to look at him over her shoulder, her smile a combination of hesitancy and a siren's invitation.

'A nightcap?' He moved closer, allowing himself the pleasure of stroking her hand, his pulse quickening at her little shiver of response. 'While we talk about Jason.'

That was a starting point, at least.

Her forehead wrinkled. 'You want to talk about him, now?'

Conall moved towards the discreet bar against one wall. The prickling sensation that ran down his spine told him she tracked every step.

'What I *want* is to make love with you. But it's past time we began talking, don't you think? Besides, I owe you an apology if not an explanation.'

He turned back, half fearing she'd retreat from him again. Instead her dilated eyes and parted lips proved she felt the same hunger. Relief filled his lungs.

'Whisky, please.'

Conall smiled. Neither drank much but occasionally at the end of a long day's work, they'd share a whisky.

He waited until they were seated and she'd taken a sip before asking, 'What did he want? I have a fair idea but...'

Greer shifted in the corner of the lounge they now shared, pulling up her bare feet. She shrugged and a myriad of tiny scarlet lights winked across her body. Conall swallowed.

'Information. He seemed to think I had no concept of confidentiality or loyalty. He wanted to know who you're seeing in Singapore, what deals you're negotiating.' She frowned over the rim of her glass. 'Did he follow you to Singapore?'

It was Conall's turn to shrug. 'I have no idea but I suspect it was coincidence.' He slid closer along the sofa, palming her ankle then circling the smooth skin of her leg. They needed to talk, but that didn't mean he couldn't touch. 'What else did he want?'

To his delight, Greer stretched out her leg across his lap. Their eyes met and Conall struggled to remember his train of thought. Carefully he smoothed his fingers over her instep before massaging her sole.

Greer's eyelids lowered as she sank into the cushions. Instead of answering she asked a question of her own. 'Is he always like that?'

'Greedy, entitled and infuriating?'

She chuckled and some of the tension wrapping around his neck and shoulders eased. If Jason had scared or hurt her,

Conall wouldn't answer for his actions. 'Yes. And stupid too, to think I'd betray you with him.'

'He wanted you?'

Of course he'd wanted her. She was beautiful inside and out. She was also the most effective, insightful person in his employ. He hoped that, over time, she'd take a much higher profile role.

Conall's hand tightened and she stretched out her other leg, offering a second foot to be massaged.

'It was a bit clumsy, really. He said he wanted me but he couldn't really have expected me to say yes.'

'You'd be surprised. An excess of self-confidence and wealth can be attractive.'

Greer's eyes narrowed but this time not in pleasure. 'He also said you were used to him taking things off you.'

Conall put his glass down with careful precision, then turned his attention to massaging her feet. He hated talking about his family. He preferred not even to think about them. But if he'd overcome his abhorrence and told Greer about his relatives perhaps she wouldn't have let his half-brother corral her alone.

'I'm sorry. I should have warned you.'

'You weren't to know he'd be there.'

'I knew you'd meet my family eventually. They had to find out we'd married sometime.'

Those indigo eyes held his steadily. 'He said another guest mentioned you were here with your bride.'

'If I had my way, neither of us would have anything to do with my relatives.'

'Does this have anything to do with why you kept our marriage secret?' There was an edge to her voice.

'Partly. I grew up in the full, intrusive glare of the public eye, and while things are much better now, I remember what it's like to have people turning your private life into news stories. I told you that at the time. I wanted to give you time before the press got you in its sights.' He frowned. 'Didn't you believe me?'

Greer shifted her weight as if to sit higher but he held her foot firmly, running both thumbs up the centre of her sole until she sighed and sank back.

'I did. But I also wondered if you thought I wouldn't make the grade in public as a rich man's wife. My background is so different.'

Shock gripped him. 'You thought I was ashamed of you?'

She looked away. 'I didn't know. You said it was to protect me but I couldn't help wondering. I'm your PA, remember? We come from different worlds.'

Conall stared, trying to process the idea. 'You're the most phenomenal person I know.' Her gaze locked on his and he *felt* her surprise. 'How could I be ashamed of you?'

But not everyone had been raised to believe the world was theirs for the taking. Greer wasn't shy or self-effacing. She seemed comfortable dealing with everyone, from colleagues to wealthy and powerful business contacts.

Yet one of her core competencies was the ability to hide her thoughts and feelings. He'd only learned recently how much she hid behind an air of calm.

'I'm sorry,' she murmured. 'I shouldn't have read anything else into your actions. But you took me by surprise when you suggested marriage. Everything happened so fast and I was playing catch-up.'

He exhaled. He remembered only too well her reticence about marrying and his secret indignation that she didn't immediately say yes.

For him their marriage couldn't have come fast enough. When Greer became pregnant and spoke of keeping the baby, maybe giving up her job to care for it alone, he'd realised how much he needed her in his life. He couldn't watch her walk away, especially with his child.

Conall knew what it was like to be young and vulnerable, without a protector. When his mother died he'd been shunted into his father's so-called care. If anything happened to him he wanted Greer and their child to have every legal and financial protection.

'I've never been ashamed of you, Greer, and I never will. I *have* wanted to keep you safe.' He shook his head. 'I should have explained better, especially about my family.'

'I'm listening.'

'My father has five children by four women and Jason's probably the worst, if you don't count my father.'

'Jason said you were used to him taking things from you.'

'Not for a very long time.' At her enquiring gaze he continued. 'The last one was my first serious girlfriend, when I was eighteen.'

'But he's years older than you!'

'Twelve years.' At her horrified stare he shrugged. 'I'm the youngest and there's a gap between me and the rest. But we were taught to be competitive at everything. Besting one of our siblings at something was applauded. Losing was weakness.'

'What did she see in him? She had you and he was so much older. And why would he do such a thing?'

Conall smiled, warmed at Greer's astonishment that any female would prefer Jason. 'I was a kid, albeit a kid with big plans. He was already established and very wealthy.'

Still Greer stared.

'My family isn't like others. When we were young our father never gave us support or love. He made the rules and we obeyed. People talk about strict disciplinarians but he was in a league of his own.' Conall had no intention of going into detail.

'For him, life is about winning at all costs. Triumphing over everyone else. Wielding power and accruing wealth. But he's short on ethics, happy to bribe or browbeat people. He moulded us into mini versions of himself.

'He supported all of us until we finished our education. But meanwhile we spent every vacation working without pay, and I do mean working. Jason was a jackaroo on a cattle station my great-grandfather established. I was a chainman for a surveyor working on a new road through the Pilbara.' It had been one of the harshest yet most beautiful environments he'd ever experienced.

'He wanted to toughen us up and above all he fostered competition between us. People ask who will inherit his business. What no one outside the family knows is that it will go to the one who has the most net wealth. Everyone's scrambling to make their own business bigger and better. He set up a perpetual competition between us and believe me, it's dog eat dog.'

Conall had never shared that with anyone. But it felt good, telling Greer, as if he bared some shameful secret he'd been too scared to reveal, only to find she didn't judge him for it.

For instead of retreating, she slid her feet out of his hold and moved to sit beside him. 'You're in competition with each other? All the time?'

'For years I was. That was drummed into me—succeed at all costs, beat everyone else, come out on top. It was a way of life for all of us. But a couple of years away from the old man and things changed. *I* changed.'

Conall watched her closely, wondering if she'd believe him. 'I realised I have no interest in inheriting his money. I know some of the rules he broke, the palms he greased and the people he took advantage of to get that money. I opted out. I go my own way.'

'But your siblings don't?'

He lifted one shoulder. 'They don't confide in me. We're not close.'

Greer's sputter of laughter made his own mouth tug up in a rueful smile. 'That's an understatement!' Then her expression sobered. 'It's hard to take in.'

'You can understand why I don't discuss it. Even as a child I knew we weren't *normal*.'

Her hand closed, warm around his. 'You shouldn't lump yourself with your family. You're not like them.'

Thank God she thought so! Since she'd pushed him away he'd begun to wonder if she saw the ugliness he'd tried so hard *not* to let grow inside him. He strived *not* to be like his old man but sometimes, when he was strategising his next commercial move, focused totally on winning, he wondered.

Was it any wonder he hadn't shared this with Greer?

'Jason's trying to stymie your business deals here?'

'Or somehow cut me out and take my place.' Conall saw her dismay and curled his hands around hers. 'It's okay, Greer. Lee might have invited him to the party but he wouldn't work with him. Jason doesn't have what it takes. He's not me.'

Her eyes danced. 'I've always liked your confidence.'

He was confident all right, when it came to sealing a profitable deal.

But you haven't been so successful in your personal life, have you?

Greer hadn't jumped at the chance to marry him. And instead of turning to him when tragedy struck, she'd left him. He'd never felt so alone. Even now their marriage didn't feel secure. They teetered between needing each other and treating each other like strangers.

No more.

They had so much to discuss, but at least they'd begun talking. Greer had listened and not turned away from the ugliness he'd kept to himself so long. He hadn't shared that because he felt it tainted him.

'Is that what you like about me?' He leaned close, letting his intent show. He lifted her hand and peppered it with kisses.

'Not all.' Her eyes darkened. 'No one kisses like you.'

That was better.

Conall kissed his way up her arm, pausing at that sensitive spot in her elbow, making her squirm and sigh. Goosebumps prickled her skin as he reached her shoulder and grazed her flesh with his teeth. She shivered in response.

He put his hands on her knees, pushing her dress higher. Her thighs were warm and smooth. 'Just my kisses?' He nuzzled his way across her collarbone.

Greer's head fell back as he kissed her throat then worked his way to her ear.

'What else do you like?'

She cradled his head, pulling him closer, her tender need a balm to his wounded soul. A flush warmed her features and her slumbrous expression made his rising erection heavy.

'Everything. With you.'

Not breaking her hold, he levered himself off the sofa enough to swing her legs along it then settle over her, in the process shoving her skirt to her hips. He found damp silk between her thighs and pressed the heel of his hand there. Her hips rose, pelvis twisting against his touch.

His pulse catapulted higher. 'Tell me what you like, Greer. What you want.'

'You, hard inside me until I can't feel anything else.'

Her words unleashed everything he tried to hold back in one sudden, searing blast. She didn't stop there, holding his gaze as she breathlessly described how she wanted him to take her the first time, and the second. And what she wanted to do to him.

Conall couldn't remember pulling back but found himself kneeling astride her, fumbling at the fastening of his trousers, simultaneously yanking his wallet from the pocket, scrabbling for a condom.

'Undo your dress.'

His voice was so ragged as to be almost incoherent. But she reached behind her as he shoved his trousers down. He was rolling on the condom as Greer pulled her arms free of the dress and shoved it down to her waist.

Incendiary heat blasted Conall. That excuse for a bra was pure sin. Strapless, made of see-through lace and barely covering her nipples, it took him past careful, beyond needy and into must-have-her-or-die.

He froze, not trusting himself.

Greer looked at his bobbing erection and pouted. Pouted! 'You haven't changed your mind?'

A rough growl filled the air. He realised the noise came from his constricted throat. Words were beyond him.

Taking his weight on his arms he moved off the sofa, provoking a protest from her.

He pulled her up to a sitting position and swept her legs off the seat and onto his shoulders as he knelt. One tug, the sound of tearing, and her underwear was gone.

Conall didn't pause to acclimatise her to his touch. He went straight to her core, tracing folds, finding her nerve centre and caressing her there, feeling that delicious quiver of response as her muscles tightened and her pelvis lifted against him, so beautifully needy.

Her arousal scented the air. She tasted like every dream come true and when she shouted his name, her fingers tight around his skull as she shuddered and quaked then dissolved, Conall felt like he'd burned off some of the doubt he'd carried that he could win her back.

It was a start.

'More,' she breathed.

'Yes.'

He was already moving, sliding her thighs off his shoulders as he straightened. She looked gloriously wanton in the remnants of her red dress, yet—did he imagine her eyes held something other than lust?

Any hope he'd had of finding restraint faded. He'd wanted to taste her breasts and tease them free of that barely there bra. Later. His groin was so tight he felt like he was about to combust.

Sliding his hands beneath her, he tilted her up towards him. Greer reached down, guiding him and he thrust home. She took him as deep as he could go. Until there was nothing but her, this woman who eclipsed everything else.

Conall was drowning in a sea of lapis lazuli, waves lapping around him, warm and silky smooth.

For a moment he held there, awed, until stillness was impossible. They moved together, Greer's brow knotted in concentration even as her eyes glazed. Another thrust and the gentle waves became a maelstrom of pleasure, pulling him deeper, harder, drawing the very essence of him.

Greer shouted his name, fingers digging into his shoulders and still she held his gaze so he saw everything she felt, *felt* everything she felt as they exploded, shattering into oblivion.

Except it wasn't oblivion, because she was there.

The woman he loved.

Conall tasted the confession on his tongue, opened his mouth to share it, but through the blur of ecstasy, reason returned. He couldn't blurt the truth suddenly. He didn't want to scare her off. Every time he'd thought they were on solid ground, he'd almost lost her.

He needed to understand why she'd run from him before. Why she tiptoed around the idea of marriage. Then he'd overcome her fears and change himself to be the man she wanted, a man she trusted. Not a man she hid from.

He'd win her and keep her. Whatever it took.

CHAPTER THIRTEEN

Greer stretched languidly, feeling the heavy silk of her robe slide across bare skin. She shot a glance towards Conall, munching on chilli ginger prawns. Instantly, as if sensing her regard, he turned his head, gaze meshing with hers so that slow-coiling heat stirred anew in her stomach.

He was bare-chested and she watched the play of his muscles as he ate. Just the sight of him beside her at the small table was sensual, arousing.

They sat in a pool of light. Beyond them, the open doors to the terrace let in the balmy, humid night air and a view of city lights. It was well past midnight but neither had eaten at the party and they'd woken hungry.

She could get used to a private chef preparing five star gourmet feasts on call.

But it wasn't the food or the luxury service on her mind. It was Conall. Tonight he'd revealed a history that made her ache for the grieving child he'd been, taken from a loving home into a place where no child belonged. She sensed he'd held back a lot more than he'd revealed in order to spare her.

His story had made her upset and protective. She'd dearly love to tell Fraser Abercrombie and the world some home truths about his unfitness to be around children. He didn't deserve a family.

'You look very fierce, sweetheart. What's wrong? If it's

Jason, don't worry. I'll make sure you never have to deal with him again.'

There it was again, his protectiveness. How was it Conall had grown into a caring, decent man so unlike his loathsome brother? They'd both suffered the same sort of upbringing. Such a childhood must have affected them both.

An idea lodged in her brain. The more she pondered the more she wondered if it could be true. Could his difficult upbringing have made him averse to having a family of his own?

'Why didn't you want our baby, Conall?'

Finally the words were out. The ones she hadn't dared say before, when she'd decided she'd rather have Conall as a husband than not at all. It had been wrong accepting his proposal, knowing he didn't want a child. But she'd been selfish and needy. Now she understood they had no real future without honesty. She had to understand what made him tick.

He stiffened, shunting back from the table. 'I *did* want our baby!' His voice throbbed with feeling and she saw a pulse pound at his temple. 'Getting your message that you'd miscarried, then coming home to find you gone...' He ploughed his hand back through his unruly hair. 'It was the darkest time of my life. I'll never forgive myself for leaving that day.'

Greer felt her eyes widen. He'd told her he was sorry about the baby, but in such terms she'd assumed he felt sorry for *her*, not his own loss. This was so much more. 'You weren't to know I'd miscarry. *I* didn't know.'

'But you needed me.'

'I wish you'd been there, Conall. But neither of us were to blame.' It had taken her long enough to accept that.

She wrapped her arms around her middle and said carefully, 'You really wanted our child?'

He sat rigid, chin up. 'You think I'd lie? About that?'

She'd never known him to be dishonest. Which meant he *had* wanted their child. Yet that made no sense.

'But you didn't always feel that way. Not in the beginning.'

Something shifted in his face. His posture changed and his mouth flattened. For the briefest moment he looked away then immediately back to her. 'You knew that?' Regret laced his words, and surprise. 'I never said it.'

'You didn't need to. It was in what you didn't say.'

There'd been no joy, nothing but practical if kind support. Did she want to keep the child? Really, was she sure? Did she feel well?

'You did all the right things. Made sure I looked after myself and got good advice. You didn't shirk in supporting me.' He'd even come to her first scan. 'But there was no excitement. You did what needed to be done.'

He might have bought a stunning engagement ring but there'd been no romance about his proposal, just a recitation of the reasons it made sense to marry since they had a baby on the way.

Slowly he spoke, his expression sombre. 'You're right. I didn't want the baby at first.'

Greer found herself pressing one palm to her abdomen, as if protecting the baby she no longer carried. It was what she'd already known, yet it pained her to hear.

Conall's stare flicked to the gesture then to her face, his own tightening. 'I'm sorry that hurt you, but you wanted the truth. As for why…' He paused. 'At the time I couldn't have told you. At first it was simply the shock of a life-changing event, something we hadn't planned for.'

Silly as it was, Greer took heart from the fact he said *we* not *I*.

'But you're right, there's more. It wasn't something I'd given any thought to. All my focus has been on building my business, first because it was expected, later because I wanted to create something independent of my father. Different to the way he worked.'

He lifted one shoulder. 'I have few memories of life before the Abercrombies and no treasured recollections of my time with them. No fun with siblings, just competition and cruel games. For years the idea of family turned my stomach.'

Greer covered his hand with hers. How had she not at least guessed? But while they'd communicated so well over other things, neither had revealed much of their past.

'That sounds horrendous.'

As an only child she'd thought it would be fun to have brothers and sisters. At least her mother had loved her and done her best for her. They'd been a team.

Conall's other hand clamped hers as he leaned close. She took comfort in his warm touch and steady gaze.

'I suppose my upbringing made me stronger, more self-reliant. But the idea of having a family scared me. It brought back things I'd rather forget. Yet as time went on, as I experienced our baby through your excitement and your eyes, things changed. I began thinking about the future, how we could build something different to what my father created.'

'To show you could do it better?'

'No!' His dark eyes glittered with shock. 'No, for us and our child. I found myself wondering what sort of father I'd make and hoping I'd do a reasonable job.'

Greer's heart ached. For what he'd missed out on with his family and what he'd suffered. For the fact he doubted himself as a result. Then there was his pain over the baby they'd lost. It shamed her that she'd had no inkling he cared so much. How blinkered she'd been.

'You'd have done a fantastic job, Conall.' Her voice was soft with the depth of her feelings. 'Whenever you set your mind to something, you succeed. If it's important to you—'

'It was. No matter how I felt in the beginning, I *cared* about our baby. I began to wonder what he or she would be like, and imagine us all together. Why do you think I sold the penthouse and bought the house? You'd said you wished you'd had a big yard to play in when you were young. I wanted that for our child.'

Greer's heart somersaulted. She remembered them strolling in the botanic gardens months ago. She'd mentioned how much she enjoyed the wide green space, saying she'd have loved a house with a yard when she was little.

'I'm sorry, Greer. All this time you thought I didn't want our baby. I thought, hoped, you hadn't realised how I felt in the beginning. We were both shocked by the news, weren't we?'

She nodded. 'I didn't feel maternal to start with. I couldn't believe I was pregnant. I'm so used to planning everything and the baby wasn't on my schedule.' She shook her head. 'But once the news settled, I knew I wanted it. My mum and I were close. I wanted that with our baby.'

She'd wanted more, including a husband who loved her, but she'd take this one step at a time.

Conall's voice deepened, brushing like suede over sensitive skin. 'I wish I'd made my feelings clear earlier, sweetheart. Maybe then you wouldn't have felt you needed to deal with your grief alone.'

'*I'm* sorry, Conall. I was so wrapped up in how I felt and sure you saw our baby as an obligation, I wanted to hide away. It must've made it harder, me leaving like that.' She tried to imagine his feelings, arriving back from the US, upset about the baby, only to find her gone. 'I was selfish. It's no excuse to say I didn't realise how much.'

'Don't talk that way.' He wrapped his arm around her, drawing her close. 'You didn't know. You were hurting.'

'We were both hurting, but I acted like it was my prerogative alone.'

A warm hand captured her chin, turning it up to meet his black gaze. It glittered, as if sparks of fire lit it from within.

'Stop that. We both made mistakes. I should have been open about what I felt.' His smile looked close to a grimace. 'That's something I've never learned to do. My whole training was in suppressing emotions. That's why I held back from talking about this, instead of forcing the issue. I'm not comfortable talking about what I feel. I was trained to see that as weakness.'

He looked into her eyes. 'Let me say it now. Our child was a wonderful gift. I didn't appreciate that at first but I came to. And if I'd been in any doubt, losing the baby made me realise exactly how much I wanted it.'

'Oh, Conall.' She cupped his jaw with her hand, wanting to ease the raw pain she read in his face.

'When you came back to Sydney from the mountains you didn't want to discuss the miscarriage. I respected that but I was relieved too. The last thing I wanted was to talk about feelings. In case you said you wanted to leave me.'

'Conall!' She goggled at him. He cared that much? Her pulse galloped as she grappled with his revelation.

'When you had the accident, I had to keep my feelings to myself until you remembered, or until it became clear you weren't going to remember and I'd have to tell you. You were vulnerable. I didn't dare admit what had happened. I've wanted so long to be up-front with you. But the only way we seemed to communicate easily was in business or in bed.'

The truth of his words hit home. How often had she pushed him away when he wanted to talk about the baby?

Greer rose abruptly and instantly Conall followed suit. 'What is it?'

'Hold me, please?'

A crooked smile curved his mouth and she felt it tug at her very being. 'Gladly.'

But instead of simply wrapping his arms around her, he scooped her up and carried her to a nearby sofa, sitting down with her cradled in his lap. His warmth surrounded her, both his strong body and his air of certainty that she found so reassuring. Greer put her arms around him and snuggled close.

'I wasn't sure I wanted children,' she admitted. 'I loved my mother dearly but the little I know about her relationship with my father was negative. We moved from town to town, even crossed the country to avoid him. Because of that, we didn't have long-term friends. We were on the move too often to put down roots and struggled financially. But I learnt the value of hard work and education. I put my career first. *That* was my idea of security.'

With her head against him, she felt Conall's voice vibrate through his chest. 'I can relate. That was me too.'

Greer wondered if that was one of the things that initially drew them together.

'But when I got pregnant, my priorities shifted. Partly it was the chance to have the sort of relationship my mother and I shared. Maybe it was the realisation I was growing a new life inside me, *our* child. I wish I had words to describe how that felt.' She pressed closer and was gratified when his hold tightened. 'My career was still important but it no longer seemed vital. Not like the baby.'

'No. Not like our baby.' His deep voice burred across her skin and burrowed inside. He shifted his grip, holding her away from him a little so he could meet her eyes. 'Would it upset you to tell me about that day?'

Greer felt something in her chest collapse, pain welling. But this hurt was for Conall. Because she'd shut him out. She hadn't thought he'd want the details of the day she miscarried. Now, to her shame, she saw how wrong she was.

They held each other as she told him everything. She clung tight when his breaths grew uneven, offering him comfort as much as he gave it to her.

Afterwards he told her that the day he returned from the

US was the day the legalities had been completed on the harbourside house. He'd been eager to get the trip out of the way so he could surprise her with their new home. How excited he was about the baby. The plans he'd had.

As they talked about their child, Greer found a surprising peace.

When, exhausted, they eventually returned to bed, it was knowing they had meetings in just a few hours.

Yet Greer didn't fall asleep quickly. She lay spooned against her husband, his breath stirring her hair and his arm around her waist. She revelled in the new intimacy they'd discovered, the way it drew them closer rather than pushing them apart. As sleep drifted closer, she found herself smiling.

They'd taken an important step, talking about their loss, about feelings. That was a first. For a long time they'd shared passion and work, good times and challenges, but never their deepest emotions.

She clung to the idea that maybe, after all, there was hope for their marriage.

CHAPTER FOURTEEN

NEXT EVENING GREER looked concerned. 'Are you *really* sure about this? Turning down the invitation to celebrate the deal you just finalised tonight?'

Conall gestured for her to precede him, following her into their hotel suite.

'Absolutely. Lee's accepted my invitation to celebrate as our guest tomorrow. His wife and key staff will all attend.'

He didn't add that he'd told Lee before today's meetings even began that tonight he had a vital private matter to attend to. One he couldn't afford to delay.

As he'd been watching Greer chat with one of Lee's legal team at the time, his new business associate had looked between the pair of them, nodded and murmured something about the importance of putting family first.

Conall had grasped the older man's hand, thanking him warmly for his understanding.

'Don't worry,' he said now to Greer. 'The hotel's restaurant is already booked for the private function and the head chef is preparing a special banquet.'

Greer stopped in the middle of the sitting room and shot him a questioning look.

'I had a junior staff member organise it. It's time the Sydney staff took over some of your more routine work. You have more important things to deal with.'

At work Greer was much more than an assistant. With a

little more experience she'd be a valuable negotiator for future deals, if she wanted that. Meanwhile, he didn't want her spending hours double-checking catering preparations. He needed her attention focused elsewhere.

On them.

He'd been on tenterhooks too long. It was time to resolve this. Crossing to the silver ice bucket, he lifted a foil-topped bottle, watching her eyebrows lift as she recognised the renowned vintage.

She moved closer. 'You were very certain of success.'

About the business, yes. As for the rest... It was a wonder his hand didn't shake as he stripped the foil from the bottle. He felt enlivened and terrified. 'We have things to celebrate.'

At least he hoped they would have.

Once the wine was poured into delicate champagne coupes, he led her onto the balcony and the magnificent view over city and sea.

Greer lifted her glass with a smile. 'To your business success.'

Conall raised his glass, holding her gaze. 'To us.'

He watched her momentary surprise, yet she didn't demur, but drank the golden liquid. He sipped the wine, bubbles bursting on the roof of his mouth.

Today had been a commercial triumph, but he found he didn't care. Only his sense of obligation to those who'd worked so hard for this deal had made him attend today's meetings. He'd wanted, more than anything, to forget work and concentrate on Greer.

Now, finally, it was *their* time. He put his glass on a nearby table.

'Conall?'

'There's something I want to share with you but I have one question first.' Her gaze searched his then she nodded. 'Why are you ambivalent about our marriage?'

Her eyes widened but not in repudiation of his words. His heart sank as he drew in a sustaining breath. He'd told himself he'd imagined she was dismissive about their relationship. But he'd been right. Adrenaline shot into his blood as dismay gripped him.

Greer put down her glass with a decisive click then rested her elbows on the balustrade, looking out over the city. She'd taken off her jacket and wore a straight black skirt and a navy camisole top in some silky fabric that caught the light. Even in office clothes, frowning, no woman he knew could hold a candle to her.

'We married because I was pregnant. Because you wanted to protect your baby, not because you wanted *me*.' Her head whipped around, eyes of deepest blue snaring his. 'Now there's no baby, no glue to hold us together. Of course I'm ambivalent about our marriage.'

Not want her? No glue to hold them together! He refused to believe it. He *knew* she felt something for him. She had to.

Initially, maybe it had been lust… No that wasn't right, even in the beginning there'd been far more between them than physical attraction. They understood each other. Surely he hadn't been wrong, believing she cared about him.

'What if I told you I didn't propose marriage just because of the baby?'

Her gaze grew wary but she didn't look away. Her chin lifted. 'I wouldn't believe you. I was there, remember?'

Slowly he nodded, thinking over what he'd said and done. How he could have said and done it so much better. How much he'd left out. He swallowed hard. 'I owe you an apology.'

Her head jerked back as if slapped, her eyes too big for her face. 'For making the mistake of marrying me?'

'Never that.' Her pain made him bleed inside. He moved in, palming her jaw and feeling her tremble. 'I didn't tell you the whole truth. I married you because I love you.'

'Don't!' Her voice was a raw whisper as she shook her head.
'Hear me out, Greer, please.'

'There's no need to pretend now, Conall. The baby's—'

'This isn't about the baby.' He cupped her face in both hands so she had to meet his eyes. 'I admit that in the beginning, I thought of marriage as the right thing to do for you and our baby. Believe it or not, from the first I wanted to protect you both, even when I wasn't sure I wanted a child. But you didn't instantly accept. In fact, you seemed doubtful.'

'People don't have to marry to look after their child.'

'No, they don't. But I wanted to. So then I had to think about *why* I wanted to when you apparently didn't. Why I couldn't rest until you agreed to marry.'

The haunted look in her eyes was like a fist slammed against his heart. Conall dropped his hands and eased them around hers, threading their fingers together.

'I told you I was raised to be strategic, pragmatic and competitive. My father sees any emotion other than greed unacceptable. I have the vaguest recollection of my mother's love, a sense of warmth and the world being a safe place. But there's been no love in my life since then. That's why it took me a long time to realise I love you.'

He paused, letting the words sink in, waiting and hoping she'd return the pressure of his hands, showing she believed. And that his love mattered to her.

Suddenly Conall was breathless.

But Greer's only movement was to tilt her head, looking down at their joined hands, her lustrous dark lashes veiling her eyes.

What was she thinking? How did she feel? He couldn't bear the silence, waiting for her response. 'Even then, when I understood my feelings, I was wary of telling you. All those old lessons in hiding emotion came into play.' Finally he admitted, 'I was scared to tell you in case you didn't feel the same way.'

That made her look at him and for the first time since he'd started talking, a thread of hope wound its way around his heart.

'I can't imagine you scared.'

His bark of laughter cut the thick evening air. 'Scared? I've been petrified. The longer I've put off telling you how I feel, the harder it's become. There never seemed to be a right time. But now I need to know.' His hands tightened around hers. 'Will you let me try again, to be the husband I want to be? The sort of husband you deserve. Even if you don't love me, I know you *care* for me, Greer. We're good together and if you give me time, I can make you happy.'

'I want to, so much,' she whispered, her throat working convulsively. She looked overwhelmed.

'I would *never* hurt you, Greer.' He waited, frowning. 'Sweetheart? How do *you* feel about *me*?'

Was it possible he wasn't the only one scared to reveal his feelings? Now, as he stared into her achingly beautiful eyes, he caught a glimpse of something that stole his breath.

'I love you.' She enunciated the words clearly, the sound sweeter and more moving than anything he'd ever known. 'I fell for you the day I walked into your office and by the end of the week I knew it was more than physical. I've loved you for ages.'

Joy began to bubble in his veins as shock seared him. 'You've known all this time?'

She nodded. 'You're not the only one wary of emotion. I never expected to feel anything like this. And then, knowing you'd married me because I was pregnant...'

'It was more than that, my darling. It's been more than that for a very, very long time.'

There it was again, that gleam of hope and shimmering excitement in her gaze. Yet even now she held firm. 'How can I know that? How can I be sure?'

Conall dropped his hand and reached for his wallet, thumbing it open and extracting a piece of paper.

She took it, eyes round with astonishment. 'The scan. *You* have this! I thought I'd lost it.'

She traced the small, grainy shape that had been their baby and his heart nearly broke at her tender expression.

'I found it on the floor of the penthouse when I got back from the States. It must've fallen out of your bag when you left.'

'You've been carrying it all this time?'

He nodded.

'Surely that just proves it was the baby you cared about.' Yet her expression had softened and he felt a powerful shift in the energy between them.

'Of course I cared. But the reason I kept the scan, the reason I felt so strongly, is because it was *our* baby, *your* baby. I'm not like my father, who's frankly a womaniser. I'm a one-woman man. He values his children only to perpetuate the myth of his own power. I loved our child because it was *ours*, yours and mine. Because I love you. I will always love you. I never imagined one, single person could make me feel whole the way I do with you.'

Her wobbly smile was the most wonderful thing he'd ever seen.

The touch of her fingers stroking his cheek almost turned his knees to water. What he felt for her was so powerful. It was everything he needed.

'If you want proof that I love you, I can't provide anything concrete. Just my promise to keep loving you all the days of our lives. If you'll take the chance on trusting me, I promise not to let you down.' He stopped, needing to drag more oxygen into overworked lungs. 'I'm asking for a leap of faith, Greer. I'm trusting my heart to you.'

Warmth enveloped him as she closed the gap between

them, pressing near, her soft contours fitting against him so perfectly it defied words.

'That's fair. You've had my heart for so long.'

'Greer.' The word ached with all the love he hadn't let himself express before, not verbally. Because he'd feared she didn't feel the same for him, a man who knew so little about softer emotions.

He wrapped his arm around her, his other hand tugging her hair free so it fell around her in a scented curtain. Anchoring her head with his hand he brushed his lips across hers before tenderly, slowly kissing her with all the reverence and love he'd never been able to share.

Her response was everything he could ask for. His wife—his wife!—was his perfect match. She completed him and she kissed like an angel. No, not an angel, a temptress.

Conall pulled back, his eyes on hers. 'Tomorrow we celebrate the deal with Lee and our teams. But tonight is for us. We'll celebrate something more important. Our love.'

He'd always thought her eyes were like gemstones but tonight they shone brighter than any precious stone. 'It *does* deserve celebration. What did you have in mind?'

Conall didn't hold back his smile. He'd never known such happiness. 'Let's see how the evening unfolds. We can start by taking this champagne somewhere more comfortable.'

Her sideways glance under lowered eyelids was pure invitation. 'Good idea.' She picked up the glasses. 'I'll carry these while you get the bottle.' She was already walking across the terrace, the gentle undulation of her hips in that pencil skirt going straight to his libido.

He thought of how incredibly alluring he found her impressive organisational skills and quick mind. She was sexy, competent, and she loved him.

He grinned from ear to ear. What more could a man want?

Conall strode after her, swiping up the bottle. 'Lead on, Mrs Abercrombie.'

She didn't waste time on words, simply smiled over her shoulder as she stepped into the bedroom.

He'd never moved so fast in his life.

EPILOGUE

'Organised mayhem, isn't it?' Amy Huang murmured, leaning sideways in the garden seat to make herself heard over the noise.

Greer laughed. 'I take it as a compliment that you can see it's organised. I suspect there'll be a scrum when the food comes out.'

Conall had been right. The rambling garden of their harbourside mansion really was made for children to enjoy.

Ahead, a ragtag group of them squealed with excitement as they raced through the shrubbery in a game that seemed to combine hide-and-seek and chasing. A smaller group, each clutching a balloon, skipped after an elf, headed for the story time bower set out under a huge purple-blue jacaranda tree. Some little ones, supervised by parents, were fishing for rubber ducks in a pond. Meanwhile the line-up for pony rides snaked along the edge of the grass.

This was the second year Greer and Conall had hosted a spring party for preschoolers, their families and school staff.

Last year Grace had been a preschooler. This year she asserted she was all grown up, since she was in big school. Now Logan was the preschooler. Greer had last seen him racing into the undergrowth with a tribe of other kids, grinning from ear to ear. Grace, of course, was waiting for another ride.

'They're all going to sleep well tonight. May will probably

be out like a light in the car.' Amy grinned. 'Joe and I might even have the whole evening to ourselves.'

'Enjoy it while you can.' Amy's second child was due in a month.

'I intend to. I...' A shout drew her attention to the fishing pond where her husband and daughter were holding up a rubber duck. She laughed. 'It looks like May struck lucky. I'd better go and congratulate her.' She levered herself out of the chair. 'While I remember, I'll give you a lift to stretch class next week, yes?'

'Absolutely.' Greer smiled but decided to stay where she was a little longer.

It had been a busy morning and it was good to sit for a while. She'd put in more hours than usual at work this week, helping Conall finalise details of another community project, this time a cooking school with residential accommodation for homeless young people. He'd scolded her about her hours but she, like him, felt personally invested in the project.

Next week she'd go back to her part-time hours. Then the week after that the Lees from Singapore were staying with them.

Movement caught her eye and she turned to see a familiar tall figure stride towards her, a little boy with tousled dark hair clinging to him.

Her heart quickened. Her beloved Conall was more handsome with each passing day. In jeans and a pale polo shirt that accentuated his lean strength, he stood out from every man here. She suspected Logan would be the image of his father when he grew up.

Conall caught her eye and his slowly unfurling smile made her melt in all the usual places. But she focused on her little boy.

'Here she is.'

At the sound of his father's deep voice, Logan looked up

and instantly Greer held her arms out, seeing his crumpled mouth.

'Logan skinned his knee and wanted to show you.'

Conall lowered their son onto her lap. Greer gathered Logan in, smiling as he gently touched her baby bump and said, 'Hello, bub,' before snuggling close against her.

She shut her eyes, inhaling the scent of little boy and fresh-mown grass. When she opened them it was to meet Conall's tender gaze.

That familiar sense of connection pulsed between them and she smiled, reaching out her hand so he could enfold it in his. They were a team in every way. Any doubts she'd ever had about him not wanting children, or not wanting her were long gone. There couldn't be a more devoted husband and father.

She looked down at her son, who so rarely sat still. 'Are you going to show me your knee, Logan? Is it very sore?'

He lifted his head, all trace of tears vanishing as he smiled. 'No, Mummy. Daddy put a dinosaur strip on it and now you've given me one of your special cuddles.'

'Your daddy's very clever, being so prepared.'

Long fingers tickled the palm of her hand as a deep voice said, 'Years of practice.'

'Will you kiss it better now, just in case?' her son asked.

Given the size of her pregnancy bump, bending that far would be hard, so she pressed her fingers to her lips then to the dinosaur bandage.

'Hey, Logan!' a little boy called from the garden. 'Are you coming?'

'Wait for me!' Logan shouted then leaned up to give her a kiss. He was already sliding off her lap as he explained, 'I promised to show Harry my secret cubby. Bye, Mummy. Bye, Daddy.'

Then he was off, whooping as he raced to his friend, injury forgotten.

Conall laughed. 'I wish I had that much energy.'

Greer leaned towards him, stroking his lean cheek. 'Poor thing, has the big day warn you out?'

In answer, Conall half rose, scooped her from her seat and settled her across his lap as he sat down again. Dark eyes danced as he held her close. 'Never, when you look at me like that, sweetheart.'

'Smooth talker.'

He waggled his eyebrows. 'Only with you, my love.'

Then his lips met hers and Greer kissed him with all the love in her heart. A love he returned unstintingly. Her husband showed her daily, in a thousand ways, how much he cared.

When Conall pulled back enough to meet her gaze his eyes were shining. 'Later.'

She nodded. 'Later.'

Then hand in hand, they rose and joined their friends.

* * * * *

Did you fall head over heels for
Boss's Marriage Agenda? *Then you're certain to love these other intensely emotional stories from Annie West!*

Unknown Royal Baby
Ring for an Heir
Queen by Royal Command
Stolen Pregnant Bride
Forbidden Princess's Billionaire Bodyguard

Available now!

MILLS & BOON®

Coming next month

MY FIANCÉE PROMOTION
Emmy Grayson

Sera stares at the newspaper with horror etched onto her face.

'What...who took that?'

'One of the event photographers. Once they realised who I was, they decided to make a quick buck.' I toss the newspaper down on the coffee table on top of a stack of books.

She sighs, her hands coming up to her temples. 'The damage is done. I'll submit my resignation on Monday.'

Knots form in my chest, tighten. 'No.'

No, only something drastic will repair this.

A frown draws her dark golden brows together. 'Then...I don't understand. What can we do?'

Something stirs inside me at her use of the word *we*. I may not know the woman standing in front of me like I thought I did, but her dedication to Hawke Financial is one thing I don't doubt.

The one thing I'm counting on.

'I do have a proposal.'

'Okay.' She nods, blows out a harsh breath. 'Okay. What do we do.'

'We get engaged.'

Continue reading

MY FIANCÉE PROMOTION
Emmy Grayson

Available next month
millsandboon.co.uk

Copyright ©2026 Emmy Grayson

COMING SOON!

We really hope you enjoyed reading this book.
If you're looking for more romance
be sure to head to the shops when
new books are available on

Thursday 21st May

To see which titles are coming soon, please visit
millsandboon.co.uk/nextmonth

MILLS & BOON

FOUR BRAND NEW BOOKS FROM
MILLS & BOON MODERN

Indulge in desire, drama, and breathtaking romance – where passion knows no bounds!

OUT NOW

Eight Modern stories published every month, find them all at:

millsandboon.co.uk

TWO BRAND NEW BOOKS FROM
Love Always

Be prepared to be swept away to incredible worldwide destinations along with our strong, relatable heroines and intensely desirable heroes.

OUT NOW

Four Love Always stories published every month, find them all at:

millsandboon.co.uk

LET'S TALK
Romance

For exclusive extracts, competitions and special offers, find us online:

- **f** MillsandBoon
- **X** @MillsandBoon
- **◉** @MillsandBoonUK
- **♪** @MillsandBoonUK

Get in touch on 01413 063 232

For all the latest titles coming soon, visit
millsandboon.co.uk/nextmonth